LAUREN L. GARCIA

Assassin's Mercy (Chaos Moon #1)

For ls-d, wherever she is...

Contents

Thanks for checking out my book! Visit me at laloga.com/newsletter to be the first to know of my next release, get excerpts & deleted scenes, and find your next great fantasy romance read.

1

Hide Your Heart

The cavern's shadows clung to Verve, binding her in darkness and squeezing her heart like a vise. By the One god, nighttime was bad enough, but prowling along the shores of one of Aredia's underground rivers was like being buried alive. Her breath also struggled in the shadows' grip but she ground her jaw against the feeling. *Stop fretting and just* do *the job*, she told herself, and pressed on, silent.

In theory, Verve only ever had one chance to kill a mage. If she bungled that first opportunity, she'd have pissed off someone who could—and would—shoot fireballs or throw lightning spears her way, and then she'd be too busy trying *not* to get burned to worry about making that nice clean kill. But no matter how they died, the world would be free of one more magic-user. A few new scars were a small price to pay.

At least, according to Danya.

Ahead, Verve's target and his companion chatted as they set up their camp. Their voices echoed through the massive underground chamber, and the light from their campfire danced over the cavern walls. Verve came around a bend in the black, rippling water to assess the situation. Two men—a mage and his ally—sat beside a small fire, burning merrily without fuel. The hair on the back of Verve's neck prickled at the sight of the magic-made fire and she swore inwardly. A part of her—a stupid part—had hoped this mage might *not* be the type who could manipulate fire, but of course, her luck was shit. As usual.

Best not to worry about her terrible luck and focus on the task before her. Fire-wielders were tricky, but not impossible to take down — with the right equipment. Best of all, once she did her job, she could get out of this damp, dark sodding cave, and never think about it again.

Verve smoothed her gloved hands over her hematite gear one more time. Both her hood and close-fitting jacket boasted an intricate pattern of dark-gray hematite beads, which Verve had sewn on herself. The jacket hung to her thighs, shielding her upper legs as well, and her boots had hematite fittings. The hematite would prevent mage-fire from burning her to ash — at least for a few minutes. Long enough for her to gain the upper hand.

She eased forward. Mage-made flames meant her daggers would have to stay in their sheaths for the initial strike, so her crossbow was already in her hand, along with a hematite-tipped bolt she'd not yet loaded. If her aim was perfect, the mage would be dead before he hit the cavern floor. But if the shot didn't kill the mage immediately, the hematite would slow him down enough for a quick thrust of her dagger. Then she'd just have the other fellow to capture, per Danya's orders. Soft-spoken and unarmed, Verve's target seemed mild-mannered enough. *Seemed.*

Stalagmites thrust up out of the rocky ground, concealing her from the mage's view. But the other fellow, her true target, stopped talking, inclined his head, and Verve froze.

"What is it?" the mage asked, glancing around.

Her target didn't respond at first, but his gaze landed on Verve's location. Twin stars burned briefly in his eyes before he glanced away. She swore mentally again. *Ea's tits.* Her heart pounded; surely the sound would echo off of the cavern walls.

A faint feeling tingled at the base of her spine: a sensation of a single finger stroking up her back. And with the feeling came an awareness, a sense of recognition, like seeing someone you sort of knew from across a crowded room.

Magic? There was no other explanation. As one of Atal's Chosen, Verve had met—and killed—plenty of mages in her twenty-four summers, but had never encountered one with this sort of… bizarre mind-magic. But the evidence shuddered over her skin: she now faced two mages, not one. Her patron, Danya, had passed on faulty information, but that would be no excuse for failure. Verve had no choice but to bring in this fellow alive.

Fine. But her fingers trembled as she eased the bolt into its seat of the crossbow.

The second man, the secret mage, murmured, "We're not alone."

Fire bloomed at the first mage's fingertips. "Get behind me, Celidon."

Nothing for it. Verve aimed through a slit in the stalagmites. *May the One god forgive me*, she prayed, bracing herself, and pulled the trigger. The kickback shoved the weapon's butt into her shoulder, but she'd grown used to the impact well over a decade ago, when she was only eleven. A strangled cry echoed in the cavern as the mage staggered backward, grabbing at the bolt now protruding from his chest. His companion dove for cover behind another rock formation—the fools had made their camp out in the open—but Verve was already on her way.

Black water rippled around her as she slipped toward them. But the mage caught sight of her before she could duck beneath the water. As she stepped onto the other shore, water sluicing down her sides, he gave a cry of pain and fury. But the fire at his fingers flickered and died as the hematite muted his magic.

"Who sent you?" he gasped, struggling to stand despite his injury. Magic fire flared again at his hands, but briefly.

Verve unsheathed one of her daggers—an old style sentinel's dagger, hematite fortified with iron—grabbed the mage's hair, and wrenched him to his knees. She steeled herself, as she always did, for the moment when her prey's life would end by her hand.

"Please," the other fellow said, stepping forward. His eyes were dark like her own, but a strange light flickered in their depths. "Please, don't do this," he added. "You don't want to do this."

Her reply was steady, even if her heart was not. "I'm sorry," she murmured. "It's not personal." She punched her dagger into the mage's throat. He crumpled to her feet, blood streaming over the cavern floor.

"Karel," the other fellow cried and fell to his knees, moaning, clutching his head as if he'd been kicked. He said other things, before she gagged and bound him, but Verve shut her mind to his voice, his fear, his pain. The ache in her chest, the gnaw of her heart eating itself; she shut her mind to them, too.

She had a job to finish.

* * *

Each breath came easier once Verve was out of the caverns. Early afternoon sunlight poured over her dark-brown skin, warming her all the way to her bones despite the chill of the early spring day. The underground river system may have made travel through the country of Aredia convenient—to a degree—but by the One god, she regretted each foray into the caverns.

Her prisoner sat atop the horse she'd left waiting on the surface. When Verve had wrapped the apparent-mage in iron chains, he'd cried out as if the chains had burned him. Although he was awake, he barely seemed conscious, so she'd had to pull him into the saddle like a sack of yuzah roots. At least none of that strange starlight flared in his eyes. He was still gagged, but she thought that even if she removed the rag from his mouth, he'd not say one word to the one who'd murdered his friend.

Her stomach clenched. She tugged the horse along faster. They'd made good time; she could already see Freehold's sturdy walls ahead. Soon, this job would be over.

But what about the next job? And the next? And on and on, until—

As always, she cut off the thought. *Until* didn't exist yet. Just like tomorrow.

"Ser Vervaine," one of the gate-guards called, lifting her hand. "I trust that mage is properly bound?"

Verve paused her horse and peered up at the armored figure. "Is that jealousy I hear in your voice, Sacha?"

The guard's helmet almost hid her smile. Almost. She had a lovely smile. "Of course not," she replied with exaggerated formality. "I'm simply doing my duty to protect Freehold. Someone has to, given how those moon-blooded maniacs tear through the country like they own it."

The mage-on-mage fighting had been going on for about a hundred and fifty years, since the Sundering that had fractured Aredia. Mages had once been safely contained behind hematite-filled walls, until they had rebelled, murdering the Aredian queen and casting the country into turmoil. The magic-users, finally free to wield their magic as they saw fit, chose not to help heal the land they had sundered, but rather to war with one another over resources and territory, leaving non-magic folks to band together and defend themselves. Because of Verve and the other Chosen, Freehold was one of the few safe havens for those who couldn't shoot fireballs out of their asses.

Verve winked at the guard. "Do you ever stop being so diligent, Sacha?" Sacha's neck flushed pink and Verve couldn't resist adding, "When are you off-duty next?"

Sacha sighed. "Not until first light."

"Well, next night you're free, I'll buy you a drink and tell you the story," Verve replied. "But I must check in with Serla Danya now."

"And I thought *I* was diligent," Sacha replied, chuckling.

"Ea's balls," the second guard muttered. "Stop making eyes at the mage-hunter, Sacha. Ser Vervaine, thank you as ever for your efforts to keep Freehold safe. We are all indebted to you and all of Atal's Chosen. But please take your prisoner and move along."

Verve saluted and led her horse through the ironwood gates. They closed with a familiar groan and she exhaled. She was back where she belonged.

Freehold was a large village that dearly wanted to be called a city. No doubt it would, one day, for every time Verve passed through the streets, she saw new faces, heard new voices. Most folks parted to let her pass, whispering to each other or calling out a friendly greeting. One less mage in the world meant these people were that much safer. Verve squared her shoulders and held her head high, and the tightness in her chest that always accompanied her on a mission began to ease.

You do good things, too, she told herself.

At the edge of Silverwood Province, Freehold was one of the few places regular folks could live without fear of the magic-users' war. Danya, the Circle priest who'd taken over as town magistrate when the former magistrate had been killed by mages, had installed hematite fittings into the town's stone walls. Although the ore was rare, Danya had also ensured that every citizen in Freehold had a hematite amulet to wear as additional protection against magic. No one asked where she'd gotten the precious material. Once upon a time, there had been an old hematite mine to the west, over in Stonehaven Province, but mages had destroyed that too.

But life in Freehold was peaceful, thanks to Verve and the other Chosen's efforts. The Argus Mountains loomed to the north, standing sentinel over the town and its denizens, while the Temple of Atal rested on a small hill at the center of town. Another wall and gate protected the temple. Verve didn't flirt with any of the guards here, but hurried inside the temple courtyard. While most of Silverwood Province boasted little but saffron-colored prairie grasses, Danya had coaxed a lush oasis to grow in the temple garden, filled with fruit and nut trees.

Usko, one of Danya's other Chosen foundlings, spotted Verve across the courtyard and raced over, his bare feet slapping against the flagstones. "Back, already?" he said, grabbing at her horse's reins. He was nineteen summers, five years younger than Verve, but his round face made him seem no more than fourteen. He glanced at her bound prey and laughed. "I *knew* you would be fast. You just won me twenty silvers."

Verve lifted a brow. "That's all?" She clucked her tongue. "Surely, my skills warrant at least thirty."

"Sure." He grinned and held out his palm, calloused from years of weapons-training. "Lend it to me, and I'll share the profits with you next time."

She playfully slapped his hand and headed for the temple's interior. "Make your own profits, Usko."

He gave a dramatic sigh. "Danya says I'm not ready for a mission alone."

"Danya knows best," Verve replied by route. She dug around in one of the pouches at her belt and tossed Usko a silver coin. "Take care of the horse and help secure the prisoner, and I'll give you some more pointers next time we spar."

Usko caught the coin with practiced grace and grinned again. "Deal. And Verve…welcome back. We missed you."

* * *

Verve had timed her arrival just right. Within the temple, the evening services were still a few hours away, so she met only a few Circle priests as she slipped through the corridors to Danya's quarters. The sharp scents of clove and pine incense drifted along with Verve, guiding her toward Danya's office, where she found the head priest scribbling in a massive ledger, spectacles reflecting the lamplight. The priest's office was dark, the windows covered by thick curtains, with only a few oil lamps set at strategic places to allow Danya to see what always seemed to Verve like endless stacks of paperwork. Running a town like Freehold required a lot of time and energy.

Indeed, the priest was so engrossed in her work that Verve had to practically shout her greeting before Danya looked up.

"Vervaine, you're back." Danya tilted her head, expectant. "I trust you found success on your mission?"

"The mage is dead. The other's in our holding cells…" Something in Verve's stomach rolled.

Danya clasped her hands and peered at Verve from over her spectacles. "What's wrong? Were you injured?"

"No, serla. But the prisoner…" Verve hesitated. "There was something strange about him. He seemed to sense me, and—"

"Sense you?" Danya broke in. "How?"

Verve glanced up to see the priest studying her. "I don't know," Verve said, careful to keep her features neutral. "I just felt…like I was being watched." She shivered at the memory of *something* crawling up her spine. "You said he wasn't a mage. But I was *dripping* in hematite and he still did…something to me."

"Well, it hardly matters now," Danya said. "He's in our custody. Put him out of your mind."

"But what *was* he?" Verve pressed. "If mages have learned a new kind of magic, shouldn't we investigate? It's our job to keep normal folks safe."

Danya removed her spectacles to pinch the bridge of her nose. She was an older woman, well into her fifties, with brown skin and long iron-gray hair woven a crisp braid that fell down her back. "Can you not listen to me, even for a moment? All that matters is the prisoner. They wanted him alive, after all."

"Who's *they*?" Verve asked. "I thought Atal's Chosen worked only for the people of Freehold."

"Some questions are best left unasked," Danya replied. "Don't press this matter further."

But Verve couldn't help herself — which was always her biggest problem. "Why keep this a secret? What aren't you telling me?"

"Nothing you need to concern yourself with," Danya snapped. "And I'll warn you to keep your wits and your silence. Vervaine, you're my oldest and most skilled Chosen warrior. I took you in as a child, fed you, clothed you, and gave you a better life than you ever could have dreamed. Yet you return my gracious favor with malicious questions." She gave a labored sigh. "If you will not behave for your own good, think of the example you're setting for Usko and the others."

Verve hunched her shoulders, trying to make herself smaller. She was taller than most women and many men, but Danya could make her feel no bigger than a teacup. "I'm sorry, serla. But as you've taught me, we can't take *any* chances with mages."

Verve's deferential use of the formal address always mollified Danya. But as Danya came around the desk and touched Verve's chin to draw her gaze, Verve fought back the instinct to flinch away from the other woman's touch.

"No, we cannot take chances with mages," Danya said. "But the world is changing and I fear our little haven here will suffer."

"What's changing, serla?" Verve asked before she could stop herself. Her breath caught. "Is it Legion? Are they coming?"

The Legion of the Pure: a place and a people. A massive city-state built on the ruins of Whitewater City, several weeks' journey east of Freehold. In the Sundering's aftermath, many had fled the magic-sowed chaos to Legion, where the god Atal had supposedly returned to keep his supplicants safe from the magic-users. Everyone knew the folks of Legion hated mages, which meant Verve should have considered Legion folks allies. But even the *thought* of Legion made Verve's head light, as if she couldn't suck in enough air.

Danya's expression did not waver from kind concern. "Don't fret about Legion," Danya said. "You're a good girl, but I can tell you've been working too hard lately. My fault, I know. I push you. You're so skilled, but you are still young."

Verve bristled. "I'm twenty-four summers."

"Aye," Danya said fondly. "But sometimes to me, you are still that little heathen child I found in the orphanage." She dropped her hand and went to her desk, rifling through various stacks of paper before withdrawing a letter.

"I've news of your cousin," Danya said, returning to Verve's side. "A Sufani caravan matching the description you gave me was spotted in Starwatch Province, a few months ago."

Verve's heart lifted. She reached for the letter, her fingertips just brushing the parchment as a smile broke free across her face. "By the One! Are they still there? May I go—"

The slap across her mouth stung, and she snapped her jaw shut. Danya glared at her, although her voice was soft. "I have indeed failed to rid you of your Sufani ways, Vervaine, if you have not yet learned this lesson: Hide your heart, child, lest evil-doers use it against you. Atal demands nothing less than everything you have, and you cannot serve Him by half-measures."

Mouth burning, Verve bit back her grimace and lowered her gaze. Stupid—utterly, completely stupid—to mention the Sufani god before her patron — one of Atal's most devoted servants. Verve knew better.

And yet.

Danya waited a beat before continuing. "I need a little more time, but I'm sure we'll find your cousin soon, you poor thing. Everyone should have some blood family."

Verve nodded. Heat pricked her eyes but she refused to let her tears fall lest she receive another blow for such an emotional display.

"In the meantime," Danya continued, tucking the letter in a pocket of her robe. "I have another job for you."

"Please, not another capture." Verve tried to keep her voice light.

Danya arched a thin brow. "The very least you can do for the woman who raised you is follow a simple order."

Long years of practice helped Verve suppress a groan. "Yes, serla."

Danya went to her ledger and skimmed her finger down the open page, eyes darting over the text. "Marea Damaris, a mage famous—or infamous, I should say—for manipulating the weather in their locality."

Verve's mind leaped on the information. "A particle mage, then?"

"Aye."

Particle mages were the most common sort of magic-user, able to bend physical elements to their will. A few generations ago, most mages were particle mages and were capable of more or less the same magic: creating fire, purifying water, controlling gusts of wind or blooms of fog, making plants grow, among other talents. But after the Sundering of Aredia, mages' abilities had become more specialized. Now, most magic-users could only manipulate one sort of particle, and so had their own focuses: fire, water, earth, and so on. Which sounded easier to defeat — until you actually squared off against a mage who'd practically been born breathing fire.

"A Damaris?" Verve added, still musing. "They're supposed to be more powerful than most moon-bloods. And you say weather... What sort?" *Please not tornadoes*, she added silently.

"Lightning," Danya said, and Verve nearly grimaced before she caught herself. Danya went to the map she'd tacked upon the wall to one side of her desk, and gestured to a murky green area towards the center of the Aredian continent. "An agent of mine reported a sighting of Marea Damaris in Greenhill Province. They were last seen holed up in some backwater village. Lotis."

"Never heard of it."

"Apparently, it's little more than a shantytown in the swamp," Danya replied, sniffing. "But I've gotten reports of other mages meeting there. Rumor has it that Damaris is building support among their fellow mages, assembling a force for some nefarious purpose."

Verve's skin prickled. "Warring with another mage clan?"

"Only the mighty Atal knows what evil lurks in mages' hearts," Danya said. "But we cannot allow the mages to organize. The only thing keeping us safe from their vile magic is their desire to war with one another. If Damaris is truly trying to build an…army, I dare say we'll all be in a world of trouble."

"So I'm to eliminate this Damaris person?"

Danya looked over her spectacles at Verve. "No, you must capture and return them to me."

Capture missions were the most annoying, but—as she'd proven—manageable. There was no use complaining, so Verve nodded, her mind whirring with plans.

"I fear tracking Damaris down will be difficult," Danya went on. "My sources say they don't stay in one place for long, but keep on the move. Your best bet is to start in Lotis and comb the area. *Discreetly.*"

"I'm the soul of discretion," Verve said, keeping her voice deadpan.

"This is not a joke, Vervaine," Danya said at last. "This mage—all mages—are evil and destructive. They crave nothing but power. They are an anathema to the order Atal wishes His followers to maintain. They tore this country apart and will not stop until every one of us is dead by their hands."

Verve's blood pounded in her ears, but she kept her voice calm. "I know, serla."

"I took you in as a child, trained you to defend yourself and others against magic's treachery," Danya went on. "As I am doing with Usko and the other Chosen. No one else in this world will look after you the way I have. You and I and all the Chosen, we must stand together against the chaos of magic."

The older woman's gaze went distant. "I can still smell the smoke, hear the roar of mage-fire. Even now, I sometimes still wake in the middle of the night, thinking I'm back home, when the moon-bloods struck. But as I reach for my son and husband, I remember…" Her eyes landed on Verve. "It's the same for you, I know."

It was. Too well could Verve recall the choking, black smoke of her burning home, engulfed in mage-made flames. The wail of her mother echoed in her ears, a memory she would never be rid of. It was harder this time to fight back her tears, but she'd had a lot of practice. "We've both lost much to the mages, serla."

"Indeed." Danya squared her shoulders, lifted her chin. "But with Atal's blessing, His Chosen will stop their reign of destruction, and Aredia will know peace once again."

The mention of the mighty god, Atal, made sweat prick at Verve's palms beneath her gloves. *Atal's blessing.* Surely a blessing of any sort was impossible. The warmongering, vengeful god that had usurped worship of the rest of the Aredian pantheon after the Sundering was not known for His compassion.

Not like the One god, the oldest god, whom the nomadic Sufani tribes had once worshipped — until Legion sentinel-soldiers had tried to eradicate them from the face of the world.

Don't think about that, Verve scolded herself. Surely the One god did not care for *her* any longer, especially not here in Freehold living as one of Atal's Chosen.

So she only said smoothly, "Yes, serla."

Danya went back to her desk, her white and black priest robe fluttering with her quick movements. "I'll expect regular reports, as usual. Since this will be a more complex task than you're used to, you have three full cycles of the first moon to complete it."

"There's not usually a time limit on these jobs." Even as the words left Verve's mouth, her guts twisted. There was only one entity that would commission such a job from Danya's mage-killers. She shoved away her misgivings and added, "You made a contract with someone outside of Freehold?"

Please don't answer. Ignorance was bliss, after all.

Danya's attention was back on her ledger. "Atal is full. Three cycles from now, you must have Damaris in your custody."

"And if the mission takes longer?" Verve could not help but ask.

The Circle priest did not look up. "Failure is not an option. You are dismissed."

Verve bowed and turned to leave. But when she reached the threshold, Danya called, "And Vervaine?"

Verve paused without looking back. "Yes, serla?"

"You're going to need a boat."

2

A Real Mission

Several minutes later, Verve leaned against the corridor outside the supply room while Clo, the Temple's steward, bustled within. Something crashed; the sound echoed over the temple's walls, but Verve held her ground.

"Need any help?" she called.

"You know the rules," Clo replied, grunting. "No one's allowed in but me. I have a system."

But Verve sighed dramatically. "I'm not going to swipe, break, or otherwise endanger your precious system."

"Stay. Out."

Verve rolled her eyes, but her mind had already wandered back to her conversation with Danya. Surely the priest wasn't working *with* Legion, not after they'd caused so much chaos in Aredia. Danya was many things, but a fool wasn't one of them. And anyone would have to be a fool to get involved with the city-state and its sentinels.

The coil of anxiety in Verve's stomach tightened. Another clang sounded from within the supply room, and Verve started. Clo swore, quite colorfully, but Verve held her tongue this time. She had a free half-day until she was supposed to set out for Lotis, which meant a visit to her favorite inn and tavern, the Dancing Dove. Too bad Sacha wouldn't be available, but at least the barkeep would be happy to see her. Well, happy to see her coin.

Clo emerged, a full clutch of hematite bolts in her arms, and Verve pushed off of the wall to accept her new gear. "Thanks," she said as she gathered the bolts. "This'll come in handy."

The steward eyed her. "That scarf's looking ragged," she said. "Hasn't Serla Danya told you to replace it?"

Verve's hand stole to the dark silk wrapped around her braids, and she tried not to tuck under the hem too obviously. She rarely wore her scarf in Freehold, but she'd been so eager to get back, removing it had slipped her mind. Could Clo see the colorful embroidery on the underside? Would she demand Verve give it up?

Best to play things casual. Verve shrugged. "Later. I want to get underway."

Clo grunted and turned to leave, but paused when Verve called her name. "You don't have a boat back there, do you?" Verve asked.

The steward blinked. She was a slight woman, but Verve knew from experience the former mercenary had more weapons hidden on her than most well-to-do frips had in their armories.

Clo wrinkled her nose. "Are you pranking me?"

"Never," Verve said. "But Serla Danya said I'd need a boat for my next mission, and I have no idea where to get one."

Freehold was landlocked and several days' journey from the White River, so a boat wasn't easily acquired in these parts.

The steward considered. "This is for the job to Lotis? I'd try Cypress Edge. Small town near the Greenhill marshes, so they ought to have what you need. Wait." She ducked back into the room and emerged a few moments later with a coin purse.

"For the boat." She tossed the purse to Verve, who fumbled to catch it, and by some miracle of the One god didn't drop any of the bolts. She wouldn't dare, not with Clo scowling at her like that. Evidently, Danya's preference for minimal facial expressions didn't extend to the staff. Or it did — but only in Danya's presence.

Verve bowed to the steward. "Thanks. See you around. Atal bless you."

Clo muttered a response and stalked back to her office, leaving Verve alone — for about thirty seconds. As Verve went to her room to drop off her gear, Usko and two of the other Chosen, Brak and Livia, met her in the corridor.

"You're not leaving already, are you?" Usko asked, while the other two Chosen peered up at Verve with wide eyes.

Verve dumped the bolts on her bed. Her room was sparse: just a bed, trunk, and desk, all of it utilitarian. Danya didn't care for frivolities like color or light; most of the Chosen's rooms didn't even have a window. But it hardly mattered to Verve. She wasn't here enough to care that the room was so plain.

"I'm setting out at first light," she said to Usko. "And no, you can't come with me."

He pouted, but the expression was fleeting. "I know *that.* I wanted to see if you're free to spar. I've really been practicing my dagger-work."

"He's really good," Livia chimed in. She was younger than Usko, barely fifteen. "He almost beat Trainer Aya a couple days ago."

Verve arched a brow at Usko. "Is that so?"

Usko's shrug was too deliberate to be casual. "It was pretty close, I suppose."

"It was *really* close," Brak added, eyes wide. He was a recent addition to the Chosen's ranks: a twig of a lad at thirteen, still all knees and eyeballs. "I can't *wait* to start with daggers. Trainer Aya still has me on the stupid practice spear. It's just a dumb stick."

"A dumb stick that can wallop your ass if you're not careful." Verve pulled back her jacket to show the kids an old scar on her shoulder. "I got *that* from one of those 'dumb sticks,' when I was about your age," she told Brak. "So don't underestimate them."

The other Chosen's eyes widened as they clustered around her scars. Verve let them ogle for a few seconds before pulling her jacket back on.

She nodded to Usko. "Come on, kid. Show me what you've got."

* * *

Verve squinted in the full sun that washed over the sandy sparring grounds, tucked behind the Temple. While stone wall surrounded Atal's Temple in the heart of Freehold, only a small wooden fence marked the sparring ground's borders. This allowed the denizens of Freehold to watch the Chosen train and, as Danya had often said, "bear witness to their own salvation." Today, only a few teenagers leaned on the railing, absorbed in the action. When they spotted Verve, they jerked upright and leaned over the fence, their faces eager.

"I wish they couldn't see us," Livia murmured as the four Chosen made their way to an empty spot.

Verve replied without thinking. "Serla Danya wants the people of Freehold to know how hard we work to keep them safe."

"I know," Livia said. "But I still don't like strangers watching me. Last week, I fell and some of them laughed."

"Everyone falls sometimes," Verve replied. "What matters is how often you get up. Besides," she lowered her voice, "most of the townies don't know the pommel of a dagger from the pointy end. Don't concern yourself with what they think. Just do the best you can."

Livia beamed at her, and something twinged in Verve's heart at the eagerness clear upon the child's face.

Verve nodded a greeting to a few of the other Chosen and their trainers, who all waved or bowed to her in return. Of the Chosen, none were older than Verve, which she tried not to think about too hard. Most of the trainers were older mercenaries whom Danya had hired to instruct Atal's Chosen on the most effective mage-fighting techniques.

But no amount of training guaranteed a long life.

"No mage-targets brought out today?" Verve asked Usko as they made their way to an empty patch of ground. A few more townies had gathered, some pointing to Verve, who did her best to ignore them all.

Usko's brows knitted. "There was one in the holding cells, but he didn't survive the last training session."

"You're too good," Brak said, grinning at Usko, who shrugged, but hid his own smile.

"When it comes to killing mages, 'good' isn't enough," Verve replied. "You must be perfect. They have *magic*; we only have blades."

"*Hematite* blades," Livia said.

Verve snorted. "Hematite blades mean little when a mage can shoot fireballs at your head from a hundred paces off."

"That's what the crossbow's for," Brak chimed in. "Right?"

"Among other things." Verve glanced at Usko. "Did you bring practice blades?"

He scoffed and withdrew both of his hematite daggers. "I'm not a kid anymore, Verve."

"Oh, my mistake." She chuckled and withdrew her daggers as well. The younger Chosen scuttled off to the sidelines, and Verve and Usko faced one another.

Usko was at that age where he was at least six inches taller every time Verve saw him. Now they stood almost eye to eye, and she realized that despite his round, youthful face, he had the bearing of a grown man. But he was still a child in many ways, and when he lunged at Verve with all of his considerable strength, she sidestepped him as easily as wind through prairie grass.

He grunted and turned to face her, his eyes narrowed in concentration. Verve grinned. "Try again. But this time, mean it."

Another lunge, which Verve avoided again, except this time she whirled around to kick his legs out from under him, sending him down to the sand with a huff. Verve stood over the boy, her dagger at his neck. "Stop messing around," she said, "and show me what you can do."

Usko bared his teeth and leaped to his feet, and drove against Verve with rapid, wild swings. His strength should not have surprised her, and for a few seconds Verve actually had to work to regain the upper hand. Sweat beaded at her brow and slicked her hands beneath her gloves, while the watching townsfolk hollered. But the other Chosen either ignored the spar while they continued their own training, or watched silently. Danya would be most unhappy if she heard *them* cheering.

Usko's strikes came faster, harder, and Verve found herself dodging more blows than she offered. But not all battles needed to be won with brute force. He was stronger, yes, but he was also still just a lad. She switched tactics, leaning into the fluid dance of avoiding getting hit while also making him work harder, faster, to even get close enough to strike her. Usko's cheeks reddened and his breath came shorter with his efforts, until at last his frustration made him sloppy. Verve parried a blow and shoved him off-balance, and he fell to the sandy ground once more. When he looked up, he met Verve's eyes over the dagger's point now over his throat.

"Fine," he huffed. "You win."

Beyond them, the Freehold townsfolk cheered. The rest of the watching Chosen, except Brak and Livia, went back to their training.

Verve flipped her dagger around before tucking it back in its sheath, then offered Usko her hand. He grunted she pulled him to his feet, and when Verve clapped his back, puffs of sand flew into the air.

"You did good," she said. "Try not to *want* to win so badly."

He swiped a hand through his sweaty hair. "Winning's kind of the point."

"Well, sure," Verve said. "But don't lose sight of the moment."

Livia wrinkled her nose. "That doesn't make any sense."

"Give it time to sink in," Verve told her.

Trainer Aya, who'd been surreptitiously watching the spar, called out, "Brak! Livia! Stop fawning and get over here. You're late."

Brak and Livia exchanged glances and took off at a run for their trainer, leaving Usko and Verve alone. Well, as alone as anyone could be while under the scrutiny of the townsfolk. Verve glanced over them—sometimes Sacha came to watch her spar—but the guard wasn't among the crowd. Too bad.

Usko cleared his throat, drawing Verve's attention. "Your mission tomorrow…"

"What about it?"

"I just…" He exhaled. "*I'm* ready for a mission. A *real* mission, like the ones you go on. I'm tired of sitting around here with Brak and the other little kids. I want to *do* something real, something good."

Verve ruffled his hair, sending more sand tumbling down his shoulders. "Training is real, and *very* good."

"It's boring. I'm ready for *more.* You think there's any chance Serla Danya would let me go with you tomorrow?"

Usko shot her a hopeful look that no amount of discipline could have chased away. Or perhaps Verve just knew him too well. She'd watched him grow from a pudgy toddler to the young man he was now.

But the hope in his face, the hope he couldn't hide, made Verve's chest get tight again, like she was back in that cavern. So her reply didn't hold the edge, the surety, it should have. "Not tomorrow, no. Don't worry — you'll be camping out in the wilderness and shitting in a hole in the ground before you know it."

His mouth twitched as he fought back a smile, but his humor seemed short-lived. "Not soon enough."

"Focus on learning as much as you can now," Verve said. "There'll be time to worry about missions later."

Liar. Verve shoved away the stray thought.

Usko kicked at the sand. "I'm not a sodding child, Verve. Don't feed me those fae stories."

Verve's heart clenched. Usko was much too young to sound that old. "Who mentioned the Fae?" she replied, keeping her tone light. "What I said was more like sage advice from a wizened elder."

He only rolled his eyes and turned away. "Whatever. Bye. Enjoy shitting in a hole."

3

The Tipsy Willow

Verve's calves ached from balancing on the raft for the better part of a day. After leaving Freehold, she'd ridden on horseback for three days and nights, camping under the open sky, until reaching the town of Cypress Edge. There, she'd procured the torturous contraption that had already dumped her into the black swamp water three times. Thank the One, her puffer smokes and most of her spare clothes were wrapped in oiled cloth so they'd *hopefully* stay dry, but she was drenched in water that smelled like the wrong end of a wild boar.

Worst of all, her long, black hair was soaked, and it took forever to dry.

Careful not to lose her balance, she shook out her braids, checked her grip on the line attached to the raft, then shoved the pole down once more to propel herself forward.

Greenhill Province certainly lived up to its name. Hilly tufts of sawgrass swayed between low pools and streams of murky water, interspersed with the occasional copse of cypress trees covered in stringy gray moss, like old men's beards. The air smelled fetid and dank, and Verve spotted more than a few huge, nebulous shapes roving beneath the dark water.

A high-pitched whine sounded in her ear. Verve tried to swat the mosquito away without taking yet another accidental bath. The blood-sucking bastards were everywhere, and all the neem oil repellent in the world didn't seem to deter them for long.

"Why couldn't Lotis be on solid ground?" she muttered to herself as she poled the raft along. She'd given up looking at her map hours ago, and had strayed east, following the directions she'd gotten from a merchant in Cypress Edge. By the merchant's account, she should have been in Lotis by now, but all she saw around her was swamp. And mosquitoes.

The cypress trees thickened, blocking the sky and surrounding Verve with their knobby knees and the creepy dangling moss. Something smelled foul—likely a decaying animal—and she wrinkled her nose. First the pitch-black caverns, now a fetid swamp. Trust Danya to *always* send her to the worst possible places in Aredia. Verve shook away her discomfort and tried to focus on her mission — and on *not* losing her balance. Again.

By the first signs of dusk, the cypress trees had not relented, only grown more dense. Shadows closed around Verve again, sending her heart-rate into a gallop, but she tried—she *tried*—to push away her fear. She wasn't a cowering child anymore, but a woman grown and capable. Besides, darkness was a hunter's friend.

If only her racing heart would believe *that* old lie.

Something huge surfaced about an arm's length from the raft. A monstrous creature stuck its head out of the water, dark liquid eyes fixed on her. Verve froze, letting the raft drift with the mild current. A long snout and a wide body ridged with scales emerged after the head, and Verve's mouth fell open. By the One god, the damn thing was longer than her raft. Surely it could swallow her whole! She held as still as she dared as the current carried her past the monster and prayed it wasn't too hungry. Her crossbow was secure at her back, and she mentally prepared to shift her balance should she need it and her bolts.

The raft floated by the creature, who watched her with unblinking eyes. Verve let out a relieved breath, then the monster dove. The wake from its movement tossed Verve from the raft, sending her with a splash into the rolling black water. Cold enveloped her, water slid into her nose and mouth, and for a few terrifying seconds she couldn't tell up from down, let alone where the swamp creature might be. The long line attached to her raft wavered uselessly. She couldn't find her footing and her chest strained with the ache of holding her breath. A flash of light caught her eye and she kicked hard towards it, arms working to bring her to what she hoped was the surface. Something scaly brushed her hand and she bit back a scream, and swam harder.

She broke free of the dark water with a gasp, and scrambled for her crossbow, which she kept loaded for emergencies while traveling. Kicking her feet to stay upright, she caught movement out of the corner of her eye and whirled to see a gaping maw and rows of jagged teeth, and fired. The crossbow bolt bounced off the creature's head and landed with a delicate splash back into the water.

Shit.

Nothing for it. Verve threw herself into swimming, arms and legs pumping as best they could while she gripped her weapon and tried to tug the raft along, and she made for the nearest bit of shore. By some miracle, her supplies were still secure, so within moments she'd sloshed to what passed for solid ground here, clutching her crossbow and the line to her raft. A glance back at the water showed the creature swimming on, unbothered by her antics, until it disappeared once more beneath the murky water.

Weak-kneed relief washed over Verve, followed by the realization that she was once more soaking wet. And the mosquitoes had found her again. Well, the good news was that the ground here was more solid than not, which meant she could walk some of the way.

She stood in place for a few moments to ensure the creature wasn't returning, then rifled through her bag to assess the damage. When her fingers brushed the familiar fabric, she sighed in yet another bout of relief as she examined the embroidery. The water hadn't touched the leaves and flowers sewn into the precious scarf: the only piece of her mother she had left. Verve resisted the urge to stroke the silk and tucked it back securely into its oiled cloth. She shouldered her pack and her crossbow, checked her other weapons, grabbed the raft's line, and continued on foot.

* * *

Mercifully, the solid ground more or less continued for the rest of Verve's journey. But by the time she spotted the assortment of ramshackle wood buildings that she prayed made up the village of Lotis, true dark had fallen and her nerves were rebelling. Every sound made her heart leap into her throat, and she couldn't stop the tremble in her hands as she adjusted the pack over her shoulder and checked over her various daggers.

She assessed the buildings again, squinting through the dim light of the odd torch to determine which dump might hold a tavern. Even the tiniest villages always had a tavern. Sure enough, she spotted a painted sign above one of the building's doors: The Tipsy Willow.

Perfect.

After a brief internal debate, Verve rummaged through her pack again and withdrew her scarf. The swathe of silk was double-sided, with one side holding intricate floral embroidery, and the other a plain, deep charcoal color. Verve's nerves eased a little when her fingers brushed the smooth, familiar material. Not that she *needed* comfort now, of course, but wrapping her damp braids beneath the scarf, leaving the dark side out, gave her fortitude a much-needed boost.

Thanks, ahmma. Although Verve had not spoken a word of the Sufani language aloud in years, even thinking of her mother brought her a flash of comfort.

Before entering the tavern, she nestled her crossbow into its case and secured the latch. The weapon's appearance often made folks wary, and she was trying to keep a low profile. Besides, she was intimidating enough that most people left her alone. Even so, as she approached the tavern, she toyed with the steel wire wrapped several times around her wrist like a bracelet.

The Tipsy Willow was on the water's edge, accessible by a dock that embraced the building like an overeager lover. Verve's boots thudded gently against the wooden dock; old fear flooded her veins at the sound. She cast a glance out over the rippling black water that blended with the trees and the night sky. She was alone. There was nothing to fear. Even so, she shuddered and slipped into the tavern.

Warmth and light greeted her, followed by the sweet, honey-citrus scent of jessamin flowers. The tavern was close and small, but held a few townsfolk, who all predictably went silent when she stepped in. She didn't blame the locals for their consternation at seeing the tall, forbidding stranger enter their home, so she kept her expression neutral as she went to the bar with swift, certain steps.

She set her belongings down and slid onto a stool at the counter, then glanced around for the barkeep. A man about her age appeared out of the back, a couple jars of something like honey in his hands. Verve's breath caught at the sight of his golden skin and long, black hair neatly braided into two tails that hung over his broad shoulders. Dark eyes, cheekbones that could cut glass, full lips…

Then he glanced up and their gazes met, and he smiled. Her stomach fluttered at the simple expression, one he gave so freely — and to a stranger, no less. His smile was *real*, and for the space of one heartbeat, she forgot everything else and simply stared at the most beautiful person she'd ever seen. How in the stars had someone like *him* ended up in this dank swamp?

He set the jars down and came toward her, but when his gaze landed on the crossbow case she'd set on the bar beside her, the line of his jaw hardened.

"No weapons allowed," he said.

Verve patted the case. "It's not hurting anyone."

The barkeep snorted. "Aye, and I'm a sodding sentinel. No weapons."

Verve bristled inwardly, but kept her face pleasant. She wasn't *just* here for a drink, after all. Better play nice with the locals.

"I've no wish to cause trouble," Verve replied, lifting her hands. "Where can I leave my belongings so they won't walk away?"

"Outside." His voice dropped to a mutter. "Preferably at the bottom of the nearest sinkhole."

Well, it was a sexy mutter, but still. He had some nerve. She bit back a frown. "Anywhere closer? I'm not made of coin. If they disappear—"

"Then leave."

Sodding hell, this man! Verve replied between clenched teeth. "After the day I've had, I *really* need a drink." She dug into a belt pouch and plunked a few damp coppers onto the polished bar. "Can't we work this out?"

He eyed the coins like they'd personally offended him, then exhaled sharply and gestured behind the counter. "Set your toys there, if you must. But don't expect me to babysit your gear. I've enough to do as it is."

"Thank you," Verve replied, stepping over to set her belongings down. "You're ever so kind. Small wonder this place isn't bustling with customers."

She carefully stowed the crossbow case behind the bar, then made to go back to her seat.

The barkeep cleared his throat. "All of your weapons, ser."

Verve lifted a brow but slid free a few of her daggers and set them aside, too.

But he stopped her again. "I said *all* of them."

She scoffed openly now, and couldn't help her glare back at him. "You can't possibly think—"

"I *know* your type," he broke in, "All. Your. Weapons."

The tavern went silent again as they stared at each other. The barkeep was taller than her, but not by much, and in the dim lantern light his skin looked soft. He had the bearing of one who'd done a lot of physical labor, but he was obviously no fighter; he didn't hold himself like he expected every interaction to come to blows. But the thin coat he wore couldn't hide the sturdy lines of his muscles, and he smelled of jessamin flowers and green, growing things. But his scowl was ice.

If she wanted information on this Damaris mage, the local barkeep was probably the best place to start. She *needed* to play nice, or at least civil. But the idea of being unarmed made her skin crawl.

Her internal debate lasted only a heartbeat before she plastered a smile on her face and tried to sound like she wasn't screaming inside. "Ah, you clever lad. Of course, I was only joking."

She withdrew the last of her daggers—one in each of her boots and another smaller one up her sleeve—and set them with the rest. He glanced at her wire bracelet, but only nodded when she gestured to the stool again.

"Thanks," he said as she settled down. At least the ice had thawed from his voice. "What'll you have?"

"The strongest whatever's at hand."

He poured a measure of dark liquor into a small glass, adding a few drops of the honey-colored liquid, and passed it her way. Verve sniffed the mixture, but smelled nothing amiss, so she took a careful sip. The warmth of the liquor hit her belly, smooth and sweet, and sent a pleasant tingle into her fingertips.

She smacked her lips and raised the glass to him. To her delight, he smiled again. "Good, isn't it?" he asked.

"What's your name?"

He paused. "Alem," he answered at last.

"It's delicious, Alem," she said, and eyed him up and down. A flush crept to his cheeks as he grinned, before he quickly turned to another patron seated down the bar.

Verve sipped for a while, savoring the flood of numbness to her limbs and the pleasant sloshy feeling gaining ground in her mind. She finished one round and ordered another. And another. Alem hesitated before giving her a fourth round, until she shoved a whole silver coin into his hand, which seemed to ease his conscience.

As she drank, she studied the tavern-goers. Most seemed harmless enough: locals who probably made turpentine or something else disgusting that more civilized places needed. A few watched her, but she saw nothing more than curiosity in their gazes, and when she caught them looking, they looked away. Good. Despite how her line of work often forced her to get chummy with strangers, keeping others at arm's length was always the smartest choice.

But mostly she watched Alem. When he wasn't interacting with her, he was speaking with his fellow townspeople, one woman in particular seated at the other end of the bar. She was probably around Danya's age—older but not old—her face lined with experience. She had a booming laugh that made Verve jump in her seat the first time she heard it. Alem laughed with her, and Verve's gaze stuck on the way his lips pulled into that easy, crooked smile.

Then the older woman shifted in her seat, and her coat fell back to reveal that her right arm was missing. But Verve hardly noticed the absent limb once she caught sight of the intricately embroidered scarf resting on her shoulders. The scarf was of Sufani make.

The room seemed to spin beneath Verve. Her vision tunneled to the distinctive patterns of leaves and moths; bits of the natural world that all pious Sufani carried with them. Once, long ago, the nomadic Sufani had covered their faces when not among their families, but that tradition—like so many other things—had died when Legion had begun hunting down those they deemed heretics. Sufani weren't a race, but a group of folks who walked the path of the oldest god, the One god — and the mighty Atal despised them for it.

Verve's hand stole to the scarf she'd wrapped around her braids, which bore similar embroidery. But of course, this woman was not her mother. Her mother was dead, like so many of their people. With any luck, Danya would find what was left of Verve's family, and then the hole in her heart would finally be filled.

But another Sufani. Here. What would a devout follower of the One god—the god of all life—think of the ruthless killer she had become? Verve's cheeks burned and she stared into the golden depths of her honeyed liquor, and tried to make herself disappear. If she was gone, perhaps the memories of smoke, screams, and fire wouldn't find her any more. If she was gone, perhaps her actions would be forgotten in time.

But the One god knew her dark heart, no matter what. She could run to the other side of the world, fly to the stars above, and the One would still know the evil she'd done.

You do good things, too, she reminded herself, but the thought rang hollow.

The older woman glanced Verve's way, and her eyes widened. Verve grimaced and focused on her drink, praying the other Sufani wouldn't approach. But her luck, as usual, was worse than terrible.

"The One is life," said a lilting voice from beside her.

Verve's heart tightened at the familiar benediction, spoken in the language of Sufa, a spark and cadence she'd not heard in—

Don't dwell on the past, she could hear Danya saying. *Focus on the here and now. Keep your mind on your mission.*

Verve tipped the last of her third—or was it fourth?—round down her throat, then glanced at the older woman. "Sorry, ser, I don't speak that."

She only slurred the words a little. The older woman glanced at Verve's scarf, then offered a warm smile. "My apologies, vidahem. I mistook you for someone else, I suppose."

Vidahem. A Sufa term of endearment. When was the last time anyone had called her that? Verve's eyes burned. She shoved the glass across the bar, toward Alem, who was watching the exchange. "Another," she called.

Alem's brow lifted. "You sure about that?"

Verve ground her teeth. "You deaf?"

Alem scowled and the older woman studied her, brows knitted.

Way to play nice. Verve bit her tongue and tried to add in a honeyed voice, "I mean, please?" But the words came out a lot more watery than she'd meant them to, and more tears burned at her eyes, struggling to free themselves. Verve fought them back, fought to keep her face from revealing her heart. "Please," she said again. "Alem. Just one more."

Before he could reply, the tavern door swung open. A gust of cool, damp air slid into the room, kicking the lamplight into frantic flickers. Alem froze, his eyes wide. Verve twisted around to get a look at the newcomer. The woman that had entered wasn't as tall as Verve, but her body was lean, hard. Black hair hung in a shaggy mop around her face, making her high cheekbones that much more defined. She wore no armor, carried no weapons, and she radiated *danger.*

Only a mage would travel unarmed. And judging from the feral look in this woman's brilliant green eyes, she was a shape-changer with a mind to cause trouble.

Verve tucked her hands below the bar and began unwinding her wire bracelet.

The newcomer scanned the room, then stalked to the bar, brushing past Verve to Alem, who remained utterly still.

"I'm looking for a mage." The newcomer's voice was a growl. A few of the other patrons scurried out of the door.

Alem shrugged. "You should keep looking."

"Damaris," the newcomer added. "Marea Damaris."

Verve's ears pricked. Was this shifter hoping to join forces with this Damaris moon-blood?

Beside Verve, the older woman cleared her throat. "Damaris isn't here, right now."

The shape-changer ignored her and addressed Alem again. "Marea Damaris was last seen in this village. Tell me where they went, and I'll leave."

"Look, I just serve drinks." Alem's voice quavered, but he held his ground. "I don't keep track of every customer. Damaris passes through here sometimes. Usually when we least expect it. But we have no way to contact them."

"Horseshit," the shape-changer snarled. She placed both hands on the bar and dug in her nails like claws as she stared down Alem. "Tell me."

Alem took a step back, hands raised. "I won't fight you. If you want to kill me for nothing, that's on your soul, but there's no one here by the name of Damaris."

A low growl emerged from the shape-changer. Verve caught a flash of scaly skin on the backs of her hands, and the wood began to splinter in her grip. What sort of monster did *this* mage turn into?

It didn't matter. Verve's body buzzed with liquor, and besides, she was *done* with mages throwing their sodding weight around. She slid from her stool and spoke to the shape-changer. "Are you deaf or just stupid? That mage isn't here." Her words sloshed a bit, so she paused before adding, "You'd best go back to whatever hole you crawled out of."

The shape-changer glared up at Verve, her lip curling. She was alluring, in a bite-your-head-off sort of way. "Back off, dreg. This doesn't concern you."

"Like hell it doesn't," Verve replied, gripping the now-unspooled wire bracelet in both hands. "You interrupted my drink."

"Tough titties."

Verve bared her teeth in a grin. "You have no idea."

Around her, the tavern had gone silent. Someone had left the door open, allowing another swamp-scented night breeze to rifle Verve's scarf. She stepped toward the mage, using her height and years of conditioning to dissuade the moon-blood from taking this bullying nonsense any farther.

But Verve's incredible luck held true. The shape-changer slid into a threatening stance, body lowered, hands splayed. Claws grew from her nails, her head and body lengthened, and rows of razor-sharp teeth glinted from her long snout. Sickle-shaped claws sprang from her feet.

Verve swore inwardly. An ummaroc: a type of drake usually only found in the most distant reaches of the world. Why couldn't it have been a wolf? They were *so* much easier to kill.

The shiftling worked fast, so Verve had to be faster. She sprang forward, flinging the wire around the monster's neck, twisting to avoid slashes from those deadly claws. She then leaped backward, using her momentum to tug the garrote tightly around the ummaroc's throat, causing the creature to stumble. Momentarily dazed, the ummaroc struggled harder, letting out a murderous screech that made Verve's stomach turn and caused the final few tavern-goers to shriek and duck under their tables.

By the One, the creature was strong, more than Verve had anticipated. The shiftling struggled furiously in Verve's grip, and despite her efforts to avoid the claws, a sharp pressure sliced down her calf. Shit. That was going to hurt like hell in a few minutes.

"Enough," Verve snarled, tugging the garrote again, adding a kick to the creature's belly for good measure. The ummaroc tried to slash at her again, but another tug at the garrotte stopped that foolishness. The mage struggled beneath the wire's unrelenting grip, mouth open, tongue already turning purple. Verve tightened her hold. "I could slice off your head like a piece of cheese, you filthy—"

"Stop!" Alem cried.

Verve whirled to see him beside her, hands still raised, eyes wide and beseeching. "Don't kill her," he added.

Heart racing, head spinning, Verve ensured her grip was secure. "She'd kill you."

"I know, but that's no excuse," Alem said. The ummaroc let out a gurgling screech and he flinched, but didn't back away. "Let her go."

The ummaroc struggled in Verve's hold, eyes wide, tongue out, claws scrabbling at the air. A few more moments, and this fight would be over.

"Please," Alem said. "There's enough death in the world."

Silly thing to say to an assassin. Verve's hands trembled and her breath came short. The unknown amount of liquor she'd consumed was catching up to her, for the room tilted beneath her feet and for a moment she forgot she wasn't the monster being choked. Alem's dark eyes seemed to swallow her whole; she could see nothing else but him. She inhaled and tasted honey.

Her hands relaxed. The wire slid free from the ummaroc's neck, but before the creature could recover, Verve sent her out of the door with a solid kick. "Find someplace else to be, dreg," Verve heard herself mutter.

Footsteps clattered over the dock, going distant, but Verve hardly noticed. The world spun, her vision went spotty, and the void took hold of her sight and her mind as she collapsed to the tavern floor.

4

A Stubborn and Foolish Notion

Verve inhaled the scents of jessamin, lavender, and sweetgrass. Her head rested on something soft, which meant she wasn't on the floor — or the hard ground, where she'd spent many nights camped out on some mission. So she wasn't dead and she had shelter. Both were pleasant realizations. But the more her consciousness returned, the more she noticed the furious pounding in her head. Although she wasn't gagged, her tongue tasted like someone had shoved heaps of dirty rags into her mouth.

After some internal grumbling, she forced her eyes to open. She was indeed inside what looked like someone's home. Colorful woven tapestries covered the walls and floor, and a small altar of the One god sat at the window opposite her. A single crystal hung from a circular wooden frame resting on the windowsill, casting hundreds of tiny rainbows throughout the little room.

"Alem," Ivet said from her side. "She's waking."

Even the quiet words roared through Verve's head like a thunderclap and she groaned, turning her face into the pillow. The throbbing increased, like her brain was a blacksmith working to outfit an entire cavalry. A door creaked, and footsteps pounded against the floor, coming to a halt beside her.

Cool fingers pressed against Verve's temple. She flinched away, but he kept his place and murmured, "Be still."

His touch was gentle and although Verve's better sense urged her to flee, she held still. Gradually, so gradually she might have imagined it, her headache meandered away, as if it had realized it had taken a wrong turn. The absence of pain left her hollow until she opened her eyes again and met Alem's gaze. His face was stoic, save a tiny smile in his eyes that sent a flutter in her chest.

"Better?" he asked.

In response, Verve twisted to look at her calf, where the shiftling had sliced her last night. Save a few odd freckles and an old burn scar from a past battle, her dark-brown skin was uninjured. There wasn't even a scar.

Her mouth went dry.

Alem was a dendric mage. The most rare of all the magic-users, dendric mages could manipulate particles of blood, flesh, and bone. Verve had never met one before, only heard stories that would curdle milk. Her ribs threatened to crush her insides, but she worked to quell the sudden, desperate urge to snap the magic-user's neck. He'd used his magic to *help* her, after all. But no doubt the moment he learned what she truly was, he'd turn against her.

Act casual, she scolded herself. At least Ivet seemed concern for her well-being. Even kindness could be a weapon in the right hands. No one needed to know Verve's true motive for being in Lotis.

But when she looked into Alem's dark eyes, what came out of her mouth was, "What in the stars and moons is a dendric mage doing here, curing cuts and hangovers?"

His lips pressed together. "There's no such thing. I'm afraid you're mistaken."

Shit. Most normal folks had no clue about dendric mages, so Verve scrambled to correct her error. It'd been a long time since she'd let herself get spellbound by a pretty face. She wouldn't make that mistake again. "I've been around. I've heard stories."

"I'm sure." He looked over at Ivet, who stood a pace away. "I told you, bringing her here was a bad idea."

"Compassion is never the wrong choice," Ivet replied. "Isn't that why *you're* here?"

Alem's eyes flickered to Verve, and he flushed again. "Point taken."

Ivet offered Verve a warm smile. "Please don't say anything about Alem's… gifts. As you can well-imagine, many lives depend upon him."

Verve nodded, but she hardly heard the words because her throat went tight at the familiar cadence to Ivet's voice. But she pushed through the feeling of homesickness. To feel homesick for a home that didn't exist any longer was pure foolishness. She sat up slowly, rubbing her eyes and glancing around the small room. Her hematite gear, crossbow case, pack, and the rest of her weapons—including her wire bracelet—lay neatly together at the foot of her sleeping pallet, covered in tiny rainbows cast by the morning light that pierced the crystal.

Surely they'd seen the hematite in her gear. But it sat unmolested and within easy reach. Which meant they didn't see her as a threat — or they had reinforcements waiting outside the door.

A *normal* person—or at least, not a trained mage-killer—wouldn't feel nervous or intimidated right now, so Verve tried to pretend. But she couldn't look at Alem—a sodding *mage*—right now, so she focused on the Sufani woman. "The shape-changer?"

"No sign after she left," Ivet said, coming closer to kneel beside Verve. Alem retreated to the other side of the room, glowering. Ivet ignored him and studied Verve. "I thank you, stranger, for your interference last night. How are you feeling?"

Verve rubbed her forehead. "Well enough. I…" She trailed off when her fingers brushed her still-damp hair — and felt the absence of her scarf. She sucked in a breath and looked toward her belongings, only to see Ivet hand her the scarf, clean and neatly folded. Verve snatched it from the other woman and tucked it into a pocket on her tunic.

Ivet smiled. Lines bracketed her eyes and mouth; all spoke of a life of laughter. Verve's heart twisted, but she forced herself to speak normally. "Thanks for the heal, I suppose."

Alem grunted.

Ivet chuckled. "He means, 'you're most welcome.'"

"I mean nothing of the sort."

Verve hid her amusement. *Focus,* she told herself. *Do your job.* To Ivet, she said, "I'm still in Lotis, right?"

"The one and only," Ivet replied, sitting back, placing her single, weathered brown hand in her lap. "Did you mean to arrive in our little corner of the world, or did the One god have their own plans for your path?"

"Not sure yet." The lie came to Verve's lips with ease. "I've been looking for work, but hadn't heard of this town until a few days ago."

Ivet glanced at Alem, then back at Verve. "Judging from your, ah, display last night—not to mention all the hematite in your gear—I take it you're a mercenary who specializes in fighting mages?"

Mercenary sounded more palatable than *mage assassin,* especially in a mage's company, so Verve nodded. Let them think what they would.

Ivet smiled so easily. "Well, perhaps the One meant for you to find us. As you saw firsthand, we have need of someone with your skills."

Not if you have a dendric mage to heal everyone. Verve kept that thought to herself and schooled her face to mild curiosity. "You have a lot of renegade shape-changers come through and try to cause trouble?"

"Not just the shiftlings," Ivet replied. "Particle mages, too. Our little village appears to be at the border between mage territories."

"Not that the other mages *need* a reason to kill each other," Alem muttered. "Or to sow chaos."

Odd stance for a mage to take about his kindred. Verve pretended to adjust her tunic as she surreptitiously studied Alem. He didn't *look* evil, but then, mages rarely did — unless they were shooting fireballs or something else objectively dangerous. Danya often lectured to Verve and the other Chosen at length about how wicked moon-bloods were, but Verve's missions outside of Freehold had shown mages were just... people. She thought of the mage she'd killed in the caverns; he'd died in fear, just like anyone.

But she'd never met a dendric mage. Perhaps they were better at concealing an evil nature. Maybe they weren't rare at all, just good at hiding.

If so, she had more in common with *this* mage than she wanted to think about.

As if hoping to prove her own point, she kept her voice conversational. "Perhaps I may be of aid. Tell me more of this area."

"I founded Lotis to be a peaceful village, secluded but safe," Ivet said. "I brought a few friends with me, and more have come over the years. Most stay. Life out here isn't always easy, but we make do. But I fear even we couldn't stay isolated forever. The mage clans have been warring with one another for this part of Greenhill for some time, but they've always left us alone. Until the last couple of weeks."

"What changed?" asked Verve. "No offense, but from what I saw last night, there's not much to fight over here. Unless they believe another mage is after their territory." She risked a glance at Alem, who stiffened. Was it guilt that flashed across his face? Or something more sinister?

"Legion," Ivet said.

The word sent a thrill of horror through Verve's veins, one she tried to ignore.

"The mage clans have always claimed whatever territory they could," Ivet replied. "But over the years, Legion's borders have spread farther south, which has pushed the mage clans' boundaries closer to us. That's all we've been able to learn."

"They refuse to speak with us," Alem added. "Usually they just attack us on sight. It's getting harder to travel to some places."

"From what we can tell," Ivet added. "There are two dominant clans of mages in the area that have been at each other's throats for some time. Legion's expansion in the north has pushed the mage's war south, and Lotis is now caught up in the fray."

That sounded about right. Much the same had happened around Freehold, which is why Danya had taken such care to establish her order of Chosen mage-hunters.

Verve forced a grim smile on her face. "A familiar story, since the Sundering. Have you considered leaving Lotis for a safer place, like Freehold?"

Alem snorted. "Safe for whom?"

"For anyone who can't heal with a touch."

Verve expected another bitter retort, but Alem's chin ducked and his hands curled as he looked at his boots. Guilt, again? What did a healer have to be guilty about?

Ivet sat up. "I'm Sufani. Like most of my people, I've spent most of my life on the move. But after I lost the arm, I wanted to settle down, build a home somewhere. That home is here. I'm not leaving."

"A stubborn and foolish notion," Verve replied. "But I can respect you for it."

The older woman chuckled. "How fortunate for me, sisa."

Longing stung Verve's heart at the Sufa word for "girl," said with the same easy lilt her parents had so often used. All she could give in return was a vague nod. "The shiftling last night… Has she threatened Lotis before?"

Too soon to mention Damaris, but Verve could be patient when she needed to be.

Alem leaned against a tapestry at the far wall, crossing his arms over his chest as he stared up at the cottage's ceiling. "No. She's new. Before her, some squabbling mages burned up most of Hadiya's barn three days ago. And last week, Berel's farm got caught between another group of shape-changers who decided her mushroom crop was the perfect place for a pissing contest."

A chuckle bubbled to Verve's lips before she caught herself and held it back. "Sounds about right. But what's that got to do with me?"

Ivet reached into her coat-pocket. Verve tensed, mentally calculating the necessary moves to disable the older woman in case she struck, but then Ivet withdrew a leather coin purse and offered it to Verve.

Within was a single gold piece, probably worth more than this entire village. Danya had a chest of these coins back in Freehold, and Verve herself had received handfuls for successfully completed jobs. Hell, the purse Clo had provided before she'd left had three times this much. Verve fingered the coin and studied Ivet. "You're serious."

"Not usually," Ivet said. "But this one time, yes. I am. Please stay and help defend us."

Alem came back to the older woman's side, but his eyes never left Verve. "She's a killer, Ivet. She had more pointy bits on her than a porcupine. And you saw the hematite in her kit."

"Those of us without magic must still protect ourselves from its dangers," Verve replied.

Alem harrumphed. "She can't be trusted."

He was right, of course, but admitting that was hardly a good business practice. But Verve knew that indignation wouldn't suit her face, so she merely flipped the gold coin toward Alem, biting back a chuckle when he scrambled to catch it.

"I'm sure your resident healer can give you all the help you need." Verve made to get to her feet, although hope struggled to find footing within her heart. A job offer like this would be the perfect cover for her true mission. But if she acted like she *wanted* the job too much, Ivet might suspect Verve wasn't as innocent as she pretended. Best to play indifferent. Best to not reveal her true nature.

They'd figure it out, eventually.

Ivet rose too, and grabbed Verve's hand. Verve's first impulse was to lock her wrist and flip the other woman back down before common sense kicked in. She *wasn't* being attacked. Not yet, anyway. So she only looked at Ivet's hand on hers, then into Ivet's eyes in a silent warning that usually made folks at least take a few steps back.

But the Sufani woman cradled Verve's hand and held her gaze without fear. "Please, vidahem. The One god has brought you here, to us, for a reason. I must believe this is it. Please."

Ivet's eyes pinned her in place. Vidahem. Before coming to Lotis, when was the last time Verve had heard that gentle word?

Everything she wanted, laid at her feet. So why did Verve's legs itch to run the other direction and never look back?

Mind on the mission.

As carefully as she could, Verve extricated her hand from the Sufani woman's grip. "Keep your gold, ser."

Ivet's shoulders sank and Alem scoffed. "See what I mean? Folks like her care only for themselves."

No winning with him, it seemed. Verve took no small amount of pleasure in her next words. "I'll do the job for three silvers."

A fraction of the original offer. Ivet beamed. Alem glared. Verve tried to smile despite her innate sense of what was to come.

Everything until now had gone just as she wanted. Too bad in Verve's experience, that meant the worst was yet to come.

5

Answers

Lotis was only slightly less depressing in the daylight. Verve followed Ivet through the village's "streets," which were an odd mixture of floating boardwalks and dirt paths that wound through the homes and businesses of the locals. The surrounding swamp still looked murky and unpleasant, even with shafts of sunlight pouring through the cypress trees, but Verve didn't mind so long as the sun was out.

"Does it flood often?" Verve asked Ivet as they crossed over a wooden boardwalk that connected Ivet's home to an open space at the village's center.

"Some parts do during the storm season," Ivet replied. "But the floating boardwalks help to keep the worst of the water at bay. Hadiya's working on a way to pump out any buildings that might flood."

An image of the horrible, scaly creature made Verve shudder. "I suppose you're taking your lives in your hands—ah, hand—by living in a swamp."

Ivet chuckled. "Perhaps. But our location keeps the undesirables away. Well, it used to."

Alem trailed behind Verve and Ivet, silent and judgmental. Verve ignored him and kept her face passive. They passed a small home built right on the water, on top of what Verve imagined was a floating foundation of some sort. An older fellow sat outside, fingers deftly working a loom, blending together vivid shades of crimson, orange, and saffron. He glanced up at the sound of footsteps on the dock and smiled in their direction while his milky

41

eyes stared straight ahead.

"Ivet, I was wondering when you'd be by," the fellow said by way of greeting. Given the gray in his neat beard, he was well into his fifties. "I hear Alem trudging along with you. But who's the third? Not that stranger I heard about last night?"

Ivet paused, and Verve realized she'd not told them her name. She had a few pseudonyms she'd used in the past, but keeping track of lie after lie always gave her a headache.

"I'm Verve." She bowed, then immediately wished she hadn't, for surely she looked like a moron, bowing in greeting to a blind man.

He smiled. "The One is life. Welcome, Verve. I'm Dannel. What brings you to Lotis?"

Another Sufani? Verve's heart tightened and she couldn't find her voice for a few seconds.

Ivet replied, "Verve's a mercenary. She's going to help us with our little mage problem."

Alem scoffed. Dannel's fingers worked his loom as he said, "Are you a mage, Verve?"

"No, ser." Verve stared at his hands, deftly weaving the strands of fabric in a perfect medley of colors. The emerging pattern reminded her of sunsets over the Silverwood plains; too deliberate to be placed by luck. "Are you?"

"Only a little," Dannel replied easily.

Verve's fingers twitched for her daggers, but she forced herself to be still. Dannel seemed harmless enough, but an instinctive flash of warning flared at the back of her mind. Thank the One—or rather, Atal—for Danya's training in concealing her expressions. Otherwise, Verve's eyes would have bulged out of her head. *Two* mages, living among regular folks? And if there were two, there were probably more. How many and what their abilities were remained to be seen.

Heedless of her internal struggle, Dannel continued. "Lost my sight when I lost a fight with Legion, oh, a decade ago, now. But the One god blesses me still, for each color sings its own song, and my fingers know every tune. But my feet still itch something fierce," he added with a sigh. "Sometimes I miss life on the move."

The mention of Legion made Verve's heart clutch. To her side, she caught Alem watching her intently.

"I'm sorry," Verve said to Dannel, for she could think of no other response.

Dannel shrugged. "Don't be. I'm better off than most." He toyed with a strand of orange thread. "You have a lot of experience killing my kind, I take it?"

"Too much, some might say," Verve replied. "Not nearly enough, according to others. But I will do my best to help you now." She hesitated, then glanced at Ivet. Now seemed like an appropriate time to fish for more information. "That shiftling last night was looking for a Damaris, right? Are they truly nearby? I've heard tales…"

Ivet tensed, but Alem replied immediately. "Marea Damaris isn't here now, but sometimes passes through."

Dannel laughed aloud. "I'd not wait around to meet them. If you see Damaris, run the other direction, unless you want to end up like a lightning-fried egg."

Verve made herself chuckle, too, but studied Alem surreptitiously. He gnawed his lip and shoved his hands in his coat pocket, clearly uncomfortable with the mention of Damaris. Verve filed that information away for later as Ivet bid Dannel goodbye and led Verve through Lotis.

"It's best if you see the more recent places the renegade mages attacked," Ivet was saying as they passed by another few buildings. Many sat dark and silent, in varying states of damage and disrepair.

"Lots of empty buildings," Verve said. "Have many folks left recently?"

"No one lived here at all until about five years ago," Ivet replied. "That's when I stumbled on this abandoned village and realized its potential. Managed to convince a few others to join me. From there, we've grown a bit. Slowly, you know, because of all the warring mages in the area. Travel can be difficult, sometimes. But slow progress is still progress."

The scent of burning wood strengthened as they drew closer to the edge of the village.

The barn had probably once been in the best shape of any building in

Lotis before mages had gotten a hold of it. Half of the barn stood sturdy and proud, the sides smooth and even, the roof secure, the double doors held closed with a lock. Which was pointless now, as the other half was little more than charred rubble. The barn's owner, who seemed to be in their late forties, wrestled with some giant wooden contraption, trying to pull it beneath the non-destroyed part of the roof.

Verve didn't think, only sprang forward and grabbed part of the contraption, and together she and who she assumed was Hadiya dragged the ridiculously heavy thing across the space.

"That's far enough." Hadiya blew out a breath, then scowled at Verve. Old but angry pink scars covered one cheek and part of their temple, making their scowl seem harsher. "We're not paying you to move my shop supplies, I hope."

"You're welcome," Verve replied, and bowed a greeting.

Hadiya grunted and looked at Ivet. "This one's mouthy. I don't like mouthy."

"Verve is also quite skilled," Ivet said, clearly fighting back a smile. "Right, Alem?"

He was silent.

"Mind if I have a look around?" Verve asked Hadiya after Ivet formally introduced everyone.

The barn's owner waved a hand. "Be my guest. I'd say don't break anything, but that seems foolish now, considering. Sodding mages," they added in a mutter, then glanced at Alem. "Present company excepted, of course."

Verve broke free from the group to examine the barn. Someone, probably Hadiya, had moved the surviving tools to one side of the space, but judging from the charred lumps of wood and tools covered in ash, the fire had devastated most of their belongings. What must have been a cozy loft on the barn's second level was now about half splintered, crumbling wood.

"What do you think you'll find in this mess?" Alem asked, approaching Verve.

She skimmed her gloved fingers over the burned edge of an outer wall. Still warm. Only mage-fire could retain such warmth after a few days.

"Particle mages caused this damage," she said. "One that manipulated fire, and another that shattered the wood. And they were fighting another…" She picked through the rubble until she found a set of distinctive slashes in the fallen remains of an inner wall. "A shape-changer. A… bear, I think. Not a powerful one, though, or there'd be more blood, deeper claw marks."

"You can tell all that just from looking?" Alem asked.

Surely that wasn't *awe* in his voice. Verve lifted her chin. "I'm right, aren't I?"

"Yeah, he was a bear," Alem said. "He chased the others through here."

"Growled something fierce," Hadiya added. They'd come with Ivet to watch Verve look around. "Woke me up from a dead sleep."

"You live in the barn loft?" Verve asked.

"No, the house next door," Hadiya replied. "But I'd fallen asleep at work here that night. Thank Ea, the shiftling's growls were loud enough to rouse the dead, for if not, I might not have made it out with my viol before the bastards set my beautiful barn ablaze." The ire died from their voice as they added, "Seen enough sodding mage-fire to last me ten lifetimes."

Their old scars told a similar story, one Verve knew too well. "Mages killed my family," she heard herself say, and the others looked at her. "I've seen enough of their magic, too. I'll find the ones who did this, ser, and make them pay."

"Don't care about vengeance," Hadiya muttered. "Just want to live in peace."

"As do we all," Ivet added.

Alem cleared his throat. "How'd you know the shape-changer died?" he asked Verve. "We couldn't find any bodies."

Verve nodded absently, still searching. The villagers' regard sat heavily upon her, and she had the odd urge to prove her skill further — without killing anything. No doubt there'd be plenty of *that* in her future.

She glanced at the claw marks, the charred wall, then stepped past the barn, making her way to the water's edge, where reeds stood thick and tall. The wind shifted, and carried with it the scent of death. Sure enough, the shiftling's body lay burned, buried in the reeds where he'd likely dragged himself after the particle mages' attack. Animals always hid themselves when near their next lives.

"Sweet Mara's mercy," Hadiya breathed, peeking over Verve's shoulder. "That's the shape-changer?"

"Like I said, he lost the battle." Verve tugged at one of the dead mage's arms and examined his hands. Even partly submerged in water, blood had crusted beneath his nails. "But I'll wager he gave the particle mages something to remember him by."

She dropped the arm, where it flopped with a splash back into the water, then glanced over at Alem, who stared at the dead mage like he was going to puke. But surely, a healer had seen worse.

Verve rose and dusted off her gloves on her trousers. "Ivet, you said something about a mushroom farm?"

The Sufani woman, too, looked heartsick, but she nodded briskly and gestured with her single hand. "Aye. Follow me."

A few minutes later, Verve stood in the center of the strangest forest she'd ever seen. Dozens of tree trunks, stacked on each other like log cabin walls, sat in neat rows beneath a canvas canopy. Red and yellow-speckled mushrooms in various states of growth bloomed from each trunk. Another canopy covered wooden shelves that held buckets filled with some sort of peaty material and hundreds of tiny, blue-capped mushrooms. Still more types of fungus stretched out farther, each growing in its own way, no doubt carefully tended by the petite woman named Berel, who stood beside Ivet, wringing her hands.

"I've repaired most of the damage, as you can see," Berel was saying. "But the renegades *destroyed* my spore prints from those Dilt strains I managed to get last summer." She gestured to the splintered remains of a small shed, which Verve began to examine.

"A group of shape-changers," Verve murmured, fingering a tuft of wiry hair that had gotten caught on what was left of the door frame. "A boar — a big one. And… A lion." She knelt to examine a paw print the farmer hadn't destroyed during her quest to salvage her livelihood. "And a deer of some kind. Bigger than a fleet, but similar."

She followed the path of destruction deeper into the farmer's steading, Alem and Berel at her heels while Ivet watched from afar. Verve didn't consider herself a master tracker, but a week or so later, these mages had left a trail that even blind Dannel could have followed.

"They fought here," Verve said, glancing around at the splintered remains of the mushroom logs. "The boar gouged the deer—part of their antler broke off—" she picked up the piece of antler and tossed it to Alem, "but the lion caught the boar, probably by the throat, given the amount of blood. Boars are tough, though. It must have gotten free and run off..." She straightened and looked into the thick forest about twenty meters away, where a telltale patch of broken branches heralded the boar-mage's escape. "And the lion and deer continued fighting. The lion..."

"Won, I imagine," said Berel, glaring at the broken logs. "Wish they'd killed each other."

"They might have," Verve replied. She scuffed the dirt with the toe of her boot to reveal a bloody claw and another piece of antler. "The prints are too far gone to tell for sure now, but I'd wager the shiftlings continued their fight to the last. Just not here," she added, looking back at Berel. "Did you see them?"

The mushroom farmer shuddered. She was older than Verve, in her late thirties, and wore a colorful shawl reminiscent of Dannel's weaving. "No. Klaret and I were still asleep. She'd just returned from a hunt." Her voice broke. "If she'd still been out there when those... those mages attacked..."

Alem put a hand on Berel's shoulder, and the farmer leaned into his side, tears streaming down her face. "It's all right," the healer murmured gently. "You're safe, now. Klaret's safe."

"But for how long?" Berel asked. She looked at Verve with red-rimmed eyes. "You'll kill them all, won't you? Tell me you'll kill those monsters."

"We can't sink to their level," Alem said. "Verve agreed to *protect* Lotis, not go looking for trouble."

"Trouble's already found you," Verve replied. "I agreed to do whatever's necessary to keep Lotis and its people safe." She dug around in her coin purse. "If you don't like it, I'll return the fee and be on my merry way."

Alem glowered, but Verve had judged Berel correctly, for the other woman pressed her palms together, beseeching. "Stay. Please. Do what you must. I can't live like this any longer. I just want Klaret and I to be left in peace."

Alem ground his jaw. "So do I, but more death isn't the answer."

"Alem," Ivet said softly. "This is where your road has led. Will you turn back now?"

Something passed between them, some tension Verve couldn't name, so she filed the information away for later.

At last, Alem shook his head and looked away. "Just don't… kill unless you must," he murmured to Verve. "Please."

Some strange inclination made Verve nod, made her reply just as gentle as his request. "I never do."

6

Fortifications

"Alem, finish showing Verve around, would you?" Ivet said when the three of them returned to Lotis's center. "It's my turn to help with lunch."

Alem glanced around. "Isn't Owen supposed to help you, too?" He tensed, and on instinct, Verve reached for one of her daggers. "I haven't seen him all morning," Alem added.

Ivet swore softly. "He must have run off again. That boy, I swear."

"It's all right," Alem said, sighing. "I'll find him."

"Take Verve," Ivet replied wryly. "Maybe Owen will listen to someone armed."

With that, the village's founder hurried toward the tavern, leaving Verve and Alem alone. Verve glanced at the dendric mage. "Who's Owen?"

"Another lost soul who found himself here." Alem gestured to the boardwalk ahead and they began to walk. "He's fourteen summers old — just a lad. Klaret found him and his little brother, Lio, about three months ago. They were alone on a raft. Their parents…" His jaw tightened. "Dead."

"More victims of the warring mages?" Verve asked.

"Unfortunately. There's another orphan here, a little girl named Kinneret. She's the youngest member of Lotis. Six summers old." Alem's steps echoed on the boardwalk with heavy thuds. "Kinny's mother was a particle mage — killed by one of the shape-changers. I couldn't save her. No idea where

49

Kinny's da is, but she's safe if he ever comes looking."

"Six summers." The sun was high and warm, but Verve shivered anyway. "Is she a mage?"

"Yeah," Alem replied. "So is Lio. Not Owen, though."

"Strange," Verve said. At Alem's look, she shrugged. "I've never heard of mages and regular folks living together like you do in Lotis. Peacefully."

"*Regular* folks," he muttered. "Who are they, I wonder?"

Verve did not rise to the bait. "I suppose you all live here together because none of you are powerful enough to survive on your own."

Alem shoved his hands in his coat pockets. "Aye, that *must* be it. Certainly not because even us filthy moon-bloods desire to live in peace."

The harsh edge to his voice sent up her hackles. "I never said that."

"You implied it."

Verve lifted her chin. "I'm *sure* you and the other mages here are the exception, but even you must realize your kindred are monsters."

Alem scoffed. "High-handed words coming from someone who makes a living from death. What lies do you tell yourself so you can sleep at night?"

Verve halted, one foot on the boardwalk, the other on solid ground. Her heart was racing, but beneath the sun, she knew nothing but anger. "Mages aren't regular people, Alem. Even a healer like you has more power than anyone has a right to, and you can't even turn into a beast or throw fireballs — that I know of. All morning, you've shown me how mages have made your home bleed. Well, I've traveled far and wide, and the story is the same everywhere. Those who don't have magic are at its mercy, and those that do are too busy fighting for power or territory to worry about those that don't. And you dare to judge me for doing what I do?"

He stepped closer, within arm's reach, but there was no fear in his eyes. "*Ivet* hired you. Not me. If I had my way, you'd already be gone. More death isn't the answer to our troubles."

"Maybe not. But I'm the only answer you have right now. And to answer your question, I sleep just fine." Well, that was a lie, but Verve wasn't about to spoil her victory.

She'd never backed down from a challenge and wasn't about to start, so she stepped close enough to smell him: honey and citrus, and a faint, warm scent of tea. She shook away the silly observation and added, "What's your damage, anyway? I'm guessing you have your own tragic past that brought you to Lotis?"

Alem's brows drew together before he looked away, back at the village behind them. "Not really. I just…" He flexed his hands, and Verve couldn't help but admire the muscles of his bare forearms. "I just don't understand why they fight each other. The other mages, I mean."

He nodded to the path ahead that paralleled the water, and they continued to walk away from the village. Verve scanned the area but found no sign of danger — or a missing teenager. "Like I said, they fight for territory, or resources. Mages have no leaders, so they war with one another for control."

Alem skimmed a hand over one of his braids. "Control of what? Aredia is broken. Legion will overtake us all, soon enough."

The mention of Legion clamped an icy fist around Verve's chest, chilling her to her core. She fingered one of her daggers. Alem had thrown a fit when she'd tried to take her crossbow out this morning; she'd relented — this time. Not again, she vowed. She was nothing without her weapons.

"Does Legion trouble you here?" she asked.

"No, thank Seren," Alem replied. The mention of the mage moon made Verve glance up, but the scarred second moon was nowhere to be seen. Atal, the first moon, had just started to wane, and now dipped toward the tree-line.

Three full cycles of Atal, Danya had said. Verve tried to relax. Plenty of time to complete her mission; then she could leave this stinking swamp and never think of Lotis or Ivet or Alem ever again.

"If Legion does come," Verve said softly, "you'll all be lost."

"I know," he replied, voice grim. "I just wish my fellow mages would realize it, too."

Several minutes later, Verve and Alem stood under the open sky, surrounded by marshes. From here, Verve couldn't make out Lotis, just the dense trees that sheltered the small village. She shaded her eyes with her hand and peered across the marshland.

"No sign of Owen," Alem said. "So, what are you looking for?"

"Fortifications," she replied. At his visible confusion, she tried to elaborate. "The best way to win a fight is to avoid one. And yes, I see the irony of someone like me saying that, but I speak from experience."

Another crooked smile tugged at his lips. "You read my mind. What sort of fortifications do we need?"

Alem was actually kind of charming when he wasn't being an ass. She tried not to smile back. "Everything. I'm good, but you need more than a single fighter to defend Lotis. You need actual defenses, preferably several layers of them, surrounding the village. You'll need folks keeping watch too, at all hours. And you'll definitely need a shelter in the village itself." She paused. "Can anyone else fight?"

"Not really. Klaret's a hunter, but mostly with traps and lures. Hadiya can be scary, but they're no warrior." Alem studied her as if seeing her for the first time. "What else do you recommend?"

A warm feeling bloomed in Verve's chest, but she tried to ignore it as she toyed with her wire bracelet, considering. She had a wealth of information to draw from—Danya had spared no expense on her training—but she'd never expected to apply that knowledge in such a practical way. "Traps will suit our purposes pretty well. The right traps in the right places would make any would-be invaders think twice about sticking around. At the very least, they'll buy the rest of you some time to retreat." She glanced over to see Alem looking at her with an expression she couldn't read. "What'd I say to offend you now?"

"*Our* purposes."

Sod it all. She pursed her lips. "I meant *your*. I'm just the hired blade." She shielded her eyes from the sun again and continued. "The swamp itself can—and should, really—keep people away. Are there any natural defenses *you* could take advantage of?" She thought of the huge swamp creature with a grimace.

Alem toyed with one of his braids, a faint smile on his mouth. "Maybe. I..."

He trailed off at the sound of a snicker. In one fluid motion, Verve unsheathed her daggers and slid into a ready-stance, body braced for a fight. "Get behind me," she began, but Alem was already shoving past her.

"Owen," he called, pushing through the tall grasses. "Owen, I heard you!" He reached a particularly thick area and dove forward. A squeal sounded, then a few muffled curses, and the grasses trembled.

Verve rolled her eyes and sheathed her weapons. Moments later, Alem reappeared, dragging a lanky, dark-haired boy by his muddy shirt collar. "What in the moons are you thinking, running off alone?" Alem grunted as Owen struggled in his grip. "You could be—"

"I know, I know," Owen snapped, wrenching out of Alem's grasp and dusting off his shirt with exaggerated motions. "I could've been burned alive, or eaten alive, or something-else-horrible alive." He blew out a breath, then caught sight of Verve. "Who's that?"

She ducked into a half-bow. "I'm Verve. You must be Owen."

The boy looked at Alem. "She's the mercenary Ivet hired? The one who fought that shape-changer?" Alem nodded and Owen's eyes rounded as he looked back at Verve. "Is that hematite on your gear?"

She bit back a chuckle. "Aye."

"Does it really stop magic?"

"Sometimes," she replied. "Though if the mage is strong enough, hematite won't be as effective."

Owen's gaze landed on her daggers. "Those are sentinel daggers, aren't they? I've heard about them. Did you get them from the Legion sentinels?"

Alem's face had gone stony at the mention of hematite, and Verve had to work for a reply. "They were a gift," she managed at last. "I believe they're older than Legion." At least, she hoped, although the sentinels of Legion were known as the fiercest mage-hunters on the continent. For all Verve knew, Danya may have gotten these daggers—indeed, all of her hematite gear—from Legion.

Best not to dwell on that.

Verve tried to smile at the lad. "How do you know so much about hematite?"

Owen hunched his shoulders. "Sentinels killed my mama and da. I wanted to understand why."

Verve's heart squeezed, and her next words were soft. "Have you figured it out?"

The boy sniffed and swiped his nose with his sleeve. "Not yet."

Alem put a hand on Owen's shoulders, drawing his gaze. "Owen, you know you're *not* to leave Lotis on your own, and definitely not without telling anyone where you've gone."

"Aye." Owen looked at his boots. "Sorry, Alem. It won't happen again."

That was a lie if Verve ever heard one, but it wasn't her job to discipline this kid. She waited for Alem to scold him again, but the dendric mage only embraced the lad, squeezing him tight. "I know you want to help, Owen," Alem said softly. "But if anything happened to you, Lio would be all alone, and the rest of us would be heartbroken. Please, don't run off alone again."

Owen leaned into Alem, eyes shut. "I'll try."

Now, *that* was true.

* * *

Hours later, back in the village, Verve stood with Ivet and Alem outside the Tipsy Willow. The late afternoon sunlight cast the painted sign in fresh, vivid colors, but the tavern itself had seen better days.

"Hadiya's barn would make a better shelter," Ivet said, sighing.

Verve pursed her lips. "Clearly not, since mages already burned half the damn thing to ashes. Is there no other structure that could be fortified? You'll need a place to retreat if more renegade mages tear through here again."

Alem skimmed a hand along the tavern walls. "It's cedar. It holds up against the damp. Doesn't that count for something?"

"Sure," Verve replied. "If the mages attack with raindrops. But it seems the local moon-bloods prefer fireballs." A flash of metal on the tavern roof caught her gaze. "What's that?"

Alem didn't look to where she pointed. "Busted weathervane."

His tone brooked no more discussion and the errant piece of metal sticking straight up out of the roof didn't seem worthy of more inquiry. But it was still odd.

Verve glanced at Ivet. "I know the answer, but I've got to ask: have you any hematite?"

Alem grimaced, but Ivet shook her head slowly. "'Fraid not. That stuff's far too rich for the likes of us." She skimmed a glance over Verve's jacket and hood, where flat hematite beads winked in the light. "I see that's not a problem for you, though."

Hematite: the dispelling stone, one of the few natural elements that could withstand magic's effects. The ore had once been far more common before the destruction of the hematite mines well over a century and a half ago.

"Hematite's pretty necessary in my line of work," Verve replied. Guilt tugged at her, but she shoved it aside. It wasn't her fault these folks barely had enough coin to buy salt.

"What about brushthorn?" Alem asked. "It's a local weed, fairly resistant to flames. We could mash it up, make a paste, patch up the walls like tar."

"Brushthorn…" Verve considered. "It's common here?"

Alem nodded. "And then some. I'm constantly trying to keep it out of my garden."

"You'd need a lot," Verve replied. "And it wouldn't solve the problem of the mages who can dismantle wood with a touch. But it'd be a good start."

Alem beamed at her and her stomach did a weird, tumbling dance that she blamed on all the liquor she'd consumed last night.

"Stone would be good, too," Verve said to Ivet. "Got a bricklayer nearby?"

Ivet chuckled. "Unfortunately not. Though there are some clay deposits to the north, according to Klaret."

"Clay's better than nothing," Verve replied. "It can supplement the brushthorn. But really," she glanced around the village again, "walls would be best. Nice high ones of stone and hematite."

"If we had the coin for *that*, we'd not be living in the middle of nowhere," Alem muttered.

An image of Freehold's sturdy walls came to Verve's mind. She'd never considered how valuable such walls were — or how difficult they must have been to fortify with hematite. But somehow, Danya had scraped the coin together.

"Well, it's something to consider." Verve looked at Ivet. "You should also set up some sort of warning system—a bell or other loud noise—that will notify anyone within earshot of trouble, and recall them to the safe house. And you'll all need to practice, of course."

Ivet's brows knitted. "Practice?"

"Aye, you know, run drills. Make sure everyone knows what to do when trouble comes." Verve gestured to Lotis's center, where Lio and Kinneret were playing with Owen, who pretended not to watch the three adults. "Especially the little ones, or anyone who can't move easily and quickly. Get them to safety first, so you only have one place to defend. It's just common sense."

Ivet and Alem only blinked at her, and Verve was torn between laughter and bewilderment. "Have I stuck my foot in my mouth?"

"No," Ivet said, shaking her head. "It's just… well, to be honest, I feel a bit foolish for not thinking of this sooner."

"You've started now, which is what matters," Verve replied. "Best not to dwell on past mistakes."

Sound advice. Too bad she'd never take it. Besides, a lifetime of murder for coin and country was much more than a *mistake.*

It's not murder if the targets are evil, Danya had told her, so many times.

But standing in the center of the ramshackle village, among these gentle—if odd—folks, while the little mage kids chased each other in circles… Nothing *felt* evil. Nothing even felt off. In fact… Wait, was she actually… enjoying this task?

Verve mentally shook away her confusion. She wasn't here to make friends; she was here for a job. An *actual* job, not the fantasy she was crafting. Sure, it was pleasant to use her skills and knowledge for something other than killing, but she was still at work. She could see Danya's scowl, feel the burn of her patron's palm against her cheek for slacking off.

"I suppose," Verve ventured, "you've not had to worry overmuch about defenses, if Marea Damaris spends time in Lotis. I'd wager even the meanest shiftlings won't want to cross paths with a mage who can wield lightning."

Alem's cheeks darkened, but before he could respond, a shout pierced the late afternoon air. Verve whirled to see a stranger tearing through the village, feet pounding over the boardwalk. Berel followed, her hair wild, her eyes round.

"Get the children inside the Willow," Ivet said to Alem, then she started forward. "Klaret," she called. "What's wrong?"

"Mages," Klaret replied as she and Berel approached. "'Bout a quarter mile out. Heading here."

Berel filled in the details between gasps. "It's the same ones who tore up Hadiya's barn!" She looked at Verve. "Now's your chance to prove your worth, eh?"

Energy flooded Verve's limbs, but a sense of calm laid over her, as always happened right before a battle. After all, she'd trained most of her life for moments like this. Killing mages came as naturally to her as breathing.

Alem had already ushered the children into the tavern, and had then darted away to find Dannel. Other folks had started appearing, faces creased with curiosity, then apprehension when they realized what was going on. Ivet waved them toward her, but most just milled about in confusion.

We'll work on that, Verve thought. "Get everyone inside the Willow," she said to Ivet. To Klaret, she asked, "You saw them using magic? How many and what sort?"

Klaret nodded, then held up two fingers. "Particle mages." Three fingers. "Shape-changers."

"I think one of them's an urslan," Berel added. "Sodding giant bear. And you saw a lycanthra, didn't you, love?"

Klaret nodded grimly.

Shit. That's what I get for wishing for wolves, Verve thought. Well, it'd make for an interesting evening. Verve looked at Alem, who was helping Dannel inside the tavern. "I'm going to need my crossbow."

He started. "You're going to fight *five* mages? By yourself?"

"Yes, which means I need my *fucking* weapon," Verve hissed. "We've wasted enough time, and I can't leave you all unguarded. If I hurry, I can convince them to take their fighting somewhere else—"

A storage shed near the edge of town exploded in a shatter of splinters and wood chips. A deep, primal roar echoed through the air, followed by a snarl and the acrid scent of burning fur. The villagers screamed and ducked, until Ivet shoved the final few through the tavern door. Verve swore and clutched her daggers—she didn't recall drawing them—and made for the sounds of mage fighting. Crossbow or not, she had a job to do.

7

Monsters

Verve's boots pounded over the boardwalk. Her options were dismal. Mages were most easily vanquished when taken by surprise, but that tactic was out. Now her main objective was to keep them *away* from Lotis's inhabitants.

She rounded a corner and came upon the scene. As Klaret and Berel had reported, two particle mages faced off against three shape-changers: a spotted panther, a lycanthra—a huge wolf from the northern country of Cander—and another massive predator called an urslan, which was basically the most terrifying parts of a bear and a lion combined.

Sodding mages. Why couldn't any of the shiftlings turn into something cute and cuddly? At least most of them could only change into *one* other form.

None of the mages noticed Verve right away. They were all too far up each other's asses to spare attention to a pathetic non-mage dullblood like her. Well. They'd sure as hell take notice once they smelled the hematite she wore. But for now, they circled each other in a patch of solid ground they'd tamped down. Fire licked up one mage's arms while the other particle mage flexed her fingers, her calculating gaze darting to the wooden boardwalk the panther was about to step upon. No doubt this mage was planning to splinter this boardwalk like she'd done to the storage shed. The urslan already bore a nasty bit of singed fur along its side, and both mages had their share of scrapes and scratches.

Verve's fingers itched for her crossbow, but of course, thanks to Alem's annoying pacifist ways, that wasn't an option at the moment. Fine. She could improvise.

The particle mages were objectively the most dangerous to Lotis, given their ranged abilities. Given how they stood back-to-back as the shape-changers circled, they were probably prepared to defend each other to the death.

Verve gripped her hematite daggers, quickened her pace, and all but flew between the shape-changers, heading for the particle mages. She side-stepped to avoid a swipe of the panther's claws, whirled, and struck the fire mage's heart before either particle mage realized what was happening. The fellow cried out in agony—hematite blades hurt mages more than steel—and collapsed to his knees, blood pouring from his wound. The other particle mage shrieked and lifted her hands, and Verve ducked and rolled as a spray of splinters from a nearby tree pummeled into her like a thousand tiny spears.

The hematite in her gear kept the worst of the splinters at bay, but a few struck through to her skin. Pain needled Verve's cheeks, arms, and upper back, but she fought the feeling away. Pain was a weakness she could ill-afford. She sprang upright, a dagger in hand, and lobbed it toward the other particle mage. But her aim was sloppier than it should've been; the blade only skimmed the mage's arm, making her stumble but not fall.

Meanwhile, the shape-changers circled, confusion clear in their move-ments. They could definitely smell the hematite she wore, and so understood Verve was *not* an ally come to aid them, but regardless, they seized the opportunity she presented. The urslan fell upon the second particle mage. Even injured by mage-fire, the urslan was formidable; it only took a single bite at the mage's throat before she fell to the ground, unmoving. The panther made short, similar work of the male fire mage, finishing the job Verve's dagger had started.

But the lycanthra stared at Verve with the unnerving, brilliant green eyes of most shape-changers: a gift from their ancestor, the first shiftling, Eris

Echina. Now that the particle mages were down and Lotis was safe for at least the next thirty seconds, Verve could concentrate on keeping herself alive. She and the giant wolf circled each other. By the One, this creature was massive; each paw was bigger than Verve's splayed hand. The panther and the limping urslan joined the enormous wolf in facing down Verve. Blood speckled the creatures' faces, and each one studied her with eyes that held too much caution for mere beasts.

But mages *were* monsters, in whatever form they took. It was people like Verve, people who fought back against their magic and their chaos, who deserved to survive. Verve steeled her nerves, adjusted her grip on her daggers, and pressed forward.

"Verve!"

Alem's voice made her heart plummet. She spared a glance in the sound's direction: a clump of thick marsh grasses. "Get out of here," she cried.

In response, a familiar case rolled out of the grasses, bounced over the torn ground, and came to a halt at Verve's feet. By the One, her crossbow!

The shape-changers paused, faces tilting in confusion in a manner too reminiscent of *real* animals. Verve almost laughed. She kicked the case away from the shiftlings and launched herself after it. She'd practiced withdrawing and loading her weapon in almost any scenario, so within seconds she had a bolt ready to go, with more clutched in her hand. But the shape-changers' confusion was short-lived. No sooner did Verve load a hematite-tipped bolt than the urslan charged forward, the others close on its heels. Verve scrambled backward, aimed, and fired. The bolt landed with a satisfying *thunk* in the urslan's shoulder.

The creature's gait faltered as it rumbled in alarm; hopefully the shoulder wound and the mage-fire burn would slow the urslan enough for Verve to get away with only losing a little blood. But of course, the urslan continued its assault. Some shiftlings were tougher than others. Verve ignored her spike of fear and tried to lead them through the marsh, toward the murky swamp — anything to get them farther away from Lotis. Moving through the soggy marsh ground was like slogging through pudding, but at least the terrible footing meant she and the shape-changers were on more even ground. But nothing lasted, so she scanned the nearest scraggly trees, searching for a suitable perch.

The shiftlings followed, snarling, jaws wide and teeth gleaming in the fading light of the late afternoon. Sweat pricked between Verve's shoulder blades as she loaded another bolt and fired. This one struck the panther's chest. The creature howled in pain and the others looked over at their fellow mage. Verve seized the opportunity and scrambled up a young pine tree: the best and closest option. The damn thing rocked and swayed beneath her grip, for it was too skinny to support her weight for long, but she needed *some* distance between herself and those pointy bits. A second after her boots had left the ground, the lycanthra snapped at the space she'd once stood.

Legs aching with the strain of the fight, not to mention balancing on the swaying tree, Verve fired again — the panther's death scream echoed through the trees. The lycanthra circled the pine, occasionally leaping up at Verve with a ferocious roar that sent chills through her heart. She fired and fired and fired, until she ran out of bolts. The panther was dead; the lycanthra wounded but still walking. But not for long, given how it couldn't put weight on the leg she'd pin-pricked with bolts.

Her arm burned; one of the shiftlings, she thought the urslan, had given her a nasty cut, but it wasn't fatal. She'd see to it later. They were well away from Lotis now and Verve's pulse sang with victory.

A low growl made Verve look back to see the urslan at her eye-level. The monster towered on its hind legs, teeth covered in bloody foam as it screamed its fury. That's what she got for celebrating too soon. She drew her daggers again, pushed off of the tree, and leaped upon the urslan. The creature roared, but the combination of wounds from Verve's assault and the loss of its allies had depleted the shape-changer's strength. That was the only good thing about shiftlings: they wore animal form, but they could be demoralized like any human. Fights with shiftlings were best won by breaking their human spirits.

Verve slashed the urslan's side, then leaped away, but her injury made her too slow and the beast got in another swipe at her leg. She'd feel that one later, too. Palms slick with sweat, she shoved her daggers in their sheaths and grabbed her crossbow, pausing only to tug a bolt free from one of the dead mages. She danced away from another swipe of the urslan's claws, aimed, and fired. The bolt struck true, piercing the urslan's eye. Even the strongest shiftling couldn't survive a shot to the skull. The monster cried out, staggered backward, bloody and beaten, and collapsed. As the urslan shifted back to its human form—a ragged-looking woman—Verve punctured her throat.

No more time to waste. She snatched her smallest dagger free from her boot and lunged for the lycanthra, who had given up the fight to collapse beside its panther ally. In death, the panther had turned back into its human form; the lycanthra now lay beside a slender man with a mop of sandy hair. At Verve's approach, the giant wolf snarled at her, but didn't have the strength to stop her from completing this kill, too. The wolf melted away, leaving another young man in its place. His features echoed those of the former panther.

Breathing hard, she stood over the dead mages, ensuring that none rose again. Magic was not to be trusted and she'd seen mages come back to life from the shores of the river of death.

Movement out of the corner of her eye made her glance over to see Alem watching from the reeds. His face was gray and his wide eyes were fixed on the mages. Verve glanced back at the fallen magic-users — was one still alive? But she saw only the bodies. And blood. A lot of blood. Not just on the mages, either, but all over her. By the One, she was painted in gore.

The sound of retching made her look back at Alem as he ducked into the reeds. Verve said nothing to him, only pulled her bolts free of their targets and collected the rest of her weapons. That fight wasn't her best work, but it wasn't her worst either. She hadn't even needed to use her bracelet this time.

"You all right?" she called when she couldn't hear Alem's heaves any longer.

He emerged from the reeds, mouth twisted in disgust. He didn't look at her, but knelt by the dead mages. Verve's stomach flopped. "The villagers?"

"They're fine," he said in a hoarse voice. "They're safe."

Verve glanced at the bloody mages, trying to understand his revulsion. "Surely you've seen worse, being a healer and all?"

Alem shuddered, pressed a fist to his mouth, but managed to control himself. "I've never seen anything like this," he murmured, and started back for Lotis.

After a beat, Verve followed. Despite her injuries, her steps should have been light. She'd done good work, and only bled a little. Surely it was Alem's reaction that was extreme.

But as she trudged back to Lotis, Verve couldn't shake the feeling that she'd left one monster too many alive.

* * *

Hours after Verve's battle, the pyre flames shot upward, licking the night sky. Verve stood just within the circle of light cast by the fire and took another swig from the bottle of liquor she'd liberated from the Tipsy Willow's stores. The mages' souls were heading to their next lives now that their bodies were well on their way to being ash. Ivet and Alem both had insisted on burning the bodies, including the mage who'd wrecked Hadiya's barn. Much to Verve's bewilderment, the other villagers had agreed.

But not all battles were worth fighting. Instead, Verve savored the burn of liquor down her throat, and the pleasant fuzzy feeling in her mind that made the end of a long workday somewhat bearable.

Despite the blazing pyre, most of the Lotis villagers were in a mood to celebrate. Ivet and Dannel's influence, perhaps, for Sufani often held rowdy celebrations during funerals, when emotions were high.

The folks of Lotis had congregated closer to the Tipsy Willow, where Berel and a few others had set up some tables outside. Dannel strummed a gitar while Berel passed around plates of something that smelled delicious, and the villagers sat together as they ate. A bubble of laughter rose from Berel; several other villagers followed suit. The sound was a little too loud, amplified by relief. The young ones sat amidst the elders, eagerly diving into their plates. Owen cast occasional glances over his shoulder, either at

Verve or at the pyre, but remained seated with his fellow villagers. Alem was nowhere to be seen.

The scent of roasted turkey wafted Verve's way and her stomach rumbled, but the thought of eating anything made her guts turn. She took another drink from the bottle.

Hadiya appeared with a viol and sat beside Dannel, and after a few hushed murmurs, the viol joined the gitar in song. The little girl, Kinneret, squealed with delight and jumped up from her seat, dancing in the spontaneous, joyous way of children. A smile tugged at Verve's mouth before she could help herself, so she took another pull of liquor.

"You must be hungry," Ivet said. The older Sufani bore a heaping plate of turkey, mushrooms, and some vegetables Verve couldn't immediately identify. Ivet offered the plate, but despite Verve's grumbling stomach, she didn't move.

Ivet glanced over at the pyre. "Keeping watch, eh? Do you ever stop working?"

Verve tried not to smile at the gentle mockery in the other woman's voice. "Where I come from, if you stop being careful, you die."

"Where I come from, you'll die no matter how careful you are. So you may as well live in the meantime." Ivet offered the plate again. "Please, eat something. You've had a long day. And have you asked Alem to look at those cuts?"

The plate was heavy and warm, and in Verve's semi-drunken state, she couldn't find a reason to refuse any longer. She tucked the bottle into an obliging coat pocket and dug into her meal. "Alem's a mage," she said between mouthfuls. "And I'm dripping with hematite. His magic won't do anything for me."

Ivet chuckled. "Aye, but armor comes off. Or have you taken to eating the stuff like the sentinels do?"

An edge of worry tinted Ivet's voice, but surely that was just the liquor telling lies to Verve's ears. No one, even Usko, ever worried about her, not really. Sacha, back at Freehold, sometimes said she missed Verve, but that was just pillow talk.

"I'm reckless, not stupid," Verve managed to reply after swallowing a bite of mushroom. "Hematite rots your innards and kills your brain. I don't eat the stuff."

"Thank the One for that," Ivet replied, smiling.

"Thank the One," Verve echoed. The words emerged as a whisper, and she couldn't help but foolishly glance around to make sure Danya hadn't overheard her heresy.

For a few minutes, they watched the villagers. Alem had appeared, bearing a tray and several mugs of what Verve assumed was ale. He moved with grace through the others, at once dancing *and* carrying the loaded tray without spilling a drop. When he set the tray down, he glanced over at Verve and Ivet. Something passed over his face, something Verve's muddled brain didn't want to recognize as concern. Ire spiked through her. Did Alem think she was going to hurt Ivet?

And why shouldn't he? Danya's voice whispered in her mind. *You're a killer.* No doubt he'd never look at Verve without seeing her covered in the blood of those mages. Nor should he. It was better for everyone that met her to keep her true nature in mind.

The turkey suddenly tasted like ash. Verve stared at her plate without seeing it. The fire, once warm and inviting, now burned too hot. Screams echoed in her mind. The scent of smoke and charred bodies threatened to send up what food she'd eaten, and the darkness beyond closed in around her.

A soft touch at her shoulder made her start. Ivet watched her. "Vidahem? Are you all right?"

Verve ducked out of Ivet's reach. "There a privy around here, or do you lot just go off the side of the dock?"

She slipped away before Ivet could answer.

Outside the bubble of warmth and light, Verve shored up her spirit against the night. She sat with her back against the remains of Hadiya's barn, her dinner cooling on the ground beside her, a puffer in her trembling hand. Smoke from the burning dried thalo leaves rolled inside thin paper trailed toward the night sky, toward the rising quarter of the moon, Atal. The waning moon was like a lidded eye watching Verve's every move. She took another draw from the puffer and released the smoke in a stream. A wave of calm lapped over her, dulling the sharper edges of her thoughts. After a moment, she withdrew the bottle she'd taken from the Willow and drank deeply. By now, her brain had turned into something resembling the soggy ground that had probably saved her life earlier.

"Thank the One," she said aloud, and leaned her head back against the barn.

"There you are." Alem's voice broke through her stolen calm.

Verve closed her eyes, hoping to shut out his anger. "Sorry. I'll pay for the bottle."

He scoffed and came to stand before her. "I don't give a shit about the bottle, although…" He sighed. "That's top shelf. You've expensive taste."

Verve bared her teeth in a mocking smile. "I'm good for it."

"What are you doing out here, alone?"

"I can look after myself."

"I'm well-aware," he murmured.

Eyes still closed, she took another hit from her puffer. "Someone's got to keep watch while you lot cavort."

Alem snorted a laugh. "Is that what you're doing out here?"

Verve cracked one eye open to regard him. Standing over her as he was, he blocked her view of waning Atal. "Don't you have anything better to do than scold the woman who saved Lotis?" she asked.

"You got some pretty nasty cuts back there," he said after several heartbeats. "Have you treated them yet?"

Verve patted the bottle. "It burned at first, but I don't feel anything now."

He harrumphed. "At least let me look."

"Wounds heal."

"Not without help, sometimes." But he didn't move, didn't try to touch her as Ivet had. Why did that fact disappoint?

"While I'm wearing my gear, your magic can do nothing for me," she said slowly, carefully. Would he understand? "And I'm not about to strip for you.

Or anyone, for that matter."

He slid down to sit beside her, still not touching. "I wasn't implying you should strip, Verve."

Maybe you should. The thought ambushed her, and she couldn't help but glance over at the solid lines of his arms and legs, at the sharply angled cheekbones that belied a soft heart.

Then he said, "The road you're on? I've seen where it goes. And it terrifies me."

A laugh sprang from her tongue, almost making her drop the puffer. "Then why keep liquor here at all? And why work as a barkeep, unless you like judging your customers?"

"Nothing wrong with a little relaxation at the end of a long day," he replied. "But there's a line between 'just enough' and 'this will kill you one day.' And this," he gestured to where she sat alone with the bottle, "has crossed it. And I just… Hate to see anyone suffer."

"Suffering's part of life." She took a long draw and blew out the smoke. "Besides, people in my line of work don't live long enough to die of natural causes."

He was silent. "Do you truly believe that?"

"Why do you care?" she shot back, though she wasn't really annoyed. She'd been called worse. She almost laughed again. "You're not perfect, either. What kind of a healer pukes at the sight of blood, anyway?"

He scrubbed a hand through his hair, mussing his neat braids. "Yes, I've seen blood before, Verve. But what you did today was a slaughter. You… destroyed those mages. Completely."

For some reason, she couldn't look at him. "Am I mistaken," Verve said, "or was I not hired to protect this village?"

"Protect, sure," he replied. "You had some great advice. Ivet's already making plans based on what you told her, and Dannel's already threatening to weave you a shirt or something." He sighed. "But they didn't see what you did today."

"Dannel can't see anything," Verve said, and snorted at her flimsy joke.

Alem rubbed the base of his thumb like he was deep in thought. "How does someone learn to fight like you do? What kind of a life have you had?"

Something inside her balked at the gentle earnestness in his voice, so she sucked down the final bit of puffer and glared at him. "I survive. I always have. One day, I won't. Until then..." She flicked the final bit of the puffer into the darkness. "I get by. Same as anyone."

Alem exhaled. "Nothing about you is the same as anyone else."

In another moment, she might have been flattered, but here and now his words landed like crossbow bolts in her heart. Heat tore at her eyes, clawing its way through the puffer smoke and the liquor, and the darkness tightened around her neck, strangling her in shadows. Her breath quickened and her feet itched to get up, to run away, to put the shadows behind her.

But no matter how far or how fast she ran, the darkness always nipped at her heels.

Instead, she looked back up at Atal. Three full cycles was too many. She could finish the job in one. Then she'd be gone — the sooner the better.

"I have some herbs in my garden," Alem said carefully. "No magic needed. If those wounds get infected—"

Verve stood, cutting off his words.

She dug in her belt and withdrew one of the silver coins Ivet had given as payment. She pressed it into Alem's palm and tried not to enjoy the feel of his skin against hers. "For the bottle," she said. "Please tell Ivet I'll sleep in the barn tonight. And keep your advice to yourself. I don't need it."

8

Different Faces

Two days later, well after the mages' pyre had burned itself to ashes, Verve tried not to tear out her hair in frustration.

"I said, *leave* your belongings at home," she called to the nearest group of Lotis villagers, who struggled to run to the tavern while dragging bulging packs.

One of the villagers turned to glare at her. "These candle holders are family heirlooms. I can't *leave* them!"

"It's just a practice drill," Verve hissed through clenched teeth. "Candlesticks will be the *least* of your worries if rogue mages decide to burn down your house."

"But I already left *all* my winter clothes," the villager whined. "You expect me to leave my great-grandfather's heirlooms too?"

The warning gong rang out again, the sound echoing over the marsh and drowning out Verve's reply. The pounding in her head, already fierce at the futility of this mission, worsened.

"Oh, Hadiya found the gong!" Another villager came up beside the others, also sporting an enormous pack of belongings. "It's louder than I remember."

"Just get to the Willow," Verve said, jabbing her thumb in the tavern's direction, where most of the other Lotis villagers were converging.

The two stragglers made to move, but the first one paused and glanced back toward her home. "Drat. I forgot my spare set of boots."

70

"Forget your sodding boots," Verve shot back. "Go. *Now.* If this were real, you'd both be incinerated already."

Both villagers scoffed, then Ivet's voice sounded behind Verve. "You heard her," Ivet called. "Get a move on!"

Ivet's commanding tone did the trick, and both villagers scrambled toward the tavern. Verve glanced back to see the village leader standing at the edge of the floating dock that led to Dannel's front door.

"You're the last, vidahem," Ivet said to the old fellow. "Are you coming or not?"

Dannel stood just outside the door, clutching at his loom. "Aye, if Verve will help me with this."

Maybe Verve could have humored him, but the damn loom stood as tall as she did. Judging by how it didn't budge when she threw her weight against it, the sodding thing probably weighed about ten times as much as the old man. No way Verve could move it on her own. Besides, that wasn't the point of this drill.

Mage or not, Verve *couldn't* yell at the old blind fellow. Which left her with only one option. She said, in her gentlest voice, "Ser, there's no time—"

"I can't leave my loom," Dannel broke in as Ivet tried to guide him toward the tavern. "Please!"

The clanging gong sent another spear of pain through Verve's temples, but she fought back the instinct to drag the old codger along by force.

"Hurry, Verve," Dannel called. But there was a distinctly jovial edge to his voice, one that made Verve want very much to hit something. Preferably with one of her daggers.

She let go of the loom and glared (uselessly) in Dannel's direction. "It's just a drill! And besides, you don't *need* your sodding loom! And if this *was* real, you'd be wasting valuable time by dragging along everything you—"

The gong rang out one last time, and the ensuing silence swallowed the rest of Verve's words. She pinched the bridge of her nose. "Never mind. The drill's over."

"So it is." Dannel slipped out of Ivet's grasp and guided himself back to his seat beside the loom. "Pity. It was a good idea, though. Maybe it'll go better next time."

He hummed as he plucked at the threads, while Verve stood by, stunned speechless. Sodding mages.

She glanced at Ivet, who offered her a small smile. "Well, we got *almost* everyone," Ivet said.

Verve bit her tongue and slid a hand over her scarf, which she'd wrapped around her braids today. *Don't yell at the old people.*

"I think," she said through a clenched jaw, "*some* folks don't yet understand the concept of 'practice drills.' Dannel, if—no, *when*—mages attack Lotis, there won't be time to save every precious bauble. Human lives are more important than any possession."

"Funny words, coming from a mage-hunter," Dannel replied lightly as he worked.

Verve's face warmed. "Point taken, but I'm here now, and trying to help."

"Human lives over trinkets," Dannel continued, as if Verve hadn't spoken. "Careful, sisa, your Sufani is showing."

Sisa — an affectionate Sufa word for a child. Verve's jaw unhinged as more heat flooded her cheeks. She shot Ivet a look, but the village leader only met her gaze steadily. Beyond them, the rest of the villagers began to stream out of the Tipsy Willow, chattering in a mixture of excitement and annoyance.

This was all too surreal.

"I'm not—" Verve began.

But Dannel clucked his tongue as he wove together strands of violet and indigo. "You are one of us," he said. "Even *I* can see that."

Verve's insides went cold even as fire pricked behind her eyes, and it took her several moments to find her voice. "I'm not a Sufani any longer. My family is gone."

A memory flickered at the surface of her mind: not smoke and screams, like Danya always spoke of, but the sound of heavy steps on wood. Darkness covered her eyes and mouth, and she couldn't take a proper breath.

Ivet's soft touch at her elbow made her start. The older woman gave her a small, sad smile. "We've all lost those we love," Ivet said. "But it gives me some comfort to know they're in the One god's keeping, and have moved on to their next lives. I like to think we'll meet again."

She studied Verve with a gaze full of hope, and Verve went cold all over again. She drew back, her hand instinctively touching her scarf. "If the One cared about Sufani so much, why are so many of—" She couldn't bring herself to say *us.* "—them gone?"

"Legion's cruelty knows no bounds," Dannel muttered. "They hunted our people down, scattered them across the world like chicken feed. All because they love a different god than we do."

Legion. Verve shut the word out of her mind. Mages had killed her family. *Mages* had burned her home and shattered her old life. Legion, and its patron god, Atal, were just in the background.

Lest she think too hard about any of this, Verve glanced at Ivet. "Well, Atal has blessed *my* life in many ways."

Somewhere, she thought Danya was nodding in satisfaction.

Ivet's smile held no warmth. "No doubt. Atal's ways are a mystery to me, but then, I'm not one of his Chosen." She hesitated. "Did Atal bless you with that lovely scarf you wear?"

Verve's fingers flew to the silken fabric again. "No. This is…" She flushed. "A family heirloom."

To their credit, neither Dannel nor Ivet commented on her hypocrisy. Instead, Dannel extended his hand. "May I?"

Weird, but Verve wasn't about to object. Carefully, she removed the scarf and handed it to the older fellow. He smoothed his fingers across the material, humming softly as he turned the scarf over to stroke the embroidered flowers.

Verve shot Ivet a look she hoped meant, *What's going on?* But Ivet just smiled.

"Beautiful," Dannel said at last. "The embroidery is exquisitely done. And only on one side, of course."

Verve's brows knitted as he handed the scarf back. "What do you mean?"

"It's a common Sufani technique," Ivet explained. "One side is plain, to blend in among the kotahi."

Kotahi. The Sufani word for *outsiders* ran like a shiver over Verve's skin. She could not recall the last time she'd heard it.

"That charcoal gray does the trick, indeed," Dannel added.

"How did—"

"I told you," Dannel interrupted. "The colors speak to me."

Verve blinked. "Right."

"And the other side," Ivet continued, reaching to touch the edge of the scarf, which Verve still clutched. Bathed in sunlight, the embroidered flowers gleamed. "The true side, filled with wonder, with the beauty of our world, which the One god gave us." She met Verve's gaze again. "We have all learned to wear different faces to survive, haven't we, Verve?"

Verve stood frozen, staring between the elder Sufani. Knots tightened in her belly, her throat, behind her eyes, and suddenly she could not bear this conversation any longer. She mumbled some nonsense about scouting, then turned tail and fled away into the marsh.

Not even a month into her mission, and she was losing sight of her true purpose here. Danya, the other Chosen, and all the innocents of Freehold were counting on her. But instead of focusing on her task, Verve had allowed herself to get caught up in the villagers' petty lives.

Well, no more. She was here to find Damaris, and kill mages in the meantime.

Nothing else mattered.

9

Asylum

Days after the last practice drill, the gong crashed in earnest, the echo bouncing off of the newly fortified sides of the Tipsy Willow. Verve paused in her exercises—she'd been sparring with a training dummy Hadiya had scrounged up—and glanced toward Ivet, who'd sounded the alarm.

"I thought we didn't schedule a drill for today…" Verve's question died on her tongue as Ivet gestured to the path that led out of Lotis. Klaret and Owen were sprinting toward the village.

Verve's heart stuttered. "Is it Damaris?" she called hopefully.

Owen pointed behind them. "Renegade mages!"

Verve swore. In the two weeks since she'd fought those other shape-changers, no other rogue mages had dared show their faces near Lotis, although Klaret had reported seeing a couple particle mages fighting each other a few leagues from the village.

Of-sodding-course, there'd been *no* sign of Marea Damaris. Verve was starting to wonder if the moon-blood was just a mass hallucination. If—*when*—she found this mage, she'd need to press Danya for a bonus.

Villagers rushed past her to the Willow. Verve allowed herself a moment of pleasure to note that only a few of them carried unimportant trinkets. Progress. Owen helped Dannel up and toward the tavern, where Lio and Kinneret were already safely ensconced for their daily studies.

After grabbing her weapons, Verve met Klaret outside of Dannel's house. "Just two shiftlings," Klaret said before Verve could ask. "But they're chasing a couple."

"A couple of what?" Verve asked, loading her crossbow. She glanced around, but didn't see Alem. Where in the stars was he?

"More mages, I think," Klaret said grimly. Her gaze fell toward Berel's home, then she relaxed at the sight of her lover rushing up with Hadiya. "Not sure what's going on, but they're all headed this way."

It was the most Verve had heard Klaret speak since she'd arrived. Verve nodded her understanding and pointed to the Willow. "Get to safety. I'll handle them."

Klaret shot Verve a grateful look as Berel and Hadiya bounded up, then the three villagers rushed to the tavern. The wind picked up; the tall, cotton-like clouds that had drifted over the sky all morning had darkened to iron gray, and the air bristled with energy. As Verve hurried down the path that led out of Lotis, Ivet called her name.

Verve slowed but didn't stop. "Get to the shelter. I'll return when it's safe."

"Be careful," Ivet called in Sufa.

Verve rolled her eyes and replied in Sufa before she could stop herself, "No promises." The second the words left her mouth, she regretted them, for even shaping the familiar tones made her heart try to collapse in on itself. Damn Ivet and her kindness. Verve gritted her teeth and pressed forward.

The gray clouds had thickened by the time Verve found the mages, who stood upon a small grassy island between cypress trees, black water rippling on all sides. A couple, perhaps only a few years older than her, clutched one another as another trio of shape-changers circled them, pressing them to the center of the tiny island. Verve had never seen these lion shiftlings before, but she recognized the other shape-changer as the sodding ummaroc — the sickle-drake she'd kicked out of the Tipsy Willow her first night in Lotis.

"Back again, eh?" she muttered. "Good thing I wore your favorite bracelet."

None of the mages noticed Verve, so she eased herself into the dark water, silently praying she'd not meet another swamp creature, and made her way through the shallow marsh toward her targets.

"Please, let us go," one of the mages cried as the shiftlings circled. He had tawny skin and dark hair, but even from afar, Verve could see his bright green eyes. Another shiftling, then. But his companion had dark eyes. No mage-fire flickered at her deep-brown hands, but Verve figured this particle mage wasn't without her own skills.

The ummaroc snarled and her targets flinched. Still silent, Verve eased herself onto the little marsh island and readied her crossbow. She'd only get one shot at surprising the moon-bloods; better make it count. Too-well did she recall the ummaroc's tough skin, so she aimed instead for the nearest lion. As the ummaroc dove for one of its targets, Verve fired. Her aim was true. The lion had no time to even squeal as the bolt embedded itself in its throat. As the creature collapsed, it shifted back into its human form, and the other lion roared in ear-splitting fury. The ummaroc whirled to see Verve, then to Verve's immense confusion, leaped into the water, away from Verve — and away from Lotis. Maybe she'd seen Verve's wire bracelet.

No such luck with the second lion, who turned on Verve with bared teeth and claws. Verve ducked out of the way of those massive paws, whipped out a dagger, and drove it home into the lion's shoulder. The creature roared again, the sound blending with a distant rumble of thunder. Verve rolled away from another swipe; a rock jabbed into her back, sending a dull pain through her spine. She leaped at the lion again, using her own momentum from the roll to drag the embedded dagger down the lion's side. The shiftling screamed again, but this time the roar faded into a human wail.

Both shiftlings lay dead and the ummaroc had not returned. But the other mages, the ones the shape-changers had been hunting, were also nowhere in sight. Verve swore and glanced around. Her stomach rolled at the sight of the couple rushing directly for Lotis, hand in hand. She allowed herself a second of debate before she aimed her crossbow at the shape-changer.

The particle mage glanced back. Her eyes rounded as she spotted Verve and she froze, raising her hands as if in surrender.

"In Seren's name," she cried. "We claim asylum! Please, we mean you no harm."

Her fellow stood at her side, panting hard. "Asylum," he repeated breathlessly. "Please, have mercy."

Crossbow still loaded and aimed, Verve strode toward them. Her boots squelched over the spongy ground, the whipping wind tore at her damp braids, and she could not suppress a thrill of satisfaction when the mages shrank away from her. "Give me a *good* reason to spare your lives," she growled.

"Please," the woman begged, hands still raised. "We mean no harm. We heard Lotis was a safe place, and we thought—"

"Safe *from* dregs like you," Verve broke in as she closed on her targets. "Not *for* you."

Tears streamed down both mages' faces. "We don't want to fight," the fellow said, his voice shaking. "We just want to live in peace."

"I've heard that sob story before." Verve aimed between his eyes. "You'll have to be more convincing." She pressed her finger to the trigger.

"Verve, stop!"

Ivet's voice made Verve freeze. She glanced over to see the village leader—and Alem, of course—hurrying up the path that led to Lotis. "Get back to the village," Verve said as they came running up. "I've got this."

"I heard them claim asylum," Ivet said, pushing past Verve and going to the mage couple. Alem, too, stood between Verve and the mages. Like *she* was the villain here. An unexpected twinge of hurt bloomed in her heart, but she refused to lower her weapon.

"Please," the woman was saying to Ivet. "We came here in good faith. We didn't mean to lead the others to you."

"You know those other mages?" Ivet asked.

"They're of my clan," the man said. "We were all on the same side. Or we were, until Ellory—the sickle-drake—showed up."

Verve scowled. The fellow was obviously lying. Folks said anything to avoid death. But Ivet didn't seem to feel the same. She glanced over the two mages, then at Alem. "They're injured."

"Not for long," Alem replied. "Thanks, Verve, but we can handle this. Your work here is done."

Verve hated how relieved she felt at his words. She kept the emotion out of her voice as she adjusted her grip on her crossbow and addressed the male shiftling. "Ellory is the ummaroc?"

He tensed at the movement of the weapon, but nodded. "Aye, she's an Echina, but she's from the north. One of the strongest shape-changers I've ever seen. Our clan welcomed her as kindred. At first."

"What changed?" Ivet asked softly.

The two new mages exchanged glances before the man ducked his head. "It's shameful. We started…" He shuddered. "We started working for Legion. Capturing other mages from enemy clans and selling them to the mage-hunters."

The mention of Legion was like a bucket of ice water tipped over Verve's head. Her vision went blurry and her breath came short, and she had to brace her legs so she wouldn't collapse. When she could look up, she caught Alem watching her. He lifted a brow, but she shook her head. *I'm all right.*

"Ellory set the others on that path," the woman was saying, placing a hand on her lover's arm. "She convinced them to work with Legion. You know those Echinas… They're wild. Uncivilized."

The man's mouth quirked in a smile as he looked at his companion. "Aren't we all?"

She gave him a warm look. "Sometimes."

"Just how many Echinas are there?" Alem asked, frowning. "And are you *all* related?"

The fellow winced. "Echina isn't exactly a family name. It's more like an… identity that most shape-changers choose."

"The shiftlings don't pay as much attention to bloodlines as particle mages do," Verve added. "It's in the name: shiftlings *shift* their loyalties, depending on whatever will serve their best interest."

The shape-changer glared up at her. "Not all Echinas even like each other. You're not being fair."

"But I *am* speaking truly," Verve replied.

"Oh, yes, a mage-hunter's an expert on loyalty," he shot back. "As long as there's good coin involved in killing people, you're as loyal as they come."

"I *defend* innocents from your kind." Verve jerked her crossbow toward him, just to make him flinch.

Ivet placed a hand on Verve's crossbow, pushing it down. "Your names? I'm Ivet. This is Verve, and that's Alem."

"I'm Nori," said the woman. "I'm a particle mage of the Amago family. And this is Kyon."

Ivet smiled. "The two of you are star-crossed lovers, then?"

Nori raised her chin. "Does it matter? We've heard a Damaris owns this territory."

Verve's interest piqued. "Your family's allied with the Damarises?"

"Particle mages stick together." But Nori didn't look convinced when she glanced at Ivet. "Will Marea Damaris kill Kyon for being a shiftling? Or will you give us *both* asylum? This stupid fighting started before I was born. I never wanted any part of it. I don't care who controls what territory."

Kyon added, "And I damn sure don't want to work for Legion like the rest of my clan."

Ivet tensed and looked up at Alem, who nodded once, the motion so small, Verve easily could have mistaken it for a trick of her eyes.

Ivet bowed a greeting to the two newcomers. "Do not fear the mage called Marea Damaris. They know friend from foe. If peace dwells in your hearts, you will be welcome in Lotis."

Alem glanced over at Verve. "Put that away, if you please. We don't need it any longer."

Verve eased off of the trigger, but didn't unload the bolt. "What will Damaris say when they meet these two?"

He rolled his eyes. "None of your business. Watch our backs, will you?" With that, he slipped ahead and began questioning the two new mages as the group made their way to Lotis.

Verve slowly followed, keeping her eyes on the thick forest, and the darkening stormy sky. The whole way back, Kyon and Nori alternated glancing back to watch her every move. Verve didn't blame either for their caution.

10

Power's Price

Despite Verve's protests, Ivet allowed the newcomers to waltz into the Tipsy Willow like they belonged there. By the time Ivet had them both seated, with a couple of Dannel's woven blankets around their shoulders and steaming mugs of tea in their hands, Verve decided this was another of those battles that weren't worth fighting. Even so, she kept both eyes on the newcomers from her place by the door.

Well, that was sort of a lie. Most of her attention was for Alem as he sat with the new mages, bare hands pressed to their wounds while he worked his quiet magic. Verve had only seen him heal a few times, but she couldn't help her fascination. The nasty cut at Kyon's bicep scabbed over, then the skin knitted itself back in place. A clean heal; there wouldn't even be a scar.

The One is life. A memory of Verve's father and mother, heads bowed as they murmured that Sufani benediction, floated to the surface of her mind, unbidden. The One god loved all life, and so too did the Sufani. Or at least, they strove to. Love was hard to come by when Atal's followers were hell-bent on hunting your people into extinction.

She swallowed the lump in her throat. Her family was gone and surely even the One god had no love for an assassin of any sort. It was Atal, Danya's god, whom Verve served now. Only Atal, who craved order and stability, would accept the path Verve's life had taken. To walk among the kotahi, the non-Sufani, she'd had to become one of them.

No going back now.

When Alem was done, Kyon studied his arm and gave a low whistle. "Thank you. I've heard of dendric mages, but never seen one in action. You're quite skilled."

Alem gave him a small smile. "I'm just glad to help. Nori, let me see your cheek."

Idiot, Verve thought, her gaze never leaving Alem. *One day, he'll heal the wrong person, then he'll be in a world of trouble.* Dendric mages were rare, which meant they were valuable beyond measure. Alem was a fool to use his gifts so openly, and with a smile, no less.

A gorgeous smile, but a foolish one.

Raindrops intermittently pattered against the tavern's tin roof in a cozy contrast to the warm lantern light within the Willow. Many of the villagers had chosen to ride out the storm in the tavern. To one side, Owen and Lio read a book with Berel, while Dannel softly strummed his gitar. Hadiya and Kinneret played a simple card game.

Thunder rumbled in the distance. Verve glanced out the window, but saw nothing beyond the approaching storm. The worst of the rain hadn't yet arrived, but the world outside was dark and gray, enough like nighttime to make her shiver.

"Verve?"

Her heart kicked up at Alem's voice, and she glanced over to see him standing close. Ivet now sat with the two new mages, the three of them deep in quiet conversation.

"What's wrong?" Verve asked.

He gestured to the tavern door. "Can I get your help? I need to prepare some more herbs, and it'll be quicker with two pairs of hands. If we hurry, we can beat the rain."

She glanced over at Ivet again. "I shouldn't leave."

"Why...? Wait, let me guess..." Alem cocked his head as if in deep thought. "Because those nasty moon-bloods are just waiting for a chance to strike, right? The moment you turn your back, that's when they'll let their true colors show."

"Exactly." Verve gave him a feral smile. "So glad you see things my way."

He rubbed his temples. "They're not evil, Verve. I promise."

"According to Ivet," she drawled, "Marea Damaris, not *you*, will judge friend from foe. Right?"

A flush crept to his neck, but he gave her that easy smile. "I can make my own judgements. Look, will you just help me? Everyone else says my herb mixture stinks."

"You sure know how to entice a girl." But Verve's curiosity—sure, *that's* all it was—got the better of her, so she agreed. After casting one last look at Ivet, Verve followed Alem out of the Willow and into the electric air. They darted through the village, dodging raindrops, until they reached Alem's home: a modest cottage on the far side of Lotis, surrounded by a rickety fence. Alem led her through the front gate and past the neat rows of various plants, many of which Verve recognized as being rare, or at least not local.

As Alem wrestled with the door, Verve's gaze caught on the mass of vines climbing along a set of trellises that took up much of the garden. Tiny yellow flowers bloomed among the green leaves, and even in the rain, the scent of citrus and honey was overpowering. "What are those?" Verve asked, pointing.

Alem tugged on the ring-shaped door handle, but the wood just bowed outward and remained stubbornly closed. He grunted. "Sodding thing always sticks when it rains… Oh, those are jessamin blossoms. Their nectar makes the most delicious honey — well, it's not *true* honey, but it tastes enough like honey, so no one complains. My parents always grew them. I suppose a place doesn't feel like home unless I can make my own jessamin honey—"

The flow of his words cut off as Verve reached over to help him before they got soaked. Alem went still as she placed her gloved hands next to his, gripped the polished brass handle, and tugged. After a heartbeat, he tugged too, and while the door groaned in protest, it refused to budge.

Thunder rolled again, making the cottage shudder. Verve shot Alem a wry look. "Is this normal, or shall I break a window?"

He gave a helpless laugh and one of those easy, open smiles. "A little worse than normal. Let's try one more time before we commit property damage."

She ripped her gaze from his mouth back to the recalcitrant door and braced herself. "On three."

"One," Alem said as he slid beside her, the sides of their legs just barely touching. Warmth radiated from him and his breath came a little too short for someone not sprinting.

Verve swallowed. "Two."

The scent of honey blended with the fresh green smell of his garden, and Verve inched just a little closer to him. Just to adjust her grip on the handle, of course.

They said in unison, "Three—"

The word whooshed out as the door sprang open, sending both Verve and Alem stumbling backward over the grass. She careened into his solid chest as he let out an "oomph," and they collapsed together in a lavender bush. Another clap of thunder rumbled through Verve's bones as she tried to scramble to her feet, but her legs caught in the lavender bush and she nearly fell again. Until a strong hand gripped hers and pulled her upright. Alem's palm was calloused in some places, but smooth in others; evidence of a varied life.

"Thanks," she breathed.

"Sorry about that," he said. "I guess I need a new door." He gave her that crooked smile she was starting to hate because she liked it so much.

Suddenly it was of the utmost importance that she brush away the lavender leaves from her coat. "Not the first time I've fallen," she replied, not looking at him. "Doubt it'll be the last, either."

"Right," Alem said just as thunder rolled again.

He went back to the cottage and stepped inside, beckoning her to follow. Verve paused at the threshold, assessing the interior for any unpleasant surprises. A single room greeted her. Drying herbs hung from the rafters, neatly bundled together and organized by type. Shelves of books, scrolls, and various jars filled with unidentified substances lined the walls. A flimsy ladder led up to a loft, which probably held his bed. Like Ivet's home, Dannel's colorful weavings hung in every available space.

No sign of danger. Thunder crashed outside, the rain clattered harder, and Verve closed the door.

Alem had gone to a long desk that took up one entire side of the cottage, and dug through neatly labeled jars filled with dried herbs. The hearth was dark. Verve stood out of the way while he dumped various herbs onto the desk. He whistled softly as he worked, stopping only to murmur to himself as he sorted through the herbs.

"Bucksbalm, for pain relief," he murmured. "Cat's claw, to ease any inflammation. Oh, where's that rosewood root…?"

Verve cleared her throat. "Is this the stinky part?"

"That's in a few minutes, once we steep these," Alem replied.

"So you asked me here to stand around, or…?"

He winced. "Sorry. I got distracted. Will you please get a fire going and set that cauldron up to boil?"

She obliged, grateful as much for a way to keep her hands busy as for the warmth and light of the fire. Once the fire was lit, she maneuvered an iron hook over the fire, then placed an iron cauldron already filled with water on the hook.

"Thanks," Alem said as he dumped several handfuls of his herb mixture into the water. "We'll let that steep for about twenty minutes. I'll get the rest ready."

Rain pounded outside. Verve eased closer to the fire. "Anything else I can do?"

"Keep stirring," Alem said, nodding to the mixture. He handed her a long wooden spoon. "Don't let it boil over. I'll have my hands full over here."

He withdrew a pair of scissors and a length of thin cloth and began cutting sections off, folding them into neat squares. Again, Verve couldn't stop looking at his forearms, or noticing the deft, confident movements of his agile fingers. He'd shown the same gentle strength with the new mages as he'd healed them.

Heat swam through Verve, so she focused on stirring the now-bubbling herb potion. A bitter, acrid scent drifted up from the herbs, underscored by something sickly sweet. The mixture smelled strange now, so heat and water probably wouldn't improve the situation.

But right now, everything was… quiet. Cozy, like she could just kick off her boots and curl up on the nearest chair with a cup of tea. The storm-darkened sky felt distant, like she and Alem were in another world.

One she didn't want to leave.

She shook the foolish notions away and shot another glance at Alem, humming off-key to himself as he worked.

"How are those wounds?" he asked her suddenly.

Verve flexed her arm. "Just a few fresh scars now."

"If you'd let me help you, they'd have healed cleanly. You have enough scars."

"I have as many as I have." She glared at him. "Too bad if the sight offends you."

He ducked his head. "Shit. I'm sorry. I know I get too pushy, sometimes. It's just… I can't tell you how many folks I've healed from what should have been totally avoidable injuries. People get reckless, and they don't think about how fragile they are. It's like we're all made of glass, you know? My magic may heal what's fractured or torn, but there's only so much I can do when someone's dead set on destroying themselves."

The earnestness in his words softened some of her more annoyed edges. "That may be true," she replied. "But you can't force your way of thinking on anyone else. No matter how much you want to — or how much you think they need to hear it."

"Easy for you to say when you're not the one fighting the Laughing God for every life that passes through your hands." The scissors trembled in his grip. "I just… If the One god or Seren or whoever gave me this power, that must mean I'm supposed to use it, right?"

She stirred, careful not to slosh any of the mixture over the cauldron's sides. "You shouldn't flaunt your abilities so freely. You'll regret it when the wrong person discovers how valuable you are."

"What's the alternative?" he asked. "Let people suffer to save my skin?"

Verve watched the bubbling mixture, trying to ignore the bitterness in his voice, one matching her own. "Sometimes, suffering is an enemy you can't escape."

He was quiet. "Would you hunt me down, too? For the right price?"

She gripped the spoon handle like it was one of her daggers. "Do you really want me to answer that?"

"I guess that's answer enough."

Was that disappointment in his reply? She ground her jaw. Even if it was, why should she care what he thought of her?

Neither spoke for a few moments. Verve stared at the roiling water and the herbs within, and tried to wrestle with the echoing turmoil in her own heart. When she could stand the sound of the storm no longer, she cleared her throat. "Your parents kept a garden?"

"Aye, a huge one," he replied, a smile in his voice. Like Ivet, Alem smiled so easily. As if on a whim, he set down the scissors and cloth, and approached Verve. He pulled back his coat to show her a tiny gold jessamin flower pinned to his shirt. "My mother loved them the most, I think. My father liked them because he found them practical, but my mother had a deep fondness for anything that smelled good and tasted better. Most of what I know of herbs, I learned from her."

"When did they pass on to their next lives?" Verve asked.

He toyed with the pin. "How do you know they're gone?"

"I heard it in your voice."

He looked at the cauldron without seeming to see it. "I was eleven summers. My village—I was born near Fash, in Silverwood Province—had held on throughout all the mage fighting. We were isolated enough not to attract too much attention. Until the sentinels from Legion came. They were sweeping the province, searching for places they could fortify against the chaos caused by the mages — or so they said."

Verve kept her gaze on the bubbling mixture in the cauldron; she could guess how this story would end. Alem continued, pushing the words out quickly. "They promised protection, but in exchange, they took everything: our coin, our crops, anyone old enough to hold a sword. They learned what I was and tried to take me. My parents…" He took a shaking breath. "They resisted."

"And Legion doesn't care for resistance," Verve said softly.

"No." Alem's voice turned distant. "They killed my parents and burned our farm to ashes. But I managed to slip away. I ran… Oh, for a few days, I think. It's all a blur, now. I ran until I couldn't any longer. It was the very beginning of winter. At one point, I saw a burning light ahead, through the forest. I followed it. But I must have been near the river's edge—near my next life—for I don't remember reaching it. I only remember waking to see a man, very old, with the bluest eyes I'd ever seen. They glowed like the fire. The sight of him terrified me at first, then he spoke, and I…" Alem sighed again. "I wasn't afraid any longer. He saved my life, brought me to Pillau, to the home there for orphans."

"Pillau?" Verve couldn't keep the surprise from her voice. "You lived in the Blue City?"

"Aye, and it's even more beautiful than the stories," he said, grinning.

"I've never been that far south," she admitted.

"I've lived all over Aredia," he replied. "And I've never found anywhere I loved as much as Pillau. Lotis is the only place that comes close."

"You could return to Pillau."

"Lotis is my home now," he bit out. "These people depend on me."

"Someone with your talents could find work wherever you wanted," Verve replied, frowning. "Why stay here?"

"Other than it being my home?"

Point taken. Verve collected some of the bubbling mixture in the spoon and sniffed cautiously. A whiff of what must have been rotten feet hit her nose, and she pulled a face.

She glanced back at Alem. "Why'd you move around so much?"

He shrugged. "Lots of reasons. But I like Lotis. A lot, actually."

Verve wrinkled her nose, and it only had a little to do with the fetid stink emanating from the cauldron. "What's so special about Lotis, anyway? It's a sodding swamp."

"There's beauty here, if you know how to look."

She rolled her eyes. "Tell that to the giant monster that tried to eat me almost the second I touched the water."

"Monster…?" He considered, then laughed aloud. "Let me guess: longer than a canoe, barrel-shaped body, scales, big teeth?"

"So you've met before."

"It's a swamp chomper," Alem replied, brown eyes twinkling with merriment.

Verve scoffed. "You're mocking me? Really? After I've selflessly fought my gag reflex just to help you?"

"I would never dream of mocking you, Verve," he replied, chuckling. "Swamp chompers are very real. They're like… big cows that live in the water. They eat river grass."

She pursed her lips so she wouldn't laugh. "Then why the pointy teeth?"

He shrugged. "The grass is tough? I'm not sure, but I know they're harmless." He chuckled again, glancing at her. "Scared *you*, huh?"

As close as they were, she could make out the stubble at his jaw, and she wondered if his lips were as soft as they looked. She shouldn't have smiled, let alone said, "I screamed like a babe."

"Sorry I missed that," he replied, gaze fixed on her. "I've a feeling you don't often get scared."

I'm scared all the time. But the truth remained locked behind her teeth. Verve turned her attention back to the mixture, which had thickened somewhat, the water now a deep plum color. "Please say it's ready. I'm about to open a window."

He peered into the cauldron and nodded. Together, they removed the cauldron from the hook—carefully, with mild spillage and copious swearing—and set it upon a stone trivet.

"We'll let that cool," Alem said as he brought over a slotted spoon and a clean bucket, lined with cloth. "In the meantime, we'll pull out the herbs to dry a bit, then wrap up the poultices."

Verve wielded the spoon while Alem wrapped the soggy mixture in several layers of clean linen. Outside, thunder rolled and rain pounded, but within the cottage, Verve hardly noticed the storm. At one point, she got a little too warm and stepped away from the steaming mixture, gently daubing her temples with the scarf she kept wrapped around her braids. Her hair was long past due for a good wash, but the process of unbraiding, untangling, washing, drying, and redoing the braids took forever.

When she looked over at Alem, he looked away quickly, a flush creeping up his neck. "Beautiful," he said. "Your scarf, I mean."

Warmth bloomed in her cheeks. She was still too close to the steaming herb mixture. But that didn't account for how her heart leaped in her chest. "My mother embroidered it," she said.

"It looks like the ones Ivet wears. Is it Sufani?"

"Yes."

When she said nothing more, he turned back to the poultices. "Your mother must have been very skilled."

Must have been. Of course, it was easy to guess that someone like Verve didn't have a loving mother waiting for her in some comfortable home. But, Alem hadn't pressed her for information. Weirdly, this set her more at ease, which in turn made her wary all over again. By the One god, living in her head was exhausting.

A bright burst of lighting flared behind the curtains as the storm pounded at Alem's back door. Verve's pulse leaped in response, so she went to the cottage window and brushed aside one of Dannel's weavings to squint through the downpour. More lightning flashed, illuminating the nearby trees. Hadiya's barn was within sight; a streak of lightning danced upon a metal rod atop the structure. Verve recalled seeing another metal rod on top of the Willow.

"What in Ea's realm is going on?" Verve asked. "Why's there so much lightning?" Her breath caught. Oh, stars and moons, was Damaris actually *real?* Everyone acted so cagey when the "powerful mage" was mentioned; Verve had started to wonder if this mage was just some tale the locals had cooked up.

Alem came to stand beside her, wiping his hands on his trousers. "It's not magic, if that's what you're wondering."

"But the lightning is *related* to Marea Damaris?" No use trying to play coy any longer. Verve needed a proper answer.

"How much coin will you get for bringing them in?" Alem asked suddenly.

"It must be a lot, otherwise you wouldn't have stuck around." She opened her mouth to argue, but he shook his head. "I know why you're really here, Verve. Ivet knows, too."

Was this another battle not worth fighting, or one she'd already lost? It was getting harder and harder to tell the difference. "There *is* good coin in bringing in a mage like Damaris," Verve finally admitted. "But the proper authorities have reasons to want a mage like that in their custody."

Alem snorted. "'The proper authorities.' What does that mean? Who has the right to say if someone else should live or die?" His voice dropped to a murmur. "What has Damaris done other than protect us?"

Verve tried to ignore the bitter edge to his words. "The world is terrifying right now," she said quietly. "People are scared. And magic is strange, which makes it dangerous, which only strengthens the fear that most folks live with every day."

He hugged himself and looked at the floor. "Magic doesn't *have* to be dangerous."

She skimmed her fingertips over the hematite buttons on her coat, savoring their polished surfaces. "But it can be. Surely I don't have to tell you that."

"Being afraid doesn't give anyone the right to hunt folks down like animals," Alem replied. "For coin, no less."

She met his gaze. "Wouldn't you pay to keep your loved ones safe?"

To his credit, he did not look away. "I must believe there's another way — a way without bloodshed."

"Is that what *Damaris* thinks," Verve mused, "or just Alem?"

His jaw tightened. "Marea Damaris is beyond your reach — beyond anyone's reach." He paused, toying with the flower pin on his shirt. "If you can't find them here, will you leave?"

Was that sorrow behind his words, or hope? Verve couldn't tell one from the other, sometimes.

Would she leave? If she didn't, someone would eventually come looking for her. Hell, Verve should have sent an update by now. No doubt Danya was immensely curious how this job was going. Except if Verve returned to Danya empty-handed, her failure would be punished. So that wasn't an option.

But the other option left a taste in the back of her mouth that reminded her too much of the healing herb mixture: bitter, but probably for the best.

Verve said, "I suppose my absence would make your life easier."

Lightning flashed again, followed seconds later by a distant rumble of thunder. Alem looked at her, and there was no mistaking the heat in his gaze, the expression that made her heart fling itself at her ribs, as if trying to reach him.

"Easier, perhaps," he said. "But definitely less interesting."

11

The Meridian

A few days after the storm, more visitors came to Lotis. Verve had spent the day scouting the surrounding area, searching for traces of a lightning mage's presence, and so did not learn of the newcomers until Owen, breathless, found her on her way back early that evening. She'd risked the raft again, for it made travel quicker and easier—assuming she didn't fall off—and so she poled along beside the marsh bank as Owen reported the news.

"Ivet called one of them a 'meridian,'" Owen said as he trotted along the bank, parallel to Verve.

Verve frowned. "Never heard of them. Are they a mage?"

"I don't think so. Well, maybe," he admitted. "Ivet said something about meridians being able to 'pull out the truth like a rotten tooth.' The meridian—she said her name was Sohvi—looks… strange. Her eyes sort of glow, sometimes."

Glowing eyes. Verve recalled Alem's story of the old man who'd rescued him as a boy. And her own encounter in the caverns, with the man she'd brought to Danya. Misgiving pricked at the base of her spine. "And the other?"

Owen grinned. "Hasina. Judging from the axes she's wearing, she's either a warrior or a really dedicated woodcutter. You'll love her. Maybe you can spar together. Or she'll turn out to be evil, and you'll fight each other."

Owen added. "Either way, I want to watch. I bet I could learn a lot."

It was easier to lower her guard around the kid. He reminded Verve of Usko in some ways. Too eager to grow up; too young to realize the error. "I hope the former," she said.

But she was prepared for the latter.

After arriving back at Lotis, she tied up the raft and checked her weapons — just in case. Walking into the Willow with her crossbow loaded would probably not go over well—Owen had said Ivet had offered the newcomers shelter for the night, which meant they were guests—but Verve ensured the rest of her weapons, including her wire bracelet, were hidden but close to hand.

She entered the tavern, where Owen had already returned. Inside, many of the Lotis villagers sat in a semi-circle around the newcomers: two older women. One had thick silver braids draped down her back, while the other sported close-cropped, white hair. As Owen had reported, a pair of sharp axes rested at the short-haired woman's belt, and Verve frowned at the sight. Why had Alem not confiscated *her* weapons?

Come to think of it... where was Alem? He wasn't behind the bar or among the other locals here. Perhaps he was in the storeroom. Still, Verve approached the group on wary steps.

"Ah, there you are," Ivet called, beckoning her forward. "I'll apologize now for letting strangers among us—she's very protective," she added as an aside to the newcomers, "but you must meet our new friends."

The woman with the braids glanced over at Verve. Her eyes were brown, surely, but for a moment, they glowed like twin stars. The sight froze Verve in place. Magic. It must be. But what sort of mage had glowing eyes?

The meridian regarded Verve with interest. "You are Vervaine."

It wasn't a question. And Verve had not told Ivet—or anyone here—her full name.

She kept her features impassive and gave a shallow bow. "You must be Sohvi."

The warrior, Hasina, shifted, gaze locked onto Verve. The meridian inclined her head and the glow in her eyes faded, leaving them a predictable dark brown. "You have recently come to Lotis?"

"Yes," Verve replied.

No one else spoke. All the air in the tavern seemed to have evaporated. Why did Verve feel like she was under investigation?

"From where?" Sohvi asked. Her voice was melodic, but Verve could hear a polished, keen edge. And Hasina stared at her like she'd caught Verve in bed with her lover.

Verve strolled through the tavern as if she owned it, hoping her bravado would ease some of the tension and give her a moment to collect her wits. She went behind the bar—still no sign of Alem—and poured herself a drink before replying. "I get around. You?"

"Our home is in Pillau," Sohvi said, her gaze sliding to Ivet. "But we have traveled far."

"I imagine so," Ivet replied, nodding. "Are the stories true?"

What stories? Verve tensed as she waited for Sohvi's response.

"Depends on the stories," Sohvi said, a smile in her voice. She cast a glance at Hasina. "I drag my poor anchor all across Aredia."

"Yes, poor me, indeed." Hasina's grin transformed her face as much as the fondness in her voice. So they were lovers, or something like it. Verve stored the information away. Stranger, though, was the term "anchor" in this context. Was Hasina a sailor or something?

Verve took another draw from her mug, savoring Alem's jessamin-sweetened ale. She preferred liquor, but something about these two newcomers made her want to keep her head clear a while longer. When she looked up, Sohvi stood on the other side of the bar. Hasina spoke to the others; by the cadence of her voice, she was telling them some story that had them all enchanted.

Sohvi studied Verve. "I know you."

"Most people don't like to admit that," Verve replied, drinking again.

Something flashed in Sohvi's eyes. Not that weird glow, but something else. Anger. But her voice was steady as a river. "Hasina and I are seeking another meridian. A dear friend of mine. His name is Celidon."

"Get behind me, Celidon."

Verve's fingers tightened around the mug's handle as the memory flared to life. She'd stalked the mage and his strange companion, followed them beneath the ground, across the underground river.

"No one here by that name," she managed at last, and took another sip.

"So I hear. But *you* know where he is, Vervaine."

Verve tried to give a dismissive laugh. "I think you've got the wrong idea, ser. I'm not your friend's keeper."

"No." Sohvi's eyes glowed now, bright enough to sting. "But you are Karel's killer. I saw you. Cel showed me everything, right before you took him into custody, right before you clapped him in irons and cut off our connection. And now," she leaned forward, piercing Verve with that star-bright gaze, "you will tell me where Celidon is."

The mug slipped from Verve's hand. It hit the floor and shattered, and the tavern went silent again. Verve tried to move, tried to back away, but Sohvi's gaze held her in place as much as her memories of the encounter in the cavern. Her heart tore at her chest, her hands shook, her breath came short, but she could not run away, nor hide. All she could do was stare at the meridian and fight back the urge to confess all of her sins.

"I… d-don't know what you mean," she stammered at last.

Sohvi's eyes glowed brighter, blinding, searing. Verve couldn't look away. Was no one going to intervene?

Why should they, when she was in the wrong? Why should anyone help a monster?

Verve was alone, as she'd been for so long. She would always be alone.

She deserved to be alone.

Sohvi's voice sounded in Verve's mind, as though the other woman spoke aloud. *Where is Celidon?*

The words echoed in her brain like a hundred gongs ringing. Verve couldn't shut them out, couldn't ignore them, couldn't hide or run away. Her throat burned with the truth, and eventually, it clawed its way free. She lost.

"Freehold," she whispered. "He's in Freehold."

The glow dimmed. Sohvi leaned back, a satisfied tilt to her chin. She glanced over her shoulder, where Hasina stood, watching the two of them. Verve hadn't noticed when the warrior had gotten up.

At Sohvi's look, the warrior nodded, then looked back at Ivet. "I'm sorry, ser, but it appears we'll not be staying the night after all."

To Verve's shock—and relief—the Lotis villagers seemed not to have noticed the… whatever had occurred between her and Sohvi. Ivet did give Verve a mildly curious glance, but seemed otherwise unconcerned. "I'm sorry to hear that, but of course, you must be quite busy."

The meridian and her warrior left, but Verve hardly noticed. She tried to sweep up the broken ceramic from her mug, but her hands shook and her head was light, and she couldn't work the broom properly.

Ivet returned, coming around the bar. "Verve? Are you all right?"

No. Verve nodded briskly. "I'm fine, Ivet. Just tired. And clumsy, it seems."

Ivet gave her a warm look. "Vidahem, you work too hard. Besides, I didn't pay you to clean. Go rest. We'll take care of this." She shooed Verve out from behind the bar and called someone else over to sweep.

Verve didn't look at anyone as she slipped outside, sucking in the evening air that was still a little too cool for spring. The meridian was gone, but Verve could still see her eyes, burning like stars.

She swiped at her cheeks and stared at the moisture on her fingers. When was the last time she'd wept?

Atal hung on the horizon like a lidded eye. The waning moon reminded her of her mission, so Verve dug her nails into her palm. She had to focus. The pain broke through her stupid self-pity, brought her back to her senses. Even so, her hands trembled as she fished out her tinderbox and another puffer from her pocket.

She lit the puffer, and a few deep draws brought her a sense of calm once more, chasing away the memory of Sohvi's star-bright eyes, of Celidon's pleas for his life.

"It was just a job," Verve said to no one. "It wasn't personal. It was for the greater good."

All true. So why did she still weep?

* * *

Verve meant to find Alem once she'd finished her smoke, but instead she returned to Hadiya's loft, where she spent the nights it wasn't raining. There, she opened a bottle of Dilt brandy from her personal stores, and the rest of the evening faded into a blur. Although the barn's roof had seen better days, the charred opening gave Verve a perfect vantage point to watch over the road leading into Lotis. Or so she told herself.

She saw no trace of the meridian and her anchor. Had they truly left? If they were hoping to ambush Verve, they'd find more trouble than they bargained for.

But the memory of the meridian's glowing eyes made Verve shudder. She lit another puffer to chase away the recollection.

When true night fell, Verve lit the lanterns she'd brought up here, casting the small space in a warm, comforting glow. As she finished, footsteps sounded below. Someone had entered the lower level. Verve's muscles were loose at this point, but the thought of a fight wasn't unwelcome. It'd be good to do *something* with this nervous energy, after all.

"Who's there?" she called.

"Just me," Alem replied.

Verve's heart soared but, she tamped down the feeling. "What's wrong?"

The ladder creaked as he climbed to the loft. His head popped up, his long hair hanging loose around his shoulders as he inhaled, then regarded her. "Care for some company?"

She waved a hand. "Step into my parlor."

The loft was fairly large, but most of it was too damaged to be of use. After much inspection and testing, Verve and Hadiya had figured out that one side was structurally sound. So when Alem clambered up the ladder and stepped onto the loft platform, the wood thankfully didn't do more than creak in protest.

He carefully picked his way toward Verve, sniffing the air again. His gaze fell to the almost-empty bottle beside her and he raised a brow.

She gripped the bottle to her chest. "It's not from the Willow. Calm down."

"I wasn't…" He sighed and dropped to a seated position by the windowsill, leaning on one elbow to gaze at the moonless sky. Both Atal and Seren had set by now, but each moon would appear again in its own time.

"I heard you met our guests," Alem said.

Verve took another draw from her puffer. "You could say that. Didn't see you there, though."

He grunted. "What'd you think of them?"

Verve considered. "Hasina's strong, and could probably best me if she caught me by surprise. But I'd bet that I'm the more creative fighter. No doubt she's more… particular with her morals than I am. Sohvi…" She fingered the puffer. "I'd have to kill her first, and quickly. She's no mage—as far as I could tell—but still dangerous. A jab at her throat would do the trick. Messy, but effective. I could probably defeat them both within five minutes, given the right circumstances. Ten, if they caught me unawares. But most people don't manage that."

Alem's eyes rounded as he stared at her. "Ea's tits and balls…"

The shock in his voice meant she'd let a little too much of her nature slip free. Cheeks burning, Verve retreated to her bottle, downing a huge swallow in what she hoped was a casual manner.

"I meant," Alem said slowly, deliberately, "what did you think of them as people? Not how you'd…kill them."

"What else is there to know about someone?" The words sprang free before she could stop them.

Alem's gaze fell on the bottle again. "Have you ever met a meridian?"

The heat in her cheeks somehow correlated with how her voice became more slurred. "Why's everyone so sodding fixated on whether I've met someone with freakish glowing eyes?"

He skimmed a hand through his hair, which fell around his face like a silken curtain. "Never mind." He got to his feet. "I shouldn't have come."

"Wait." She stood, too, and promptly bonked her head on the low, slanted roof. Grimacing, she went to him, straightening when she reached his side, where the roof was at its tallest. "Alem, I didn't like them," she admitted. "They…bothered me."

His brows shot up. "They hurt you?"

"No, I wasn't hurt." She tried not to notice the way his forearms flexed as he tightened his hand into fists. "But the meridian did something to me; used some kind of magic I've never encountered."

"She pulled the truth from you?" Alem asked. When Verve nodded, he seemed to consider his answer. "Meridians have that ability, though I'm told only a few can manage it."

Her head throbbed; she pressed her fingertips against the sore spot. Alem's eyes darted to her fingers, then to her hematite-embedded coat. The question hung between them, unasked, and Verve was almost drunk enough to answer it.

Almost.

Alem glanced out the window again. "I realized what Sohvi was the second Owen described her to me."

"You don't like meridians?"

He gave a soft, bitter laugh. "Much the opposite." At her confused look, he folded his legs and sat back down. She followed, blowing the puffer smoke out of the window as he continued. "Meridians can live much longer than normal folks. The man who saved me when I was a boy — he was a meridian. One of the first ones, so I later learned. His name was Milo. He was…kind. Gentle. He discouraged fighting, even shouting in anger. He always tried to bring peace to anyone in a conflict. When Milo discovered my abilities, he encouraged me to use them for good things: to heal, to comfort, to ease pain."

Alem leaned his chin on his hand. "Most mages used to be able to do what I can: to manipulate a body's particles. Most of them used that power to heal. But some…" He took a deep breath. "Some, I'm told, used it for ill-deeds. They could dismantle a body, piece by piece. They could destroy someone from the inside-out, steal their energy, their magic, indeed their very life, with a simple touch. So you can understand why dendric mages like me were hunted down and destroyed. Eventually, so Milo said, the ability grew more rare, until it all but vanished."

None of that had occurred to Verve, and she couldn't suppress a shudder at the images his word evoked. "And I thought mages throwing fireballs or turning into giant bears were bad."

"Hardly the worst evils magic can do." Alem offered her a crooked smile, which faded quickly. "Growing up, my parents taught me to fear my magic. They were terrified using it would get me killed — or worse. Instead, it got *them* killed. I hated who I was for a long time after. Milo helped me learn to like myself, even embrace my abilities. But he always cautioned me to use my powers to heal, not to harm." He sighed heavily. "I wanted so badly to be a meridian like him. Meridians help people; they heal the spirit. They make the world a better place."

Well, that sounded strange, but interesting in an even stranger way — like how her target Celidon had somehow sensed Verve right before she'd taken him prisoner. "So they *are* mages?"

"No. Meridians acquire their abilities later in life, usually after years of training and preparation, and a recommendation from another meridian."

Verve considered this. "'Acquire their abilities?' What's that supposed to mean?"

Alem shook his head. "I don't know the specifics, but their powers have something to do with," his voice dropped to a whisper, "the Fae."

Verve stared at him, then threw back her head and laughed. "The Fae? Those creatures in the children's tales? I thought you were too old to believe in glimmer stories."

"Laugh all you want—"

"Oh, I will," Verve giggled.

"I've seen meridians work their own sort of magic," Alem went on. "But while they're powerful in their own rights, their connection to the Fae has odd consequences. Like… they can't touch iron. It burns them or something."

This gave Verve pause, for Sohvi had mentioned iron rather scornfully. And Celidon had reacted badly at the iron chains she'd bound him with. "You've seen iron burn a meridian?"

"Well, no," Alem admitted. "But Milo spoke of it."

Weirder and weirder. Verve hummed in thought. "What sort of magic do meridians do again?"

"They have some sort of connection to the Fae realm, and use it to heal wounds—not physical ones, but scars on people's minds and hearts."

None of that sounded like either of her encounters with meridians. Verve sniffed at her bottle of Dilt brandy, in case someone had spiked it with something stronger. Much stronger. "You believe all of this fae shit?"

"I saw Milo use these powers a few times when I lived in Pillau. The meridians have a…haven there, called Mirrormoon."

"Well, they sound perfect for you," Verve replied. "Why didn't you join them?"

Alem's jaw tightened. "They don't allow mages in their ranks."

Verve pursed her lips. "Seems foolish. You're already a powerful healer. What's the problem?"

He sighed heavily. "Milo never quite explained, not to my satisfaction, anyway. He only said 'I'm sorry, but I made a promise.' As best I can figure, mage magic doesn't mix well with meridian abilities."

But that was clearly a cold comfort. Verve had an urge to put a hand on his cheek, to pull him close, though what comfort *she* could offer, she had no clue.

The puffer was done, so she eased a little closer to him and told herself it was the liquor buzzing in her head that made her silently urge Alem to meet her eyes. "I don't care how old *and-or* wise this Milo person is," she said. "If he rejected *you*, he's a sodding fool."

Alem gave her a thin smile. "He wasn't, but thanks. But maybe you can understand why I wasn't so eager to meet with Sohvi today."

The mention of Sohvi brought Verve's last mission roaring back to life in her mind once more, for all that she'd hoped to obscure the memory with smoke and liquor. She pulled away, drew her legs up to her chest, and hugged her knees. Alem's quiet admission resonated in her heart and she wanted to reciprocate somehow. But how? And more importantly, why?

If he knows more of what you are, Danya's voice whispered in her mind, *he'll turn his back on you. Hide your heart, Vervaine, lest it betray your life.*

But Danya wasn't here, and the night outside the window made Verve want to retreat further into the pocket of light she'd created with her lamps, one that had drawn Alem like a moth to a flame.

Slowly, she tugged the words up from her bitter depths. "Sohvi came here looking for me."

Alem's head shot up. "Why?"

She gnawed at her lower lip. "My last mission…I killed a mage, and took his companion prisoner. I think that fellow was a meridian."

"Was?" Alem's voice darkened. "You killed them."

"No," she shot back, too quickly. "I only brought him to my patron, who'd set me on the job. He was alive, last I saw. But Sohvi seemed to know this, somehow. She knew…" Her throat tightened and she couldn't look at Alem, or the night sky outside. Instead, she tipped the last of the bottle's contents down her throat. She couldn't ignore her past, but she could drown the memories of it, at least for a night. Hadn't she earned one night of peace? "She came here to find me. I put you all in danger."

Alem slapped the bottle out of her hand, sending it out the open window. The absolute nerve! Verve glared at him. "What d'you think you're—"

"I can't do it any more," he interrupted, glaring right back. "Watch you drink yourself into oblivion every time something upsets you. How you've not died of liver poisoning is beyond me, but this," he gestured vaguely to her, "needs to stop before the worst happens."

Slowly, she rose, careful not to hit her head again. Each movement was focused, controlled, deliberate. Her hands trembled, but it was with the fury that now coursed through her veins. "I came here to help Lotis," Verve said through gritted teeth. "And I think I've made some good progress on that front. How I spend my *own* time isn't *your* concern."

He stood too. His eyes on her were hot iron, searing into her soul. "You came here hunting a mage. You stay, I assume, because it benefits you somehow. Every time I think otherwise, I regret it."

"That's on you," Verve shot back. "Not me. I've never pretended to be what I'm not. If you see something else…" She spread her hands. "Also on you."

As she spoke, the memory of Danya's voice rang through her mind. *Do you see? This is what happens when you open yourself to others. Turn away now, before it's too late.*

Then Alem said softly, "Verve, you're killing yourself."

Maybe it was the liquor. Maybe it was the puffer. More likely, it was some combination of the two — along with her own overly dramatic heart. The words came to Verve's lips before she could stop them. "I died when I was six summers old, Alem. Everything since isn't real."

His breath caught, and he stepped closer, one hand outstretched. "It doesn't have to be that way, Verve. You can change." He left the last unspoken: *I can help you.*

Verve shook her head. "The worst has already happened. I'm beyond help." Heat tore at her eyes, so she turned away and drew her hood up, thankful for the cover.

Alem stood still, then his footsteps sounded as he headed for the ladder. "Coward," he muttered.

"Arrogant ass," she hissed, but when she looked back, he was already down the rickety ladder and she was alone again.

She lit another puffer, and another, and sucked each one down in a few inhales, until the burning in her eyes receded and she fell into a deep, dreamless sleep.

12

Favors

One month—one full cycle of Atal—had passed, and Verve was no closer to completing her job than when she'd first arrived in Lotis. As for her plans to have already been gone by now... Well, perhaps Danya had been right to give her three cycles of the hunter's moon to get this done. If Damaris was a false name for Alem, Verve had to either turn him in or find another mage she could claim was the infamous magic-user. Neither option held much appeal.

But neither did the threat of Danya's displeasure. So the hour before dawn, Verve's steps dragged as she prepared to slip out of Lotis for a day of lone scouting. If nothing else, she could ensure no nearby renegade mages were planning anything they'd regret — like an attack on Lotis.

But honestly, her heart wasn't interested in hunting evil mages, not when Alem had taken residence in her brain and, like some vagrant squatter, had refused to leave. A coward, he'd called her.

Her mouth twisted in a grimace as she gathered her supplies for the day, including her weapons. Alem was one to talk, though they hadn't said a word to each other in the week since the argument in her loft — in *Hadiya's* loft.

Verve made it down the ladder, but the moment her boots hit the floor, her instincts warned her of another presence nearby. Whirling, Verve met Klaret's quiet gaze. The other woman lifted a hand in greeting, then gestured at the open door behind her.

"Should have knocked," Klaret said softly. "Sorry to scare you."

Not likely. But protesting would belie that fact, so Verve kept her reply nonchalant. "Forgiven. Everything all right?"

Of all the Lotis villagers, Klaret was the least prone to casual visits.

"The traps are all in place, in the places we discussed," Klaret said. "Just thought you should know, since you're always out scouting."

That was fast. They'd only mapped out locations for the various traps a few days ago, and Klaret had said she'd need more supplies before crafting the various snares and other nasty surprises to leave for rogue mages.

But the best thing about Klaret was that she didn't seem to care about praise and could figure out most of the finer details of a plan on her own. So Verve only bowed. "Great work. Thanks."

Klaret nodded. But as she turned to leave, she cast Verve one last look. "Oh. Owen wants to see you."

She gestured outside the barn, where Verve could see the lad pacing in the pre-dawn light. What in Atal's name was going on?

As Klaret hurried off to her daily tasks, Verve met Owen outside. The moment he spotted her, he clasped his hands before him. "Okay, hear me out before you say no."

Verve groaned. "It's too early for this."

"You don't even know what I'm going to ask!"

"Does it matter?"

Owen met her eyes. "I just… Look, Verve. I've seen you fight mages—"

"What?" Verve groaned again. "You can't keep sneaking out, Owen. Pacifist or not, Alem *will* kill me if you get hurt."

"I said, hear me out!" Owen took a deep breath and continued. "You're so skilled with those daggers. I have to learn, too. Teach me. Please."

He stared at her with huge brown eyes, like a puppy hoping for table scraps. Verve bit back her first response, which was to scoff and turn away, and instead tried to keep her voice quiet. She had to let the kid down easy.

"There are so many reasons why that's a bad idea, Owen," she began. "For one thing, no one starts off with metal blades. For another… I've had years and years of practice. I began when I was not much older than Lio is now."

"Which is why I've got to *start*," Owen replied. "I'm already so behind. And look what I found!" He pointed to the side of the barn, where two practice spears leaned against the wood.

Dawn was just creeping over the sky. Verve had a full day planned, but it needed to get started already. She couldn't delay just to satisfy Owen's ego.

But just as she opened her mouth to refuse again, he added: "You won't be around forever. I have to be able to defend myself — and Lio. Please, Verve."

"Absolutely not." Alem came marching from the direction of his cottage, some kind of droopy potted plant in his grip. "Owen, get back to Ivet's. You've got lessons soon. Let Verve do her job."

But the lad stood his ground. "I've given this a lot of thought, and I'm making the right choice." He looked at Verve again. "Please?"

Alem looked at her too, and for a moment, Verve swayed between polite and firm refusals. Then Owen's words returned: *You won't be around forever.*

If I do one good thing here, maybe it'll be this. The boy deserved a fighting chance. "Fine," she said to Owen. "One quick lesson before I head out. Depending on how you do, we'll go from there."

Owen whooped and darted to grab the practice spears, while Alem gave her a *look*. Thank the One god looks *couldn't* kill — if they could, Alem would definitely make the deadlier assassin.

"Better wooden spears than metal blades," Verve murmured.

Alem's brow creased. "I suppose."

The lad returned and tossed Verve a spear, and they spent a few minutes going over the basics like grip and footwork. Alem muttered, "call me when the bleeding starts," and trudged off with his potted plant. Verve tried to ignore him and focus on Owen, whose movements were energetic, but utterly without finesse. That was expected of a novice, of course, but the bright eagerness in his eyes made Verve uneasy. He missed every feint, stumbled over every parry, but nothing dimmed the hope in his expression.

He's just a kid, her better sense whispered after he fell to the dirt again. *What are you doing?*

Teaching him, as he'd begged. Teaching him to take care of himself. He and Lio were alone, after all. No one else would watch over them.

Right?

"Shit!" Owen's cry snapped Verve out of her distraction. The lad clutched his hand, where red splotches had appeared at his knuckles. He bit his lip and winced as tears slipped down his cheeks. "Shit," he hissed again. "That really hurt."

Verve dropped her spear and approached him, her heart in her throat. "I'm sorry, Owen. I wasn't—"

"It's all right," he said, sniffing. "A little blood's part of the learning process, right?" He gave her a watery smile that made her want to hit something.

"What happened?" Alem said as he came jogging up. His gaze fell on Owen's hand, and his eyes narrowed.

"The spear slipped and stung me," Owen replied. "I'm fine."

"I'll be the judge of that." Alem took Owen's hand and rested his own across the boy's knuckles. As the dawn light fell over them both, Alem's brow furrowed in concentration, while Owen's shoulders relaxed.

And Verve stood aside, guilt churning in her guts.

Stupid.

At last, Alem drew his hands back. Not a trace of the injury lingered on Owen's skin. The boy flexed his hand, then grinned at Alem. "Thanks."

Alem ruffed his hair. "Any time. But let that be a lesson to you, all right?"

Owen bit his lip and glanced at Verve. "Actually… I want to try again."

"Absolutely not," Alem said before Verve could speak.

But the lad ignored him. "Verve? I think I know what I did wrong. I could—"

"What part of 'no' don't you understand?" Alem broke in.

"It's not up to you," Owen shot back. "It's up to Verve."

"Verve isn't responsible for your wellbeing."

"I'm fifteen," Owen snapped. "I'm old enough. Come on, Verve. What do you say?"

They both looked at Verve, who wanted nothing more than to disappear. She was the last person in the world who should have any part of taking care of another. But she couldn't admit that to Alem, and she couldn't face

Owen's eagerness any more.

"I must go," she said, edging away. "Lots to do today."

Without giving either of them a chance to reply, she turned and darted away, out of Lotis.

* * *

As Verve slipped out of Lotis, she passed by Nori and Kyon, the latter in his antelope form, as they stood watch on the outskirts. No telling if these newcomers were trustworthy, but Ivet had insisted they participate in Lotis's fortifications. Both mages tensed at Verve's approach. She ignored them—as they no doubt wanted her to—and soon she was out of their sight, out of the village's sight, and alone in the marshlands of Greenhill Province.

Out here, beneath the open sky tinged with hints of the day to come, Verve could breathe easier. The incident with Owen faded from her mind as she wove through the patches of solid ground with familiar ease, avoiding the places where the marsh grasses looked deceptively firm. As she went, blackbirds chirped warnings to one another, and more than a few turtles plopped beneath the water, fearful of the human's passage.

Using her own map, Verve had divided the area into sections, and spent each day searching a particular area for traces of renegade mage activity. The nearest village was Mara's Hope, well over three hours' journey away by water. Verve had already resigned herself to spending several nights camped out if she ever needed to take her search to Mara's Hope. But first, she would properly scour this area.

As she traveled east, she got a clear view of the rising sun; how it painted the grasses in shades of pink and gold, how the brilliant light reflected off of the pools of water that lay between the tall marsh grasses. The birdsong brightened with the sun, accompanied by a chorus of cicadas and croaking frogs. A spring breeze tugged at Verve's hood, bringing her the clean scent of water mixed with the musky, earthy smell of the marsh itself.

Alem was right. It was beautiful here.

Verve came to an expanse of water too broad to leap across and spent a few moments searching the depths for signs of malicious life. She saw no snakes, swamp-chompers, or anything else that might want to harm (or humiliate) her, so she carefully stepped into the shallow water. Cool but not cold, the water didn't reach the top of her tall boots, which was a mercy.

As Verve waded through, a snort of laughter sounded from the shore. She sprang into action, drawing her crossbow and aiming for the direction of the noise. "Show yourself," she called. "And I might let you walk away."

The tall grasses parted, revealing Usko, teeth bared in a brief but delighted grin. "And to think I was jealous of you for this assignment."

Verve swore and stowed her crossbow. Conflicting emotions squared off in her heart: delight at seeing a friendly face; anxiety, for there were only a few reasons Usko would be here, and none of them were pleasant.

She sloshed ashore, and they clasped hands in greeting. "What are you doing?" Verve asked.

Usko glanced around, face impassive. "Trying not to gag at the stink. And I'll never get this mud off of my shoes."

Verve gave him a mock-punch on his shoulder. "Going soft, huh? Danya won't like that."

His mouth twitched like he wanted to frown. "No, she won't. That's…kind of why I'm here."

"You could have just sent a message. I'd have gladly met you."

"You're one to talk. We've not heard a whisper from you all month. Danya was getting worried about you, so she sent me to make sure you weren't dead."

Verve tried not to roll her eyes. "Sure. Worried about *me*. Not my mission."

"That, too." Usko studied her, his gaze scraping up and down her form. "You don't look dead. Any luck finding Damaris?"

Verve's stomach flipped, so she gestured to the ground ahead, which was solid enough to walk upon for a bit. "Not yet, but I'm making progress. Tell Danya she'll have her mage before the three months are up."

Usko nodded and toyed with his coat, where new hematite beads sewn into swirling designs gleamed upon the dark fabric. He was moving up among the ranks of Atal's Chosen. "Look, Verve… Danya wants to talk to you. She's… unhappy you've not reported in."

Verve paused and glanced over at him. "I still have two months. And how in the stars and moons am I supposed to report in? There's not a fleet rider station for leagues out here, and the trip back to Freehold isn't exactly quick."

"I know," Usko said, palms lifted. "But Danya's worried about you. We all are."

He'd already said that, and Verve didn't believe him any more the second time. But the concern in his gaze was real. As the sun rose higher, Verve studied her younger counterpart. Aside from the new gear, she recognized the hilt of the sword he now carried as being the work of Freehold's best weapon-smith. But his round cheeks bore a fresh scar, and he was leaner than Verve recalled. How had his life been in the past month?

He looked at her, eyes wide, and his youth struck her more than it ever had before. Nineteen years was too young to kill for a living.

But he started younger, she reminded herself. *As I did.* The world was a brutal place to live, as Danya often said. To survive, one had to be ruthless.

Verve kept these thoughts from her face and tried to sound confident. "Thanks for your concern, but I'm safe and on the job. Tell Danya—"

"You don't understand," he interrupted. "Danya wants to see you. In person. Now."

Ice bloomed in Verve's veins. "Impossible. I'm—"

"You can come back, just for a visit," Usko said, hands clasped before him. "She just wants to talk to you. She has…" His lips trembled. "A mission for you. A little one. But you must return now."

Verve stared at him, her mind already racing ahead. "I'm already on a mission."

"Danya has another one for you. Well," he amended, "sort of."

"What are you talking about?"

Usko blew out a breath. "Look, Danya asked me to come all the way out here to give you this message. You don't have to be difficult, Verve. Just…do as she says, and everything will work out."

Something in his voice gave Verve pause. She took his gloved hands in hers, met his gaze directly. "What do you mean, everything will work out?"

He flinched, tried to slip his hands free, but Verve held him fast. "This is my first proper mission on my own," he said at last. "I can't fail, Verve. I just can't. You must go back. Please."

Verve's gaze caught on his fresh scar, and her own cheek burned at the memory of Danya's slap. She released Usko and stood back, her heart suddenly beating too fast. "Very well," she said, her voice cool. "I'll return as soon as I can. I'll need a day or so to tie off some loose ends here, then I'll head back to Freehold."

Relief shone through his eyes, but he did not smile at her as he once might have. "Oh, Atal, thank you, Verve! I have to get back now, so please hurry, all right?"

Her chest ached at the joy in his voice. Danya would crush that soon, too. What would be left of the jovial boy she'd once known? But to Usko, she only said, "I will. I promise."

13

By Necessity

Verve and Usko parted ways, and by midday she was back in Lotis, pacing outside of Ivet's home while she waited for the village leader to return. Ivet spent most mornings either at the Willow, teaching the children, or darting from one home to another, dealing with whatever issues cropped up in the village.

"Ah, there you are," Ivet said, striding up, a stack of schoolbooks tucked beneath her only arm. "Berel said you wanted to speak to me."

Without a word, Verve took the books from Ivet's grip and the older Sufani woman flashed her a warm smile before ushering into the modest cottage.

"Set them down anywhere," Ivet said. "I'll make us some tea. We'll sit outside; it's nice today. Not too hot — yet."

Verve plunked down the books on Ivet's sleeping pallet, beside another scarf of Sufani make, one she hadn't seen Ivet wear before. The embroidered butterflies were so delicate, yet realistic, Verve expected them take flight from the silk.

"You like that?" Ivet came to stand beside Verve, an iron fire poker in hand.

Verve drew her hand back; she'd been about to stroke the fabric. "It's lovely."

Ivet smiled fondly at the scarf. "It's not my best work, but not a bad showing. My da could do better, but then, few of my clan could match his skill with a needle and thread."

"You made this?" Verve asked.

Ivet waved her remaining hand and returned to the hearth, where she began tending the coals. "Aye, before I lost the arm. Do you know how to embroider?"

A memory returned. Pale linen stretched over a wooden hoop. Solid warmth at her back as she sat in her mother's lap. Daylight. Birds sang, and her mother sang along as she guided Verve's tiny hands in placing the needle and thread.

Verve had *some* skill; hell, she'd sewn hundreds of hematite beads to her jacket. But hematite was a necessary part of her job. Embroidering leaves and flowers just for their beauty was a frivolity Danya had never allowed.

"A little," Verve replied after a beat. "But I haven't tried in…a long time."

"Well, if you'd like to relearn, I'd be glad to help you. It'd be good to put this knowledge to use again. But I doubt you came here to ask about my sewing."

Verve touched her own scarf, which she'd recently cleaned, although her hair desperately needed new braids. Something felt wrong, but she didn't know what. Probably just her overactive imagination hard at work. That or her supper last night didn't agree with her. "Ivet, don't bother with the tea. Just… sit down. Please. We need to talk."

"By the One," Ivet groaned, "no good conversation ever begins this way. Very well." She nudged a few cushions to the center of the cottage, and they both took a seat. Ivet gave Verve a warm but curious look. "Now, vidahem, what's got you all twisted up in knots?"

"I have to go," Verve blurted out. "Just for a few days. A week, at most." She hoped, anyway. "And I can't tell you why."

"Can you tell me where?"

Verve hesitated. Common sense told her that the less Ivet knew about her real life, the better. "I'd rather not."

"So if you don't return, we'll just have to wonder?" Ivet's smile didn't reach her eyes.

Verve ducked her head. "I'm sorry. It's for the best."

"Does this have anything to do with the intense discussion you and Serla Sohvi had the other day?"

"You saw that, huh?"

Ivet patted her knee with casual ease. "I see everything, vidahem. I also recall hearing the name 'Freehold.' Which I'm sure has *no* bearing on your current, anxious state of mind."

She winked at Verve, who sighed over yet another lost battle. But Ivet's teasing eased the unsettled feeling in her gut, like a knot loosened, and she could almost smile. "'Course not."

"Of course," Ivet agreed. "Well, if someone from Lotis *were* to be visiting a bustling town like Freehold, I'd ask them for a favor."

This was unexpected. Verve kept her curiosity banked and said only, "Oh?"

"You've seen for yourself how we live here," Ivet said. "Usually, we can take care of ourselves, with little help from the world beyond. But we need to trade, or sell goods we make or find locally. Klaret and Berel usually go to Mara's Hope for that, but if you're going to Freehold..."

A vision of herself slogging piles of Dannel's weavings as came to Verve's mind, and she fought the urge to groan. "I'm sorry, but I must travel quickly. I don't have time to bring along guests and whatever wares you've got to sell."

Ivet nodded, all agreeable, which meant Verve was in real trouble. "Of course, I would never impose. It's just... Lotis doesn't get many merchants out here, especially given the renegade mages. So every few months, we send someone to the nearest village, usually Mara's Hope, to trade for what we can't make ourselves."

"You want me to handle the trade of your goods?" Verve lifted a brow.

Ivet laughed. "I'm not paying you to strike deals on Lotis's behalf. No, Verve, I'm asking you to accompany one of us, who'll do the dealing. Then, when you've finished your business, you can both return."

"I don't know how long I'll be," Verve replied. "It may take more than a couple of days."

"That's fine. It often takes a few days to get the best deals from the merchants." Ivet's smile faded. "It's been quiet lately, but we both know that's not forever. The roads are too dangerous for most to travel alone. I'd like to send more than just two of you, but I fear that would draw too much attention." She dug out a silver coin from her pocket and offered it to Verve. "Consider this an additional assignment, if it makes you feel better."

The coin rested in Ivet's weathered palm, shining and smooth. The idea of accepting payment for *this* made Verve's stomach turn. But to refuse would insult Ivet's good nature, and offer further proof that Verve was on some nefarious mission of her own. Which Ivet probably knew anyway, but Verve owed it to her to keep up the charade. She plucked the coin from Ivet's hand and tucked it with her others, silently vowing to spend it on rare dyed wool for Dannel, or some new books for the children. Something useful and welcome.

"Good," Ivet said, making to rise. "I'll let Alem know and you can set out at first light."

"What?" Verve leaped up and offered Ivet a hand, pulling the older woman to her feet. "No, I can't... Alem and I..." She blew out a breath in frustration while Ivet regarded her with a steady gaze that missed nothing. "We... had a disagreement."

"You don't say," Ivet replied in a dry voice. "Well, that would certainly explain why he's been sulking around the Willow's distillery lately. He made the mistake of snapping at Hadiya, but they showed him the error of his ways."

A smile tugged at Verve's lips, but she kept it at bay. "They did?"

"Not your concern, of course," Ivet said, eyes twinkling. "But you and Alem are both somewhat-sensible adults, and I'm sure fully capable of putting your *disagreement* aside for a few days. Right?"

"Right," Verve echoed, suddenly too focused on the idea of Alem moping after their fight to mind that Ivet was manipulating her.

"Wonderful." Ivet nodded to the door. "Let's break the news to him together, shall we?"

But Verve's feet refused to move as her better sense shoved aside her more squishy feelings toward Alem. "Have you been to Freehold, Ivet? They have no fondness for mages there. Someone like Alem wouldn't be welcome.

Perhaps Klaret would be better suited…"

She trailed off as Ivet cocked an eyebrow. "Fair point, but I think I'll let Alem make that choice for himself," Ivet said. "If he refuses, I'll ask Klaret."

She slipped out of the door, beckoning Verve along after. Verve followed, her heart a tumble of conflicting feelings.

* * *

Alem was on his knees in his garden, up to his elbows in dirt. His tunic hung on the fence where he must have tossed it, leaving his upper body bare save for sweat and sunlight. Verve's mouth went dry at the sight of his muscular torso, and what better sense she'd shored up while following Ivet here flew out of her mind. So she only stood by, mute as a stump, while Ivet explained the situation. He cut his eyes to Verve once or twice, and when Ivet finished, he reached for his shirt to scrub it over his face.

"Freehold," he muttered. "Never been. Heard stories that'll curdle your milk, though."

"They're true," Verve heard herself say. "And someone like *you* shouldn't *want* to go there."

Alem twisted his shirt in thought. "As long as I don't openly use magic, no one can tell what I am. Besides, if I can navigate a city like Pillau, I can handle Freehold."

Verve's stomach clenched at the thought of Alem within those stone and hematite gates. "They don't kill mages on sight in Pillau." She looked at Ivet. "Do you think Klaret would go?"

Alem shook his head. "Klaret's no good with people. She's comfortable with most of us, but she'd be miserable in a city like Freehold. And if Berel goes, Klaret will follow, and the weight of three people is more than our vessel can handle."

"What about Hadiya?" Verve offered.

Alem winced, but Ivet replied, "If I grew an acorn for every time they swore they'd never leave Lotis, I'd have an entire forest by now." She sighed. "What I wouldn't give for my arm back."

"You're too valuable to risk," Verve said.

Alem nodded. "Aye, Lotis can't afford to lose you."

Owen was too young, Dannel not in the best health, and the two new mages presented the same conundrum as Alem. One by one, the rest of the villagers were considered and discarded. Verve could not recall the last time she'd had to arrange travel with another person — not a prisoner. Aside from her brief visits to Freehold between jobs, she was usually alone. She'd never minded before coming to Lotis.

"It's all right," Alem said after he and Ivet had talked in circles. "I'll go. I just take care and keep my abilities under wraps." He cleared his throat. "I should probably wear some hematite to blend in. Perhaps Verve has some to spare?"

"I've plenty," Verve said, and he gave a grim nod.

"Right. Well, it shouldn't take long to gather what we've got to trade. I've been inventorying my stocks, tallying what we're low on."

He did not say "we're almost out of liquor, thanks to Verve," but he didn't need to. And when he seemed to meet Verve's gaze with effort, she hated herself a little more for the sight. She mentally stamped out the feeling. She paid for every drink she took. No doubt Lotis's treasury was brimming with her coin.

Which…wasn't as noble a thought as she'd wanted it to be. Best not dwell. Best move on, focus on her new task.

At dawn the next day, she and Alem, and a wide canoe filled with bundles and bags, departed Lotis. As they paddled against the current, Verve glanced over her shoulder at the humble homes, at the floating boardwalks, at Ivet, Dannel, and some of the kids waving goodbye. All familiar, now.

Too familiar.

With a deep breath, Verve faced forward and threw herself into the repetitive motions of paddling. She wasn't ready for the task ahead, but she could pretend as well as anyone.

* * *

During the journey through the swamp's winding waterways, Verve and Alem mostly spoke only when they couldn't avoid it, which left Verve far too many opportunities to think. That was rarely a good thing.

So while she wasn't exactly *relieved* to arrive at Freehold, the dilemma of moving their goods from the canoe to the landlocked city made for a welcome distraction. If not for the Zhee trader they met at the closest dock in a neighboring port town, Verve supposed she and Alem would've had to drag the canoe to Freehold's gates. As it was, Alem hired the trader's wagon, and after unloading and reloading their cargo, then squeezing into the back of the wagon and being jostled about like sacks of sullen potatoes, they reached their destination.

As Alem made arrangements with the trader for the return trip, Verve approached the gate guards. Luck was with her again, for Sacha was on duty. The other woman murmured something to her fellow guard and then swaggered over to Verve, one hand on her sword hilt.

Verve paused, her own fingers reaching for her crossbow before she stopped herself. "Well met, Sacha," she called, lifting a hand in greeting. "You're looking well."

"Fine thing to say to me, after you left without so much as a 'see you later,'" Sacha shot back, a frown on her full lips.

Verve flushed. "Sorry about that. I meant no slight, but my work—"

Sacha broke into a laugh, and Verve relaxed. "Ah, I couldn't say it with a straight face," Sacha replied, giggling. "Wouldn't it be funny if I really cared about such things?"

You mean, if you actually *missed me?* Verve forced a chuckle at the guard's joke. Sacha meant no harm; their relationship was casual by necessity. It'd never bothered Verve before.

Sacha stepped closer, eying Verve up and down with appreciation. "But I still wonder if you'll ever have time to pay me a *proper* visit?"

The gravel crunched as Alem came up behind them, the trader from Zheem and her wagon close on his heels. Suddenly the mild spring afternoon felt too warm. Verve tried to smile. "I'd love to, Sacha. I'll do my best."

Sacha gave an exaggerated sigh. "That's a *no*. Honestly, what am I to do with her?"

She said this to Alem, who cocked an eyebrow at Verve, but replied to the guard. "Throw her in irons, maybe?"

"Oh, fantastic idea," Sacha said, beaming.

Verve cleared her throat and gestured to the wagon. "I hate to rush you, but can we...?"

"Go on, then." Sacha waved them through the gates, but not before she shot Verve another knowing look and a wink so obvious that even blind Dannel could have seen it.

Cheeks hot, Verve trudged beside Alem as they entered Freehold. To his credit, Alem said nothing until the Zhee trader pointed them toward the market. It was time to go their separate ways — for now.

"We'll meet for dinner at that inn you mentioned," Alem said to Verve. "The Prancing Dove, right?"

"Dancing Duck," Verve muttered.

"Right." Alem glanced back toward the guard station. "Look, if you have somewhere else you'd rather stay while we're here, I don't mind. I'm a big boy. I can—"

"I'll see you tonight," Verve broke in.

He nodded, then shot her a wink. "By the way, she's adorable."

"Shut up." She turned to leave.

"I mean it," Alem continued. "But in all seriousness, I'm glad you have... someone. Everyone needs people who genuinely care for them."

Verve paused and glanced back at him. He'd tucked several of her hematite amulets beneath his shirt, and he looked about as non-magic as the rest of Freehold's population. The thought struck her that if anyone else knew what he was—Sacha, included—they'd not hesitate to tattle to Danya or the magistrate — or just run him through with their own blades.

Her hands tightened into fists. She would *not* let that happen.

"Sacha's just a friend," she said, coming back over to Alem, holding his gaze. "We have fun together, sometimes, but nothing more. I don't *have* her. Or anyone, for that matter. Just for, you know, general information."

Now *that* was a supremely foolish thing to say. Indeed, Alem's eyes widened and he seemed at a loss for words, and Verve tried not to be too visibly pleased at the fact.

"My mistake," he murmured, and gave her that crooked smile again, the one that sent her heart galloping over the open plains.

"Don't worry about it," she said. "Be safe. I'll see you later."

14

Shortcomings

After her time spent in Lotis, under the open skies of Greenhill Province, the Temple of Atal felt too confining. As Verve passed through the familiar corridors, the walls seemed to close in around her, making her breath come a little shorter. But that was a foolish thought, of course, so Verve dismissed it.

Harder to ignore were the glares of the other Chosen and their trainers. No one stopped what they were doing, of course, for that would make their interest too plain, but Verve knew the language of stolen glances, lifted brows, and hardening jaws.

"Trainer Aya," Verve said as she passed by the mercenary on her way to Danya. "Nice to see you. How's it going?"

The hired blade stared at her, lip curling in distaste, before she shoved past Verve and continued down the passageway. Verve frowned after her. The mercenaries Danya had hired to train Atal's Chosen weren't the friendliest sort, but they were at least on speaking terms with their charges. Aya had given Verve more than one scar in their training bouts, but each scar was a lesson learned. And besides, she thought Aya had liked her.

The cold shoulders continued as Verve made her way deeper into Atal's sanctum. Even Usko, when she passed by him and some of the others his age in the dining room, didn't acknowledge her greeting.

He'd said the other Chosen were worried about her, but they damn sure weren't acting like it, even a little.

A hive of wasps swarmed in Verve's belly. Was Danya coming down even harder on emotional displays? But the buzz of warning within her told her otherwise, and although she didn't need the reminder to be careful, she got the message loud and clear.

Danya was not in her office. Verve frowned at the cramped room, which was cleaner than she'd ever seen it. Some papers and scrolls lay neatly stacked on a shelf, but Danya's desk was all but bare — save a small hematite statue of Atal. Verve studied the statue—a grim-faced man wielding a sword—before heading back into the Temple itself. No sign of the head priest in the main hall, nor the infirmary or the dormitories. At last, Verve came across Danya in the temple garden, seated before another statue of Atal, this one in the garden's heart. Verve passed by manicured shrubs and stately bushes and knelt beside Danya without a word, for the priest detested interruptions when at prayer here. Verve knelt until her knees ached and the overpowering scent of blooming blush-roses made her nose itch, but she did not move.

"I see you've not forgotten me, after all," Danya said at last.

Verve ducked her head but kept silent. If she spoke before Danya gave permission… Well, at least the scars from *that* lesson only marred her spirit, not her flesh.

Danya waited several long minutes before she spoke again, a smile hidden in her voice. "First things first: I received news of your cousin. As of last week, they were still in Starwatch; a merchant reported dealings with the Sufani family we've been looking for."

The news plucked Verve up and flung her into the ether, making her dizzy, confused, and for a few seconds she only stared dumbly at the lush garden grass.

"I have a name, too," Danya said.

Verve risked a glance up. The afternoon light filtering through the garden trees cast Danya in a warm, golden glow as she beamed at Verve. "Morwen," Danya said.

Morwen. Verve turned the syllables over in her mind, searching for familiarity, but the name meant nothing. But Danya's expression was expectant, so she ducked her head again. "Thank you, serla. Do you know exactly where in Starwatch Province they can be found?"

"Oh, far to the north," Danya said. "Close to the border with Cander. But you know how those Sufani vagabonds wander aimlessly."

Danya added a smirk that made Verve's fingers itch to pull out one of her daggers.

The priest sighed. "I fear they'll have left by the time my letter reaches the area. But I had to try, for your sake. You deserve a family, Verve."

Better if Danya had buried a blade in her heart than voice the hope that Verve had long since tried to shut out of it. But Danya knew which wounds had not healed and could be pressed just so, and how the ensuing pain would block out all other things from Verve's heart. Hope, joy, grief, rage… They warred within her, each desperate to find purchase over the rest, and she could not speak for longing.

Danya allowed her a few seconds to absorb this news, then continued, her tone all business. "Usko said you're *still* trying to find Damaris?"

"He spoke truly, serla," Verve replied, still half-focused on the name *Morwen*. "I've made good progress, but the mage is difficult to track down. However, within the next two cycles of Atal, I will—"

"You've already taken too long," Danya interrupted.

"That's not fair," Verve snapped before she could stop herself. "You said—"

Heat stung Verve's lips before she registered Danya's blow. She pitched to the side, catching herself with her gloved hands, blinking back sudden tears. *Idiot*, she scolded herself as she collected her wits. She could take down the most ferocious shiftlings, but let this old hag slap her once and she turned into a sniveling child.

"The mission has changed," Danya went on calmly, as if they were sharing tea in her garden. "I require Damaris within a fortnight."

Verve winced. "I'm sorry, serla, but that won't be possible—"

Another blow landed at the site of the first; this one hurt even worse, and something warm dribbled down Verve's cheek. But she dared not move, hardly breathed, as Danya grabbed her chin and forced their eyes to meet.

"Time runs short," Danya said, her voice still quiet and too calm. "You've wasted a month lollygagging in Lotis, befriending the locals. Usko only spent a day in observation, but he learned quite enough. He saw you among the villagers."

Verve's eyes lidded as despair clutched her heart. Usko… But of course, his loyalty was to Danya. Loyalty — genuine or coerced. The result was the same.

But if he'd watched Verve acting friendly with the Lotis villagers, what else had he seen? Her mind raced to the morning she'd met Usko. Sparring with Owen. Her own inattention, and then Alem had…

Shit.

Danya chuckled. "Oh dear, do you think you've made friends in that backwater dump?"

"No, serla," Verve managed. "But I have had to seem friendly to gain their cooperation. As *you* have taught me."

She braced herself for another slap, but Danya released her chin. "You care about the rabble there, don't you? My poor Vervaine," she sighed. "I have taught you everything you know, therefore I know you better than you know yourself. You cannot hope to fool me."

No. Danya's words were wrong. This was *all* wrong. The truth tore at Verve's throat, fighting for freedom. "I'm not—"

But Danya continued, heedless of Verve's protest. "Do you know why you have *not* found Marea Damaris?"

Oh, this did not bode well. Verve kept her voice as neutral as possible. "Please enlighten me, serla."

Danya eyed her, searching for sarcasm, but Verve was adept at keeping a straight face — most of the time. At last, Danya said, "Obviously, Damaris is using a false name. That's the other reason I wanted to speak to you, especially since you *refused* to take a few minutes and send a letter to let me know your status. How I have fretted this last month! But I have it on good authority that Marea Damaris is even more powerful than we feared — and that their abilities are a far cry from those which were first reported."

Verve's heart beat faster in her chest, surely loud enough for Danya to hear. *Play dumb*, she told herself. *Don't think of Alem.* "What do you mean, serla?"

"Marea Damaris is no mere particle mage," Danya said. "They are dendric. A rare and deadly creature, to be sure. Have you encountered such a moon-blood during your time in Lotis?"

Alem.

Verve's mouth fell open, but she managed *not* to spill his secret. No way Usko had gotten a good enough look at Alem's healing of Owen to understand what he'd seen. She could still find another mage to pass off as Damaris. "I thought dendric mages were just legends."

Danya waved a hand dismissively, and it took every ounce of Verve's control not to flinch away. "More mage lies," Danya replied. "Usko did some scouting over at Mara's Hope and learned the truth from a merchant: Damaris is a dendric mage living in Lotis. Surely, you've encountered them by now?"

Worse and worse. Verve swallowed the bile rising at the back of her throat. "I have encountered some mages. But none have claimed to be Marea Damaris."

True enough. But Danya knew her too well. Danya always knew when she lied outright.

Indeed, Danya studied her, gaze sharp. "You understand, of course, that if any dendric mage were to be discovered in Lotis, regardless of what name they used, the other Chosen and I would be forced to apprehend the monster — and exterminate anyone found to be in alliance with them. It is the burden of my role in Atal's world."

She leaned forward. Verve braced herself, but Danya only patted her shoulder. "The world is cruel, Vervaine, especially for those of us without magic. We are at the moon-bloods' mercy, and Atal knows they will not show us any. But," she sighed, "every time I think you've learned this lesson, you prove me wrong."

Verve ducked her head. "I know the world is cruel, serla."

Too well.

"Aye," Danya said. "But despite your shortcomings, you have found your true path with me. This life is hard, I know, but you are perfectly suited to it, as if Atal Himself crafted you specifically for these tasks. Don't you realize that, Vervaine?" She didn't wait for a reply. "You are a killer, but there are many in this world undeserving of the gift of life. Thus, you are an instrument of Atal — one of His true Chosen." She beamed at Verve. "This path you are on is the right one for you, the *only* one. You know that, don't you?"

The response came without thought, carved as it was into Verve's deepest self. "Yes, serla."

Danya smoothed a hand down her immaculate iron-gray hair and smiled again. Why did *she* get to smile? "My poor girl," she said as she toyed with one of Verve's bedraggled braids. "I can see the last month has not been kind to you."

Verve's wire bracelet winked in the sunlight. How easy it would be to wrap its length around Danya's neck, to draw it tighter and tighter, until the Circle priest's face turned purple, until her eyes bulged and her tongue swelled, and…

More foolish fantasies, best dammed before they flowed too far. Verve's jaw tightened. "I'm fine, serla."

"Good. See that you remain so." Danya folded her hands in her lap. "Usko should have told you I have another job for you? It's the final portion of your previous mission. You're to escort our prisoner, the man named Celidon, to a contact of mine to the east, near the White River."

"The White River?" Verve knew better than to allow shock into her voice, but some things were unavoidable. "That's Legion's territory."

"The region is in dispute," Danya replied. "But as long as you play your role, Legion will not trouble you on this mission."

A heavy weight pressed against Verve's chest, like an urslan had sat upon her. Even deep breaths brought no relief. *Legion.* The word echoed like drumbeats throughout her whole self.

"My dear child, are you truly frightened?" There was mockery in Danya's voice, hiding beneath the honey-sweetness. "After all you've been through, the very mention of Legion turns you positively gray. Well, you worry for nothing. Just follow my instructions and don't trouble yourself overmuch about the details."

Verve couldn't spare the energy to care about the barely veiled insult. Her mind had flung itself back to her childhood. She was a little girl, shuddering in the darkness, while shouts and jeers sounded all around. The scent of smoke made her eyes water, but she dared not close them against the shadows. She was too warm; sweat beaded her skin, stung her eyes along with the smoke.

Danya's touch on her arm chased the memory away. "I should remind you," the priest said gently, "that although Legion's reputation is…fierce, its mage-hunters work hard to keep us all safe. We are not so different from them."

It took every ounce of self-control Verve possessed not to rip her arm out of Danya's reach. "As you say, serla."

Danya's eyes narrowed, but her voice was still gentle. "Time is of the essence. A pair of odd strangers have been spotted in town; I believe the prisoner's people are looking for him."

Sohvi and Hasina. Fear flashed through Verve's veins as Danya continued.

"You'll leave at first light to take the prisoner. Return to your little village, after, but know this, Vervaine: I *will* have the head of whichever power-mad mage has taken over Lotis. You have two weeks from now to deliver it, or I'll send the rest of the Chosen to succeed where you have failed. You know how *eager* Usko is for a true test of his skills. He's come a long way from the sniveling little boy you found in the gutter. Now, I think he'd even be a match for you. But I would dearly hate to find that out, wouldn't you?"

Verve's blood roared in her ears. Surely, she misunderstood what Danya was getting at. Right? "What do you mean, serla?"

"Aren't you paying attention?" Danya gave a *tsk-tsk* of disappointment. "If you fail, if you decide you'd rather take your chances somewhere else in Atal's realm, I will order Usko and the others first to burn Lotis to the ground, then to hunt you down to whatever corner of the world your filthy little vagabond heart drags you. Do you understand *that*, Vervaine?"

Verve was ice; she was fire. Her mouth opened, but no sound came out.

Danya smiled, sweet as any grandmother. "I think that's *more* than fair, child, after *all* I've sacrificed for you."

* * *

Perhaps it was because of Verve's reputation—or more likely, Danya's—but Ivet's silver coin went farther in Freehold than Verve had anticipated. Far enough, at least, to drown Verve's thoughts with the strongest liquor she could coax the barkeep to bring up from his stores. Another of the Dancing Duck's patrons was a known puffer vendor, happy to oblige Verve's request. After the day she'd had, she deserved a bit of fun, so she whiled away the afternoon and evening in a haze of blissful oblivion, her back tucked safely against the Duck's far wall.

She saw Alem enter at supper time and glance around. But she'd carefully positioned herself behind a column and a group of large Canderi men, whose massive shoulders blocked her from view but allowed her to keep watch. Alem studied the bar's patrons, then spoke to the barkeeper, whom Verve had given a few additional coins to play dumb should anyone inquire about her.

Just so. The barkeeper shrugged masterfully and went back to filling the mugs before him. Alem frowned, glanced around again, then slipped into a seat alone. He waved to a server and ordered. Tea, no doubt, or something else wholesome. Verve chuckled to herself between puffs. Sure enough, the server returned later with a mug of something steaming, and a plate of roasted lamb. Alem dug in, but not with enthusiasm. And he didn't stop looking for her.

Verve's heart twisted, but that was easily rectified with another few swallows from the bottle at her elbow. After a day like today, she deserved a tiny treat. Besides, she couldn't face Alem right now, at least not while she still suffered any illusion of sobriety.

Alem finished his meal and drank his tea, but after no sign of Verve, he finally gave up and headed up the stairs to the room they'd rented for the night. Room, singular. Verve didn't let herself think about that, either.

She stayed put until last call, when the barkeeper gave her *that look:* get out before I make you. Smiling a bit too wide, Verve plunked down another silver—she didn't mind flaunting a little in Freehold—and made her swaying way to the stairwell, which seemed a lot longer and steeper than she remembered. But the puzzle only mildly perplexed her as she climbed up to the rented room. With any luck, this next bit would be painful but quick, then she could be on her way. With any luck, Alem would understand.

Luck. Verve snorted a laugh, leaning against a stranger's door for support. The person behind the door grumbled something about drunken assholes, but Verve ignored them and continued.

Alem's room was dark, which made sense, given that it was after midnight. But the window was open to allow the warm night air entry. Atal rose, a waning crescent climbing past the horizon. *Two weeks,* Danya had said. Atal would be dark; Seren, the mage moon, would be at her strongest. A bad omen or a good one? Surely Verve was the last person in the world able to tell the difference.

"Verve?" Alem's voice rose, hazy with sleep.

She eased into the room. It only took two tries to lock the door behind her. "You shouldn't leave the window open. Anyone could sneak in and slit your throat."

"Thanks. I wasn't having nightmares yet." He sat up from his single bed, watching her. "Where in Ea's realm were you? I waited…" He trailed off, inhaling. "What happened?"

She ignored him and leaned out the window, savoring the night breeze on her face. It was easier to ignore the dark when her mind was little more than a pleasant slosh. "I have to go."

"What? Where?"

"You don't need to know that," she said. "But I'll be back here in a few days. Then we can return to Lotis."

The bedclothes rustled as he got up. His steps over to her were soft, but not silent. He hadn't been trained to slip across a bedroom without sound. Alem came to the window beside her, staring at her with that intensity only he could manage. "Verve, what are you talking about? You *had* to come here, so we came. Now you say you must go somewhere else? Why? What's going on?"

"Nothing you should concern yourself with," she replied, keeping her voice calm. "I'll leave you with plenty of coin, so you can hire some help to return should the need arise. I'm sorry for the short notice, but I promise you, it's for the best you not know anything more."

A new thought struck her, one that made her swear again. If Usko had gotten a good enough look at Alem back in Lotis, and then saw him here in Freehold... "In fact, you shouldn't linger at all. And wear a hood when you go out. And for the One god's sake, don't use your *fucking* magic out in the open. I don't care how hurt someone is. I'll—"

"You're hurt," he broke in. "What happened?" His hand lifted as if to touch her face.

Like a sodding idiot, her fingers stole to the mark Danya had left earlier, verifying his observation. The bleeding had stopped, but the moonlight must have revealed too much, especially to a healer with a weakness for lost causes.

"Nothing important," she said. "Assassin training. Really violent. I'll spare you the gory details."

Only Alem could take her shoulders and coax her to face him, as gently as if she were a broken bone he needed to set. "What's really going on?" he murmured. "Did your... employer do that to you?"

She relaxed in his grip and allowed him to move her. But she could not meet his gaze. "It doesn't matter."

"Verve." He moved closer, so there was only a breath of space between them. This close, she could smell tea when he said, "It has something to do with that meridian, doesn't it? Celidon." Her silence was answer enough, and he swore softly. "Whatever's going on, you have a choice, Verve. You can choose to walk away."

Yes. But if she made that choice, Usko would be the one tasked with hunting her down and killing her for the transgression. Verve's life was a grain of sand, a pebble in her own shoe. But Usko and the other Chosen... Even if Usko was completely loyal to Danya, the act of hunting and killing

Verve would haunt his steps forever. He was a good lad. He deserved better. They all did.

Despite her earlier fortifications, her lips parted and tears burned behind her eyes. A little gasp escaped her and she shook her head, trying to turn away. "I'll be back as soon as I can," she choked. "Please, Alem. Please, just listen to me this one time."

"I always listen to you," he whispered, moving with her, not allowing her to look away. "I think I hear things you don't mean to say." He took her hands in his, cupped them like they were something precious, something worth keeping safe. "You're better than who you pretend to be, Verve. Stronger. Whatever's wrong, whatever weight is on your shoulders, you don't have to bear it alone."

She wept openly now, like the babe she was. "You don't understand."

"I want to." Soft lips pressed to her fingertips. "Verve... Please help me understand."

Alem was stubborn, yes, but also sweeter than the nectar he made, and kinder than anyone had a right to be. But Verve knew she could only push him so far before that kindness eroded. It always did when she was involved. She was a liar and a killer, the very worst the world could offer, and Danya was right. She was cruel by necessity.

Alem knew this, somewhere deep inside his spirit. And if not, he'd learn soon enough, and be better off.

"Alem?"

He squeezed her fingers with tenderness, and there was no small amount of hope in his whispered, "Yes?"

"What's your real name?"

He blanched. "My...? What are you talking about?"

"You heard me."

Now he stared at her, and she forced herself to stare back, silently daring him to lie. At last his brows knitted in confusion and he said, "Alembic. Alem's just a nickname. My parents were too poor to have family names, so just Alembic. Why?"

Maybe it was the liquor, or the puffer, but she heard only truth in his words: a truth she'd tried to hide from. He wasn't Damaris. But he was her target now.

She couldn't look at him any longer. No matter what happened, her fate was already written. Fighting destiny was a fool's hope.

With the greatest effort, Verve withdrew her hands from his tender grip. She scrubbed the tears from her eyes, then dug into her belt pouch. She placed the silver coins in his hand and ensured her gaze was hard enough not to let his confusion, his hurt, penetrate. "Keep your head down and get out of Freehold the instant you're able. Take care of yourself and don't worry about me. I have a job to do."

15

A Job Well Done

Verve spent the night back in her tiny room in Atal's temple and left before first light. The trip to meet Danya's contact passed in a blur that she blamed on her hangover. Thank the One for the two fleet deer that bore Verve and her prisoner; they made swift (if stomach-jarring) progress away from Freehold and over the Silverwood prairie. Sunlight assaulted Verve today, so she kept her hood up and squinted over the saffron-colored grasses, trying not to think about how much she missed the shady swamps of Greenhill Province — where Lotis lived.

She and her prisoner had left Freehold before dawn, so they arrived at the meeting place as the cicadas sang the world to sleep at dusk. The White River flowed about half a mile away, twisting like a snake through the grasslands. Verve pulled the meridian, bound with iron chains, from his mount and set him down upon the grass. The fleets' tack came next, and for a little while, she only had to think about caring for the large deer after a day of hard travel. Danya's contact was to meet them here soon; Verve planned to spend the night to let the fleet rest, then return to Freehold at first light.

As she rubbed the sweat from each fleet deer's brindled coat, Celidon watched her. The month spent in Danya's custody had not been kind: he was thinner and grayer than Verve recalled, bruised in shades of purple and yellow where the chains had touched his skin. His eyes were brown, without a trace of the flickering light she'd seen in Sohvi's, but even in his filthy, battered state, he emanated an aura of calm.

Once the fleets were cared for, Verve turned her attention to supper: nuts, cheese, dried meat, bread. Simple fare, no fire needed, but Clo the quartermaster had packed only enough for one. Frankly, none of it looked appetizing. She studied the food spread on a cloth, then glanced back at the meridian.

"Hungry?" she asked.

He blinked. "Does it matter?"

"That's why I asked." She offered him the dried meat, which would be the most filling and the easiest for him to eat with bound hands.

He hesitated, but his stomach snarled and at last he accepted, shoving the food into his mouth, gnawing like a wild animal. Verve turned her attention to the cheese, but watched him from the corner of her eye. *My dear friend, Sohvi* had called him.

All day, Verve had been expecting to turn around and find Sohvi and Hasina close on her heels, hoping to make a desperate rescue. But there'd been no sign of the other meridian, or anyone else hell-bent on rescuing Celidon. Verve drew her crossbow and surveyed the surrounding prairie again. Other than rippling grasses, there was no sign of pursuit.

Stomach in knots, she turned her gaze more northward, toward Legion's territory. And like a fool, she hoped.

For a few minutes, Verve saw nothing, and almost started to believe that Danya's contact wasn't who she feared. But then something gleamed in the distance and Verve's fingers tightened over her crossbow. If she squinted, she could make out riders moving closer. Danya's contact and their escort, no doubt, heading straight from Legion's turf.

Run, her heart whispered, but Verve ground her teeth against the bile rising in the back of her throat. She was not a child any longer. She was on a sanctioned job for an established priest of Atal; as far as the Legion folks knew, she was an ally. Even so, she ensured her Sufani scarf was safely tucked away in her bodice. *Hide your heart, child, lest it betray your life.*

The knots in her stomach had tightened, which meant her meal held even less appeal now, so she went back over to the meridian. "Still hungry?" she asked, offering the bread.

But he did not accept this time. "What game are you playing?"

"No game," she said. "You just look like you need a good meal."

"And whose fault is that?" he snapped. Fire flickered in his eyes, just for a second. "Are you trying to make yourself feel better about killing my anchor and taking me prisoner? Do you know what Legion will do to me?"

Her breath caught. "It's not personal—"

"Go fuck yourself," he broke in. "That *is* personal. How dare you think to soothe your guilt by sharing this," he kicked the bread away, "with me? You think a hunk of bread will help you sleep at night?"

The war within her heart waged on. Shame won, burning through her blood, and her reply came out through a clenched jaw. "You don't understand—"

He laughed aloud, the sound hollow against the fading daylight. "I understand enough. I know you, Vervaine. I looked into your shadowed heart when we first met. I see what you are, perhaps more clearly than you do. A liar, a killer, a monster." Again, his eyes blazed briefly. "You have suffered, perhaps, but you have dedicated yourself to making *others* suffer, too. And for that, you deserve whatever grisly fate your precious Atal has in store for you."

"I'm...sorry," she stammered.

But he scoffed and rattled the chains around his arms. "No, you're not. You just don't like feeling bad about the evil things you've done. You're not sorry, and Karel is still dead, and I'm soon to follow. And nothing ever changes."

The sun crept closer to the horizon. The riders were closer now, still out of earshot, but they would be here soon. Verve fought for simple speech, but did not question why she wanted to defend herself to her prisoner, of all people.

"Nothing will ever change," she said. "So we must change ourselves to fit the shape of the world."

"If you truly believe that," the meridian said, "then you have already lost whatever battle you think you're fighting."

They stared at each other, the meridian and the assassin. Something wet trickled down Verve's cheeks, but she didn't move to swipe the tears away.

Celidon's regard sharpened, but he said nothing. Even chained, sick, and weak, he lifted his chin and met her gaze with defiance. And for the second time in her life, she saw what true courage looked like.

Courage wasn't a priest cloaked in black and white, teaching children how to kill. Courage, true courage, was being broken, shattered, yet still building a life in a new place. Courage wasn't Danya; it was Ivet, Dannel, and the other Lotis villagers. It was her mother, father, siblings, and all the Sufani who'd gone to their deaths with their heads held high.

Alem had been right. Verve *had* a choice. Too bad this one was the last she'd ever make.

Hoofbeats sounded in the distance as Danya's contact drew closer. Another glance showed how the waning light glinted off of the approaching soldiers' hematite armor.

Somewhere in the back of Verve's mind, hematite-covered boots thudded over a wooden platform.

She looked back at Celidon, saw the alarm that crossed his features, and before she understood what her hands were doing, she grabbed the key at her belt and reached for the lock dangling from his chains.

"What...?" He sucked in a breath. "This is a trick."

No, it was suicide. But perhaps in her next life, Verve might have a chance to rectify the absolute disaster she'd made of this one. A strange sense of calm enveloped her. At least she'd go down fighting those Legion bastards. That was something.

I'm sorry, Alem. I'm sorry, Ivet, Usko.

Ahmma. Apaah. *Mother. Father.* They'd gone to the One god long ago; perhaps the One would let her join them again.

The iron lock clicked open; the chains slithered to the ground with a clatter. Verve swallowed her fear and met the meridian's eyes. "Sohvi and Hasina can find you now. I'll keep Legion occupied. Go."

As he rose on shaking legs, starlight burned within his eyes. "You know Sohvi...?"

The hoofbeats were louder; the ground started to tremble. Was it already too late? Had she bungled this choice, too? Verve shoved the meridian toward the nearest fleet. "Go!"

The sky darkened as dusk relented to nightfall, and the ground thundered. Celidon heaved himself up on the deer's bare back. Verve reached for her crossbow, then thought better of it. She would say he'd tricked her, somehow used his powers on her to free himself. They'd believe the tale long enough for the meridian to get a head start.

Celidon finally sat upright, leaned over the fleet's neck to urge the creature forward, then a crossbow bolt punched into his back.

Someone wailed in Verve's voice, "No!"

The meridian gasped as he slid from the fleet's back and crumpled to the prairie grass. The fleet bellowed in fear and darted off, but Verve ignored the creature as she dove for Celidon. An iron-tipped bolt protruded from his chest, the wound already bright crimson.

"No," Verve cried again, pressing her hands to his chest, trying to stop the relentless surge of blood, but she may as well have tried to stop the tides.

"Vervaine." Star-bright eyes met hers. Celidon gasped again and clutched at her bloody fingers with his own. "Help me," he whispered. "Please."

"I can't," she said. "I wish I could. But I can't. I'm sorry."

For all the good it did.

"No," the meridian said. "Help me save the… space between stars."

The Legion soldiers drew closer; the ground quaked against their weight. Verve wept openly now. He was dying and spouting nonsense, but she couldn't fight this battle any longer, either. "I'll do whatever you want. Just tell me."

"Good." He gripped her fingers tighter; his star-bright eyes dimmed. "It shouldn't…be this way."

An invisible hand crept up her back, sending a thrill of warning through her whole self. The world around her exploded in sound, color, sensation: Celidon's blood, sticky and cooling on her hand; warm spring air caressing her wet cheeks; roaring thunder of the Legion soldiers, bearing down upon them.

Bitterness, grief, eager desire, relief… They warred in her heart and all around, and she could not tell where she ended and the rest of the world began. Celidon's head sank to the ground. Verve fell backward, dizzy, overwhelmed by her senses.

The Legion soldiers closed in around her.

* * *

"What have you done?"

Verve opened her mouth, but could not find her voice through the relentless fury lashing upon her mind. Two sentinels held her upright by her biceps. Their hematite gear pressed against her back and sides, hard, unyielding, more so even than the swords pointed at her heart. The sentinels had fallen upon her and Celidon's body with blades already drawn. And if she moved now, if she sagged into the sentinels' grips, the blade their leader held at her throat would sink home.

But right now, death would be a relief.

"Answer me, cur!" The Legion sentinels wore helmets that concealed their faces, casting their eyes in shadows. The one shouting at Verve must have been their leader, given the commander's insignia on her armored shoulder.

Verve could not collect her wits enough to reply. Her eyes stung with fury, but it was a fury unlike any she'd ever experienced. Her blood boiled as the emotion pummeled her harder than Danya's most vicious blows ever had, but she knew, somehow, the rage she felt wasn't just hers. What had the meridian done to her?

Along with this strange, borrowed fury, the world itself was sharper, clearer, than she'd ever seen. Seren, the mage moon, had risen, casting a brilliant silver light over the golden prairie that threw every blade of grass into stark relief.

Drugged… The meridian must have drugged her, somehow. Or used his bizarre magic. Verve slid her gaze to the Legion sentinel commander to tell them, but received a blow to the jaw instead.

"Answer me!"

"I'm trying," she managed. "Calm…down."

Another blow, this one strong enough to send even the sentinels holding her stumbling backward. Pain bloomed at her temple and her head spun. Dimly, she could hear the sentinels arguing amongst themselves as they searched Celidon's body and the sparse campsite.

The Legion commander grabbed her face, wrenched her head to look at the meridian's body. "What happened? How did he escape?"

A pang of loss cut Verve to her marrow. Images flooded her mind: Celidon, laughing at some silly joke; Celidon, gazing at the expanse of open ocean; Celidon, leaning his head against Karel's shoulder.

Their faces, their very spirits, were as familiar to Verve as her own. And they were dead. She'd destroyed them both.

A killer. The thought was hers, but not. Foreign, yet familiar. *A monster. That's all you are. And now I'm trapped here, too.*

"What are you talking about?" she slurred.

The Legion commander kicked her shin. Something cracked, then heat flooded her leg. "Sodding useless dreg," the soldier snarled. "I knew dealing with that bitch of a priest was a mistake. Now we've wasted an entire day on this filth."

The commander must have given a signal, for the sentinels holding Verve dropped her without warning. She blinked up at the night sky. Stars pin-pricked the void, but her gaze stuck on the indigo-velvet space between the distant lights; what secrets lay hidden in the ether?

"Your orders, ser?"

Another blow, this one at her side. The stars danced before Verve's eyes as the commander said, "She's as useless to that Freehold priest as she is to us. Kill her, but make her suffer first."

The sentinels closed in around Verve. The air stung with their eagerness, with the violence in their hearts. Blows fell upon her, at first like rain, then like pounding hail. Boots slammed into her legs, her sides, her head. Her vision went white and spotty; she tasted copper on her tongue. Pain blocked out everything else, but each time she started to sink into oblivion, something shoved her back to consciousness. And that unfamiliar voice in her mind snarled, *No. You won't escape any longer.*

The sentinels stomped on her fingers, snapping bones like twigs. Someone snatched her hair to pull her up, and her scalp exploded with fire. They held her fast, while another two—or maybe more—drove armored fists into her stomach, her throat. They laughed and jeered and called her every ugly name they knew.

And through it all, she could not move, let alone fight back, and that foreign but familiar voice sneered, *This is your reward for a job well done.*

At last they tired of their sport. One sentinel sank his blade deep into her stomach, then they picked her up and slung her body into a section of tall grass they had not trampled. They rode away, taking the fleet deer too.

Verve inhaled and tasted dirt. She'd landed face-down. With every ounce of effort she could manage, she rolled on her back so she could see the night sky again, the stars and the inky spaces between them, all filled with possibility. How foolish she had been to hide from the night.

All warmth seeped from her body, and she could not take a proper breath. Cold… She was so cold, like she'd never been warm, never even seen fire, let alone felt the kiss of sunlight on her cheeks.

Alem, she thought, marveling at the sky despite the ice in her limbs and the searing fire in her gut. How clearly she could see now. Everything was better when he was at her side.

Alem, I'm sorry.

16

Space-Between-Stars

If pain was a warning that something was wrong, it was pointless when it was everywhere, all at once. If the One god was real, why would they let someone suffer like this?

Suffering begets suffering, came that strange but familiar voice. *Surely you know this better than anyone.*

Verve moaned.

"Here!"

Footsteps came lightly over the ground. A new presence parted the tall grasses and knelt at her side. "Oh, gods, are we too late?" Alem's voice was hoarse. "Verve? Can you open your eyes? Can you hear me?"

"Let me," said Sohvi.

A warm feeling pooled around Verve's heart at the sound of her friend's voice.

Wait. Her friend? Sohvi was a stranger, and a hostile one at that. Why did she feel like a friend now?

"Be easy, relah," Sohvi murmured, her palm brushing Verve's cheek. The southern slang word for kin echoed in Verve's head, but before she could wonder too much, Sohvi's voice spoke again, this time in her mind. *Let me in.*

Verve had little choice. Sohvi's awareness brushed hers, gentle as her touch, and the strange new voice in Verve's mind—the one that had chided her—keened with grief.

Cel's gone, and he left me trapped within this...killer.

I know, Sohvi replied, sorrow tinting her words. *But he swore an oath to preserve you, and so he did. To the end.*

Better to be dead than one who brings death. The presence coiled in on itself, wracked with bitterness.

Vervaine, Sohvi said. *Can you answer me?*

Verve opened her mouth, but her swollen tongue did little more than flop against her teeth. Even that minor movement sent pain shooting through her head with renewed force. She moaned again.

"You're hurting her," Alem said. "She's near the river's shore, close to death. Question her later, if you must, but let me work *now.*"

"Keep your distance," Hasina said in a low, dangerous voice. "Watch for Legion's return."

"Oh, go fall on your axe," Alem shot back. "If not for me, you'd still be wandering around the province looking for Celidon. Now get out of my way."

Alem. Verve tried to say his name, but her mouth still didn't cooperate. But it didn't matter, for then he was at her side again, hands grasping hers.

"But she's *dripping* in hematite," Hasina began.

"Shut up," Alem hissed. "Your part's done. Let me handle mine."

Verve desperately wanted to smile. Warmth flooded her, like sunlight pouring through each vein. The throbbing pain that had taken over her body eased enough for her head to clear a little. Her vision focused; Alem's features came into view as he knelt over her, eyes closed, face pinched in concentration. Black hair stuck out at odd angles from his braids and sweat beaded his upper lip.

"I told you," she croaked, "not to worry about me."

His eyes flew open as he stared at her. "Sorry to disappoint."

She managed a smile. "You've never."

Sohvi cleared her throat. "She's well enough to speak now?"

"She's out of danger — for the moment," Alem said, cradling Verve's hand. "But I'll need to work on her a bit more before we can move her safely. Must you interrogate her *now*?"

"The first few hours after a meridian's death are critical," Hasina said as Sohvi came to Verve's side once more. "Sohvi needs to understand exactly what happened to Celidon, and for that, she needs to speak to Verve."

Alem's jaw tightened, and he jerked his chin. "The bloodstains over there seem pretty damn explanatory to me. I'm sorry your friend is gone, but Verve is *alive* and I intend to keep her that way."

"Be easy, Alem," Sohvi said. "There may be a way I can help her, but I must examine her first. It will not take long."

Alem stared at the meridian, and Verve could not remember a time when anyone had argued for her safety as he'd done. At last he said, "You have two minutes."

Sohvi nodded and looked back at Verve. *Show me what happened,* Sohvi said in Verve's mind. *Show me what happened when Celidon died.*

Only some of that made sense. Verve frowned up at the meridian, trying to recall. "Legion came…"

Save your voice, Sohvi said to Verve, the words still echoing softly in Verve's mind. She pressed the fingers of one hand to her temple. *Think over the memory, and I will see.*

Recalling the encounter with Legion was almost worse than experiencing it. But Sohvi sat calmly through Verve's remembrance, somehow, and when it was done, the meridian exhaled and sat back on her heels.

Hasina came over, her steps silent despite her multitude of weapons. "Well?"

"As I suspected," Sohvi said. "Celidon passed his Fae spirit to the assassin."

"She has a name," Alem ground out.

Sohvi nodded absently, her gaze on Verve once more. "It's not supposed to be this way," she said bitterly. "Becoming one of us is an honor, a privilege, one that takes years of training to even begin to understand. And now it's been thrust upon her with no warning."

Alem had not let Verve's hands go, but at this, he went still. "Wait… You're saying Verve is a meridian now?"

"So it seems." Sohvi looked at Verve. "That voice you're hearing, that unfamiliar presence you feel… their name is Space-Between-Stars. It is this Fae's soul that Celidon joined with yours."

Space-Between-Stars. Well, Verve had heard weirder names. But she refused to entertain any thoughts about her—their—situation beyond…

I don't want it, Verve managed to reply. *Take it back.*

"It will take some time to acclimate," Sohvi said aloud. "But you are a meridian now, Vervaine."

A ripple of dark humor echoed in Verve's mind as Space-Between-Stars laughed. Sohvi *took too long to find us. You and I are now bonded until your death. As far as you're concerned, our bond is forever.*

* * *

Verve could not recall being helpless like this, not in many years. Over the next few days, she watched the sky a lot, for Alem and Hasina had placed her onto the Zhee trader's wagon that Alem had hired. And once they'd left the wagon behind, Verve stared up at the brilliant blue sky as the world drifted past the new, larger canoe Alem had acquired. No one spoke to her much, which made sense, for she faded in and out of consciousness. The trip back to Lotis might have been a dream, if not for the searing pain that returned whenever Alem's magic wore off.

Throughout the entire journey, Verve could sense Space-Between-Stars's disgust at their new host, like the bitter tang of bile in the back of her throat.

Later, she woke in the dead of night, wrapped in shadows, confined in an unfamiliar place. Disoriented, Verve cried out in Sufa.

Then Ivet was beside her, pressing Verve to her chest, murmuring soothing words in their shared tongue. "Easy now, vidahem. Be easy. You're safe. You're home."

Love flowed from Ivet's bright spirit — there was no mistaking the feeling. Love like Verve had not known since that horrific day almost two decades ago; a mother's love for her lost child. Tears sprang to Verve's eyes and she was too weak to stop them from soaking the older woman's tunic.

But Ivet only held her close, stroking her hair. "You're safe, Verve. You're home."

Sunlight poured into the room when Verve surfaced again. At first she could only stare at the wooden beams of Ivet's cottage, where tiny rainbows danced, cast by the crystal hung in the window.

As she watched the rainbows, a memory surfaced. She was one among a group of supplicants, kneeling in prayer inside a cavernous temple overlooking a city she'd never seen before. Voices rose in unison all around her.

"The One is life, and life's mysteries are boundless. Mortals such as we cannot hope to fathom the true nature of the One, but there is always harmony in the One's creations. As a shaft of sunlight pierces a crystal to create a multitude of colors, so did the One provide us with our gods, who are present in our daily lives, who watch over us and protect us when we have the greatest need."

The Promise of the One. An ancient prayer, set down by the first settlers of Aredia, over a thousand years ago. And while Verve didn't think of the other gods very much, the understanding that worship of the One had once been widely practiced brought a sense of comfort, like a warm blanket wrapped around her shoulders. This memory was older than her, perhaps even older than the Sundering.

Where the memory itself had come from, she could not say.

She hurt all over, but the pain was languid, and when she lifted her arm to examine her once-broken fingers, they flexed and moved with only a dull ache.

Dead. She should be *dead*, but for Alem.

"Vidahem?" It was Dannel, seated across from her, fingers twined in his lap. "Are you awake?"

She sat up, slowly, allowing the dizziness to pass. "Dannel? What are you doing here?"

He beamed. "By the One, it's good to hear your voice. Alem's a skilled lad, but still… we've all been worried sick. I about had to fight Hadiya for my shift by your bed, then Owen and Berel wanted in. But the real surprise was

Klaret. Never heard her insist on *anything*."

It took Verve a few seconds to wrap her mind around what he was saying. "You all…kept watch over me?"

"Oh, Alem would have never left, but the poor lad about drained his magic dry to pull you from the river of death. And Ivet…" Dannel exhaled. "Well, it'd take a stronger man than me to say no to that woman when her mind's set on something. She'd be here now, but Klaret and Hadiya practically had to drag her off to rest."

Oh, no. This wouldn't do. Verve shoved back the blankets and made to stand. But then a spike of concern leaped from Dannel as he came forward on sure steps. The sudden, bizarre sensation of feeling *his* emotions made her legs buckle, and she hit the floor, groaning. He held out his hand and Verve, after a second of hesitation, accepted, and allowed him to help her to her feet. Dannel's relief sprang up like the first flower of spring.

What in the stars and moons was going on?

"I'm so glad you're here," he said, squeezing Verve's hand. "I feared I'd never see you again. Well," he laughed, "you know what I mean."

His joy was a palm cradling her heart. The shock of the shared feeling struck Verve mute until she managed, "Thank you."

Dannel beamed again and released her hand. "Stay here," he said in a mock-serious voice. "Or else Ivet will cut off my hands and I'll really be blind. I'll let her know you're awake."

With that, he made his way out of the cottage, leaving Verve alone. She stumbled back to the bed and collapsed in the pile of blankets. Outside the window, birds and crickets chirped, and somewhere, Berel led Lio and Kinneret in an off-key version of a children's song. Sunlight gleamed off of the nearby marsh water as if diamonds floated on the surface, and the air was warmer than Verve recalled. Everything in Lotis was green and full of life.

Within Verve's mind, her new passenger relaxed. Although she could not hear Space-Between-Stars at the moment, the Fae's impressions had not faded. Much the opposite. But despite displeasure with the morality of their new host, Space-Between-Stars savored every breath, every sight and sound. Through this delight, the constant weight upon Verve's heart eased somewhat.

Ivet approached; Verve sensed the other woman's worry like pinpricks down her back. But along with worry, love swelled like a sunbeam through the clouds. Verve sucked in a breath at the intensity of the feeling; it left her disoriented, dizzy. Ivet *loved* her. How? Why? What had Verve done to deserve anything so remarkable as *love*?

The cottage door opened, and Ivet entered. "Verve," she said in a watery voice as she approached.

Verve's smile came to her face with ease. "The One is life."

Ivet's joy at the familiar greeting was boundless, like the sky. She wrapped Verve in her arm and held her close. Verve sank so easily into that warm, comforting embrace. "I'm sorry," Verve whispered through her tears.

Ivet hugged her closer. "For what?"

Verve pulled back and rubbed her eyes, but Ivet placed a hand on her cheek in a silent offer of support. Verve said, "For making you worry."

"Oh, that." Ivet made a dismissive motion. "I'd worry about the tides being late. It's my nature. You've done nothing wrong."

Verve swiped at her eyes again. Gods above, perhaps her head had been injured worse than anyone thought, for her to weep so much.

Unless…

Ivet loved her. Dannel cared deeply for her well-being. So did the others who'd sat with her while she rested. Verve understood these things had happened, but what they signified seemed impossible.

Unless it wasn't. Unless the people of Lotis genuinely *cared* for her. Not what she could do for them, but for *her*.

Words failed her for a few moments until she choked out, "Is Alem all right? Dannel said…"

She trailed off at the sudden tension radiating from the other woman. "Alem is resting at his home," Ivet said. "The damage those Legion bastards did to you sure put him through his paces, but he healed you in the end."

Alem had almost killed himself to heal *her*. Guilt spiked, but she refused to let it take purchase in her heart, at least not until she made sure Alem would really be okay. Then she could tear him a new one. "I'd like to see him."

Ivet squeezed her hand. "I figured as much. Let's go."

* * *

A peek in the cottage window showed Alem wasn't in his bed, the stubborn mule, but Verve could sense his presence nearby: a distinctive blend of sweet and bitter, like jessamin-laced ale. There was another sensation, too, like the instant before a lightning strike. Whatever it was made Space-Between-Stars perk up, and then Verve understood she was sensing magic. A smell, a taste, a feeling; the awareness of Alem's power filled the air around him, drawing her closer. Within her spirit, the glimmer's interest sparked to a flame — hungry for fuel.

This meridian-thing was getting weirder and weirder. How was she supposed to live her life with this constant flow of others' emotions? And now, it seemed the Fae spirit living alongside her own had a taste for magic.

Verve gritted her teeth. She could handle this. Even her crossbow had been new once. With practice, she could learn this new power, too. And now that Danya (hopefully) thought she was dead, she had a fighting chance.

After only a little begging, Verve convinced Ivet to leave her alone at Alem's garden gate, and Verve limped around the humble cottage, following the heady trail of Alem's magic. She found the dendric mage behind his cottage, hair loose, eyes closed, seated on the ground between neat rows of lavender and blooming glosswing flowers. There were blue-gray smudges beneath his eyes, but otherwise, he looked whole.

She took a single step his way. "Alem?"

His eyes didn't open, but a feeling burst free from him, like water from a broken dam. She tried to analyze the swirl of emotions pouring into the space between them, but before she could, somehow he staunched the flow.

"Verve," he said, blinking into the sunlight. "What are you doing up? You should be in bed."

"So should you."

He gave her a smile that did not reach his eyes. "How are you feeling?"

"Alive." She took another step toward him, drawn not only by the pull of his magic but also by her own silly heart. "How did you find me the other day?"

He plucked a weed and twirled it in his fingers, his gaze going distant. "It was strange. I was in Freehold, arranging the last couple trades, when I felt… No, I *heard* your voice. In my mind. You were…" He gave a shaking inhale. "You were calling my name, but you sounded… Verve, you were dying. I could hear it in your voice. No, I could *feel* it, feel you…"

His cheeks colored, and he focused on the weed in his hand. "I raced out of the market and headed for the gates. No idea what my plan was. I suppose I was going to steal a horse or something." A thin smile crossed his face. "But then I spotted Sohvi and Hasina. Apparently, they'd been searching around Freehold, looking for their friend. The man you captured."

Space-Between-Stars's anger flared, aimed at Verve. An answering shame coursed through her and she leaned against the garden fence, as much to shift her weight as to distract herself from the feeling. "But *how* did you find me?"

He did not reply immediately. "It was like…there was a cord tied between us. All I had to do was pull, and it led me right to you." He scoffed and tossed the weed down. "It sounds stupid, I guess, but it worked."

"Sohvi couldn't manage it?" If they were both meridians now, then surely…

Alem shrugged. "She said she could sense Celidon, but after he died, I think she was too…distraught to sense much else." He glanced up at her, squinting through the sunlight. "How does it feel to be a meridian?"

All around them, lacy butterflies danced over the yellow glosswing blossoms. A warm breeze brought the scent of water, of new grass, of the soapwort the villagers used to wash their clothes. But beneath all of that, or perhaps only mingled within it, was a sense of peaceful occupation, relief, joy: the emotions of the Lotis villagers. They were happy because Verve and Alem were safely home.

Home.

She'd lost her last home at six summers old. After that, there'd been no other place that she could consider *home*. Not until now.

"Strange," she said at last. "But good. Sometimes, anyway."

"What do you mean?"

She skimmed her fingertips over a lavender bush. "I can…sense emotions from other people. At least, I think that's what's going on. I'm glad Lotis is so small. I think it'd be…noisier somewhere like Freehold."

Alem nodded thoughtfully. "Milo sometimes spoke of sensing others' emotions. He taught me a little of how to shield my own." His voice turned grim. "Came in useful when living near meridians."

That explained what he'd done when she arrived. How much else did he know? She said, carefully, "I think my Fae spirit hates me."

Alem went still. "Why?"

"Why do they hate me, or why do I think they do?"

"Either."

Verve pretended to study the nearest plant, a leggy dandelion with about half its fuzzy puff missing. "Probably all the killing I've done."

She could almost hear Space-Between-Stars's snarky response, *You think?*

"Milo once told me the Fae are highly empathetic beings," Alem replied after a beat. "It wouldn't surprise me that the one you've joined with isn't thrilled with the arrangement."

Great. "What do you think Milo would say to someone in my case?" Verve asked.

Alem gave her another of those not-smiles. "I think he'd say give it time."

Verve smiled at him, but he looked away again, shoulders hunched. Confused, Verve took another step closer, so they were within arm's reach of each other. "Did I thank you?" she asked.

He shrugged. "I'm a healer. Healing kind of comes with the territory."

"You did more than heal me, Alem."

He flinched at the sound of his name, and still would not meet her eyes. "As you say."

With her new senses, she groped for his emotions, but found only an impenetrable wall, a severe contrast to the surge she'd sensed a few minutes ago. Her heart picked up its pace. "Alem, I can tell something's wrong. You can't hide from me."

With effort, he pushed himself to his feet. "You shouldn't poke around people's heads without their permission."

"I wasn't—"

"Maybe you don't mean to," he broke in, "but you *are*. How would you feel if some random stranger could look into your heart, your soul, and see *everything* you wanted to keep hidden?"

A memory of the glimmer's voice echoed: *You can't escape any longer.*

But she tried to keep her calm. "I'm not a stranger."

"That's worse," he said. "Because you should know better. Look, meridians spend *years* learning to control their abilities, so they don't accidentally influence other's emotions."

Her attention snagged on his words. "Meridians can…influence others?"

"That's what I always heard." Alem studied her. "Sohvi said you must take care with this new power."

Verve tried not to scoff. "I can figure it out on my own. I've spent enough time around mages. I understand how magic works. This can't be much different."

No, and her new abilities could be even *better* than magic, for if she could sense the Lotis villagers, she could sense others, too. Which meant no more ambushes, no surprises. She would know when someone lied, perhaps even be able to dig out the truth from their mind.

Danya most likely thought her dead, but if not, Verve would know if—or when—Atal's Chosen came *near* Lotis. And if Danya got wind of Verve's survival, she would indeed make good on her threat; she would send Usko and the others after Verve. And Verve would be forced to kill—

She cut off the thought and tried to focus again on her new abilities. If she could sense magic itself… No mage would be able to get close enough to Lotis to damage anyone or anything.

Alem made a sound of frustration. "You *need* to contact Sohvi and the other meridians. Sohvi said you could find her when you were ready — she said you just had to *look*. But she also made a point to say that you'll need help to deal with these new abilities, to parse through all the memories from

Space-Between-Stars's previous hosts."

"Well, where is Sohvi?" Verve made a show of looking around. "If it's *so* important I need her help, why'd she abandon me?"

Abandon was too strong a word for the absence of someone Verve didn't know very well and liked even less, but it fit — for Celidon, who'd been Sohvi's friend. And now it fit for Verve, who now shared Celidon's memories.

More emotional baggage. Just what she needed.

Alem studied her. "Look, I don't have all the answers, all right? But I think Sohvi was just as… confounded by all of this as you are, so she needed to consult the other meridians. But I don't really care about her. What I do know is *you* need to learn how to manage your gift."

Verve scoffed. "Gift? This was forced on me. By rights, I can use it how I please."

He took a step toward her, then seemed to think better of it. "Between what I learned from Milo and what Sohvi told me on the trip back here, I've come to understand that being a meridian is mostly responsibility. You're now the bearer of an additional spirit; you may not actively *feel* Space-Between-Stars all the time, but their spirit is within you, still, and so is all the knowledge they've learned from their own lives, and all the different hosts they've had. You're in charge, but it's not *just* you behind those eyes any longer, Verve."

The truth in his words echoed like a massive bell clanging within her spirit. The weight of those old memories, relics of another time, sank into her bones, filling them with lead. It was too much. All of this was too much. She needed a puffer. She *really* needed a drink—by the One, she deserved *some* fun after the last few horrific days—and needed to sit with this new reality.

But she couldn't say that to Alem, who clearly expected her to be some paragon of virtue now.

"What's your damage?" she asked. "Is it because the meridians didn't want you to join them? Are you jealous of me?"

"That's…" His gaze fell to his bare feet. "Completely true. I just didn't realize it." He scrubbed a hand over his face. "How much of a jerk was I?"

She tried not to smile. "No more than usual."

"Ah." He winced. "Sorry about that."

"You can make it up to me by helping me understand all this bizarre fae shit. How did meridians even start, anyway? Why would Fae want to join with human souls?"

But even as the words left her mouth, she knew the answer: to taste life, and all it offered. She could recall vague memories of an ethereal world of shadows and light — the realm of the magical creatures known as the Fae. The nature of the Fae's magic meant they could not survive in the physical world: a world of sunlight on skin, or the sound of rain, of the thrill of a lover's touch. So a long time ago, some of them had made a pact with some humans: to share their abilities in exchange for the joy—and pain—of life itself.

And it was this knowledge, more than anything else Verve had experienced so far, that cemented her new reality. There was no way she could know any of this on her own. All the Fae legends, all the glimmer stories… All true. If she searched her glimmer's memories, she found Celidon's, and the meridian before him: Jocasta.

And Space-Between-Stars, the Fae who linked them all.

Now she was part of the tale.

The notion was too big to fit into her body. Verve stumbled back, tried to catch herself on the fence, but failed.

Thank the One, Alem was there. Too bad he was also weak after their shared ordeal, so when he grabbed her, he lost his footing and they collapsed together in a lavender bush. The sweet, astringent scent overpowered her, making her cough, and when she finally looked at Alem, he had bits of purple stuck in his hair.

"We've got to stop doing this," she managed.

"Lavender's pretty tough, but point taken." He grabbed the fence to pull himself up, then offered her his hand. She grasped it, found her footing, and allowed him to pull her to her feet. They stood close together amid the lavender, and again, his spirit bloomed before her senses, stronger than the surrounding herbs. They stood closer than friends should, but there was still a space between them. His breath was warm on her cheek.

Alem could hide his magic and his feelings, but he could not hide the heat in his gaze. And as she stared into his dark eyes, awareness of yet another feeling cascaded over her, through her, a riptide that pulled her out to his ocean.

"I don't have the answers, either," she managed. "But I'm trying."

"I know," he said, and took her hand. His own was warm and calloused, if a little dirty. "And I'll help you, however I can. I'll try to keep the bad behavior to a minimum."

"Not *too* much," she replied, winking, and he flushed.

17

Playing Possum

The next day, Verve woke to Ivet's cheerful voice from below her loft.

"Verve," Ivet called softly. "It's almost midday. Are you still asleep?" Excitement sparkled through the Sufani woman's presence.

Rubbing sleep from her eyes, Verve crawled to the edge of the loft and peered down. "What's wrong?"

Ivet beamed up at her, clutching at a rucksack hung over her shoulder. "Nothing. Come down. I have a surprise for you."

There were a host of reasons Ivet might be here now, but only one seemed feasible. "I'm not awake enough for another embroidery lesson," Verve said. They'd had a few before Verve's ill-fated trip back to Freehold.

"Oh, bother," Ivet said wryly. "That's disappointing. Of course, I certainly have no *other* reason to rouse you back from the almost-dead than to test your hand-eye coordination with a needle and thread."

Verve groaned and flopped back down. "Ivet…"

The ladder creaked as Ivet clambered up. "The rhyme was unintentional. I can't help myself sometimes. By the One, when did you start you sleeping like the dead? I've been calling you for a few minutes."

"Strange," Verve said, covering her mouth as she yawned. "I usually don't sleep so soundly." Space-Between-Stars' influence, perhaps, or maybe she was just still healing from her encounter with Legion.

"Sleep that deep means you must have needed it." Ivet gave Verve a look of concern. "You haven't been getting into the Willow's liquor stores again, have you?"

Heat crept to Verve's cheeks; she cast a furtive glance at her collection of empty bottles, hidden beneath several wads of hay. "Not since before Freehold."

Ivet eyed her. "There's no shame in getting lost in a bottle — or in puffer smoke, for that matter. Happens to a lot of folks, especially in a world like ours. But I worry, sometimes, that you'll get so lost, you won't find your way out."

The lilt of Ivet's Sufani accent came through more clearly now than Verve had heard before, and her compassion slipped into Verve's awareness like an arm around her shoulder. And within Verve's spirit, Space-Between-Stars softened, as if Ivet's kindness had made the Fae forget—just for a moment—how much they hated Verve.

She couldn't meet Ivet's gaze. "Thanks," she mumbled. "I'm... okay."

She turned her attention to the pile of dirty laundry she'd been avoiding. She was almost out of clean socks, so she'd have to borrow Berel's washtub again soon. The thought made her strangely giddy. How long since she'd been able to make even the most mundane plans for the future? Hell, how long since she'd slept as deeply as she had since returning to Lotis?

"I don't know how much you care for festivals," Ivet went on after a moment. "But today's the spring equinox: Ea's Day."

These days, most mention of the old gods like Ea was kept to the more exciting holidays, occasional swears, and a few dedicated worshippers. As Sufani, Verve's family had only ever cared about the One god, and Danya had only ever allowed the Chosen to worship Atal.

A flicker of recognition from the depths of Celidon's memories sparked understanding within Verve. "Ea... They're the protector of animals. You celebrate Ea's Day here?"

Verve grabbed one of her tunics. Clean enough to wear? She inhaled a distinct sour odor, gagged, and tossed the tunic away. Hopefully Space-Between-Stars' tendency to heighten smells, sounds, and sensations was in full swing here; hopefully she didn't smell *that* bad.

Ivet smiled. "We do, indeed. The festival usually lasts three days, but we're humble folk here, so we only manage one. But we go all out — as much as we can, at any rate. We've little in the way of proper costumes, but Kinneret will look so dear in her mouse ears. And Lio decided he could forgo the fire drake costume in favor of a robin — Owen found him some feathers." She lifted a brow. "Hadiya made a gorgeous turtle shell from a fallen cypress for me to wear. And I brought this for you."

She plunked down the rucksack, which Verve eyed warily. What sort of animal did the Lotis villagers think suited her? Within the bag was a...

She withdrew a felt possum tail and gaped at Ivet. "You're joking."

"Not at all. Possums eat all sorts of pests and they don't get the mouth-foaming sickness. Besides, I think they have an adorable, if strange, way about them."

Verve skimmed her fingers over the soft tail, noting the fine stitching. "Are you trying to tell me something?"

Ivet chuckled. "Nothing I haven't said already. Nori made the tail. Turns out she's quite a skilled seamstress."

With the tail was a pair of round gray ears attached to a leather headband, and a small furry cape that might very well have been a real possum, once. Verve stared at the pieces and didn't know what to think. So she only said, "Thank you?"

"You're welcome." Ivet's eyes flickered over Verve, her dirty laundry, and the stack of hay in the corner. "I know this may seem... odd to you. Alem told me what happened to you at Freehold, besides getting the shit beaten out of you by those Legion bastards."

Verve's hand stole to the cut Danya had given her on her cheek, but not even a small mark remained. Alem was nothing if not thorough. "What exactly did he tell you?" Verve asked.

Ivet's brows knitted, and a look of pure rage passed over her face, although it dissipated immediately. "He didn't know many specifics, but from what he said... Well, I don't blame you for wanting to leave whatever life you had before. So I spoke to Dannel, Hadiya, and the others; we all agreed you deserve some fun, and we wanted to show you how much we appreciate what you've done for our little village." Her voice softened. "Alem's told me what he knows of meridians, so I know you feel… Well, you *feel* more than most. Seems like a blessing sometimes, and a curse, others. Tonight, we all hope to give you a little of the former."

Love pulsed from Ivet, soft but strong enough to stun Verve into silence. Never in her time with Danya had anyone acknowledged her suffering, let alone wanted to help her through it. And in return, Ivet wanted nothing more than her happiness.

Verve skimmed her fingers over the tail, trying to work out a response that Ivet deserved. All she managed was, "That works for me."

"Alem also said your injuries were fatal," Ivet added quietly. "He said Legion left you for dead."

"Sure felt like it."

Ivet didn't so much as blink. "Will your patron be missing you, then?"

In other words, how dangerous was it for Verve to remain in Lotis? She was free; she ought to leave this place and never look back, as much for their benefit as for hers. But she could only shrug.

Ivet's soft touch at her hand coaxed her into meeting Ivet's eyes. "Verve, I want you to know there's a home for you in Lotis, if you want one. And if trouble comes for you, well," she smiled, "it's a good thing we're all nice and fortified, isn't it?"

Something swelled in Verve's chest again. She couldn't speak for longing, so she only nodded.

Ivet patted Verve's knee. "You take such good care of us all, Verve. You carry all our weights on your shoulders, like the possum mothers do with their kits. Or are they cubs? I can never remember." She paused. "Will you join us at the celebration? You don't have to wear the get-up."

Verve stared at the other woman, her heart too full to reply immediately. Instead, she slid the ear-headband on. "I'd be honored."

Ivet's joy lit the world. "We're so glad to have you."

* * *

A bath, a change of clothes, and a good meal worked their own kind of magic, and by that evening, Verve deemed herself presentable enough for the equinox celebration. The children had helped collect firewood, so Klaret and Kyon had set up a huge pyre in the heart of Lotis. Hadiya had dragged out tables and chairs from the Willow; Ivet, Owen, and Berel were busily laying out platters piled high with food. To Verve's new meridian senses, the air in Lotis shone with anticipation, happiness, relief; like sunlight glinting off of spring leaves.

But Verve couldn't bring herself to join the celebration just yet, so as the final preparations unfolded, she finished a puffer in the shadow of Hadiya's barn. Danya thought she was dead, which meant she was free — for now. But what that would mean in the future, Verve could not say, anymore than what being a meridian would mean.

Well, right now, it meant the others' emotions danced through Lotis like fireflies. They beckoned her, but she held back, her feet held fast by the tumbling nerves in her stomach. When was the last time she'd been to a celebration of any kind? The people of Lotis had welcomed her with open arms, but nothing good lasted. They were happy now, but the only constant was change. Surely any moment they would realize she wasn't worth their kindness and cast her out on her own.

"How about here?" It was Alem, guiding Lio and Kinneret in placing bundles of flowers. They'd already decorated the tables of food and had moved on to Hadiya's home.

Kinneret, who did indeed look adorable in mouse ears and a tail, held up a garland of red, purple, and yellow wildflowers. "Here?"

"Perfect," Alem replied as he wrapped twine around the porch railing to hold the garland in place. To Verve's amusement, he wore a racoon tail and a pair of pointed, furry ears, and someone had drawn a black nose and whiskers on his face. "Lio, where should we put those daffodils?"

Lio, wearing feathers and a felt beak, squinted through the fading light. "Verve! Come help us!"

Alem glanced up at her, and she tensed, wanting him to call her over, but not yet ready to venture out. But he only gave her a warm smile and said to

Lio, "Verve will help if she wants. Lio, how about you add the daffodils to the ones Kinny just put up?"

But Lio ignored Alem and darted away from him, making a beeline for Verve. The kid had to tilt his head pretty far back to look up at her, so she knelt and tried to make her face friendly. "Are those real marsh robin feathers?" she asked.

He beamed. "Yes! Owen found them for me, see?" He twirled, flapping his arms, delight and contentment rolling off of him in waves.

Kinneret, not to be left out, hurried over. "I'm a mouse! I wanted to be a lion, but Ivet said we have enough of those around here."

Their eagerness danced like sugar on the tip of her tongue, and she chuckled. "I agree. And besides, who needs lions when we have mice and marsh robins? You both look wonderful."

"You're a possum," Lio said sagely. "They sleep all day and come out at night."

A little too accurate, lately. Verve laughed again. "Sometimes."

"Sorry," Alem said as he came up. "You turn around for one second, and they're gone."

She couldn't help herself. "Nice tail."

He blushed, which was more than a little gratifying. "You too," he replied, grinning.

Then it was her turn to blush, so she reached for one of the garlands he carried. "Pretty flowers," she said, trying not to sound too awkward. "Did you grow them all?"

"We found them in the woods," Kinneret said. "Alem took us out *really* far, but we're not supposed to tell Ivet."

"Tell me what?" Ivet said as she approached. A large but thin turtle's shell hung at her back, and she had leather turtle-flippers sewn onto her gloves.

Alem flinched. Verve bit back a laugh. But the village leader only smiled at the two children and beckoned. "Come along. We're about to eat."

Both kids shrieked with joy and raced past her, making a beeline for the table now loaded with food. Ivet rolled her eyes fondly, then glanced between Verve and Alem. "Join us whenever you're ready."

As Ivet went back to the others, Alem cut his eyes to Verve. "You don't have to join us unless you want to." He held out his hand and smiled. "But I'd really like it if you did."

The apprehension she'd felt while hidden in the barn's shadows faded away with that smile. She was free; she could stay in Lotis, maybe try to build something good. The life she never knew she wanted lay within her grasp.

All she had to do was take it. Verve slid her hand into his and grinned. "Let's go."

18

The Path You're Walking

Nobody in Lotis knew how to sit in a chair. Instead, the villagers perched on upturned or fallen stumps, or blankets, or the tables themselves. They chattered and called out to one another, trading exaggerated stories and friendly jibes, and exuding a sense of camaraderie that Verve had never experienced before. Their contentment, their joy, rippled through the air like a warm summer wind. And as Verve spent time among them, an answering contentment radiated from her, like sunlight.

Strange.

But it doesn't have to be. The observation was not hers, exactly, but for the first time in her recent memory, she wanted it to be. She was the only one here armed—well, except maybe Klaret—and even the tiny dagger tucked in her bodice seemed silly now. Her meridian senses told her no danger was near: no murderous mages—or anyone else—approached Lotis. They were all safe.

And *that* was the strangest feeling of all.

Verve leaned against the Willow's fortified walls; the fireproof brushthorn paste dried solid and thankfully didn't smell too bad. She'd destroyed a towering plate of turkey, roasted mushrooms, and various vegetables before moving on to dessert. She was considering a third helping of rice-and-honey pudding, when Ivet started to sing.

It was an old Sufani melody, at once lilting and forlorn, as many of the Sufani songs were. Grief and joy traveled side by side, after all, and knowing one allowed you to appreciate the other. Too well had the Sufani learned those lessons.

Ivet's voice was sweet, clear, strong. After a few stanzas, Dannel joined her, adding his rich baritone. The words, which Verve had not heard since she was Kinny's age, resonated through her body, all the way to her frayed spirit. She could not speak, could hardly breathe, while Ivet sang. Tears slipped down her cheeks, but she could not move to brush them aside. All at once, she was back among her family, safely tucked within the shelter of their wagons around the perimeter, surrounded by people who loved her. There was a soft touch at her loose hair as her mother stroked the tight curls and coils. Her father sang deep as a river and strong as a current, while her brothers and sister bickered over the last bites of pudding.

A sense of loss cut Verve straight to her heart, straight to her soul, but this time, she let the feeling wash over her, through her. There was pain, yes, but there was also joy and love, which she'd closed herself off from for too long.

No one in Freehold celebrated like this, at least not in a way that Verve had ever seen or taken part in. The god Atal had only a few holidays, and those were full of dreary words like *penance* and *obligation*. Every so often, the Chosen would drink too much and spar for fun, but there was always an air of competition and fear among them. And despite Danya's nebulous promises of some cousin she'd never heard of, Verve's family by blood was gone.

Another singer joined Ivet and Dannel. Verve's throat ached a little at first, but the feeling passed as her voice warmed to the melody. Ivet beamed at her, and held out her hand, and Verve found the strength to walk over, to take that hand, and keep singing.

The song swelled, then ended, but Ivet immediately began another, a happier one. Dannel joined in, then Verve, who remembered these words too. Hadiya and Klaret joined with their instruments, and the air came alive with music.

Surrounded by joy and light, Verve relaxed, and found Space-Between-

Stars's delight at this decidedly *human* celebration. The Fae had been to parties like this with their other hosts, but from what Verve could tell, the novelty had not worn off. With Space-Between-Stars's enthusiasm, it was easy to let joy create joy; Verve relaxed further and allowed the strange warmth in her chest—was that happiness?—to spread to the others.

Space-Between-Stars fairly preened. Verve allowed herself a full smile as the dancing began.

Alem grabbed Kyon's hand and the two men twirled around the fire, laughing. Alem's face transformed when he laughed, and Verve could not look away. Nori, grinning, snatched up her mug and stood, flinging the water within upwards, then stretching out her hands. The water droplets suspended, then orbited her like floating crystals as she danced, beckoning the others to join her.

Verve nearly forgot the words to the song as she stared; she'd never seen a mage *play* with their powers like this. There was no tactical advantage to making water drops hover like glittering dragonflies. It was just…pretty. And as the villagers, laughing, jumped up to dance among the crystals, Verve grinned in bewildered delight.

As Verve, Ivet, and Dannel continued singing, Alem and Kyon parted ways so Kyon could grab Nori's waist and spin her around. Alem bowed to Berel, who giggled and accepted his hand, and then they were off. More villagers joined the dance. The bonfire cast a warm glow over the villagers, but their joy—and Verve's, too—glowed even brighter.

The song ended, but the musicians happily took up the work of revelry. Owen brought Dannel his battered lap-gitar; the instrument added a deeper resonance to Hadiya's viol and Klaret's mandolin. Someone handed Kinny a cluster of bells, which she shook as if her life depended on it.

Verve excused herself to gulp down a swig of cool water that had never tasted so satisfying. She indulged in a quick half of a puffer and a few sips of honeyed-liquor, then got distracted by the sweet rolls. Each bite was sugary paradise on her tongue. She moaned in pleasure before she could stop herself, but thankfully the music drowned out the inadvertent noise.

No sweets in the Fae realm? She searched Space-Between-Stars's memories but again found no taste, nor sound, smell, or touch. But the Fae's longing for these things burned bright and hot. Little wonder the Fae had made such a bargain with meridians. Perhaps this was why it had been downright easy to integrate her human senses with the Fae ones. Well, easy — so far. Verve was waiting for that other shoe to drop. But in the meantime, she had another sweet roll.

As she was debating one more, Alem's presence drew closer. She glanced up to see him approaching. His painted-on whiskers were smudged, but his dark eyes were merry and something like eagerness danced through his spirit — eagerness he shared with *her*.

She swallowed her bite and tried not to look too hopeful. "Hungry?" she asked when he came close. "There's enough food here to feed three Lotises."

"Ivet always has them make too much." He seemed to hesitate. "You... I've never heard you sing. You were wonderful."

"I've been called many things," Verve said, trying not to show her pleasure at his words, "But that's a new one."

His mouth pulled into that crooked smile, and her heart started dancing a jig. He asked, "Do you dance?"

"Depends on the partner." Should she offer, or wait for him to? She chose the latter, in case she was wrong about his intent.

Color crept to his cheeks—he'd also indulged in some ale—and he grinned. "Can't you sense what I'm feeling?"

The door of his heart flung open, briefly but completely. Hope glowed softly within him, a constant, along with the shimmering fire of an attraction he was still getting used to.

Verve smiled, too. "I'm not supposed to peer into other people's minds, remember?"

He rolled his eyes but obliged her. "Vervaine, would you like to dance?"

"With a *ring-tail?*" Oh, she was cruel.

He laughed. "Aye." His open palm lay between them, inviting. "Ring-tails are famously skilled dancers."

"I'll be the judge of that."

She had forgone her gloves tonight, so when she slid her palm into his, she felt every callused hill and valley. Just like before, his slender, strong fingers closed around hers with promise, and an answering shiver of anticipation flowed over her skin.

But like before, when she'd been too chickenshit to join the fun, all the contentment in the air set her on edge, and she hesitated to follow him to the other dancers. Nothing good lasted. If the villagers didn't turn on her, some new horror would surely come to claim its due.

Stop this pointless worrying, she scolded herself. She was free from Danya, "Damaris," and her old life.

Unless Danya didn't believe Verve was dead and sent Usko—or any of the Chosen—to search for proof. The priest was relentless. More than once, Danya had driven a merchant out of Freehold for trying to swindle her. What if she followed-up with Legion's report, and—

Verve's stomach dropped as the anxiety she'd tried to ignore the last few days hummed back to life. Even her "death" would not stop Danya from sending the Chosen here to find Alem. Fuck, she was such a sodding fool for thinking she was free of her old patron, for thinking—for hoping—she had found a little happiness all her own.

"Verve?"

Verve met Alem's gaze again, read the uncertainty there. Alem had seen her at her lowest, and still took her hand. He was still here. And so was she.

She would keep him safe. She would keep everyone in Lotis safe. No matter what.

For now, Verve reveled in the flutter of butterflies in her stomach when she said, "I don't really know how to dance."

His smile was softer. "Truth be told, I'm not great at it either, but we can still try. Tell you what: I'll show you what I know, and we can figure the rest out together. Sound all right?"

She squeezed his hand. "Sounds perfect."

* * *

Alem had no sense of timing and Verve's feet weren't used to following along

167

with anyone else so closely, but after a few stumbling steps, they eased into the simple dance. The others whirled around them, each pair or trio circling the fire as the musicians let loose a lively reel that made Verve's head spin.

Eventually, the music's wild pace slowed, allowing the dancers' hearts a chance to follow. Suddenly Verve and Alem were moving slower, hand in hand, bodies matching one another's rhythm. His grip was strong but not stifling, and his gaze on her held a heat she recognized but could not quite let herself acknowledge. Yet. Nectar sweetened the air around him, nectar and sweat and whatever scent was pure *Alem.* As they danced, Verve had the occasional odd notion she'd done this before, in another place and time, with another partner who looked at her with that same intensity.

A glimpse of a past life, resurfacing? Or a memory from another meridian?

"Everything all right?" Alem asked.

"I think so," she replied. "I just got a weird feeling this has happened before."

He nodded. "Milo used to call stuff like 'new-old memories.' I have to admit, it never made much sense to me. But he said it was pretty bizarre."

Verve relaxed into his arms, her steps coming more natural now. "I could get used to it, I guess."

Alem sighed as they moved in tandem. "Me too."

They danced a while longer before he spoke again. "If you're feeling better, I'd like to ask you something."

Verve's calm splintered, but she resisted the urge to turn away. Instead, she focused on not falling over or stepping on his toes. "Should I be worried?"

"You can be whatever you want," he replied. "I'm just wondering… What are you going to do now that you're free?"

He said this carefully, his face neutral as any of Atal's Chosen. Verve didn't answer right away. "I don't know," she said at last. "Probably stick around here for a while, at least until I'm sure Lotis will be safe."

"Good." He flushed. "I mean, for Lotis."

She eyed him. "Why do you ask?"

He kept the door of his spirit shut tight, but she could read the tension in his hands. "Next time you need to go after other mages," he said slowly.

"Will you try to talk to them before you… try anything else?"

She almost stumbled, but her training kicked in and she kept the rhythm. "Why?"

His brow creased. "What do you mean, *why?*"

"All those renegade mages know is violence," she said. "No one can reason with them. I've got to hit them hard and fast, before they see me coming. Anything else is just asking for death. It's been quiet lately, but I doubt that will continue. Those renegade mages could destroy Lotis with their stupid infighting. How is talking to them going to stop them?"

His tone turned infuriatingly patient for someone with drawn whiskers smeared on his face. "Well, I'm a mage. And I'm capable of talking *and* listening. So are Dannel, and Kyon, and Nori. Even the little ones can manage the feat."

"You're all different," she replied. "You're not warring over territory, or revenge, or some other foolish thing."

His grip on her hands tightened; sweat slicked his palm, but he kept his voice steady. "Aye, but we could be, if the rivers of our lives had taken a different course. Roll your eyes if you want, Verve, but you know it's true. Use your new abilities and look into any of those renegade mage's hearts; I guarantee you'll see what's plain to anyone with eyes: they're desperate and scared, and have been pushed to this point. As anyone could be."

He was right, damn him, but she couldn't back down. "I don't need to look into their hearts. I know your faith is misplaced. Yes, they've been pushed to the breaking point, but they've broken. They *are* broken." Her voice cracked. "Beyond repair."

The song slipped seamlessly into another. Alem made a noise of frustration. "They can't all be that way."

"How could they be anything else?" She almost felt sorry for him. Then he looked at her again and she saw the pity in his gaze — pity directed her way. Her breath caught. "I can't believe I'm being lectured by a man in a ring-tail costume."

"Says the possum," Alem replied. "Verve… You can't keep killing anymore. Not with these new abilities. You know that, right?"

Her renewed worry over Danya increased from a hum in the back of her mind to a roaring tornado. "What else am I supposed to do?" she snapped. "Try to make those mages talk out their troubles? Maybe hug after?"

"Each death you cause kills you, too," Alem said. "It just takes longer." *The One is life.*

Verve shook her head. "Pretty words. Yours?"

"Milo's." Alem met her gaze steadily. "You don't have to kill to survive anymore, Verve. You have a choice, but more importantly, you have a chance to *choose*. I think—"

"I'm well-aware of what you think," Verve broke in. "Since you never shut up about it."

She snatched her hands free of his and turned away, heading for her loft. Each step brought her away from the warm glow of the fire, and each step made more tears burn her eyes. She swiped them away furiously. The fire was too bright; the darkness choking. The emotions of the others were too...*much,* too intense and strange and difficult. This feel-good, finally-found-a-home, meridian-stuff was all a distraction from her real problem. She was such a fool to think she could be free — of Danya, of her past. She needed to plan, to prepare for the worst...

Footsteps sounded behind her. Alem's presence drew closer, pricked with fear but bright with courage. She couldn't turn to look at him, for if she did, no doubt she'd never stop seeing the imprint of his spirit, like looking at the sun.

"I'm sorry, Verve," he called when she did not stop. "I didn't mean to shame you. I know your life has been hard—"

She spun around to glare at him. "This isn't about me," she hissed. "This isn't about the renegade mages. This is about *you*. Danya knows you're here. She will come for you, and by refusing to leave, you're putting everyone else at risk."

"I've been down this road too many times," he replied. "There's nowhere I can go where someone won't want the power I possess. I told you; I'm tired of running."

Verve crossed her arms before her chest. "You stop running, you die."

"That can't be my fate," he whispered. "I won't let it."

She shrugged. "Then you'd better learn how to stand your ground and fight."

His gaze turned distant, and he did not reply. They stood about an arm's length from each other, cloaked in the shadow cast by Hadiya's barn. The mage moon glowed, full and high in the inky sky, and Verve shivered despite the warm air.

"Each death you cause kills you, too. It just takes longer."

Obviously, Verve had never seen this mysterious Milo, but Celidon had. And the meridian before him, Jocasta, had been friends with Milo. So their memories, now living inside Verve's head, pricked little holes in the dam of her conscience. She could hear Milo say those words, but more than that, she could *feel* the weight behind them, the weight of one who had caused his fair share of death.

She shook her head to clear away Celidon and Jocasta, but Celidon's spirit would not be so easily banished. Karel… Through Celidon's memories, Verve saw Celidon's soul-bonded die, *felt* him die, felt his bright spirit fade into pain and fear and there was nothing she—or Celidon, but they were the same now—could do about any of it. The memory resonated in her mind, dragging her down with the heavy weight of another wasted life. But the memory of Karel's death wasn't alone; he was one of so many she'd killed, now all clamoring at the surface of her mind. She tried to ignore those memories, the really painful ones, but there were so many now. Pain outweighed the good — if indeed there had been anything truly *good* in her life after *that* day.

She had to find a new way forward. But what would a new path look like for a killer like her?

And even if she could change, what good was an assassin's mercy, anyway?

Verve's feet refused to move as she and Alem stared at each other.

"You're not the only one who's lost people," Alem said at last.

She balled her hands into fists. "Hardship isn't a competition."

"That's not what I meant." He held up his hands, palms facing her. "Look, I don't know how to ask this without causing offense, so I apologize in advance."

That boded ill. But curiosity got the better of her, so she nodded. "Speak freely."

He lowered his hands and came forward, within arm's reach. His eyes never left hers. "What sets someone on the path you're walking?"

A night wind blew, bringing her the scent of burning wood, of cooking spices, of jessamin flowers. If she reached for him, would he shy away? Or would he continue to close the space between them?

"Dead family," she managed, trying to shrug. "The usual tragic past."

"What else?"

She frowned. "Isn't that enough?"

But the question was foolish. She exhaled and looked away, at the glowing mage moon high above. Atal was nowhere to be seen. Something in her heart cried for freedom, but she clamped down on the feeling with all her might. She could not break, could not let this pain in her heart flow free, because it would drown her.

Within her spirit, Space-Between-Stars murmured, *Let it flow. You do not have to bear this burden alone.*

Verve bit back a sob. Alem took her hand again, squeezing once. His touch broke the dam inside her, sending the rushing river to flood through her whole self. Memories she normally shied away from floated to the surface of her mind, but this time, she tried to face them.

"The mages came with fire, tore our homes apart, burned our lives to the ground. Then..." She frowned again, this time in confusion.

"Then?" Alem asked.

Verve closed her eyes, trying to recall. "Fire. Smoke. Ahmma told me to stay quiet, stay hidden. There was a...cellar?" No, that wasn't right. Her family had no stone houses, no cellars. Only the road and each other. "No cellar, but I remember being trapped in the darkness... There was shouting. I could hear them as they died."

"Your family?"

"Yes." Her breath came shorter now as the pace of her memories quickened. "Boots clattering on wood planks. The clink of armor, and swords, and..."

Her eyes flew open. Her heart froze in her chest.

Alem looked thoughtful. "Who had swords? The mages who killed your family?"

"No…" Verve's eyes stung again. She met Alem's gaze and saw her own shock mirrored there. "No, the soldiers who captured us."

He sucked in a breath. "Captured? Gods above…"

No. No, this was all wrong. *Mages* had killed her family. Danya had told her so many times, had described the scene so clearly, for mages had destroyed the priest's home, too. The shared trauma had bonded them like mother and daughter.

Or so Verve had always believed. A truth she'd tried to ignore bubbled up in her mind, like bile she'd tried to swallow. "The soldiers… they were sentinels from Legion."

Something warm enveloped her hands. She looked up to see Alem, tears shining on his face. Her influence? Surely sorrow poured from her like spilled wine. But he only embraced her hard, wrapped her in strong arms, and gently set her cheek against his solid shoulder.

She pressed her face into him, leaned her weight against him. He didn't buckle, only held her tighter and whispered into her ear, "It's all right, Verve. You're safe."

A kind thing to say, but she wasn't now and would never be. Not while Legion grew in strength and power. She cast her mind back to her last meeting with Danya and her stomach turned. Danya was in league with Legion, and probably had been for some time. Verve had lived in willful ignorance, and now she couldn't erase the realization. But what to do about it?

Find a new path forward.

Where the thought came from didn't matter. Verve was a meridian now. Her life had already veered wildly off course — whatever that meant for someone like her. She could fight and kill, and likely would again, but she couldn't allow Danya—or her own fear—to rule her heart any longer.

So she pulled away, enough to look Alem in the eyes. She'd failed her last mission for Danya.

Thank the One.

"I'll do it," she whispered.

"Oh, good," he said. "But I'd get more satisfaction knowing *what*." He gave her that gorgeous, crooked smile and her heart soared to the moons and stars.

I love you, she thought. But the realization was too huge to fit into her mind along with everything else, so she set it aside to examine later.

For now, Verve skimmed her fingertips along his jawline, savoring the scrape of stubble. His eyes lidded, then he looked at her, a question on his face. She brushed her thumb against his soft lips, steeling herself. "Next time warring mages bring their fighting too close, I'll…" She bit back a groan. "Try to *talk* to them before I kill them."

His smile broadened, dazzling, and her spirit glowed in reply. "Thank you, Verve," he murmured. His lips brushed hers as he spoke. "You won't regret it."

"Don't say that." She inhaled the scent of jessamin blossoms and drew him closer.

The kiss was soft, searching, more a question than an answer; a shared breath. Alem met her eyes again. "What should I say instead?"

"Nothing," she replied, and pressed her lips to his.

Fire raced through each vein, each nerve. His stubble scraped deliciously against her skin as her palms slid along the muscles of his arms. Alem gripped her waist, her back, and deepened the kiss. Verve's body melted into his, flowing over him like rain over parched earth. When they parted to breathe, he cupped her cheek in one hand, using his thumb to smooth away her tears.

"You have no idea," he breathed, "how much I've wanted to do that."

She gently bumped her nose against his, further smearing the paint. His whiskers were only smudges; she probably wore them now, too. "You talk too much."

"My deepest apologies," he said, and pulled her into another kiss.

19

Protector

Magic hovered at the edge of Verve's senses, urging her to crack her eyes open. The sky outside her window was still dark, but the brush of magic strengthened. If she concentrated, she could sense the turbulent hearts of unfamiliar mages, veering too close to Lotis for comfort. Verve bit back a groan and rolled out of her bed. Apparently, the local renegade mages didn't believe in sleeping late after Ea's Day.

She briefly lamented that she and Alem had spent the night in separate beds, but it'd been unavoidable when a giggling Berel had asked Alem to watch over the little ones while she and Klaret shared a night alone.

The memory of Alem's goodnight kiss lingered as a tingle on her lips. Verve allowed herself another moment to dwell, then forced her mind back to pulling on her gear. Once dressed, she left Lotis before dawn, while the others still slept off their revelry.

Along with endless mosquitoes, magic hovered in the air: a sizzling trail of power that Verve followed toward an unexplored section of the pine forests surrounding Lotis. Stronger, though, was the swell of emotions made by the warring mages. Even in the depths of her slumber, Space-Between-Stars's senses had caught the bitter tang of their anger. And now, while Verve prayed Alem was right and she *could* reason with the renegades, she kept a dagger close at hand and her crossbow loaded at her back.

In this part of Greenhill Province, fallen pine needles kept each step silent. Palmettos—huge, fan-shaped fronds—all but covered the ground in some places in a blanket of vivid green spikes that still hid Verve's dark clothing. When the sun broke through the horizon and shone through the pines, Verve closed in on the mages.

The anger she'd sensed earlier congealed in the air here, thicker than the heat of a summer afternoon. Anger, and no small amount of fear, which Verve felt as hot needles pricking up and down her back. A roar echoed through the pines, startling a family of whippoorwills from their roost. As the birds flew away, Verve slowed her pace and crouched, peering through the palmettos for the source of the noise — and the overwhelming waves of fury.

There. Ahead in a clearing, four mages squared off. There was the ummaroc, the sickle-clawed drake that Verve had faced on her first night in Lotis. The creature bore a scar on her neck from Verve's wire bracelet, which she'd brought along again — just in case.

Another creature, another mage, moved with the ummaroc: a saber-toothed lion, with a magnificent mane and two long, deadly tusks protruding past its fangs. The saber-tooth roared in challenge, fury spiking with the echoing sound, and the hairs on Verve's arms stood at attention. Her heart quickened, but she held her place and fought to shake away the emotions bleeding from the mages.

The other two must have been particle mages, for they looked innocuous enough. A woman with dark skin and hair, not too dissimilar from Verve's, glared between the shape-changers. "Keep your distance, if you know what's good for you," she called. "This is our territory; our home. You're nothing but filthy dregs from the tundra."

"Go back to where you came from," the other particle mage added. This one was tall and broad, the kind of person who could fill a doorway — or bash through the wall to make a new one.

Magic poured off of each particle mage, strong enough to sting Verve's eyes, but what their talents were, she could not tell.

Her hands itched to grab her crossbow. They were all so intent on one another, she could take out two before they realized what was going on. Depending on which two, she'd have a *very* interesting few minutes after that. The fight wouldn't be easy, but they rarely were, and besides, she could win.

But she'd made a promise.

"Try *talking* to them, Verve," she muttered in a nasally mockery of Alem's voice. Well, she *was* curious if this new tactic would work. Too bad curiosity wasn't one of her more survival-minded attributes. Verve eased forward, still trying to get a sense of her opponents before losing her favored element of surprise.

The ummaroc flowed into the shape of a woman with short, messy black hair and fierce green eyes. The scar at her neck stood out against her brown skin, more so than against her scales. "They can't go back, fool," she growled at the particle mages, who'd started at her sudden transformation. "Legion's taken over."

"And whose fault is that?" the huge mage replied, and lifted their hands.

A blast of air flew toward the ummaroc-mage, who ducked and rolled out of the way just in time to avoid being knocked over. Trees and palmettos blew backward with the blast, and an answering wave of power grew even headier in the air, pulling Verve forward like a marionette.

The other particle mage laughed, then raised her hands, where the air rippled with heat. No fire bloomed from her fingertips, but the heat swelled all around her, making sweat bead at Verve's upper lip. Heat flared from her belt-buckle and the daggers tucked among her gear, forcing her to spend a few precious moments adjusting her clothing to avoid being burned.

The ummaroc—still in her human form—cried out and darted away, shifting back into her animal form. The other, the saber-tooth, roared again and lunged at Door-Smasher, who shot another blast of air toward the huge lion. The heat mage—Verve dubbed her Fever—and the ummaroc now faced off, and the air between them sizzled.

It was time.

You can do this. The thought sounded like Alem. Verve summoned her courage and stepped out of the palmettos, hands raised, body poised to duck back into cover in case she needed a quick exit. But with each step, she fought for calm. Perhaps this confrontation could go smoothly.

Aye, and perhaps she'd turn into a bird and fly across the sea.

"Good morning," she called to the mages. She'd braced for at least one of them to attack her without so much as a blink, but they all froze and turned to stare at the stranger emerging from the forest. Surprise shot through them, along with renewed fear, for few but the most powerful mages—or warriors—would dare break up a magical fight.

"Who the fuck are you?" Fever hissed. The heat thickened, pricking Verve's eyes, while every bit of metal on her stung like a hornet's bite.

"I'm from a nearby village," Verve said. She tried to make her voice gentle. "I've come to respectfully ask you to take your business elsewhere."

There. Neatly said. She and Alem had gone over the words a few times last night. It'd been his idea to wish them a good morning, though the notion was laughable now, given that half of her targets were beasts.

The particle mages exchanged incredulous looks, until Fever threw back her head and laughed. Thankfully, the heated air began to cool.

Door-Smasher flashed a toothy grin. "And why should we?"

"This area's unclaimed," Fever added.

The saber-tooth snarled.

Fever scoffed. "If that's supposed to be a response, shift so you can speak in your own defense, you moth-eaten, malformed cat."

But it was the other, the ummaroc, who changed back into her human form. A powerful shiftling, indeed, to change shape so frequently. Most couldn't manage the feat more than once or twice a day. Verve searched her memory and recalled the ummaroc's name was Ellory Echina, who, among her other talents, was adept at giving Verve the most murderous looks.

"This doesn't concern you, hunter," Ellory said to Verve in a low, dangerous voice. "Leave now, and we'll let you live."

Verve could not help herself. "How's the neck?"

Ellory's fingers flew to the angry pink scar that wound almost all the way around her throat. "So you came back to finish the job, then?"

The saber-tooth's ears flicked and Ellory, who must have known the other shifter well enough to understand them, said, "Aye, she's one of Atal's Chosen, a mage killer, and no friend of ours. Or yours," she added, looking pointedly at the particle mages.

Fever and Door-Smasher exchanged looks, and then they both turned completely to face Verve, whose stomach dropped in warning. "You killed my sister," Fever whispered, her eyes narrowing.

"Aye, and my brother," Door-Smasher said through a clenched jaw.

A new flavor of ire pricked Verve's senses: peppery anger — at her. At the mage killer.

Probably should have seen this coming. The thought sounded a little too snarky — even for Verve. Actually, it sounded like Celidon, whose memories, along with Jocasta's and Space-Between-Stars's—could be lost forever if this encounter went sideways. Verve had agreed to help Celidon in his final moments, so she'd been able to take on the Fae spirit, but there was no telling if these mages would make that same choice.

You're in charge, but it's not just you behind those eyes any longer, Verve.

Her pulse quickened. She held up her hands and struggled to find her footing among the maelstrom of the mages' emotions. "I'm Lotis's protector," she said. "Your kinsfolk were hurting the village. I had to—"

The saber-tooth roared again, the sound reverberating through Verve's skull, and the huge cat paced toward her, trying to box her in with the particle mages. The beast didn't have to speak; her fury toward Verve writhed like maggots. Heat swelled in the air, slinking down Verve's throat and into her lungs, until she burned from within.

She scrambled backward, groping for her crossbow, but a blast of air threw her on her back and knocked the breath out of her. Coughing, Verve still tried to get away, but the heat thickened. Her silver belt buckle, her daggers, her sodding brass buttons — everything metal on her person began to burn, as if just pulled from a blacksmith's forge. She shrieked and fumbled for the belt, for she'd die before she cast away her daggers, but then the saber-tooth was before her, screaming its fury. Ellory had shifted again, clawed hands flexing, dagger-like teeth glinting in the rising sun.

Being surrounded by murderous mages was bad, but not impossible to handle. Verve had been in worse situations before, after all.

But their relentless barrage of fury pummeled her spirit and sapped her strength quicker than a full sprint over desert dunes. Her head spun, her heart threatened to beat its way out of her chest, and she could not think how to get away.

Until she remembered Alem, and the wall around his heart he'd built, the wall that kept out her meridian senses, the wall he'd lowered a few times to allow her to peer within.

Heat swelled; her skin burned. Another blast of air lashed her cheek, but she tried to move with the blast rather than fight it. Within her mind, she built a high wall that looked like the side of a Sufani wagon, and then hid her heart behind it. This, she could do. This, Danya had unwittingly trained her for, and while only seconds passed, the mages' fury receded and Verve's head cleared. She ducked out of the way of the saber-tooth's strike, and dove into the palmettos.

Mission failed. *I'm sorry, Alem.*

The ummaroc screamed a warning to the others as Verve sprang up, crossbow in hand. The hematite smelted with the steel kept the metal from magical heating. Verve aimed at Door-Smasher's stunned face and pulled the trigger. The bolt landed with a *thunk* right between their eyes, and Verve had another bolt loaded by the time the ground shuddered beneath the mage's impact.

She aimed at Fever, who threw up her hands. "Please," the mage cried. "I'll leave, I prom—"

The second and third bolts struck her with enough force to send her stumbling back, where she landed and did not move again.

Two mages down. The air cooled, the fury retreated into desperation as Ellory and the saber-tooth lion circled Verve, fearful but still determined.

Well, they weren't the only ones. Verve's fear beat like a drum in her mind, demanding action. But long years of training helped her think through her terror, and somewhere in the back of her mind, Space-Between-Stars's approval echoed like a struck gong.

Use the fear, Space-Between-Stars urged. *Gather it close, then release. I'll help.*

Was that… possible? If so, Verve had enough fear to take down an army. *Oh,* now *you want me to live?* she couldn't help but snark.

Humor flickered in Space-Between-Stars's presence. *Good point. Perhaps I should let you fall, and take over one of these lovely mages.*

Nice try, Verve shot back, letting her amusement color her words. *But I'm not done for yet.*

Breath short, Verve focused on the knots of fear in her belly. In her mind's eye, the emotion was a gray smoke, a haze that clouded her vision. But smoke could be cleared. With Space-Between-Stars's support, Verve concentrated, then projected her fear toward the saber-tooth, like an emotional crossbow bolt. The creature cried out, a high-pitched keen, and turned to run. Verve gave her three paces, then pulled the trigger on her crossbow, and the shiftling collapsed into a sour-faced woman.

Three mages down. Verve turned to the ummaroc, who foolishly had not fled. Just the two of them now. Ellory's fear spiked, white hot, but the creature didn't move. Verve loaded another bolt and aimed for the scar at her neck.

The ummaroc's eyes were bright green, wide, and her heart hung on its hinges, leaving her spirit open for inspection. Within, that same fear roared, thundering.

Fear and loneliness, and a desperation born of the two. Verve looked into Ellory's soul and saw her own reflected. For one moment, she seemed to float over her body; she saw the two of them facing off amidst trampled leaves, blood, scorched earth. They were two sides of the same coin. No, they were the same side of different coins, and Verve's determination to end this mage's life crumbled. Her crossbow felt leaden, like her bones, and it took all of her strength not to collapse.

"Leave, now," Verve heard herself say. "I have no quarrel with you personally, but you can't stay here."

Ellory's desperation stank like sour milk, but the shiftling turned and darted off through the palmettos, her steps silent.

And Verve stood alone again, surrounded by deaths of her own doing, and an answering regret echoed in her own heart. The crossbow slipped from her hands as she sank to her knees, and it was hours before she summoned the strength to return to Lotis.

20

Springs Eternal

Whe Verve dragged herself to Lotis later that afternoon, she sneaked not only back into the village, but up to her room in Hadiya's loft, where she'd tucked away a nice hoard of liquor and her dwindling supply of puffers. Thanks to Hadiya's ongoing improvements to the barn, Verve's makeshift "home" was no longer exposed to the elements. Four walls and a roof made sleeping more comfortable, but such structural integrity also made it more time-consuming for Verve to slip in, drop off her crossbow, and slip back out with bottles tucked in her coat pockets. She clinked a little, but not much, and a little unnecessary noise was a small price to pay for a way to numb the roil of emotions.

But why she went from "her" loft to Alem's cottage was the real question, one she didn't care to answer just yet. He wasn't home; she could sense him in the Willow, engaged in some industrious, no doubt dutiful, task. All she really knew was that Alem's cottage smelled of lavender, jessamin, and rosewood, and even though he wasn't there now, if *she* was, she wouldn't feel quite as alone.

Gritting her teeth against the pain in her chest, she slunk passed the still somewhat-battered lavender bush, wrestled open the backdoor, and stepped inside his home. She didn't bother climbing up to his loft bed, only sunk beside his hearth, where embers glowed softly. Verve exhaled and leaned her head against the hearth wall. Everything hurt from her toes to her ears.

183

Even her hair ached. The foolish fancy made her laugh, then cry out because laughing was a terrible idea when one had almost been incinerated from within.

But that didn't matter. Within minutes she'd burned through a puffer and made good progress on a bottle of Redfernian brandy, and her mind was once again a pleasant, dull haze. Thank the One, the puffer smoke didn't bother her throat. Nor did the liquor; the folks from Redfern Province certainly knew how to craft a smooth brandy. Attention summarily shifted from her horrific failure that morning, Verve would fight a battle she knew she'd win: her hair.

* * *

Some time later, the cottage door creaked open and Alem called, "Hello?"

Verve frowned over the tangle of hair in her grip. "It's just me."

"What are you…" He trailed off as he came in and found her seated on the floor, half her braids undone, two empty bottles at her side. "What in Ea's name are you doing?"

She tugged at her shredded braid, where she'd been trying to wrestle her comb free. "They're filthy. I've been meaning to clean them, but it's just so much work. Sometimes I want to just cut it all off, but…"

But she could still feel her mother's gentle strokes at her hair. They'd had similar hair, so tightly curled that it looked like a cloud when allowed total freedom. Tears sprang to her eyes. "I can't fix it."

Alem knelt by her side. "May I see?"

"Sure, but there's nothing you—or anyone—can do. I'm a lost cause."

He skimmed his fingertips over the half-done braids, then he glanced at her. "There's a lot, isn't there?"

"So much," she said. "And it's stubborn." She smiled at the waves of silky black falling over his shoulders. "Not like yours."

He chuckled and smoothed a hand through his hair. "My hair has its moments. I've got to wash it about every day, else it's a greasy mess." He glanced at her. "How long have you been back?"

"A while."

"You're hurt." It wasn't a question.

"Mostly my pride." Well, maybe more than that, as her chest ached, and she couldn't fight back a wince.

"Seems more than that," he replied.

But he didn't ask, and she almost let the moment pass by, but some defiant part of her brain asserted itself. With effort, she shrugged out of her hematite coat and hood, leaving her in a simple tunic and her leather pants. By the One, she must have looked like… well, like wild animals had mauled her. So about normal, then.

"Is there anything you can do?" she ventured, not looking at him.

His reply was warm. "Aye. Hold still, and I'll take a look." He reached for her, but stayed his hand at the last moment. "Actually, 'take a look' is misleading. I'll need to touch your skin."

"I know." She lifted her chin, exposing her neck, and tried to quell her instinctive panic at the notion. They'd kissed before, so how was this any different? But it was. "Do what you need to," she added.

His fingertips brushed her neck lightly to move her tangled hair aside, and closed his eyes, and she prayed he couldn't feel her leaping pulse.

After a few moments, he exhaled sharply and looked at her. "No lasting damage, but I reckon what's there is painful. What'd they do?"

"One of them made the air…hot," Verve replied. "Not with fire, exactly, but enough to burn with each breath. And all the metal on my kit got too hot to touch." She gestured to her belt buckle.

Alem's brows knitted. "Any pure iron in your kit? Apparently it hurts meridians."

Celidon's memory of iron cuffs clamped around his wrists made Verve want to sink into the wall and disappear. "No pure iron," she managed. "Just steel and some brass."

"Well," Alem said. "As far as I can tell, those mages did no permanent damage. Hold still."

His palm rested on her chest, just below her collarbone, and he closed his eyes again. Verve held as still as she could, trying not to breathe, and watched him. His full lips pursed when he concentrated, but his hand was steady. Magic thickened in the air around him, beckoning, but not dangerously, like the other mages' had done. No, Alem's magic was a balm, a soothing grace, like nothing else in her adult life had ever been.

At last, the pain in her chest receded; the aches all over followed, fading to nothing. Alem drew his hand back and looked at her. "Better?"

Verve nodded, tugging at the comb in her braid again, but the sodding thing was well and truly stuck. "I tried just to talk to those mages, Alem, I really did. But my reputation got ahead of me. The mages… They might have listened, but that ummaroc shiftling was with them, and she knew what I was. The others figured it out soon after…" More tears sprang to her eyes and she couldn't finish.

He was silent. What was there to say? She was a fool to think she could be anything other than what she was now. She braced for the inevitable.

"Have you seen the springs?" he asked instead.

She frowned. "It's spring outside, yes." Was *he* drunk?

He chuckled. "I meant Pilgrim Springs. Ivet says they're healing springs, but that's not quite true. Don't get me wrong, they make for a nice, refreshing swim when it's hot, but they won't heal you… Just clean you up a bit." Gently, he took her hand. "It's an easy journey. I could use a dip. How about you?"

He'd not opened his heart to her now, but he didn't have to, for she read the kindness in his expression as if he'd painted on the feeling, like raccoon whiskers: ridiculous, but sweet.

I love you. The words formed on her tongue, but she held them back. She was drunk and high and in no state to do anything so foolish as to admit the truth.

But she did smile at him. "I could use a wash. I stink."

"Oh, yes," he agreed, grinning. She stuck her tongue out at him and a deep flush crept to his cheeks. Quickly, he got to his feet and offered her his hand. She took it and he helped her up, pulling her easily.

"It's not far," he said, still holding her hand. "Let's go."

* * *

Teeth chattering, Verve summoned her courage and dunked her head again, allowing the fresh water to saturate her loose hair now that she'd gotten the comb free. She burst up out of the springs, shrieking. "What kind of cursed god makes such pretty water so sodding cold?"

"You'll get used to it after a few minutes," Alem said, laughter in his voice.

"Assuming I can survive that long." Still shivering, Verve smoothed back her soaking hair and glanced around them at Pilgrim Springs. She'd never seen water so brilliant blue; towards the center, where the spring water emerged from underground, the blue deepened to a rich indigo. But on the rocky limestone outcropping she stood upon, the water was the same color as the sky on a summer's day.

Limestone formations circled the springs, water reflecting off of the pockmarked stone in rippling bands of light. The trees were thick here, too, and some grew out of the limestone itself, clinging to the pale stone as they reached for the sky.

Alem meandered along the sandy shore. He'd shed his tunic and shoes, and his soaking trousers clung to his muscular legs. Verve had already caught him looking at her, too, but didn't mind in the least. She'd kept on her small-clothes, but had left her tunic, pants, and boots on the shore.

The strange combination of Alem's healing magic and the shock of cold water had kicked her back into a state of somewhat-sobriety. She shook out her hair again. The slap of loose, wet hair on her back was oddly unfamiliar, but not unwelcome. She scraped her fingers over her scalp, savoring the feeling—usually her braids got in the way—and sighed.

"Better?" Alem asked.

The water didn't feel as horrifically cold now, at least, but Verve eyed her comb and hair tincture with reluctance. "Better," she replied. "Almost too much. I don't really want to leave."

"Then don't." The sunlight glinted off of the water on his trim, muscular torso as he stepped further into the springs, then ducked beneath the rippling surface.

She sank to a squat, balancing on the limestone, submerging herself to her chin. Cool water surrounded her like a refreshing embrace. Damn him;

he'd been right about this, too. When he emerged, she said, "I'm sorry about today. I tried."

"I know." He shook his hair, sending water droplets flying. "Will you try again?"

She studied her hands beneath the water's surface, noting the distorted ripples. "Why bother?" She closed her hands into fists. "Why should mages trust me?"

Why should anyone?

He didn't answer right away. "It's worth another shot. You can't just try a new thing once and give up if it goes poorly."

"I assure you, I'm more than capable of that."

He wrung out his hair and didn't look at her. "So, your plan is just to keep killing others until you kill yourself with drink?"

Heat flushed through her face, despite the chilly water. "Maybe. What's your point? Why do you care so much about… about other mages?"

"I'm a healer. My job is to preserve life." He cocked an eyebrow at her. "You're Sufani. Ivet and Dannel have talked about the Sufani's reverence for all life."

"Reverence is nice and all, but it doesn't keep you safe."

"But endless killing will?"

She rose, water rolling off her in rivulets. "You don't understand."

"No," he said. "But I'm trying to. And I think…" His cheeks colored. "You've had a hard life and made some mistakes, but they don't have to define you forever. You can change. You have, already. You're better than whoever your employer wanted you to be. I've seen the evidence for myself. You're a good person, Verve."

As he spoke, he allowed his earnestness to seep through the cracks in his wall, like a comforting hand on her back. But as much as she wanted to believe him, she could not shake the memory of the mages she'd killed.

And the mention of her "employer" sent another thrill of warning through her, one that darkened her mind like storm clouds. Danya was nothing if not thorough. Eventually, Verve's former patron would send someone to verify what the Legion sentinels must have surely reported.

I should leave, she thought, then dismissed the notion. Even if Danya abandoned all hope of finding Verve, she believed a dendric mage lived in Lotis. And Alem had said he'd never leave, which meant if Verve truly wanted to protect the village, she ought to stick around.

Yes, of course. She'd stay to protect Lotis from Danya and her Chosen — no other reason. Verve rolled her eyes at *that* willful ignorance.

Carefully, she picked her way back to the sandy shore, where Alem had returned. He tensed at her approach, but held his ground and her gaze. "I know I sound preachy," he said. "But I just… I want more for you. Call me a fool, but I do."

"Fool," she said, and skimmed a hand up his arm, over his solid chest. He sucked in a breath, his eyes going darker as he stared into hers. Desire bloomed around him, thick as jessamin blossoms.

"Very well," she murmured. "I'll try to talk again. But Alem?"

"Verve?" he whispered.

She bit her lip, considering. "I know you love it here, but Danya—my patron—she knows a dendric mage lives in Lotis. You could leave — just for a while," she added when he opened his mouth to object, "just until the danger passes. You'd be such a prize for Danya. Please, Alem." She curled her fingers against his chest. "Please, leave Lotis, just for a while. It's not a coward's act to leave when danger threatens. You've lived in Pillau; you've been through those intense summer storms, right? How does the saying go? 'Hide from the wind, but run from the water.' Danya and Atal's Chosen are a flood, and they *will* destroy you if you stay."

His brows knitted, but he placed his hand over hers, pressing it to his chest, where his heart raced. "This isn't about cowardice, or bravery. This is about my home and my family. I'm not going anywhere, Verve."

Despite the tight ball of fear coiling in her belly, her heart soared again at his touch. "You're either brave or stupid," she said, "but either way, Lotis is lucky to have you. And I swear I'll keep you—all of you—safe."

<h1 style="text-align:center">21</h1>

All We Can Ever Do

The next day, Verve and the mage Nori crouched at another nearby spring, at the top of a bluff overlooking a bowl-shaped indent in the ground. Water rippled at the base; one of Aredia's underground river connected this small spring to Pilgrim Springs.

Verve was just grateful she didn't have to crawl underground for this mission. She tucked an errant strand of hair back beneath her scarf; she'd forgone the braids for now and just protect the defiant, delicate coils. "Do you recognize them?"

Nori squinted at the mages camped on the other side of the bluff. In this early evening, the other mages had lit a small fire—probably mage-made—and spoke in quiet but jovial tones that did not mask the undercurrent of anger that swirled around them.

"No," Nori murmured, and Verve's heart sank. "But they're particle mages like me. That fellow's cooking — but not with the fire."

"I can smell it." Verve fought the urge to whip out her crossbow and end this dilemma right now. It helped that Space-Between-Stars recoiled at the thought of more outright killing. "Do you think they'll listen to you if you ask them to move on?"

It was a long shot, to be sure, but Verve didn't know what else to do.

Nori had dark skin like Verve, but wore her hair close cropped and bleached golden. Now she skimmed her fingers over her scalp, brows

190

knitted. "Like I said, I'll *try*. But I can't promise anything." She shot Verve a rueful smile. "Cover me?"

"Of course." Verve hesitated. "Like we discussed, if you find yourself in trouble, give the call and hit the ground. I'll do the rest."

Nori nodded, fingers twining together. Even without a meridian's insight into her emotions, her anxiety was plain. Verve met her eyes, drawing her gaze. "Look, I'm grateful for the assist, but you don't have to do this."

"I know, but I want to." Nori smiled again, but the expression did not reach her eyes. "Kyon and I came to Lotis looking for asylum with Marea Damaris, but we never expected to find such kindness as your village has shown."

Your village. Verve's throat tightened, but she kept her face impassive as Nori continued. "I don't think Damaris is coming, but I still want to repay the kindness Ivet and the others have shown. Especially when my own people have caused so much trouble."

Verve studied her. "Few mages would admit to that."

"Maybe not to *you*," Nori replied, her brows knitting. "But most of us just want to live in peace." She glanced back at their targets and her agitation spiked, searing Verve's awareness like a bite of hot pepper. Nori gnawed on her lower lip. "I just need another moment…"

The other mages' attention shifted. They hadn't spotted Verve and Nori, but time was running out to take the advantage of surprise. And Nori looked no closer to moving forward with their plan.

Abandon this idea, Verve's training urged, but she shook the notion away. These mages were planning something, and their camp was much too close to Lotis for comfort. By the One, sometimes Owen brought the little ones out here. Were the people of Lotis supposed to hide in their homes until all the mages had murdered each other?

But rushing in and killing the renegades would be no better, and Verve had little desire to drink herself into a stupor to numb her emotions — again. So here they were.

She risked a soft touch at Nori's shoulder. "I'll cover you the whole time. And you have magic enough to defend yourself until I can arrive." She tried to smile comfortingly, but thought the expression was more of a grimace. "And like I said, just call, and I'll come. All right?"

As a last resort, she tried to inject some of her own courage into the other woman, but it was a fine line to walk without actually using her meridian abilities to manipulate Nori's mind. Verve still wasn't certain she had the mechanics right, so rather than risk removing Nori's independence, she simply tried to let her own calm confidence show. Perhaps that would be enough.

Nori took a deep breath, then flashed her a smile. "Thanks." She faced forward. "I'm ready."

Hours later, Verve and a limping Nori returned home. Nori clung to Verve, while Verve tried not to let her own ire seep through. Alem and Kyon in his antelope form met them on the road, but the moment the shape-changer realized Nori was injured, he ran to her, snuffling at her sides and whickering softly. Alem followed, face expressionless.

"I'm all right." Nori released Verve and wrapped her arms around Kyon's neck, hugging him close.

Alem glanced at Verve, who closed her fist around one of the daggers at her side. "Nori did her best," Verve said through a clenched jaw. "But it was another failure."

"I really thought they'd listen to another mage," Nori said, swiping her eyes. "But I was a fool, I suppose. Thank Seren for Verve and her crossbow."

Verve glanced up at the waning mage moon. Her crossbow case dragged at her shoulder, slowing her steps, and she couldn't look at Alem. "They barely let her speak," she said, nodding to Nori. "They thought she was a spy, or an assassin sent from one of the other clans. I suppose they weren't wrong, exactly." Her voice dropped to a whisper. "This was foolish."

Alem looked at Nori. "Can you make it back to my cottage? I want to look at that wound."

Kyon nuzzled Nori's cheek and she smiled. "Aye. Thanks." She leaned heavily against the antelope's side as they continued on toward Lotis, where someone had already lit the torches leading down the main pathway. Alem followed.

But Verve didn't move. The day's events clutched her heart in a stone vise and her head was full of blood and fighting. Her crossbow case slid to the ground with a thunk and she swayed in place, trying to summon the strength not to fall over.

And then Alem was at her side again, holding her upright. His lips brushed her forehead with a feather touch, and an answering shiver passed over her. "I can't do this," she whispered, leaning into him. "I'm not made for anything but death."

"Do you truly believe that?"

She blinked fast to fight back her tears. "I've failed, Alem. I can't..."

"You would give up so easily?"

Now she drew back, her blood pounding. *Easily?* Nori's going to have a new scar because of me. All because I couldn't..." How even to explain? "I couldn't shut out the other mages' anger — at me, at each other, at the world. It was too much, too heavy. It broke me, just like last time. Alem... I can't do this. I can't be a meridian."

Tears spilled down the side of her nose as she spoke; she furiously swiped them away.

Alem inhaled deeply. "Then perhaps you should contact Sohvi and the other meridians. Maybe they can help."

Verve shook her head. "Sohvi would just have me leave Lotis to join her and the others in Pillau."

You don't know that. The gentle thought wasn't her own, nor was it Space-Between-Stars. It was Celidon. Even in death—a death she'd caused—he showed her a mercy she did not deserve.

Her chest felt tight and hot. Despair threatened to pull her down into the void, then Alem took her hand and squeezed.

"It's okay," he murmured. "Verve, you'll figure it out. Just know you're not alone."

The tightness eased. He was right — in more ways than one. She was a meridian; a host of memories. So she peered into those shared memories and found a similar dark moment, which the meridian Jocasta had overcome.

I'm not alone. Now *that* was a strange thought, but a true one. Verve sifted through Jocasta's memories again, though she was not bold enough to search Celidon's. In Jocasta's, she found despair, but there was also hope.

And love.

Blinking, she looked at Alem, whose eyes were wide. A strange light illuminated the planes of his face, casting him in a faint purple glow.

"Oh," he breathed. "Your eyes… They're like stars."

Startled, she lost the trail of memories and the glow on Alem's face dimmed. "That's normal for meridians?" she asked.

"I think so." He hesitated. "Will you please try to just talk to the renegade mages one more time? It hasn't worked yet, but there must be a way to resolve this whole mess peacefully. I must believe that. I must—"

She silenced him with a finger on his lips. He went still, his face illuminated by the light in her eyes: proof that she wasn't the same person she'd been before coming here. Within her spirit, Celidon, Jocasta, and Space-Between-Stars echoed Alem's soft plea.

"There is always another road," Verve whispered. "That's what the Sufani teach their children. But it's up to us to find it." She sighed. "Fine. I'll try one last time."

"Oh." Alem blinked, then rubbed the back of his neck. "I thought you'd argue more. I had all these counter-arguments ready…"

Verve lifted a brow. "Save 'em. I'm sure we'll quarrel again soon. Then you'll be even more prepared for me."

A deep flush spread across his cheeks. "Nothing in this world could have prepared me for you, Verve."

Her turn to blush. She didn't mind one bit.

* * *

A few days later, Verve shielded her eyes from the midday sun as she surveyed the Tipsy Willow's outer walls. A layer of stones now covered the front in a supplemental wall. While the builder had cobbled the stones together like a slapdash puzzle, the overall effect would help further fireproof the building.

194

"Not bad," Verve said. "Where'd you find the stones?"

Ivet grinned. "Klaret found an abandoned building, half submerged in the swamp. Hadiya brought out her old wheelbarrow, and Kyon helped them dragged it here. And look," she gestured to a bulky pile of something hidden beneath a linen sheet.

Verve pulled the cloth back and found a stack of lumpy clay.

"For the sides," Ivet said in response to Verve's unasked question.

"Good work," Verve replied. "Will you…" She trailed off as a familiar presence entered her mind: Ellory. The shiftling was close and coming closer, and desperation hammered in her heart.

Verve's throat closed, but she forced herself to keep calm. "It's time to test the fortifications," she said to Ivet. "Ring the gong and get everyone inside."

"Mages?" Ivet asked.

"Just one," Verve said. "But she's a nasty piece of work."

Ivet clutched her shoulder. "Be safe, vidahem."

"You, too." Verve gripped Ivet's arm in reply. "I'll do my best."

Ivet's eyes widened, but she nodded and hurried for the alarm set up outside the tavern. The gong rang out, echoing through the village, and as Verve rushed to her room, she noted the faces hurrying past her. All accounted for, thank the One. And only a few carried non-essential items. She darted up to the loft, gathered her weapons, and raced to the outskirts of Lotis, following the swell of Ellory's emotions.

She found the ummaroc lying in one of the marsh pools, perhaps half a mile from Lotis. Upon seeing Verve—or more likely, smelling her—the sickle-drake snarled in warning, but the sound was weak — more of a gurgle. The scent of blood filled the air, but not as strong as Ellory's fury.

Verve drew up within crossbow range. A huge gash sliced down the side of the ummaroc's leg, the wound dark and ugly. Another shiftling had probably done this, or maybe even Legion. Heart racing, Verve tried to find a trace of Legion soldiers nearby, but there was nothing. Ellory's green eyes never left Verve, and her lip curled with her growl.

Verve's grip tightened on her loaded crossbow. It would be an easy kill. Too easy. Like many of her kills had been.

Ellory snarled again, but the sound faded into a whine as the ummaroc tried and failed to scramble for more solid ground. Her claws clutched uselessly at the dirt and grass, sending up sprays of each with her efforts.

Crossbow in hand, silently cursing her stupid, soft heart, Verve approached the shiftling. Closer now, she could see the whites of Ellory's eyes and the network of scars that traversed her body. The door of Ellory's mind was flung open with terror and fury, so it was a simple matter to peer within.

There, Verve found a history so close to her own, she may as well have been examining her own mind. Ellory's life had been a constant struggle, a horrible parade of loss and death that had left more than physical scars. Desperation, loneliness, fear… They were all Ellory had left of anyone she loved.

What sort of person would Ellory be if her story had been like Alem's? Instead of being orphaned and left to fend for herself, what if she'd been taken in by those who showed her love and compassion?

What if that had happened to me?

Verve could not kill Ellory. At least, not like this. She lowered her crossbow. "Change into your human form so we can talk, and I'll make you a deal."

The ummaroc gave another snarl that merged with a whine and continued to claw at the bank.

Verve exhaled. "You don't have a lot of options, Ellory." She made a show of looking around, while still checking for traces of Legion or anyone else set on murdering the shiftling. There: several leagues from here she found a tumult of anger mixed with a growing sense of satisfaction, like the sweetest wine on her tongue. Not Legion soldiers, Verve thought, but other mages. And they were heading this way.

She debated. If these other mages came looking for Ellory, they'd be too close to Lotis. If Verve let Ellory die—or killed her—the other mages would hopefully abandon their search and move on.

But then Verve would be back where she started.

Muttering a curse under her breath, Verve shouldered her crossbow and stepped closer to the struggling ummaroc, who grunted and clawed harder at the bank with each of Verve's steps. Fear soiled the air around Ellory: fear and desperation, like unwashed bedclothes. And within Verve's heart, that same fear echoed.

If she tried to change, she might fail again. But she still had to try.

"It's all right," she said in her most soothing voice. "I mean you no harm. We'll get you patched up, and—"

A piercing scream cut off her words as Ellory, still in her sickle-drake form, grabbed hold of a steady bit of land and pulled herself upright. She wobbled a bit, but her aggressive pose was clear, and Verve stared at the rows of dagger-like teeth and the blood shining on the drake's snout.

The sodding shiftling could slice her open with a kick. And here she was, staring down the monster, basically unarmed, considering how fast these creatures could move. Even Verve's garrote bracelet would be no help here.

Ellory's fear still stank up the air, but Verve knew enough of wild animals to understand that a terrified, cornered beast was at its most dangerous.

Which was all very sensible, but she couldn't help her sudden surge of anger. "You stupid, overgrown chicken, I'm trying to *help* you," she growled. "I swear to the One god, you sodding mages are more trouble than you're worth. I should just leave you to the others — who're not far off, by the way, and will eventually find their way to you."

The ummaroc snarled again, but Verve was *done*. "Forget I said anything," Verve said, shaking her head. "I hope your next life goes better."

The ummaroc stilled. Verve turned away—which in hindsight wasn't the smartest move—but right now she didn't give two shits. As she sloshed away, a human groan sounded from Ellory's position. Verve turned to find the mage, back in her human form, crouched on the marsh bank, clutching her wounded leg.

Blood gleamed in her short black hair and her eyes were wide and wet as she croaked, "Please…"

Verve ground her jaw. "Please, *what?*"

Maybe don't *antagonize the bitey mage,* her better sense whispered, but it was too late.

Ellory's eyes narrowed, then closed, and her face pinched with pain. "Please help me."

"I will," Verve replied as she returned to the mage's side. "But only if you swear to me—on whatever god you pray to—that after, you'll leave Lotis forever. The ones sniffing after you *cannot* track you here, do you understand? Leave Lotis and its people alone, and never return. Swear this, and I'll see that you're healed."

She stared at Ellory and used every ounce of her abilities to assess Ellory's emotional state as the mage considered the offer. Perhaps Verve should have had more qualms about peeking into the mage's mind, but she was well past caring about such courtesy with *this* particular magic-user.

So she couldn't help her surprise when Ellory answered immediately, her voice gravel-rough. "I swear on my ancestors: if you help me now, I'll leave Lotis alone. Forever."

They regarded each other as Verve searched Ellory's heart for deceit. She found only earnestness — and fear. Always fear.

It softened her already too-soft heart. "Good." She removed one of her hematite pendants and placed the cord over Ellory's head. The mage recoiled at the presence of the magic-dispelling stone, but did not protest. After a few awkward, fumbling moments, Verve got Ellory's arm around her shoulder, and they began the slow, painful trek back toward Lotis.

Alem was going to be thrilled.

* * *

Despite all evidence to the contrary, Verve was not stupid enough to bring Ellory into Lotis proper. Instead, she deposited the shape-changer beside an old abandoned dock on the outskirts of the village, leaving her with a promise to return with a healer. Whether Ellory would believe Verve was another matter, but on the brief trip to the dock, Verve had assessed Ellory's wounds enough to realize the shiftling wouldn't be able to do much harm to anyone in her current state.

Verve hurried back to Lotis and tracked Alem to the Tipsy Willow, where

Ivet had gathered the rest of the villagers. A veil of tension was strung taut over Lotis, obscuring all other emotions. When Verve pushed the door open, the villagers' tension spiked. Every face swung toward her, so she lifted her hands in a gesture meant to calm.

"The threat's handled for now," she said as Ivet rose. "But stay here a while longer, just in case. Alem?"

"I'm here." He had been sitting with the children and Ivet, but like the village leader, had risen to meet Verve. "You're injured?"

"Not me." She dropped her voice to a whisper that the little ones hopefully wouldn't hear. "One of the mages I tried *talking* to. Oh, don't look at me like that. I didn't hurt her. From the look of her wounds, it was another shiftling."

Alem nodded. "Let me get a few things, then show me where."

"What? No, just give me some poultices. Strongest ones you've got. Then wait here until I return." The last thing she needed was Alem using his magic in front of a known mage-killer like Ellory.

Or like you? Space-Between-Stars offered.

Verve rolled her eyes. Were all Fae so unhelpful?

Alem ran a hand over one of his braids. "My life is my own to risk. Someone needs my help. I can't turn away now. I'll be right back."

As he went for his healer's pack, Ivet caught Verve's arm. "This injured mage," she murmured. "Do you trust her?"

"Not yet." Verve thought of the roil of fear in Ellory's spirit; the one that her own spirit echoed. "But I'd like to. Either way, I won't bring her here without your permission."

Ivet studied Verve with eyes that missed nothing. "Do what you think is right," she said at last. "I trust you."

Alem returned with his pack then, and as they slipped out of the Willow's door, Ivet's words rang in Verve's ears. *I trust you.*

A strong, slender hand gripped her own; a tether to the moment. She looked at Alem, who gave her an encouraging nod, despite how his mind focused on the task ahead.

I won't let you down, Verve thought, and squeezed his hand back. Together, they pounded over the boardwalk, heading for the injured mage.

They found Ellory on the weather-beaten dock where Verve had left her. The shiftling sat with her back against an old support post, green eyes roaming over the horizon, body tense and alert for danger. Verve sensed the moment Ellory heard them, for the shape-changer's fear soared once she realized who approached.

Verve almost felt sorry for her.

"There," Verve said, pointing to the dock. "Let me go first and make sure she's still in the mood to parlay."

While Alem waited several yards away, Verve approached Ellory again. The shiftling regarded Verve and Alem with wariness but, like Verve, seemed to try to at least act civilly. Well, her life *did* depend on Verve, after all. Civility was the least she could do.

"I brought help," Verve said as she stepped on the weathered wood. "Do you still agree to our bargain?"

Ellory dipped her head in a nod, then grimaced. A pool of blood had appeared below her seat; a bad sign that the wound had not yet closed. The mage met Verve's eyes and genuine fear bled through her voice. "Will I lose the leg?"

"Let's ask the expert." Verve waved Alem forward, and he hurried up, dropping his pack beside Ellory. After some brief introductions and a few hushed questions, he removed Ellory's hematite pendant, cut away the leg of her ruined trousers, and placed his hand over the ugly wound.

"We found you just in time," Alem said after a few moments. "I can heal you, but it will go quicker if I disinfect the wound first. This may sting a bit." He withdrew one of the poultices he and Verve had made and pressed it to the wound. Ellory winced, but held still.

At last, Alem lifted the poultice and placed his palms against her skin. "This next bit shouldn't hurt," he said to the shiftling. "But it might feel odd. Please hold still."

Ellory nodded. Alem concentrated, his healing magic soaking the air all around like the scent of earth just after a summer rain. Within Verve's spirit,

Space-Between-Stars's focus sharpened, diamond-hard, as if the Fae wanted to absorb the mere presence of magic. Verve had never wanted anything in her life as much as Space-Between-Stars wanted Alem's power, and she realized at once why the meridians didn't allow mages into their ranks. Such a longing would be a distraction — at the very least.

Verve couldn't move, couldn't breathe; she could only stand in awe as the angry, crimson flesh started to heal over. The skin knitted itself together until only a pink scar remained.

The entire time, Ellory's gaze was riveted on her healing wound, until she tore her eyes away to look at Verve in wonder. "A dendric mage," she whispered. "I'd heard rumors, but I never believed… I thought the others were full of shit."

"Aye," Verve said in a low, dangerous voice. "And if you know what's good for you, you'll make sure those rumors never become anything else. Do you understand?"

"I gave you my word, didn't I?" Ellory snapped, but she lowered her gaze. "Aye. Sorry. Yes, I'll not breathe a word about your mate."

"He's not my…" Verve flushed again, and harder still when she caught Alem grinning to himself. "Don't you start," she said to him.

He sat back and winked at her. "Too late." He wiped his hands off on a cloth he'd brought and said to Ellory, "All done. You ought to rest for a few days, just to let the final bit of healing take place, but you'll be right as a rooster after that."

Ellory twisted to better see the former wound, and her eyes widened. "Ea's tits… You really did it. Thank you."

Gratitude clung to her words like spun sugar. But confusion also lingered there, as if Ellory was uncertain how to act in this situation.

Alem gave a half-bow from his still seated position. "You're welcome. Don't tell your friends."

Verve tried and failed to hide her snort of amusement, then Alem winked at her again and her stupid heart wanted nothing more than to knock him down and kiss him silly. The feeling got stronger the longer she looked at him, so she glanced back at the shiftling. "I don't sense your enemies nearby any longer. Do you have somewhere to go?"

Ellory's face clouded and she glanced toward Lotis. Verve tensed; could she allow the mage to return with them? Her stomach twisted at the memory of Ivet's gentle, *I trust you.*

But at last Ellory struggled upright. "I've always managed on my own. Thanks again." She met Verve's gaze, and something like hope lingered there. "You know, for not killing me and all."

"Keep your word, and I'll continue the trend," Verve replied.

She'd not meant it as a joke, but Ellory's mouth pulled into the beginning of a smile. "Fair enough." She hesitated. "I… owe you one."

No doubt the shiftling meant the words only as a courtesy. But Verve nodded. "I'll keep that in mind."

Ellory glanced at Alem. "Can I shift?"

"If you have the energy," he said. "Shifting shouldn't affect my healing work."

Ellory closed her eyes and melted into her ummaroc form. Alem drew back, alarmed, but Verve stood her ground as the sickle-drake bobbed her head at them, then slipped off, limping over the dock and into the tall marsh grass.

But the shape-changer's heart remained the same: gratitude and hope had overtaken some of her fear, at least for now.

A warm, sturdy arm slipped around Verve's waist. "You did a good thing," Alem murmured, close.

His lips brushed against her ear, and she shivered. "I tried."

"That's all we can ever do."

By now, the sun was creeping toward the horizon. It would be dusk soon. Verve searched for Ellory and found her still heading away, toward the forest, where she had more places to hide. No other mages had come into Verve's awareness, nor Legion, nor Atal's Chosen.

Not yet. The moon Atal hung in the sky, nearing fullness; a reminder of Verve's old life that she knew, deep down, she could never fully be free from. Danya could still destroy everything she had come to love. *Love.*

If she was going to protect Alem, protect Lotis, she needed to be at her best; she needed to be free of her fear. She thought again of Celidon and Jocasta's lives, of the sense of kinship she'd felt simply by looking back into the memories she'd taken on, albeit unwittingly.

Celidon and Jocasta's memories brimmed with their respective times as meridians. Soul-healers, meridians were apparently called. Well, if anyone's soul could use some healing, it was Verve's.

Something warm curled within her chest: a sense of rightness not entirely her own. This was no rational decision, but it was the right one — the only one. Space-Between-Stars's approval came against the Fae's will, but Verve felt it all the same.

"Alem?"

"Verve?"

She leaned her head against his sturdy shoulder, and he wrapped an arm around her and hugged her close, like his embrace could shield her from the worst of the world. "I want to try something," she said slowly. "But I... I don't want to be alone."

"That's ominous." His embrace tightened. "But you have me, Verve. Whatever you need, you have me."

22

To Stand Alone

Maybe it was an impulse of the glimmer spirit, or Celidon's latent memories, but once Verve had decided to use her new meridian abilities on herself, the urge to return to Pilgrim Springs beat against her brain. So the next morning, after again ensuring that all was well within Lotis, she and Alem went back to the spring. Rather, she raced along the forest pathway and Alem hurried after.

Verve reached the spring first. The sun had not yet broken through the canopy, so morning mist clung to the brilliant blue water, veiling it and the surrounding woods. Cypress trees surrounded the springs; strands of curling gray moss dangled from their branches into the rippling water. Water birds trilled distantly, but Verve sensed no larger creatures nearby, magical or otherwise.

Small mercies.

Within her mind and memory, Space-Between-Stars fairly danced in delight at being near the moving water. Spurred by the Fae's emotion, Verve darted across the sandy shore, pausing only to shuck all but her small-clothes, and then waded into the shallow side of the spring. Cold water brushed her ankles and calves, but she relaxed into the shock and allowed herself time to adjust. Her racing heart slowed as a feeling of calm settled over her, like warm air, scented with flowers.

Alem caught up with her, huffing a little as he sloshed to her side. "I didn't

204

think you liked it here *that* much."

Verve didn't realize she was smiling until it was too late. "Me either."

He smiled, too. "What now? How exactly does this soul healing stuff work? Milo never let me know any specifics."

Some of her calm flitted away as she glanced at the deep blue water before her. She was well and truly out of her element, but perhaps Celidon's or Jocasta's memories could assist. So she held out her hand. Alem took it, and the tight feeling in her chest eased a little at his touch.

"I'm not sure," Verve admitted, meeting his eyes. "I'm running on someone else's instinct now. Bear with me?"

He squeezed her fingers. "That would be hilarious if I were a shiftling. But, alas."

Startled into a laugh, Verve gave his chest a playful swat, and not just because he'd cast aside his shirt. He caught her wrist and kissed it, then held her gaze. "Do what you need to do. I'll be here."

Never in her adult memory had she been able to rely upon anyone else. Never had she wanted to. The idea terrified her more than even her new abilities, more than the crushing dark of the void. But it was difficult to feel afraid now, surrounded by cool moving water and shafts of sunlight, so she nodded, closed her eyes, and looked inward, following the trail of memories Celidon and Jocasta had left. She'd sifted through them several times already, mostly before she fell asleep each night: images of places and people she didn't know at first, but once she concentrated, she found the shape of their hearts molded against the souls within her. Several lifetime's worth of love and pain, all stowed within her spirit for safekeeping.

The weight of that responsibility should have dragged her down, but instead, it gave her wings.

Verve allowed the memories to flow across her mind for a while before she turned her focus further inward. She cast back through her own memories as one might dive beneath the spring in search of the mighty underground river that connected the entire world.

But although she kept her eyes open, she saw neither spring nor sunlight, but only the cloying darkness.

Boots thudded against wood. Verve's bare feet curled over that same wood — the weathered, splintery planks of a platform. The platform's sides were open and the chattering of other people—a lot of them—echoed even over the desperate pounding of her blood in her ears. Hoots and hollers sounded, shouts of "heretic" and "dreg" and other foul words she only vaguely knew, for her parents had always tried to shield her from the worst of the world's cruelty.

Everything was dark. Each breath came strained because of the rough cloth someone had shoved over her head. She'd squeezed her eyes shut because when she opened them, she saw the cloth and the meager light that struggled through, but nothing else. Her breath stank, her body stank. Her head was light and her heart hammered against her ribs.

But she couldn't breathe deeply to calm herself, because each breath reminded her of the tough, scratchy rope around her throat.

The wooden planks shivered beneath more stepping boots. The crowd's cheers grew deafening. Verve knew only some of the kotahi tongue—the languages of all non-Sufani—but even she could tell they were howling for blood. Her blood. She whimpered and leaned against the person beside her.

"Be strong, Verve," her mother, Ruzha, whispered in Sufa. "The One will watch over you." But Ruzha's body trembled.

Verve had not heard her mother's voice in nearly two decades, and now it was nearly her undoing. All the certainty she had felt this morning drained away, and she fought to free herself from this horror masquerading as a memory. The vision faded; her breath came easier.

Stay, Celidon's spirit urged. *You must acknowledge the past if you are to thrive in your future.*

Surviving's just fine, thanks, Verve replied, squeezing her eyes shut.

Jocasta's spirit slipped through her own, bolstering her. *You're not alone, Verve. We will guide you.*

Why? she shot back. *Why do you care? I'm a killer. I'm a monster. Why should you help me?*

You bear the name your mother and father gave you, Celidon said. *You are strong enough to bear this, too.*

Space-Between-Stars added, softly, *And everyone deserves a chance to be who they truly are.*

Distantly, she felt Alem's embrace and knew, somehow, he was witnessing these events too. She recoiled again, unwilling to subject him to this trauma, too, but even as she did, his steady presence glowed in her mind's eye. *I'm here,* she thought she heard him say. *I'm not going anywhere. You can do this.*

Bolstered, Verve took a deep breath to shore up her resolve, then she turned her attention back to the memories she'd buried for so long.

She regretted it at once, for she knew what would come next.

Something powerful snatched the rope around Verve's neck, jerking her away from her mother, forcing her to stand alone. The voice at the rope's other end snarled words Verve didn't understand. Her mother snapped a reply, then yelped and stumbled, breathing hard. Verve's heart thundered and she could not see beyond the thick, black fabric that had swallowed her head.

A n unfamiliar voice called out in the strange kotahi language. Verve strained to listen, and this time understood more of the words — thanks to the other meridians' magic.

"See before you the heretical Sufani," the voice called. "The filthy nomads who disgrace our true god, Atal, by refusing to honor His name above any other."

The crowd hissed their disapproval, but it was their thrum of anger that sent chills up Verve's spine.

"But our true god is not without mercy," the voice continued. "For He gives all of His children a chance to recant their misguided, false beliefs and pledge their hearts to Him. So now, Sufani, you have the choice: recant, or travel to your next lives."

A mixture of hoots, boos, and jeers rose from the crowd. Something whistled through the air, landing with a foul, wet splat against Verve's toes. She recoiled, only to slam into a set of armored legs. The legs' owner grunted and kicked her forward, back in line, and her toes squelched into the dung, making her gag. Her mother cried out in fury, but Ruzha's reward was another blow. The slap of a gloved hand against flesh echoed in Verve's heart, where seeds of rage took root.

The boots thudded before they came to a halt at the far edge of the platform. "Speak, heretic," the voice called. "Do you recant your wicked, sinful ways?"

Verve's father, Koru, answered in the kotahi tongue, his voice clear, ringing. "This is wrong. You know this is wrong."

A slap. The crowd cheered. The voice spoke again. "Do you forsake your false One god and instead pledge yourself to the mighty Atal?"

"Never," Koru answered.

No sooner had the word left his lips did more footsteps sound. The crowd hollered as Verve's father grunted. The platform shivered as if he'd fallen forward on his knees. Verve's head grew light and her vision spotty.

"Very well," the voice said. "May you find the truth in your next life."

Silence, deafening, then the sickening thwack of metal against bone, the iron scent of blood, the cheering crowd, the shrieks of anguish and fury from the Sufani's throats.

The voice spoke again, this time to Verve's eldest sister. "You there, the eldest of the litter. What say you?"

Cicely's voice wavered, but her reply was clear. "Go fuck yourself, kotahi dreg."

Her end came swiftly too, but with more cheers.

Within her spirit, Celidon and Jocasta's horror echoed Verve's. Space-Between-Stars's spirit, however, swam with disbelief and rage. *How could humans do this to one another?*

Too easily, Verve managed to reply.

Her brothers, Teo and Anu, were next. Again, she lived through the moment when each member of her family was put to the same question. Again, each one died, defiant. By the time the questioner came to Verve's mother, Verve recognized the tears in Ruzha's voice, but her reply was as firm and bright as polished steel. "I hold no other before the One god. Your Atal has no power—"

They beheaded her before she finished speaking.

At last the footsteps paused before Verve, and she braced herself. Someone grabbed her neck and pulled the black cloth away, leaving her blinking, disoriented. It'd been daylight when they'd shoved the hood over her head; now, darkness clung to the world. Beside her, the blood of everyone she'd ever loved painted the platform, their desecrated bodies twisted and still. Bile rose in Verve's throat and she ducked, gagging, only to shriek as a soldier snatched her head up by her hair and forced her to look at the questioner.

Another sentinel, fitted in the gleaming silver armor of a Legion commander, towered over her. Torchlight glinted off of their gear and danced upon her family's spilled blood.

"And you, child," the sentinel sneered. "Will you follow the path of your mother and father, and meet your next life now? Or will you choose the true path, the light of Atal, who shines above us even now?"

The sentinel gestured up to the sphere of the moon, Atal, hanging golden on the horizon. But Verve only briefly cut her eyes to the full moon. All she could see was blood.

"What say you, child?"

Her throat was dry, her heart a runaway horse. She wanted to cry, to reach for her mother, but her mother lay beside her, still and bloodied, that bright spirit extinguished. Her tears were useless.

Be strong, Space-Between-Stars urged.

But Verve was weak. She had always been weak.

She squeezed her eyes shut. *I'm sorry, ahmma, apaah, and everyone else.* "I choose Atal."

Verve opened her eyes, gasping. The sunlight blinded her, and she canted forward and the icy water at her feet hit her nerves like a punch, and sent her toppling. Someone grabbed her arm. She shrieked and twisted out of their grasp, shoved them back, but her body gave out and she collapsed into the shallow water, breath short, eyes burning with tears.

"Verve."

She couldn't breathe. She couldn't think. Sunlight rippling over water merged with the firelight gleaming on blood, and she shut her eyes against it all. But closed eyes brought darkness, and darkness brought death, and she trembled all over.

"Verve… It's all right."

"I'm sorry," she cried in Sufa. "I'm weak. I couldn't bear it. I'm sorry."

A gentle touch brushed against her shoulder blades. "You're safe," Alem said, his voice low but clear and strong. "Verve, you're safe. It's all right."

She lost track of time as Alem held her, as they sat together in the spring shallows long enough for the icy water to feel almost warm. When she could speak again, she looked into his dark eyes. "Thank you for being here, though."

He brushed his thumb along her cheek. "I would do a lot worse for you."

Verve scrubbed her face with her pruning palms and stared at the rippling water. "Legion took my family prisoner, then executed them." She shuddered. "Publicly."

"I got some of that," Alem said. At Verve's look, he elaborated. "It was like I could experience what you were remembering."

She ran a hand through her hair. "Sorry."

"Don't be." He hesitated. "Mara's mercy… I had no idea. I knew Legion killed Sufani, but that…" He gave a shuddering breath. "What happened, after?"

This she remembered too well. "They put me in an orphanage with other castaway kids. That's where Danya found me a few years later." Memories of more crushing darkness, of punishments in locked closets and kicked ribs filled her mind, but she could not bear to think of her time in the orphanage more than briefly.

Something sour rose in her throat. "I should have died with them that day. I was too weak, too scared."

"You were a child."

The sourness burned on the back of her tongue, so she jumped up and raced to the bushes to retch. When she returned, Alem stood on the shore, tears shining on his face. "You were a child," he said again, holding out his hand. "Their deaths aren't your fault. They would be glad you're alive."

"Not like this," she whispered. She took his hand, but her own felt like lead. "They would be ashamed to know their daughter is a killer. A monster."

And she was, by the One god, she was. The souls of those whose lives she'd taken pressed upon her heart and she could not find the strength to stand. Her legs buckled, and she collapsed against the sugary soft sand, too exhausted even to cry. Only now did she truly feel the weight of the deaths she'd caused, for whatever reasons she'd told herself. How many parents, siblings, lovers had she destroyed?

Too many to count.

You were just a child, Jocasta's spirit echoed. *You were lost, then exploited. It is Danya's and Legion's sin to bear.*

Celidon's spirit flared brightly in agreement. *You did not deserve that fate.*

Feel the pain, Space-Between-Stars added, notes of chagrin and recognition in their words — a far cry from the sneering fury Verve had felt from the Fae upon their joining. Apparently, even Fae spirits could change their minds. *Feel it in every part of your being.*

Easy enough, for pain was all she knew now. Alem held her tightly as she clutched her fists into the sand, closed her eyes against the soft sunlight, and wept.

Let the pain flow through you, then release it, Space-Between-Stars said. *Only then will you be free.*

Please, show me how, Verve begged.

And the Fae spirit within her said, *Open your eyes.*

23

The River

The river flowed across Verve's vision, cutting through the darkness of the void around her with threads of brilliant white, blue, gold, pink, and every other color she'd ever seen or imagined. But this was like no river Verve had ever encountered in her waking life. This river hovered above her head, a flow of energy and light, beckoning her with a faint melody she almost knew.

A filament of the river flowed within reach, so she leaned closer to examine the wondrous sight. Thousands of tiny shapes, mirrors of each other, repeating forever, made up the river's body. Each piece fitted perfectly with the others, all propelling each other toward some unseen end. Verve turned to follow the river's path and found it flowing onward, toward a massive, glowing ocean of light somewhere far away.

"Beautiful, isn't it?" Celidon said.

Verve whirled to the meridian—the *dead* meridian—who stood several paces away. A haze of light surrounded him and his eyes glowed faintly; a ghost with a mild voice. In Verve's mind, his spirit resonated with hers and she felt his grief as keenly as her own. Jocasta's presence lingered nearby, but the former meridian did not appear. Which was probably for the best, as this was all quite bizarre enough, thank you.

"What is that?" Verve asked, which was the most logical question, of course. Not "where am I?" Or "what's going on?" She'd save those for later.

Assuming she had a later.

Celidon turned his face up to the shining river of light. "Space-Between-Stars brought you here. We are in the Fae realm, once called the Shadowlands. That is the Great River, where the souls of our people—the Fae and our own—flow together for all eternity. You can hear their song, can't you?"

The beckoning melody strengthened into a song of thousands upon thousands of souls, resonating with one another; a flow of energy and life.

"Yes," she breathed, and tilted her head up to better absorb the song.

Celidon's smile held no warmth. "It's not for you. Or it shouldn't have been. But you..."

A sense of heaviness pressed against Verve's heart, and her shoulders sagged. "I never meant for any of this to happen."

"What did you think would happen when you took Karel's life?" Celidon asked.

"I didn't," Verve replied. "I just... I believed I was doing the right thing, that I was working for the greater good. All mages may not *be* evil, but even you must admit they are capable of evil acts. Places like Freehold are proof of that."

"Evil begets evil," Celidon said. "That doesn't make any of it right."

"Then what's the alternative?" Verve pressed. "Lay down and die? You know, I've never claimed to be a hero, or a paragon, or anything good. But at every turn, there's someone shaming me for the choices I've made — the choices I've *had* to make, just to survive another day. If you meridians are so powerful, why haven't you stopped mages from warring with each other? For that matter, why haven't you stopped Legion?"

Celidon stared at her, but it was Jocasta's voice that replied. "We have tried, Verve. But there are few of us, and many, many mages, and Legion grows more powerful with each passing day."

The former meridian had appeared at Verve's side. She was an older woman, older even than Danya or Ivet, with long moon-white hair flowing loose about her shoulders. Like Celidon, she shone with her own light.

"Well, that's bullshit," Verve replied, lifting her chin. "You have all this power, but it may as well be nothing at all for the good you've done. At least I use my *evil* for a good cause. Lotis is stronger now because of me. Doesn't that count for something?"

Jocasta's shoulders fell. "It does. The world needs more places like Lotis; places where hope can flourish."

Caught wrong-footed, Verve didn't know quite how to respond. "Well. Then maybe you meridians need someone like me, after all: someone who knows how to fortify, and fight back."

Celidon's jaw had tightened, but he looked at the flowing river and relaxed. "I didn't realize what you were when first we met. I should have. My folly — my pride."

"You didn't realize I was a mage-hunter?"

He shook his head. "A walking wound, not healed over. I could have looked into your heart right there, in those caverns, and healed your pain. That's what meridians do. That's what I *should* have done. If I had, Karel might yet live."

Few others Verve had ever met would so freely acknowledge their mistakes. Furthermore, she felt Celidon's regret as her own: a slow, seeping loss of energy.

"You're not at fault," Verve replied, softer than she might have otherwise. "*I* killed Karel. You could have done nothing to stop it."

Any more than you could have stopped Legion from destroying your family, Space-Between-Stars's voice echoed in her mind.

Verve started up at the figure who'd appeared at her side: a tall, stately being with curving horns and eyes that glowed like twin stars. Space-Between-Stars's skin was the inky black of night, speckled with the occasional star.

Her breath caught at the Fae's true form. "You…" She swallowed. "You're taller than I expected."

Space-Between-Stars inclined their head, dipping the curving horns in what Verve imagined was a bow. *It is… strange to see you here as well,* Space-Between-Stars replied. *You should know the other meridians have been speaking of you, debating what's to be done. No other before has joined our family without our permission. It's too late to separate you and I without destroying us both.*

Celidon nodded. "And to lose Space-Between-Stars *and* Jocasta…"

"And you, friend," Jocasta said.

The Fae turned their starlight gaze onto Verve again. *The other meridians are undecided.*

Verve clenched her fists. "Anyone else want to weigh in on *my* future? Any other souls or past selves living in my head that I've not yet met? No?" She exhaled. "I can apologize until the sun burns itself out. But I can't change the past, only try to help the future. You can talk to the other meridians?" When the Fae nodded, Verve's resolve solidified. "Then tell them this: from now on, I'll do my own thing. They don't have to keep track of me. I'll make my own way. I always have."

"No, you haven't," Celidon replied. "You may believe otherwise, but you've let your past control your present and shape your future. Will you carry on this way, as you always have? I think not. I think the weight will crush you. And I cannot say I regret it. But," he sighed again, "I have seen what shaped you, so I will try to help you."

"Your kindness overwhelms me," Verve muttered, although her mind spun at the dead man's words. "Help me, how?"

Meridians are links: between the human world and the Fae realm, between memories, between the heart and mind, Space-Between-Stars replied. *Through our magic, meridians can take on the burdens of grief, sorrow, fear, and release them to the river, to be purified.*

They gestured above their heads to the glowing strands.

That… made no sense. "Huh?"

"Love is like a river," Jocasta said gently. "Love is boundless, endless, so when the object of that love is gone, the waters churn and roil. They must find a new direction."

"What are you saying?" Veve shot back. "That I'm just supposed to *replace* people I've loved? Seems cold. Coming from an assassin, that's saying something."

Jocasta's smile held the just-enough warmth of a summer morning. "No, Verve. What I mean is that love is our natural state of being: ours and the

Fae's. It's why we worked so well together. We are all born to love, however we can." She gestured to the river of light above their heads. "Love is a river. Let it flow."

Let me show you. Space-Between-Stars took Verve's hands. Theirs were cool, light, little more than a feather-touch. But before Verve could pull free, the Fae's star-bright eyes caught hers, pinning her in place.

"Inhale and gather up your grief," Celidon said. "Exhale and release it to the river. Only then can you move forward. Inhale."

Sensing no better alternative, Verve breathed in. Grief and anger coiled in her heart, a tight tangle of knots that she could never fully untie. But she didn't have to; she had found their source.

"Exhale," Jocasta said. "Release your pain into the river; feel how it always flows."

Verve breathed out. The knots loosened, black threads uncoiling and reaching for where a light in the river flared. An answering light glowed in her own heart; a little flame of rightness. Some threads slipped free, flowing into the river, and some of the weight upon her lifted. *Good work,* Space-Between-Stars murmured.

"Again," Jocasta said.

"How long must I do this?" Verve asked.

"As long as it takes," Celidon replied.

Verve frowned. "So helpful. Thanks."

Celidon flashed her a smile that held too many teeth. "You're welcome."

* * *

When Verve opened her eyes again, she was in her room. Alem sat at her side, writing notes in a little book, humming softly. The sky beyond the windows hung in a cloudy, pale place between dusk and dawn, and she could make no sense of time.

She had only a vague recollection of returning from Pilgrim Springs. "How in the blazing void did you dress me?" she muttered as she sat up.

"You dressed yourself." He glanced up, dark eyes assessing. "Remember?"

She scrunched her face in recollection, but her memories from last night were foggy at best. "Kind of?"

"You were exhausted," he replied. "You've been asleep all day. How are you feeling now?"

She rubbed her temples. Her head ached a little, and despite sleeping so much she felt like she'd not slept in a week, but otherwise… "Good. Hungry."

Satisfaction flickered through his spirit, like the fireflies beyond her window. "That's a good sign. Mind waiting here while I let Ivet know? She made me swear to alert her the moment you woke up. I'll grab you some food, too."

While he clambered down the ladder to find the village leader, Verve went to the window—newly replaced by Hadiya—and peered outside. Storm clouds crept over the sky, brushed along by a steady wind. The moon Atal hung on the horizon, days from fullness, and Verve's stomach clenched. But she sensed nothing amiss beyond Lotis: no trace of the Chosen or Legion. No trace of anyone with violence in their hearts. Perhaps all of her work to clear the area of dangerous mages had finally paid off. Perhaps Ellory had warned her fellow moon-bloods to steer clear of Lotis, and Danya truly believed her dead.

Verve snorted. Aye, and perhaps she could swallow the moon and light up the whole world.

The barn door creaked as Alem reentered. "Ivet's busy with the little ones," he said as he ascended the ladder. "And it's about to rain, so I imagine no one will want to leave the Willow."

Verve met him at the ladder as he hefted a massive basket up and into the loft. "What *is* all this?" she asked.

Without waiting for a response, she pulled back the cloth covering and her mouth immediately began watering at the sight of pesadhi, a Sufani dish she'd not eaten in too long. She tore into the small meat pie at once, savoring the perfect blend of temerin spice and yuzah root, and the tumult of memories evoked by the familiar tastes.

As she ate, she rifled through the basket to see what else Alem had brought. When she caught the scent of honey and her fingers brushed the bundle of smooth, palm-sized dough balls, her breath hitched.

Suddenly, she wasn't in Hadiya's barn any longer, but seated at a fire, cozy between her mother and father while her elder sister and her brothers fought over the last bite of tarai: sweet, fried dough filled with crushed nuts and honey. Tears sprang to her eyes, for she loved sweets, but so did her siblings — and they were bigger. A soft movement beside her made her glance over to her father, who withdrew a single, large tarai, and handed it to her, a small smile on his lips.

The memory faded, but for once the remembrance of her family brought only a little pain.

"You don't like it?" Alem asked.

Verve sniffed — she'd been crying again, sod it all. But the realization didn't embarrass or infuriate her like it used to. "It's delicious." She swiped tears from her eyes and took another bite. "Just like my apaah—my father—used to make."

She tilted the basket toward Alem, who selected one of the pesadhi and they ate in silence for some time as clouds slowly blotted out the moon. But for once, the darkness outside didn't make Verve want to withdraw. Dusting sugar from her hands, she went back to the window and flung it open, and leaned her elbows on the sill, staring at the shifting moonlight veiled with clouds.

"Ivet said it's been quiet lately," Alem said as he came beside her. "No sign of any trouble, mage-related or otherwise."

Verve closed her eyes, searching with her meridian senses, but again, she found no trace of danger. Surely that was a warning by itself, but she was full and comfortable, and Danya felt very far away.

Even so. "I sense nothing wrong, but I'll patrol later," Verve replied.

"Good idea." Alem shifted closer so she could feel the heat radiating from his body, smell the green scents of his garden, practically taste jessamin nectar on her tongue. The memory of his kiss sent a flush through her body and an ache in her fingertips. The door of his heart was ajar, allowing her a glance within, but she resisted the urge.

"Ivet and the kids are at the Willow?" Her voice was almost a whisper.

He smiled. "Most everyone is. It's Ivet's night to cook, and no one misses her food if they can help it."

"Except you."

His smile broadened as he looked at her. "I've got everything I need right here."

Surely her cheeks would burst into flames, but she hardly cared. His voice brushed against her ears: low and soft, but filled with promises. Nerves twisted in her full belly and suddenly eating as much as she had didn't seem like the best idea.

Inhale. Verve gathered her agitation, knotted it into a tight ball. *Exhale.* She could not see the river here, but she could feel the inexorable flow — not just as a memory, but a constant presence in Space-Between-Stars's spirit.

So she breathed through her habitual urge to flee because right now, all that mattered was that she and Alem were here, together.

Tell him.

"Alem?"

"Verve?"

She gnawed at her lower lip. Her armor lay to one side of her room, but her heart was still guarded. Could she let anyone breach those walls?

You already have, Space-Between-Stars's voice whispered in her mind. The Fae was still within her, as were Jocasta and Celidon. But their presences had retreated, giving Verve much-needed space in her own head. Thunder rumbled outside, making the barn walls tremble. A storm wind caressed Verve's cheek.

Alem pressed his palm over her hand on the windowsill, surrounding her with his warmth, his quiet strength. He studied her, and within his dark eyes she saw her own reflected back, glowing like stars.

"Mara's mercy," he murmured. "You're so beautiful."

"Space-Between-Stars," she burst out.

His brows knitted. "What?"

"The Fae spirit I took on when I became a meridian," she replied. "They're here. In my head with me. I mean, not so much right now, but I don't know how much they can sense of what I sense, and I just…." She flushed. "I thought you should know before we…"

A slow, crooked smile crept over Alem's face. "Before we what?"

She rolled her eyes at his teasing. "Have tea, obviously."

"Obviously." His smile broadened, then he turned more serious. "I understand, Verve. I know you're not exactly alone. But I don't care. I'm a simple man. I just want to be with you — however you want, however I can."

Of all the things about him that made her crazy, it was the earnestness in his voice was her undoing.

Words lost their urgency. Admissions lost their weight. What mattered was the feeling of skin on skin, the heat of him pressed against her. Verve released her hesitation in a murmur that sounded like his name. Alem's eyes lidded. He cupped her cheek in his callused hand and drew her closer, but paused when they were a breath apart. "So can I kiss you again?" he whispered, the words a feather-touch at her lips.

"You'd better," she replied. "Else I'll be very cross."

He smiled against her mouth. "Well, we don't want that."

"We do not."

The kiss started gently, but something broke open inside them, pouring over Verve's parched spirit like the rain outside. She wound her arms around Alem and he embraced her in kind, sliding his hand up her spine, pressing her as close as he could. The kiss deepened. Heat swam through Verve's veins, urging her closer, harder, *more.* She wanted to drown in him, wanted to taste, to feel nothing else but *Alem* for the rest of her days.

Somehow they'd gotten horizontal. Rain pounded beyond the open window, but the barn's roof sheltered them from the elements. And in truth, Verve would hardly have noticed—or cared—had the roof cracked open and rain poured over them, for all of her attention was on Alem. He leaned over her, his embrace solid and strong, his lips roving from her mouth to her neck to the shell of her ears. A frisson of pleasure danced over her skin, pooling between her legs; a flare of desire unlike any she'd felt during other romantic encounters.

For the desire wasn't just hers; it was Alem's too, radiating off of him like sunlight. This realization made her pull back, breathless, to study him.

Breathing hard, Alem leaned on his elbows over her. "Everything all right?"

"I can feel you," she replied.

He gave her that crooked smile and shifted his hips, where he strained against his pants. "I can feel you, too."

She laughed in delight. "I mean… *I* can feel what *you* feel." She skimmed a fingertip over his cheekbone, down to his lips. "Your spirit. It's so much clearer than it was before. It's…resonating with mine." She flushed. "I can't explain it, but it's…really nice."

He gave a low hum of consideration and bent to suck at her neck, sending more jolts of sensation across her whole self. "Just nice?" he asked between kisses.

"I said *really* nice," she gasped.

"A good start." He nibbled at her neck, and she gasped again. "But let's see if I can do any better than *really nice.*"

Her head spun, her thoughts rapidly dwindled to solving the crisis of still being clothed when there was so much skin to explore between them. She wriggled out of her tunic, then her small-clothes. Alem leaned back and did the same. Thunder rumbled outside again, making the barn walls quake, then a streak of lightning illuminated the room, casting the planes of his muscular torso in brilliant white light. An answering desire swam through her chest and her belly, and the ache between her legs grew more desperate. Nothing else mattered but being with him right now. He caught her lips with his and kissed her harder than before, like he was drinking her in, and suddenly she could not bear to be alone in her body any longer.

"Alem," she whispered into his mouth. "I need you. Now."

He groaned and sat up, his eyes roving across her naked form before he met her gaze again. "I need you too. But we must be careful. Have you ever taken red orris root?"

"Are you seriously playing healer right now?" Verve rolled her eyes, but smiled. "Yes, I've had plenty recently. No surprise babes for me. You?"

"I hadn't taken any in a while," he admitted. "Until you started coming around."

She grinned. "Thought you'd get lucky, did you?"

"Never thought I'd get this lucky." He kissed her again. "Verve, I want to touch you, and taste you," he murmured. "Is that all right?"

His words, and the lust in his gaze, sent a delighted chill over her and she smiled. "I suppose."

He grinned, too, and bent to kiss her mouth again. But his lips soon moved to her jaw, her neck, down her chest to linger over her nipples. Verve arched her back, gasping at the combined sensation of his faint stubble over her skin, merging with her own pleasure at his knowing touch. While he worked her nipples with his tongue, his fingers—long and skillful—crept down her stomach, to the heat between her thighs. She was soaking wet already; his gentleness now was infuriating in the most delicious way, and she moaned aloud.

"Good?" he murmured into her mouth.

At first, all she could do was gasp his name and writhe beneath his hands, although at last she managed a strangled, *"More."*

"As you wish." His lips moved from her breasts, following the path his hands had taken down her stomach, to her hips, then down to her thighs, where he lingered for an eternity, laving his tongue against the soft skin there, making her cry his name again and again, begging him, until at last, at *last* his tongue flickered against her pearl and she truly lost the ability to think of anything but his touch.

His dark head bobbed between her legs as he lapped at her, using his fingers and his tongue with a skill she'd never have guessed from his gentle nature. And through it all, his desire for her filled her mind, merged with her own pleasure at their joining, overwhelming her in the best possible way. He delighted in being between her thighs, in tasting her, feeling her soft heat, her slickness; her own pleasure spiraled up and up, tighter and tighter, gripping her heart and mind and body, until she found her release with a cry.

Gasping, all Verve could do was stare at the barn's rafters without really seeing them. Her mind was at once blank and filled with Alem's desire — and his delight at her pleasure. He drew away, swiping the back of his hand over his mouth, and came to her side once more, lying his long body next to hers. His hardness brushed her thigh, but he seemed to be in no hurry to sate his own lust as he stroked her cheek while she caught her breath.

"If I didn't know better," he said, touching his nose to hers, "I'd say you enjoyed that."

Her heart soared and she laughed. "What gave it away?"

He nuzzled her neck, making her squeal. "You've got a few tells."

She pulled him in for another kiss and tasted herself on his tongue. Desire flared within her once more, not only an echo of his. "Like what?"

But she didn't let him answer, only kissed him again. His desire leaped, stronger, insistent, and this time she let her fingers explore his skin, dipping below his waist to brush against his length. He hissed in pleasure and moaned her name, and her vision swam with their shared desire. He found his release with her name on his lips, and nothing had ever sounded half as sweet.

I love you, her heart sang, but she couldn't form the words, couldn't think much at all beyond the shared languages of touch and taste. She let him rest for a few minutes before stoking his fire once more, and then neither of them spoke at all for some time after. And outside, the storm raged on.

Later, they lay facing one another on her bed, listening to the rain drumming against the roof. Neither one had bothered to light a lamp, but a light shone against Alem's face, showing his sleepy grin. "Your eyes are glowing again," he murmured, stroking a finger down her hip. "Feels like I'm looking at the stars."

She shivered at his touch. They were both utterly spent, but their emotions still twined together like woven threads. Alem's contentment reflected her own.

There was no sign of Celidon or Jocasta, but Space-Between-Stars preened within her spirit. The Fae had not been an active participant in Verve and Alem's lovemaking—they had not been present in her mind with enough clarity to sense any details—but they had ridden the waves of Verve's delight and pleasure, and thus, Alem's too. Now the Fae spirit drifted like a feather in the wind, pleased beyond measure.

It should have been (at the very least) creepy, but Verve only felt a warm buzz of contentment, a feeling that even the finest liquor could not recreate. She sighed, and the light shining on his face glowed brighter.

"Glowing eyes might make it hard to be stealthy," she said sleepily.

A flash of alarm flitted through Alem's spirit, but he said only, "Why do meridian eyes glow?"

"Didn't your meridian grandpa tell you?" Verve asked.

"No, but I did ask."

Alem shifted so he was on his back, and curled an arm around her. Verve leaned against his chest and pressed her ear against him, where she could hear the steady thud of his heart. "I don't know," she admitted. "I think it's got something to do with the Fae magic they use. *We* use. Everything glows in the Fae realm."

"So it's true," he breathed. "Meridians can enter the Fae realm. I heard rumors, but Milo never said outright. What was it like?"

Show him. It was no direction from anyone else, just an instinct; perhaps due to her connection with Space-Between-Stars.

So Verve closed her eyes and concentrated on the steady rhythm of Alem's heart, a song echoed by the timpani of abating rainfall outside. Inhale. She reached through her spirit and found her connection to the Fae realm in all its shadowed, shining glory. Exhale. She sent the image to Alem, willing him to see.

His soft gasp made her eyes open. He stared at her, but his gaze was distant until he blinked slowly and shook his head. "Mara's mercy... I never saw anything like that. I never could have imagined."

She skimmed a hand over his chest again, savoring his warmth and the beat of his heat. "Me either."

Contentment lulled her into sleep, soon, and the last thing she saw before her eyes closed was the moon, Atal, breaking through the clouds, shining glorious and full over the world.

24

Void

Verve winced as her needle bit into her thumb, then sucked on her wound before any blood could fall on the cloth. Although, a few drops of blood could hardly make her clumsy embroidery attempts any worse. As it turned out, sewing hematite beads onto her old gear was *very* different from embroidering leaves and flowers. Although… a bloodstain or two might have made the handkerchief more interesting.

"What are you grinning at?" Ivet said from beside her, enjoying a steaming cup of tea. "Something sinister, I imagine."

But there was only warm affection in the older woman's voice. Verve turned the little round wooden frame with the cloth stretched over it so Ivet could see the misshapen flowers. "I'm mutilating this fabric."

Ivet chuckled. "Bah. I've seen worse."

They sat together outside the Willow, on a couple of rocking chairs that Hadiya had set on the boardwalk. The village had come together, as they often did, for a shared midday meal, but afterward, most folks had stuck around the tavern. Berel and Klaret sat opposite Ivet and Verve, drinking tea and speaking quietly. Hadiya, Nori, and Dannel had gathered outside Dannel's home, discussing the state of the dock that led to his house — apparently some of the wood planks needed replacing. Kyon, in his antelope form, carried a happily shrieking Kinneret and Lio on his back—carefully and under Ivet's watchful eye—around the village's center. Owen and Alem were off foraging for some herbs that refused to grow in Alem's garden.

The sky was a brilliant blue, with only the occasional puffy white clouds drifting peacefully over their heads. Verve had a full belly and almost everyone she loved was within her senses.

She toyed with the spool of green thread, searching again for Alem. He and Owen were out of sight, but she could sense them not far off, in the forests around Pilgrim Springs.

"Is he all right?" Ivet asked.

A flush of heat on her cheeks brought Verve back to the moment. "He's well. They've had some luck finding that sassafras."

Ivet smiled. "Good lads." She sipped from her mug of tea. "I'm still trying to wrap my mind around your abilities. Does Alem know you can keep track of him when he's out of your sight?"

Her words were too nonchalant to be casual. Verve kept her own reply equally calm — a feat, given how the thought of sharing sensations with Alem made her warm all over. "He finds it a terribly practical use of my new talents."

Ivet chuckled, but her expression grew more solemn. "Otherwise, have you found any signs of danger?"

Atal's fullness had come and gone, with no sign of Danya or her Chosen. Now, as the waxing crescent of Seren hung in the sky, Verve could almost let herself believe that Danya truly thought her dead.

Almost.

That quiet murmur of doubt had kept Verve awake many nights since her near-death at Legion's hands. And although she'd done her damned best to shore up Lotis's defenses—and prepare its inhabitants for imminent danger—she could not shake the churning in her stomach whenever she thought of Danya.

Again, Verve searched for a trace of danger: a flicker of anger, a sense of violence, even the curious but weary mind of some errant traveler. Again, she found nothing, which was in some ways worse. Her stomach twisted and her fingers could only stroke the cloth in her hand.

"No," Verve said at last, glancing at Ivet. "Perhaps I should pay Danya a visit."

Ivet went still, but only briefly. "And do what, exactly?"

Best not think about that, now. "I must get to her first," Verve said. "Or else she'll come for *me*. Or, rather," she added a little too sharply, "she'll come for Damaris."

Ivet sighed. "I never cared for that name, to be honest. Alem's a good lad, but naive, at times. Still, I've benefited from their reputation. We all have."

Her gaze flitted to the roof of the Tipsy Willow, where one of the strange metal rods stood out against the blue sky. Verve frowned. "Alem started the rumor, didn't he? Is there even a real Marea Damaris?"

"No," Ivet replied. "From what I understand, mages in the Damaris family stick to the coastline. There's no one by that name here." Ivet stared into the depths of her tea. "But your Danya would want Alem for his magic, regardless."

"She'll not have him," Verve said firmly.

"How long have you known Marea Damaris was just a tale?" Ivet asked.

Verve unraveled another length of thread and worked it through the needle's eye. "Wasn't that hard to figure out. Besides, I know who *Alem* is. That's all that matters to me."

Ivet patted her knee. "I knew I liked you, vidahem."

Alem's sudden shock ripped through Verve like lightning. Before she knew what was going on, she was up and racing through the village, making a beeline for the forest, for Alem and Owen, who were unprotected. Ivet called after her, but Verve didn't hear the other woman's words. She had no time to go for her weapons—hell, she didn't even have shoes on—but she still wore her wire bracelet. But even if she'd been naked, she'd still have gone after him.

Her bare feet sloshed through the marsh, but she hardly noticed the wet. Her heart drummed with Alem's fear — no, his terror. Owen was afraid, too, and his fear strengthened with each moment, like the swell of heat from a blazing campfire. Verve reached the woods and darted down the now-familiar paths, praying to the One god with each step. *Please, keep them safe. Please, let me reach them in time.*

As she went, she tried to sense what they were afraid of, but found only a blank spot in her mind, like something had blotted out the stars. But it didn't matter. She'd find whatever it was, and it would bother no one else again.

The pine forests dampened some sounds of her passage, but her training kicked in and she slowed enough to keep her steps completely silent. As she came upon Pilgrim Springs, she tried to swallow her fear—and Alem's, and Owen's—so she could do what she did best, but her efforts were useless. When she rounded the bend and the springs came into view, she could not stop the scream that burst from her throat.

Alem lay bloody on the shore, Owen kneeling beside him. From their frantic emotional states, Verve sensed both were alive, but terrified. A figure in hematite armor stood over them, dagger raised, blood gleaming on the edge. No thoughts or emotions emanated from the figure; they may as well have been made of stone. But with a drop of her stomach, Verve recognized his armor: this was one of the mercenaries working for Danya, training her Chosen.

Verve's bracelet was already unraveled. She grabbed both ends and leaped for the mercenary's neck, where there was a small gap — just big enough for the wire to slip through and bite into skin. The merc had enough time to curse before Verve wrapped the wire around his neck and pulled backward with all of her considerable strength.

Someone screamed. Fear choked the air: not just hers, but all around her, like wildfire sweeping over the world. But Verve ignored it, because she had to finish this, and braced her feet upon the sandy shore as she tugged the wire. The merc struggled, kicking back at her with heavy, spiked boots, jabbing at her with steel plates on his armored elbows. Blows pummeled Verve's thigh and ribs, but her grip didn't waver. The mercenary's head tipped back, smashing into Verve's nose. Pain made her head spin and her vision swirl, but she still held the bastard fast. At last he collapsed to the sandy shore, gasping, writhing, and then went still.

Verve didn't let go, not for several long minutes, long enough to ensure the merc wasn't playing possum. When at last she deemed him truly dead, she pulled back her wire bracelet, wincing at the spots on her hands where the wire had cut her, too, and went over to Alem and Owen on shaking steps.

"He's alive," Owen said, eyes huge as he knelt by Alem. His training spear lay on the ground beside him. "The mercenary tried to grab Alem, but I did what you taught me and struck him from behind. But then he got a bad swipe in and Alem went down. The bastard's dead now, right?"

Verve nodded and bent to Alem. His eyes fluttered open, and he gave her a weak smile. "Are you all right?"

Tears slipped down her nose as she cupped his cheek with her bloody palm. "Don't worry about me. I'm…"

Screams still echoed in her mind. Fear drummed in her heart. The smell of smoke crept through the forest to reach her.

None of them were memories.

Lotis's warning gong rang through the trees, echoing off of the water. Verve flung open her mind and reached out for Lotis, and found the village engulfed in terror wrought by blank figures who surely wore hematite armor.

The Chosen were there.

And she wasn't.

* * *

Black smoke bruised the pure blue sky. Shouts hung in the air, interspersed with the heavy tread of boots and the snap of flames. But it was the Lotis villagers' terror that propelled Verve back along the path she'd come, fueling her steps with desperation. She'd snatched up the mercenary's dagger, but the familiar weight in her grip was a cold comfort.

Had the merc stumbled on Alem and Owen out of luck, or was this a multi-pronged attack on Lotis and its inhabitants? Fae spears and other thorny plants stuck in her bare feet; she squelched through cold mud, but nothing mattered but Lotis. Behind her, Owen and Alem came slowly. Both had urged her to return first, but a part of Verve hated to leave them behind, too, because what if the worst happened?

The worst has already happened. Because you let it. This is all your fault. The thoughts sounded like Danya's voice.

As she ran, Verve reached out with her meridian senses again, trying to assess how many of Atal's Chosen had come — and who she might face once she got there. She found only flashes of pain and terror, and blank voids in her senses. The Chosen's training ran deep. Verve knew better than most.

Her chest ached. What if she found Usko there? Or Brak or Livia, or any of the kids she'd helped raise? By the One, she was such a fool even to hope she'd ever be free of Danya.

I can't do this.

I must.

Within her heart, Space-Between-Stars urged, *there might be another way.* If only that were true.

Verve burst back into the clearing just outside of the village, close to Alem's cottage. At first, she couldn't see for the smoke. New flames blazed upon many of the structures within Lotis — except the Tipsy Willow. Fighting back a cough, Verve crouched low and tried to calm herself enough to think clearly and *not* focus on the spots of blood marring the ground. She crept around Alem's cottage to get a better look at the tavern.

About a dozen of the Chosen, their trainers, and a few mercenaries Verve did not recognize surrounded the Willow, blades at the ready while several of the mercenaries hammered the tavern door with axes. But the clay and brushthorn mixture held strong, and some of the attackers limped — Klaret's traps had worked, to some extent. Although Verve's heart ached at the idea of hurting any of her former fellow Chosen, relief washed through her limbs at the sight of the older trainers and the unfamiliar mercenaries. None of the attackers looked to be the younger sort; a small mercy.

But while Lotis's fortifications may have helped the village protect itself, Verve was the vital component. She had a job to do, one she'd sorely neglected. She had only two measly weapons, no shoes, and still had to battle the turmoil of not only her own fear, but also that of the villagers. But she was their only hope. She gripped her stolen dagger and steeled herself, then stepped around Alem's cottage.

"Hey, ugly," she called. Trainer Aya turned, and Verve allowed herself a snicker. "Tired of teaching little ones how to kill?"

The Chosen tensed, but Trainer Aya made a swiping gesture with her hand. "Ignore her," she barked. "You have your orders. Find the dendric mage."

"They're not here," Verve said as she approached her former allies, trying to inject every bit of swagger she could into her steps. "But I am. Or are you too frightened to face someone who can actually fight back?"

Trainer Aya gestured again, and three of the mercenaries peeled off from the main group to lunge at Verve, who ducked out of the way. One merc, she felled with a vicious blow to the back of their knees, another spot where their armor didn't adequately protect them. The mercenary cried out and collapsed, and Verve snatched up their axe. A weapon in each hand just felt *right*. She circled the other two mercs, assessing the situation. That first success had been mostly luck and timing; little chance either would repeat itself. But even if Verve had all of her gear, she'd be hard-pressed to defeat this many foes on her own.

One of the mercs chopping at the tavern door grunted. The wood groaned and splintered as it began to give way. From within the tavern, Verve felt the villagers' terror as if it was her own. Memories of boot steps on a wooden platform filled her mind, and for several long seconds she couldn't take a real breath.

Then the two mercenaries facing her moved in tandem. Sunlight flashed off of their hematite gear, smarting Verve's eyes and shaking her out of her reverie. They had her outmatched in gear, but she was still fast. She released her rage in a scream and drove between them, hacking at limbs and necks with graceless rage. They fell aside, too wounded to immediately rise, and Verve rounded on Trainer Aya, who met her with a drawn sword.

Energy poured through Verve's limbs, drowning her pain, fueling her fury. Her vision pooled to the fighters before her: faceless, spineless peons of Danya's, or whoever offered them enough coin. Meridians were supposed to heal, not harm, but it was too late for that. Verve gathered her anger to her, coiling like a serpent preparing to strike, then unleashed the torrent upon Lotis's attackers. Trainer Aya gasped and stumbled back, reeling as if drunk, and several of the hired blades shrieked and grabbed their heads. Verve spared the Chosen this emotional assault, but they got the message, judging from the way most of them took off running. Most of the trainers followed, leaving only Aya and a handful of mercenaries. Much better odds.

Verve stalked toward the remaining attackers, allowing the raw surge of her anger to flow around them, through them. "Leave now," she snarled, "and I might let *you* live."

A couple more of the mercs tore away, whimpering, while Trainer Aya stared at Verve, her chest rising and falling. At last, she shook her head. "No job's worth this," she muttered. "Especially not in this foul swamp. Let's go." With that, she and the remaining mercenaries hurried between the burning buildings as they left the village as Verve stood, bloody and panting, outside the Willow.

Her meridian senses still swam with rage and fear, and she could not get an accurate sense of which villagers had survived. Heart still racing, she pounded her fist against the tavern door. "Ivet? Ivet! They're leaving! Are you—"

The door flung open, revealing Berel's tear-streaked face and Klaret's frown. "She's not here," Berel cried. "Kinny got scared and took off, and Ivet went after her, and then the mercs were upon us!"

"I think she went to the docks," Klaret said grimly, pointing.

Hadiya shouldered through them, a bloody rag pressed to their temple. "Where's Owen and Alem?"

"Here," Alem called. He limped behind Verve, Owen and Kinneret with him, and those within the Willow exclaimed in joy. But there was no room for celebration in Verve's heart yet.

"We're all right," Alem said to the others' questions. "But Ivet..."

Verve went cold. "You found her?"

Alem's eyes were bright with tears. "By the docks. But Verve, she's—"

But Verve was already gone.

Please, she begged any god who would listen, *please, let Ivet be well. Let her be well.*

A single arm stuck out of the water at the base of one of the more rickety docks. Heart in her throat, Verve reached down and gently pulled up Ivet by her slender shoulders. Ivet's eyes were wide, fixed unseeing upon some distant point, and a line of blood circled her throat. A cut from a garrote bracelet, just like Verve's. As carefully as she could, Verve brought Ivet's body up on the dock and laid her atop the warm wooden planks, bleached by the sun. Verve knelt beside her, numb.

Footsteps pounded beside her as the others approached. Dannel brushed past Verve, reaching for Ivet, murmuring in Sufa.

"I'm sorry," Verve said, also in Sufa. "She's gone to her next life now."

Dannel's shoulders hunched as he pressed his face into his hands. Hadiya came next, helping Dannel to steady himself even as tears streaked their face. Berel sobbed into Klaret's chest, while Klaret hugged her close. Kyon kept the children well away from the horrific sight, murmuring gentle words to the little ones. In the distance, steam hissed like a giant serpent as Nori snuffed out the fires with her magic.

A familiar hand rested on Verve's shoulder, and she reached up to touch Alem in return. "I'm sorry," she whispered, though she didn't know whom she spoke to.

"It's not your fault, dharika," Dannel whispered, and Verve's chest ached at the Sufa word for *daughter*.

"Aye," Hadiya muttered. "It's those merc bastards."

"No." Verve brushed back Ivet's necklace to show them the wound around her neck. "This is the work of the Chosen — one of my people."

Former people. She truly was a fool to think she could escape her destiny.

Alem sucked in a breath. "They were after me, weren't they? After a fucking dendric mage..."

He trailed off as horror stole his words, heavy in the air as the choking smoke. That same feeling thickened through the others as the reality sank in. No one spoke.

"What's that?" Klaret asked, pointing to Ivet's tunic, where a slip of parchment peeked out from the soaked fabric.

With shaking fingers, Verve withdrew her map of the area, which someone had tucked into Ivet's tunic. She unfolded it and stared at the location circled with blood, near the provincial border, leagues away from Lotis. Someone had also scratched a date—three days from now—and four words: THE MAGE OR LOTIS.

"A message for me," Verve managed. "An ultimatum."

Alem knelt beside her, peering at the map. "Shit."

He had that right.

Verve's body was leaden and her stomach a block of ice. Although she clearly had work to do, she couldn't summon the strength to stand. All she could do was cradle Ivet's only hand in hers, gripping the pruning flesh like a lifeline. But there was nothing on the other end, no tether to a safe harbor.

Just the void.

25

Hornet's Nest

By some miracle of the One, Nori preserved most of the homes in Lotis. The mercenaries had set fire only to those near the center of the village. Of these, Dannel's had burned the longest, but Nori had coaxed the marsh waters up to save the older fellow's home.

Thank the One for small mercies.

That evening, after an afternoon that Verve hoped to forget, after she'd bathed and eaten, after she'd sucked down only one puffer and a single, meager gulp of Indigo Tears (she'd showed remarkable restraint, all things considered) she suited up in her loft room.

She wasn't alone.

"Marea Damaris…" Alem scrubbed his face, then leaned back against the wall. "They're not real. They never were."

Verve's hands shook as she twined her wire bracelet back to its proper place. Had Ivet recognized the weapon when one of the Chosen wrapped it around her neck? Had she been afraid? She must have been.

"No shit," Verve muttered as she fastened the bracelet. "But why'd you start the rumor?"

Alem was silent. "People are always after me — well, after my *magic*. For years, I traveled around, never staying in one place too long. I tried *not* to heal others, but using my magic like that is a part of me, like my hands or eyes. I'd swear never to heal anyone again, ever. Then I'd come across someone wounded…" He sighed. "Seren's light. I'm a fucking idiot."

"No more than I am." Verve checked over her hematite gear, looking for any weak sections. Although the sight of the dark-gray ore made her stomach turn, the armor fit her like a second skin, and she had no other options. "The lightning?"

"Metal rods on the roofs," Alem replied. "They attract lightning, enough at least to make folks think there's some truth to the rumors."

"Clever."

Alem ran a hand through his hair. "Not really. Ivet never liked the lie. She warned me the plan wouldn't turn out well, that someone, somehow, would figure out the truth, but I was so tired of moving around, and I love it here. I thought if I stayed, I could do some good — small good, but still. I wanted to build a life somewhere. And Ivet welcomed me with open arms…" He trailed off.

Verve tried again to swallow the lump in her throat as she turned to her crossbow. "A dendric mage makes for a valuable ally," she said. "One worth the risk. Everyone who lived here would be healthy."

"Staying here *put* everyone at risk," Alem whispered. "You were right. I should have moved on."

But he hadn't. And neither had Verve, and now Ivet was gone.

The crossbow needed cleaning; mud and grass had somehow gotten worked into the firing mechanism. Verve had a set of small tools she used for that purpose, but her hands trembled too much to disassemble the entire weapon to clean it properly. Another failure of her weak heart. She dug out what debris she could and set the crossbow back in its case.

Verve gathered up the bolts. "The good news is, I know where Danya will be, and when. She wants a sodding mage? I'll give her one." Alem tensed. Verve glanced over and rolled her eyes. "Not you. Obviously."

"Then who?"

"Doesn't matter." Verve examined the tip of one of her bolts. Hematite wouldn't do any additional harm to a normal person, but the bolt was still sharp enough to pierce Danya's heart. The wire bracelet winked in the lamplight; a promise of death that Verve was delighted to make good on where Danya was concerned. Maybe somewhere, Ivet would feel avenged.

You don't have to do this, Space-Between-Stars murmured from the deep recesses of her spirit. But Verve ignored the Fae, just as she'd ignored Celidon and Jocasta's similar pleas. She'd looked through their memories. None of them had ever faced what evil she did now.

She was alone once more.

Alem sat up. "You're going to kill the woman who raised you?"

"What else am I supposed to do?" Verve snapped. "Let her live? After—"

Tears burned at her eyes, and she ground her jaw to fight back the swell of emotion. She'd done nothing else since Ivet's death. Everyone in Lotis was sick with grief; the emotion roared through the quiet village louder than an army of urslans. Verve had to shut her heart against it all, else she'd go deaf.

"There's been enough death," Alem said softly.

"You don't have to watch," Verve replied. "The One god forbid I offend your delicate sensibilities, but this is real, this is life *and* death. If I don't act now, if I don't stop Danya, she'll send her hired blades here again. Is that what you want?"

"Of course not, but—"

"No." Verve slammed down her crossbow quiver, sending the bolts clattering across the floor between her and Alem. "No, there is no 'but.' There is no answer to this question but Danya's death. You don't have to condone it, or even like it, but you do have to accept it. Anything else is just naivety."

Alem's dark eyes hardened as he stared at her. "Remember Ellory? You found another way. Why can't you try that again?"

Verve held his gaze. "There is no other way. Not with Danya. I was a fool to hope otherwise."

He deflated at the truth in her words. "I know. It's just… You're *more* than a killer, Verve. You always have a choice."

A strangled laugh tore out of Verve's throat as she bent to grab a handful of the bolts. "Killer or protector, it's all the same right now, isn't it?" She brandished the bolts. "*This* is what I am. *This* is why the One god set me on this path."

Alem sprang up and knocked the bolts out of her hand. "That's horseshit, Verve, and you know it." He gripped her fingers and touched his other hand to her cheek. "Remember how you showed me your memories? That was a gift; I understand you so much better now. And I still say you can find another way."

A gentle thumb swiped away her tears. Verve bit her tongue, savoring the pain that masked everything else, then pressed her palm over his. "I'm sorry, Alem," she murmured, squeezing his hand. "But you're wrong. I wish it wasn't so. Stay here. Stay safe. I'll be back soon."

* * *

It took Verve the better part of a day to track down Ellory, deep in the pine forests to the east of Lotis. In this part of Greenhill Province, the trees blotted out all but the most determined rays of sunlight. Now, just before twilight, only meager light trickled through the pine boughs. A buzzing cicada song filled the air.

The shiftling had made good on her promise not to return to Lotis, but she hadn't left the area. Odd, perhaps, but Verve wasn't about to look a gift sickle-drake in the mouth — *especially* in the mouth.

Verve reached a pine-coated clearing and paused, ostensibly to sweep her gaze over the pines and the spiky palmettos. But her meridian senses revealed the intense curiosity prickled with irritation that was Ellory. The shiftling was close, determined... because *she* was now tracking Verve.

Perfect. Verve changed tactics and meandered toward the meeting place marked on the note the Chosen had left. For an hour or so, she kept her pace slow but steady, to show she was unafraid of the shiftling. When dusk fully settled over the pines and it was time to make camp, Verve broke the silence.

"Want to make yourself useful and hunt us up some supper?" she called. "Or shall we fight over my stale bread?"

A long snout emerged from the nearest clump of palmettos, razor-sharp teeth gleaming even in the failing light. A fat turkey hung from the ummaroc's jaws, and Verve grinned.

"Clever girl," she said. "I'll get a fire going. Settle in. We need to talk."

The turkey landed with a thud at Verve's feet as Ellory shifted back to her human form. "I gathered."

"Oh, good. I hoped you weren't getting any nasty ideas while you tracked me."

"No more than usual."

Later, they sat on either side of a snapping fire, the turkey plucked and roasting. Verve nibbled on some dried fruit while Ellory watched the flames.

"Do you eat what you hunt in that other form?" Verve asked between bites.

Ellory nodded. "But if I change back too quickly after eating raw flesh, my guts will hate me."

Verve wrinkled her nose. "Never thought about that. Now I regret asking."

Ellory flashed her a smile that was more of a grimace. "You found me on purpose, I suppose? To cash in on that favor I owe you?"

The dried mangoes lost their sweetness, and Verve could only stare at the chunks of yellow fruit in her palm. "Lotis was attacked."

Ellory tensed. "I've kept my word. I haven't come *near*—"

"It was a bunch of mercenaries," Verve interrupted. "Working with Atal's Chosen."

Ellory's green eyes widened. "Your fellow assassins? Were they after your healer friend?"

Verve grabbed the stick she'd used to get the fire going and poked at the coals. "They know a powerful mage lives in Lotis. There are… suspicions about that mage's abilities." She gave Ellory a meaningful look. "But they attacked Lotis to send a message to *me*." A deep, trembling breath did nothing to banish the memory of Ivet's fragile body in her arms. "They want me to deliver that mage — or they'll return to Lotis and claim their due."

Ellory absorbed this. "Since you're alone, I reckon you've got a plan."

"Well, I'm not alone *anymore*. Matter-of-fact, I'm on my way to meet them. *With* a mage, no less."

Ellory stared at her. "You can't be serious."

"Even for a shiftling, you're powerful," Verve said. "You can take care of yourself."

Indignation spiked from Ellory — undercut by acrid fear. "Not against a host of mage-hunters. Neither can you, by the way. Is this a suicide mission?"

Was it? The river in the Fae realm appeared in Verve's mind again, lit from within by countless Fae souls — and some meridian souls, too, she'd come to realize.

Love is a river, Jocasta's words echoed. *Let it flow.*

Verve ground her teeth against the gentle words. Love and rivers of light were all well and good, but as she'd told Alem, this was not a moment for either. People like her met these moments with force, with blood and death, so folks like Alem could live in peace. And even then, peace was never guaranteed. Evil would always grow where it could. Someone had to stand against it.

No matter the cost.

She smoothed a hand over her scarf to quell the growing agitation, hers and Space-Between-Stars, who had retreated as much as they could from her attention.

Still, she ensured the Fae knew she spoke to *them* as much as to Ellory. "I have no intention of dying," Verve said coolly, to hide the tumble of nerves in her chest. "Wanting to win a fight is normal, but distracting too. You must enter the battleground expecting nothing other than to address each moment as it comes. Your body and mind *want* to survive. At a certain point, no amount of training or preparation will help; you must trust them to make that happen. I expect no fighting from you, but you will make a *fine* decoy while I address my business with Danya." She held up her wire bracelet, letting the firelight catch upon it. "The world won't be poorer for one more death, especially that of a monster. And as you said, you owe me one."

"I do owe you," Ellory said slowly. "But you ask too much. I've steered clear of Atal's Chosen for a reason."

Verve prodded the turkey with a dagger; the meat was still too pink to eat. "So let me get this right: you'll hand over your fellow mages to *Legion's* mage-hunters, but you draw the line at putting yourself in harm's way? Or is it Atal's Chosen, specifically, you fear?"

"None of this is your business," Ellory shot back. "What does it matter, anyway? Just coerce me and be done with it. Why do I have to *want* to help you?"

Despite her sharp words, fear, guilt, and shame, warred within the shiftling, like her heart was a roused hornet's nest and Verve had chunked the rock.

"Because you're more than the path you've chosen," Verve said quietly. "You know this, Ellory. Yet you're afraid to face the truth, because it hurts too much, and because to do so would mean your entire life must change. But the truth is, change is the only thing you can count on."

Ellory's light-brown cheeks flushed and her desperation soured the air. "Fine. I'll go with you, but stay out of sight unless there's trouble. I'll be your secret weapon. You won't have to fight alone—"

"We are *always* alone," Verve broke in. "Other people are just around, sometimes. No, Ellory, for this plan to work, I need a mage with me when I face Danya."

"You're an assassin," Ellory grumbled. "Can't you just spring on her from the shadows?"

"That won't work, this time," Verve replied.

Ellory frowned. "If you don't want me to fight for you, and you're not planning on taking this Danya down *with* you, then what's your brilliant plan?"

Please, Space-Between-Stars muttered. *Do tell.*

"I have my methods," Verve replied. "As you saw during one of our other encounters."

Ellory hugged her arms to her chest. "I've seen nothing like what you did to those other mages. You felled them without weapons or magic." Her nose wrinkled. "But there's not a whiff of magic from you. You're no mage."

"Perhaps I have my own kind of magic."

"Impossible."

Verve tried to smile. "Apparently not."

She glanced around at the forest, now cloaked in darkness. Her meridian senses let her feel the presence of a dozen small creatures within a stone's throw, and double that farther away. There was nothing to fear beyond the bubble of light cast by their fire.

Then something larger moved just out of range of her senses. Something human-sized. Something familiar, but not predatory. Verve strained, but couldn't make out the presence beyond those vague feelings.

She looked back at the shiftling. "The first time we met," Verve said slowly. "You said you sought a mage named 'Damaris.' But I don't think you were looking on a whim. Who were you working for?"

Ellory went still as stone. "Why does it matter?"

"I know how good the coin can be for bringing in a mage with a Damaris's reputation," Verve went on as if Ellory had not spoken. "But I also don't know of anyone in *this* province who'd pay a mage to hunt another mage."

She'd expected the shiftling to snarl at her, but Ellory only looked away. "Maybe you don't know as much as you think."

"Definitely," Verve agreed. "But not when hunting mages is concerned. And not," she added, softer, "where Legion is concerned."

Ellory grimaced. "Damaris was going to be the last. I'd promised myself. But don't shame me for doing what I must to survive. I'd think you, of all people, would understand."

"Too well." Again, Verve peered within Ellory's heart. Not too deeply, but enough to get a better sense of the mage's guilt and despair, to understand how both gnawed at her spirit. She didn't expect to be slapped in the face by a sense of loneliness so strong it made her eyes sting.

With effort, Verve forced her voice to be somewhat normal. "By helping me destroy the Chosen's leader, you're helping other mages. *Helping,* not hurting. This is your chance to set things right."

Ellory's jaw tensed, and she stared into the fire. "Nothing will ever do that."

Let it flow.

Verve nodded. "Then this will be a good start. And…" A memory of Ivet's comforting embrace made Verve's throat swell, and her stupid soft heart ached at the loneliness pouring off of Ellory. "And after this is done and Danya's truly gone, there's a place for you in Lotis. If you want."

"Are you serious?" Ellory breathed.

"I am." Verve stroked the scarf around her hair. Somewhere, she hoped Ivet was smiling. "Favor or not, I can't *make* you do anything. This is all your choice. Say the word, and we'll part ways. Forever."

They stared at each other until Ellory exhaled and slumped forward. "Fine. I'll help you."

"Great." Verve poked at the turkey again. Perfect. She carved off a piece for herself, then offered her dagger to Ellory, hilt-first. "Hungry?"

* * *

At dawn on the third day after the attack on Lotis, Verve and Ellory reached the meeting place from the Chosen's note: a broad clearing deep in the pine woods. The clearing sat beside a tributary of the White River; this branch lay in isolated terrain, only near the ospreys and otters.

And mosquitoes.

A tiny, high-pitched buzz sounded in Verve's ear. Crossbow in one hand, she clumsily slapped the insect away, but a dozen more took its place. Grimacing, Verve slathered on the last of her neem oil. The sharp, musky citrus scent made her eyes water, but the mosquitoes retreated.

Beside her, Ellory covered her nose with her "bound" hands as she sneezed. "Seren's light, what in the blazing void is *that*?"

"Pest repellent," Verve replied.

"It's foul."

Verve winked at her. "Must be working."

"I'm more than happy to leave," Ellory grumbled. "I'm not a fan of hematite chains."

"Oh, they're not even locked. You can break out the second you want to. But for now, stick to the plan."

Ellory swore beneath her breath, adding a curse or two aimed at Verve.

But Verve ignored her and extended her senses. Besides the mosquitoes, few living creatures inhabited this area. The vague, familiar presence she'd sensed before remained; she was starting to wish it was a figment of her imagination. But that presence wasn't much of a concern, for a much greater threat was much closer to hand.

Danya.

Verve and Ellory came over a small hill and found their target. The priest stood just across the tributary, on a blackened patch of ground where all the scrub brush had recently been burned clean away. No trees hung over her head, and a nearby pile of newly felled trunks and branches created a makeshift wall behind her — close enough to cover their backs, but not close enough to trap them within a wall of fire should a mage get any funny ideas. Someone had scattered buckets of water and sand all around to further put out any fires.

Of course, Danya wasn't alone. She stood at the center of about a dozen of her Chosen, her white and black Circle priest cloak stark against the green forest backdrop. The Chosen's hematite gear created a dark-gray wall around the priest, protecting her better than any blade could. Usko stood just behind Danya, at her right shoulder — a place of high honor.

The place Verve had once claimed.

Usko's face was expressionless. All the Chosen's faces were blank — as they'd been taught from their earliest days in Atal's service. But while their expressions gave nothing away, their hearts were sharp with fury, edged with bitterness at Verve's betrayal.

Knots tightened in Verve's stomach, but she held her head high. Beside her, Ellory muttered a curse, adding, "You didn't mention the priest would have a whole sodding army."

"Not an army," Verve replied. "A family." And she'd left them.

Her plan, once sharp and clear as a blade, now seemed blurry — and beyond foolhardy. Even she and Ellory together were no match for so many skilled fighters — even if she'd *wanted* to fight any of her fellow Chosen.

No, she scolded herself. *Stick with the plan.* After all, one of the Chosen had killed Ivet. But as she stared at Usko, Brak, Livia, and the rest, her resolve dissipated like puffer smoke.

Her stomach twisted again. "Keep quiet," she muttered to Ellory. "Let me do the talking."

She and Ellory stopped at the tributary's edge, facing Danya and her Chosen. From here, Verve could sense wagons and horses nearby, but nothing worse, thank the One.

"Well met, Danya," Verve said, bowing. "Nice day for a prisoner handoff, isn't it?"

"Prisoner?" Usko hissed. "The moon-blood looks willing enough."

Verve tilted her crossbow so the dawn light caught on the hematite bolt, aimed at Ellory's head. "Open your eyes, Usko."

"You're not as funny as you think you are," he shot back. "Traitor."

Verve grimaced at the ire in his voice, and his eyes narrowed.

"Enough." Danya held up her hand, and Usko—and all the other Chosen within her reach—flinched. Closer now, Verve realized again how young many of them were; even younger than Owen. Did Danya believe she had brought these children to their deaths? Or did she truly expect them to kill for her? Both were true, and both boiled hot beneath Verve's skin.

The priest eyed Ellory up and down, then smiled at Verve. "Good girl. See what you can accomplish with a little motivation?"

It took every ounce of Verve's self-control not to aim the crossbow at Danya's heart, plan be damned. But she schooled herself to be calm — as Danya had so often forced her. "You have a gift for persuasion. I've fulfilled my end of the deal. Now, will you leave me alone?"

Danya's smile was wide. "Send the dendric mage over, and we'll talk."

Ellory shot Verve a *look* very much like the one they'd exchanged during that first brawl in the Tipsy Willow. Lip curled, hands clenched in fury, the shiftling's desire to spring an attack pressed upon Verve's heart, too. Verve returned Ellory's look with one of her own: *Not yet.*

A low growl escaped Ellory's throat, but she faced forward once more. As Verve made to shove her toward Danya, that other presence filtered through to her consciousness again, closer this time than before. *Much* closer.

Verve swore, but it was too late.

Alem stepped out of the trees behind her, hands raised. "Greetings, Serla Danya," he called. "I'm the one you want. I'm the dendric mage."

26

Tornado

odding fool! As Alem came to her other side, Verve fought down the thrum of panic that beat through her veins, and faced Danya again. "The fellow's lying. Or deluded. He's nothing — barely has enough magic to light a match. Don't—"

"Quiet," Danya broke in, and deep-seated training made Verve's jaw snap shut. Usko, radiating confusion and fear, murmured something to Danya, who studied Alem. "So *you* are the dendric mage?" Danya asked.

"I am." Fear caught Alem's spirit like one of Klaret's snares, but his voice was steady.

Ellory shifted in place, glancing between Verve, Alem, and Danya. Verve's mouth opened, but nothing came out. If she called him a liar, Danya would finish off Lotis. But if she let him go, he'd be gone.

Either way, she'd failed to protect those she loved — again.

Heat pricked at her eyes, and she could do nothing to stop the swell of bitter grief.

"Verve."

Danya's voice snapped her attention back. The priest still eyed Alem with curiosity — and a growing excitement she could not conceal. "Is it true? Or is this another of your pathetic attempts to trick me?"

Alem looked over at her, and within his dark eyes she found a plea, one not spoken aloud with words, but in the shared language of their hearts.

She heard his voice in her mind as clearly as if he'd spoken in her ear: *Trust me.*

And within her own heart, another choice emerged.

"He's the dendric mage," Verve heard herself say. The tears that trickled down her nose were real. "He's the one you want. And he's right: there is no Damaris."

"You can't trust her, serla," Usko hissed to Danya. "She abandoned us."

His hurt rippled across the clearing; a stone tossed into a still pond, and the waves struck Verve's chest as surely as a fist. She swallowed the lump in her throat.

"I know Vervaine better than she knows herself," Danya sneered to Usko. "And despite that disgusting emotional display she's putting on, she's telling the truth. But you—" She slapped Usko's cheek and he flinched back. "You will keep your silence. You are nothing without me — none of you are. Your lives are worthless beyond what worth I grant you — beyond what the mighty Atal grants you. Is that understood?"

Her voice echoed through the pines and the other Chosen bowed in unison and spoke as one. "Yes, serla."

"Bitch," Ellory muttered.

Verve's fingers tightened over her crossbow. "Agreed."

But Alem cast her another look, a desperate one, and she gave the slightest nod. He faced Danya again. "I offer myself to you, serla, so you have no need to search the area for me any longer. No other place here is worth your valuable time. Of that, you have my word."

Verve only listened with part of her mind. Although it was no doubt foolish to let her guard down, even a little bit, she had to try. Using her meridian senses and every ounce of her concentration, she focused on the tight spiral of Danya's emotions. They swirled within the priest's heart like a tornado: chaotic, but controlled by the force of her will.

Fear — that wasn't a surprise. In the time since gaining these new abilities, Verve had sensed fear from most people in some measure, some form. In Danya, fear was silent but powerful, propelling the tornado's movements without distinguishing itself from the rest of the tumult.

But Danya's fear didn't excuse her actions.

Next, Verve found anger. This, too, she had expected. Anger was the dust and debris shaping the howling dark tunnel of wind that laid waste to the landscape of Danya's spirit. Anger — at mages, at the world that had allowed the magic-users to run amok, at the everyone else who cowered in fear when faced with that wild power.

Anger at... herself? This was odd. Verve spared a second to ensure Alem was still speaking—he was waxing eloquent about his healing abilities—then she delved back into Danya's heart, searching for the source of the priest's self-directed rage. Since she wasn't able to physically touch Danya, the memories she found were at first fuzzy and vague, and she could make no sense of them.

Space-Between-Stars, she called. *Can you untangle this?*

A breath passed, then another, and she thought the Fae who shared her soul would not answer. Until they replied, *Prepare yourself.*

Gradually, as Verve surrendered to the flow of Fae magic, her past connection with Danya allowed her meridian senses to strengthen. Just like before, when Alem had peered into her memories with her, she saw Danya's memories through Danya's eyes.

A little boy with Danya's ears looked up at Verve. "Mama?"

He couldn't have been older than six summers, but his body was too light, just like Ivet's had been. Blood trickled down from his nose — which Verve knew looked just like his father's. Danya's voice came from Verve's throat. "Dear heart..."

His voice was faint against the backdrop of roaring flames, of trampling soldiers, of screams. "Mama," he whispered. "I'm tired."

Verve held him close to her chest, trying to shield him from the chaos in the rest of town. She said, "It's all right, little one. Sleep now. I'll be here when you wake."

The boy's eyes fixed on her. "Why are you sad, Mama?" He struggled in her grip. "What's going on?"

"Hush." Verve pressed him closer. Danya's silent prayers echoed in her mind. *Gods above and beyond, keep him safe. Please. I'll do anything...*

"Where's Papa?" the boy—Benin—murmured.

Verve's own eyes stung as her heart swelled, aching with fresh grief. A man's face appeared in her memory. Royden: round cheeks, a thick beard, a smile that always touched his blue eyes, even in his last breath when he'd told her not to be afraid. Tears trickled down her face as she cradled her son and the memory of her lost husband.

A scream jolted Danya back to a reality where mage-fire burned all around her shattered home. But the moon-bloods were all too busy warring with each other to care that a child lay dying of wounds they could have healed — wounds they had caused, albeit indirectly.

"You'll see Papa soon," she said, her voice achingly calm. "I promise. Rest now, Benin. I'll be with you. Always."

The memory receded, but Danya's grief still twined with bitterness, sharp as that moment when she held her dying son. And Verve, whose kill count numbered more than everyone in that little village, understood *why*.

Verve blinked, and the pine trees came back into focus. The sun still climbed up through the forest, sending beams of light across everyone. Verve inhaled the scents of neem oil, of the charred earth Danya's Chosen had prepared, of sweet spring flowers blooming nearby.

"What are you doing?"

Danya's voice struck Verve like a slap. She met her mentor's tear-bright eyes and realized she was still weeping, too.

"Tell me," Danya added, balling her hands into fists. "Tell me what you're doing to me! And why are your eyes glowing? What foul magic has corrupted you?"

Without waiting for an answer, she gestured to one of the trainers, who barked an order. The Chosen splashed across the stream and formed a circle around Verve, Alem, and Ellory, daggers, crossbows, and spears aimed at the trio. Several of them snatched Verve's weapons away, including her wire bracelet, leaving her unarmed. Usko stood closest to Verve, and his gaze on her was iron.

But Verve ignored him, ignored all of them, and only stared at Danya. Grief was a reason, not an excuse; grief did not absolve Danya of her many sins. But it sure as hell made Verve less inclined to kill her.

Which definitely complicated the whole "kill your evil mentor" plan.

Didn't you say something earlier about change? Space-Between-Stars mused. *Something* truly *profound?*

Verve rolled her eyes. *Don't remind me.*

But the moment of light teasing offered her a reprieve from the grief of Danya's memories, and she replied with more calm than she'd expected. "Benin. Royden. Danya, I'm sorry for what you lost. I wish I'd gotten a chance to know them."

Danya's eyes widened at the acknowledgement, then narrowed. The whirlwind of fury, grief, and bitterness strengthened, howling above all other thoughts and feelings, and Verve stumbled, blown back by their force. The sharp tip of Usko's dagger dug into her lower back as the Chosen leveled his weapon at her.

Is this what family is supposed to be? The thought sounded like Celidon and Jocasta.

And Ivet.

No, of course not. The bonds Danya had woven between herself and the Chosen were no more real than the false cousin "Morwen" she'd tried to sell Verve. But it didn't have to be this way.

"You're 'sorry?'" Danya hissed. She paced forward, shoving past her Chosen to stand within slapping distance of Verve. "What do you know of that word, you disgusting little maggot? I've sacrificed everything for you—for all of you—but you threaten the peace we've built with...*magic* of your own? What have you done to me?"

Verve fought not to flinch back. Beside her, Ellory growled. Alem, too, looked at Verve with wide eyes, but within them, she saw no fear, not anymore. Not like she felt in Danya.

Another vision came to Verve then, but not one manifested by her meridian powers. This was the thread of a thought she followed to its end. Danya was her, and she was Danya; they were bound by trauma. Whether that bond was real or imagined made little difference, because only the binding mattered: the relationship an adult had shaped with a child tied them together with knots that could never be untangled.

Only cut.

If Verve didn't sever those bonds, she'd never grow into the person she wanted to be, the person Alem believed in. The person Ivet had loved.

Verve glanced around, trying to get a better sense of her bearings, but her movements were slow, like wading through molasses. Behind her, Usko jabbed his dagger into her back again, at the exact right spot against her armored jacket to send a spike of pain through her. "Do it," he muttered. "Give us a reason to strike you down. Hurt her, and you're dead."

Verve tried to overlay calm over Usko, but her concentration was in tatters from peering into Danya's memories and she could do no more than sense Space-Between-Stars, let alone channel the Fae's power again.

"This doesn't have to be your fight," Verve began, but he pressed the dagger's point forward again, harder, and the ensuing pain made her cry out and drop to her knees before Danya.

Ellory snarled again, and made to lunge, but the presence of a dozen or so loaded hematite crossbows made her hold still. Alem, too, lifted his hands, his jaw working in fury as he glared at Danya.

"You claim to protect the innocent," Alem said to the priest. "But all I see are children who've been taken advantage of by the one who should have protected them. How your god must hate you."

"Alem, stand down," Verve cried, but Danya gave a signal and one of the other Chosen, a girl not much older than Usko, grabbed Alem's wrists and clapped hematite bracers upon them.

Tears still streaming down her face, Verve looked over at Danya. "There's no reason to hurt anyone else. I'll go with you. Do what you want with me, but show them mercy. Please."

A shadow fell over Verve as Danya came closer, looming over her, glaring down like some vengeful god. "Mercy?" Her voice was too soft, too gentle. "What do you know of that, ruthless killer that you are?"

"You made me this way," Verve choked.

"Perhaps, but you never questioned me, or asked me to change. How was I to know you weren't happy? I've done so much for you, child, and this is how you pay me back? With accusations and attacks?"

Verve's mind spun. Danya's words were lies, of course, but the tornado had gripped her heart and she couldn't find her footing enough to argue. Long years of obedience, of coerced loyalty, of bows and deference, made her lower her gaze as her own bitterness pummeled her spirit.

Danya smiled. "Usko," she said, gesturing to Alem and Ellory. "Finish them."

"No," Verve cried, but she wasn't the only one.

An animalistic shriek pierced the air as Ellory shucked her hematite chains and melted into her ummaroc form. Shock tore through the group like lightning. Stunned at the sudden appearance of a sickle-drake in their midst, the Chosen scrambled back, their tight formation momentarily broken. Even Danya gasped.

Ellory snarled and stepped in front of Alem as if to shield him, but one of the Chosen recovered first and aimed his crossbow at the ummaroc. His aim was true; the bolt landed in Ellory's shoulder with a sickening *thunk*. She screamed and canted backward, momentarily disoriented, and another Chosen, a young girl, leaped toward her, daggers in hand. A slash, a streak of bright crimson against Ellory's nose, and the shiftling collapsed, unmoving.

Then Alem stood alone over Ellory, his chest heaving, his jaw tight, his hands clenched into fists. "I'll never work for you," he said to Danya. "I'll end my own life first."

"Enough of this shit."

Verve whirled to see Klaret, Hadiya, and Kyon in his antelope form leap from a thick stand of palmettos. Hadiya brandished an axe while Klaret carried a wicked-looking machete. All three of them emanated pure fury.

"If you harm Alem and Verve," Hadiya growled to Danya. "You'll feel my axe in your skinny little neck. So call off your pups, Priest, else I'll really give you something to pray for."

Klaret grunted in agreement while Kyon stamped the ground in warning. A laugh bubbled up in Verve's throat at the ridiculous sight of two villagers and an overgrown goat facing down the daggers, crossbows, and spears of Danya's Chosen. But her amusement was the grim sort, gallows humor, for the Chosen would definitely destroy them. More deaths on her head.

Heart twisting, she called to Jocasta and Celidon. Surely one of them had encountered a situation like this in their time as a meridian. *Please,* she said through their ethereal bond of spirit and memory. *Please tell me how to fix this.*

A warmth, like a hand squeezing her shoulder, was the only reply. And while Verve would have preferred a weapon of some kind, their presences bolstered her more than a shining blade in her hand.

Well, mostly.

Meanwhile, Danya smiled at the Lotis villagers. "Another mage. Good. Legion will be so pleased." She gestured again to the Chosen, who converged on Kyon, Hadiya, and Klaret, herding them together with Ellory and Alem. "On my word, kill the bumpkins, but take the shiftling and dendric mage alive."

The villagers drew up back-to-back, their stances ready, their faces grim. Verve's heart threatened to beat its way out of her ribcage. She scrambled to her feet, only to meet Usko's dagger. Behind her, Kyon squealed and Hadiya shouted a litany of curses, but Verve couldn't move for Usko's weapon pressing against her chest.

Danya's hand on her shoulder made her start. Danya's grip was strong, unyielding, as she spoke into Verve's ear. "This is your last chance to stop this madness. One word from me, and your friends will live."

The air was thick with the iron scent of blood. Was Ellory moving? Verve couldn't tell. Klaret cried out and Hadiya cursed again, and Verve trembled.

"What do you want?" she managed.

Danya squeezed her shoulder. "Legion *only* wants the dendric mage. And I only want *you.* Return to my side and convince him to come with you peacefully, and your darling little village will be safe. Forever."

27

Transgressions

Verve's insides went hot and cold all at once. She stared at the lined, weathered face that had once been the closest thing to a parent in her memory. Yes, Danya had doled out more than her share of blows, but she'd been generous in other ways — and not just in coin. There'd been birthday celebrations, festival days piled high with sweets, new clothes and trinkets after a job well done. Danya had taught her to read and write, abilities that few could claim.

Perhaps sensing Verve's weakness, Danya squeezed her shoulder again. "I'm sorry for losing my temper, before. I didn't mean those things I said."

Lies. So why did Verve still ache to believe them?

Danya continued. "Your pleas have not fallen on deaf ears. You and I can start anew, Vervaine. You clearly want more freedom; I can give it to you. Anything you want can be yours. We can forget the past and forge a new future — together."

A grunt of effort made her glance over to see Alem kneeling over Ellory. But even though he wasn't looking at Verve, his spirit calmed her, anchored her in her own resolve, in her own certainty.

Jolted back to her senses, Verve glared up at Danya. "I'll never forget what you've done—what I've done—and nor should I. But you're right about a new future. You just won't be in it."

She risked a glance at Alem and the others. They all still breathed, thank the One, although Hadiya bore a nasty gash on their arm and Klaret had a bruise already forming on her jawline. There was blood on Kyon's hooves and horns, but he seemed unharmed. Alem still knelt over Ellory, face drawn in concentration.

The Chosen circled everyone, an impenetrable wall of blank faces and shuttered hearts, peppered with spikes of fear and fury. Perhaps Danya was a lost cause. But the other Chosen—the lost children of Aredia—needed someone to fight *for* them — not the other way around.

Within Verve's spirit, Space-Between-Stars whispered, *Agreed, Verve-the-Protector.*

"She doesn't own you," Verve called, trying to inject reassurance into her words even as the Chosen closed in. Where she wavered, the Fae soul joined with hers bolstered her resolve, adding more strength to her words as she spoke them.

"Danya doesn't really know your fates or control your destiny. Her grip on you is an illusion she's created, but you must believe in it for it to work. She depends on you, although she claims that you're nothing without her. But the truth is the other way around."

Flickers of doubt sparked through the Chosen. A few of them cast glances at one another and back at Danya, who stood alone in the charred circle. "How frightened Vervaine must be," Danya called, "to speak to her kindred like children."

"They *are* children, you insufferable twat," Hadiya hissed.

Usko shouldered through the group to stand before Verve. "You're lying," he said. "You left us, and now you regret it. You'll say anything to save your own sorry skin." He held up a pair of daggers and tossed one her way. The weapon landed at Verve's feet, sunlight dancing on the hematite and steel edge. Usko leveled his remaining dagger at her. "I will not let Serla Danya suffer your rebellion any longer. Face me now, or die a coward."

Verve stared at the dagger, then looked back at Usko. His jaw was tight, his eyes narrowed, but his hands trembled. And her meridian senses showed her the full spectrum of his fear, and his grief at facing one of his kindred.

The door of his mind hung open, but she did not step across the threshold.

One of Atal's Chosen he may have been, but he'd never had another choice.

Time to change that.

"Usko," she said, softly. "Do you truly want to fight me?"

"Shut up, coward," he cried. "Fight, or die."

Verve shook her head. "It's a simple question. What do you want, Usko?"

The dagger in his grip trembled harder and his words came out choked. "What I want doesn't matter."

Verve managed a smile. "That's a lie, Usko. Probably the worst lie she's ever made you believe was real. What do *you* want?"

His lips quivered, his eyes brightened with unshed tears.

"Do you really want to kill me?" Verve asked him, then glanced around at the other Chosen, who all stood frozen as they stared at the scene unfolding before them. "Same to all of you. Is this the life you want? Or is it all you think you deserve? I did, once."

She looked at Alem, who spared a glance from his attempts to heal Ellory. When he met Verve's gaze, he flushed and smiled. Despite everything he had to grieve, joy radiated from him at their shared glance, giving Verve the strength to do what she should have done from the start.

At the edge of Verve's vision, Danya tried to slip away, only to find a wall of her Chosen. None moved to let her pass.

Verve seized the opportunity. She gathered up her old grief and new joy, and sent both out to the Chosen. Soft gasps sounded from the younger ones, the ones Danya had not yet battered into stoicism. But when the older ones relaxed the grips on their weapons, a new feeling sparked among them, like little candles brought to life, and Verve truly believed she could do this. Yes, there was grief and anger and fear, but there was also joy, and hope. Verve grasped the feeling and Space-Between-Stars helped it to resonate in her own heart.

"I thought I deserved nothing better than what Danya offered," Verve said to them. "But I see now that lies are all she gave me. So I'm done with Danya, with the life she's created for me. You can be, too. There's another life waiting for each of you, if you want it.

"You are not bound by destiny or fate — only by the choices you make.

And you can choose to change."

Usko's hand fell to his side. The dagger dropped to the earth, silent. All around him, the other Chosen lowered their weapons, while the little candles of their hope flared brighter. Usko rubbed his face in his hands, then peeked up at Verve. "Can I… come with you?"

More tears sprang to Verve's eyes. She smiled and held out her hand. "You'd better."

One of the Chosen cried out in alarm. Verve whirled in time to see Ellory, bleeding and still in her ummaroc form, barrel toward Danya, who was trying to slip away again. Sudden horror erupted from Danya, but she had no time to run. A few of the Chosen leaped to defend the priest, but the sickle-drake was fast, too fast; Ellory dove past them and fell upon Danya. The priest screamed one last time. A single snap of the ummaroc's jaws, and Danya was gone. Ellory drew up, blood coating her muzzle, a fresh scar streaked along her snout, and looked over at Verve.

The attack had happened so fast, Verve barely registered what was going on even as her gaze fell on crimson blood marring the pure white side of Danya's cloak. The sudden absence of Danya's presence was like the moment after a blow; she felt nothing but a faint tingle. No doubt pain would come soon enough.

Ellory stared at her, then slipped into the palmettos, and out of sight. Verve sensed the shiftling's roiling emotions but cast them out of her mind. Ellory had made her choice. Some of the other Chosen converged on Danya's body, but no one wept.

A warm hand rested on Verve's waist, and she leaned into Alem. "I'm sorry," he whispered. "I only managed to heal Ellory a little. I didn't think she had enough fight left in her to…"

"It's all right," Verve replied when he trailed off. "You did a good thing."

Hadiya, Klaret, and Kyon came up beside Verve. "What now?" Hadiya asked as some of Atal's Chosen milled around their former leader.

Verve glanced over at Usko, who was one of the many who'd not gone to Danya's body. He gave her a small but hopeful smile, which she returned. To Hadiya, she said, "We're going home."

28

Her Next Life

Several days later, Verve and Usko stood before Ivet's pyre with the other Chosen and villagers. It'd been a slow, painful slog back to Lotis with injured in tow, but thank the One, none of the Chosen had perished during the confrontation.

Usko glanced over at Verve as she lit another puffer. "You're crying again?"

She hugged his shoulders, making him tense. "It happens."

"Danya would say…" He trailed off. "But that doesn't matter anymore, does it?"

The flames danced up into the night, where the mage moon had swelled to fullness amid a starry sky. In Verve's mind's eye, the river of light in the Fae realm flowed on, bolstered by one more flickering spirit that burned brighter than any star.

Goodbye, Ivet. Until we meet again.

Verve exhaled a stream of puffer smoke into the starry sky. The grief that pressed upon her heart did not relent at the beautiful sight, but that was fine. Although Ivet had gone on to her next life, a part of her would be with Verve forever. "Danya's body is gone," Verve said to Usko. But she'll always be with us in some ways."

"Good and bad ways, I guess," Usko said as he glanced around at the others. Half of Atal's Chosen had returned with Verve and the villagers back to Lotis, while the rest had remained to burn Danya's body. Livia had been among them, and when questioned about her plans, had said only, "Without her, I'd still be on the street. So we'll send her to her next life, and then start our own. We're free now, thanks to you."

Verve had invited Livia and the others, but they'd made their choice. Perhaps one day, they would make another.

But for the moment, the integration was going well enough. Most of the Chosen stood clumped together, watching the pyre with varying degrees of confusion. A few had taken to nibbling on the provided food, and Verve made a mental note to ensure they helped clean up after. Everyone had been painfully polite so far, so she wanted to ensure cooperation from the newcomers as soon as possible.

"I didn't kill her," Usko said suddenly, nodding to the pyre. "Danya sent some of the others here with the mercs and trainers, to send you the message. But I..." He trailed off, shame curling around his spirit as he added, "I told Danya about the dendric mage, and how you seemed to care for the people here." His voice dropped to a whisper. "I was just following her orders. It wasn't personal. But I'm sorry."

So this was why the poets said irony was bitter. Verve shut her eyes, took several deep breaths, and allowed some of her grief to wash over Usko. "Is this worth whatever reward Danya gave you?"

The tears that slid down his nose were answer enough.

She hugged his shoulders as he swiped his eyes. They both watched Ivet's pyre, then Usko asked, "Who was she?"

Verve's throat tightened. "The leader of Lotis. A Sufani, like me. But most of all, a good, kind person whose heart was open to everyone."

"Well said." Dannel came up behind Verve and she took his hand. Usko eyed the gesture, then his gaze fell upon Dannel's pale eyes and his own widened. Dannel, unaware of the younger man's regard, gave a heavy sigh. "I'll miss her so much. But she's on to her next life, now. I hope it's a good one."

"Me too." Verve squeezed Dannel's palm. "Up for some singing later?"

He gave her a sad smile. "Of course. We must send Ivet off with a song." He glanced over at Usko. "You, lad, do you sing?"

"Uh…" Usko looked at Verve, who shrugged. "I don't know, ser."

Dannel chuckled. "Well, care to find out?"

"It won't hurt," Verve stage-whispered to Usko. "I promise."

"If you say so," Usko replied, brows knitted.

Dannel chuckled again and patted his shoulder. "Good lad."

He asked Usko another question, drawing the boy into conversation, so Verve slipped away to find Alem. He stood with Owen and Hadiya a little way off from the pyre, speaking in low, urgent tones. At Verve's approach, Alem's spirit brightened and he held out his hand, beckoning. She slipped her palm within his and allowed him to draw her closer.

"What's the word?" she asked.

Hadiya crossed their arms, their expression grim. "Klaret's replaced the sprung traps, and added several more. The Willow took a helluva beating, but we've already planned repairs — and a few upgrades I've been planning. Kyon and Nori are scouting now. Your little murder family aren't so keen on the mages, but I think we'll all get along in time."

"If they stay," Verve replied. "Some may choose to move on. But of those who stick around, I'll see if anyone wishes to take on a new role. The village needs a proper guard."

Alem ran a hand through his long hair. "More warriors, eh?"

"Protectors," Verve said, a little sharply. "They're skilled enough to manage the job. But I want to first give everyone the option of doing something else. No one should have to kill for a living."

He nodded. Although his grip on hers was firm, his mind was far away, as it had been in the days since the confrontation with Danya. Verve had been so busy getting the Chosen settled, she and Alem had not had a chance to speak more than a few words.

Hadiya glanced between them, then over at the cluster of Chosen, milling about near the food, although no one had taken more than a few bites. "Ea's tits and balls, do they need an invitation to eat? We didn't cook all day for the stuff to be looked at. Come on, Owen. Let's show them how a proper feast is done."

With that, they slipped away, leaving Alem and Verve conveniently alone.

Verve glanced over at Alem, who gave her a faint smile. "Sorry if I've been distant." He made a vague gesture. "I'm just… overwhelmed."

"Me, too."

Hand in hand, they watched the pyre in silence.

At last, Alem said, "Verve… I know I gave you a lot of grief about your profession, even though I benefited from your abilities. It was unfair of me, and I'll try not to do it again. I never meant to condemn you, personally, but I know I hurt you more than once. I'm sorry."

She stared at him, and he allowed her to see his true heart: the turmoil of grief and guilt and bitterness. But overlaid upon these was love, sparkling, directed at her.

"You had your reasons," Verve managed. "And I wasn't exactly warm and fuzzy to you — most of the time. The One god knows I gave that grief right back to you."

"I deserved it," he replied. "After you left to meet Danya, I thought about what you said, about protecting and killing, and fighting back."

Heat flushed her cheeks. "I say a lot of stupid shit when I'm angry."

"None of it was stupid," he replied. "But more than that… From the day we met, you *showed* me what it meant to truly protect what you hold dear. You made Lotis stronger, and I saw how you cared about more than just killing. So that night, when you left to find Danya, I realized I couldn't let you kill for me—or anyone—ever again."

His shoulders slumped. "You were right. I started the Damaris rumor to keep Lotis safe, but all I did was risk everyone's safety. If I'd left Lotis ages ago, Ivet would still be alive."

Verve squeezed his hand. "Don't travel that road, Alem. It won't take you anywhere you need to go. And besides," she offered him a soft smile, "if you'd left, we never would have met."

Some of the bitterness tumbling in his spirit eased, and he returned her smile. "And what a tragedy that would have been."

Something bubbled in her heart at his words; it took her several heartbeats to recognize joy. "Before I met you, no one had ever tried to see the best in me, or wanted anything for me but what I already had. You and Ivet both…"

She trailed off, throat suddenly too full of words to speak one. Alem hugged her close to his solid chest, enveloping her in his warmth, in the scents of jessamin and lavender. Verve embraced him too, as tightly as she could, for he was the strongest person she knew.

"Ivet loved you," Alem whispered in her ear.

Like the vast river of light and energy in the Fae realm, love did not have a beginning or an end; it just flowed through each spirit it touched, leaving an indelible mark.

"I love her, too," Verve said, then drew back and looked into his dark eyes. "But not how I love you."

He stared at her, then a huge grin spread over his face. "Really?"

"Let me show you." Verve drew upon her meridian abilities and allowed the full force of her love to pour over him, shining like the sun at its height. A brilliant light illuminated his smile as he cupped her cheeks and kissed her, hard.

When at last they parted to breathe, Verve's eyes still glowed, showering light upon the darkness all around them, and within her own spirit, too.

* * *

Sohvi returned to the area several days later. Verve, who'd been scouting for danger, sensed the other meridian's presence at Pilgrim Springs, and went to meet her. She found Sohvi swimming while Hasina watched from the shore.

"Not a swimmer?" Verve asked as she came over.

"Someone's got to keep an eye out for snakes," Hasina replied, pulling a face. "Besides, that water's fucking freezing."

Verve chuckled. "You get used to it."

Even fairly early in the day, the air was already thick with the heat of late spring. Verve shucked her boots and waded into the chilly water, sighing in pleasure as it crept up to her calves.

Seeing her, Sohvi swam over and clambered back to shore, water sluicing off of her. "Do you know why it's called Pilgrim Springs?" She continued without waiting for an answer. "It's named for the first person who went to the Fae's realm in the spirit world — and returned to ours. Do you know how he managed the feat?"

This time, Sohvi actually waited for a response. Verve searched Space-Between-Stars's memories and found the recollection, strange though it was. "He had Fae blood?"

"Among other things." Sohvi glanced around, a faint smile on her lips. "This place is beautiful."

Verve nodded. "I agree. But something tells me you didn't come all this way just for a dip and a history lesson."

Sohvi adjusted the scarf covering her thick braids. "Flowing water is sacred to meridians, for it strengthens our powers."

"Good to know," Verve replied. "But I'm still wondering where this is going."

"Meridians are all connected, in many ways," Sohvi said slowly. "The longer we know each other and work together, the stronger those bonds are. However, the Fae spirits we've joined with also share a lasting, strong connection with each other. Seaglass, the Fae I've joined with, felt the experience that Space-Between-Stars shared with you: the confrontation with your mentor."

Heat flooded Verve's face, and it wasn't just because of the season. "I made the right call, with Danya."

"I know." Sohvi hesitated. "You have become a fine meridian. I was... wrong."

Verve allowed the words to hang in the air for a moment. Although a part of her wanted to gloat, a larger part of her was still raw with grief over Ivet's passing and the loss of her old life. The latter was a good loss, in many ways, but it was still a loss.

So she only gave a slight bow and ensured her smile held as much warmth as the spring water. "Whatever bet you made, I hope you didn't lose your ass *too* badly."

Hasina snorted a laugh. Sohvi shot her a reproving look before continuing. "You've exceeded everyone's expectations." She sighed. "Especially mine.

I admit, I treated you harshly, although my actions were not without justification, given your…history."

"Fair enough." Verve studied the tiny brim fish as they gathered around her toes. "Did you come here to apologize?"

Hasina coughed into her hand, but this time, Sohvi ignored her. "No," Sohvi said, lifting a brow. "I came to offer you a place among us, at our sanctuary in Pillau. There, you can learn more about your abilities, and meet the others. There aren't many of us, even with our anchors," she gestured to Hasina, "but you and your anchor would be welcome."

Verve frowned. "My… what now?"

"Anchor," Hasina said. "Your tether to the physical world. The Pilgrim's anchor helped him cross over from the Fae realm back here. Most meridians have an anchor. We keep the meridians grounded so they don't get lost in their abilities."

"The dendric mage," Sohvi added, as if all of this was painfully obvious and Verve was being deliberately obtuse. "The *healer*. He's your anchor. I can sense the connection between you, even now."

"Being an anchor is no simple job," Hasina added. "Meridians can get lost in their abilities."

As Verve knew, all too well.

"But it is rewarding," Hasina added, "to be a part of something larger than yourself."

Rather than reply, Verve cast her mind out, seeking Alem. She found him intent upon his garden, as he prepared an assault of ladybugs to face a particularly stubborn gang of aphids. Joy flared from him at the brush of her awareness to his, along with a questioning sense of, *is everything okay?*

Verve allowed her own joy at their connection to reach him, along with a mental nod. *Everything's fine. Give those aphids hell.*

Determination swirled through him. *I intend to.*

When she looked back at her fellow meridian, Sohvi was smiling. "You make a strange pair, to be sure, but I suppose the One god has mysterious ways."

Verve blinked. "Meridians worship the One?"

"The One is life," Sohvi answered, as if it were obvious.

A familiar tightness in Verve's throat almost staunched her reply. "I thought only we Sufani believed in the One."

The One is older than even my people, Space-Between-Stars replied.

"There are many things to know about meridians, and still more we are learning, each day," Sohvi said carefully. "Will you come with us on our journey?"

Verve's heart ached at the earnestness bleeding through her words. "I've made a life here," she replied. "And I have no wish to leave just yet."

Hasina and Sohvi exchanged glances, then Hasina said, "We stopped at Freehold on the way to Lotis. The place was buzzing with news that the Chosen have vanished. There are rumors that they killed the head priest of Atal's temple, then fled. Everyone's panicking about rogue mage attacks, but the magistrate said that hasn't been an issue in some time."

Sohvi nodded. "Your doing, I believe. Apparently, most consider this area protected."

"Must be a nice change," Hasina added. "The Freehold magistrate was relieved, actually. Seems like your Danya made life difficult for a lot of folks."

But Verve could not quite allow relief to take root in *her* heart. "We may be safe from the Chosen and renegade mages, but Legion attacked me once. Do you think they'll come back to finish the job if they learn I survived?"

"You're nothing to them," Hasina replied.

But Sohvi's expression darkened. "Let me show you something."

Suddenly, she and Verve stood alone in the vast stretch of black beneath the glowing river of the Fae realm. Verve twirled around to get a better look at the mighty river of light; each step, each movement, was easy and free, like her body was lighter and stronger here.

"What's going on?" Verve breathed. She'd been too astonished to do more than gawk the last time she'd visited the Fae realm.

"Meridians dwell partly in the spirit realm," Sohvi said. "Physical sensations aren't as strong here, so it may feel easier to move. But I brought you here to show you something else."

"Where's Hasina?"

"Back in the physical realm," Sohvi said, a touch of irritation in her voice. "Only meridians can travel here. Don't fret: Hasina will keep watch over our bodies. This is why we have anchors. Come on."

"I wasn't fretting," Verve muttered. "But it's sodding weird, isn't it?"

Sohvi gave a faint smile and beckoned for Verve to follow. The two meridians made their way along the shining river, leaping in huge bounds toward a small beacon of light to one side. It glowed brighter as they drew closer, and the light poured over Verve's heart, as much a part of her as her blood and bones.

"This is Lotis now that a meridian calls it home," Sohvi said, gesturing to the beacon. "Lotis and its inhabitants are under your protection."

"That's…fine," Verve replied, breathless with wonder. "But I'm not sure I could do much good should Legion make their way here. Their attack on me was," she shivered, "ruthless."

Sohvi nodded. "If you concentrate, if you learn how to better use your meridian abilities, you can shield Lotis from Legion's soldiers. If you do this, they will not trouble your people again."

Verve considered. "You said the meridians have a home in Pillau, right? Ever thought of expanding to Greenhill Province? I know a nice, quiet little village that takes on strays. And it's never a bad idea to have a second location."

Sohvi's brows furrowed. "An interesting proposal. I'd have to speak with the others, but it could work."

"Great." Verve offered her hand, and Sohvi accepted. "Celidon would be proud."

Sohvi studied her, then looked back at the river. "I know."

* * *

Later, after Sohvi and Hasina had left Lotis, after everyone else had stumbled off to sleep, Verve and Alem retreated to his cottage. Since she'd relinquished her loft to Usko and the other (former) Chosen, she'd taken to sleeping at

Alem's. While Alem stoked the coals glowing in the hearth, Verve unwrapped her scarf and shook out the cloud of her curls. Taking care not to damage or tangle the strands, she gently scraped her nails over her scalp, sighing in relief.

"You don't want the braids anymore?" Alem asked, still kneeling by the hearth.

Verve skimmed her scalp again, savoring the feeling. "Maybe one day. They're beautiful, but a lot of work. Besides, I have other ways I'd rather spend my time now."

She gave him a knowing look and tugged off her tunic, tossing it by the door with her pants and boots. He'd shed his shoes and shirt already, and his muscled torso glowed almost golden in the growing firelight.

Over dinner, she'd told him of her conversation with Sohvi and Hasina, and since then he hadn't stopped beaming. "Ah, yes," he said. "Doting on your beloved anchor, right? Tell me, is that a meridian habit, or just a Verve one?"

"I'm still not sure I like the nautical term." An image of the river of light came to Verve's mind, and she shrugged. "But it fits."

"Well, *I'm* as pleased as a racoon in a midden heap," Alem said.

Verve rolled her eyes, fighting back a smile. "You would be."

Grinning, Alem curled up on the soft, woven rug before his hearth and held out his hand. "Say it again?"

Verve came to him and he wrapped her in his arms, tucking her into the shelter of his body, enveloping her in love, comfort, safety. Once foreign, now the feelings were as familiar as the scent of jessamin blossoms, as the sound of rain, as the feel of her palm within his. She wriggled her body closer, pressing as much of herself against him as she could. A soft groan slipped from him, accompanied by an answering flare of desire that ran unchecked between them.

So settled, Verve leaned her head back into him. *I love you, Alem.*

The words were not spoken aloud, but in her new silent speech, resonating like cicadas singing to the sunset. Love reverberated between them, a joy made that much stronger when shared.

Delight burst from him, a starburst, a shaft of sunlight split into dozens of rainbows. Strong arms wrapped around her and he breathed into her ear, "I could get used to this whole anchor thing."

"I already am," she whispered back, nudging him with her hip.

He gave a soft groan, then kissed and nibbled at her neck, sending shivers of pleasure across her entire body. "Verve," he said between kisses, "I love you, too."

The words thrilled through her. She would never tire of hearing them. So she turned so they were face to face, the warm hearth glowing at her back, and ran her hand down his torso. He closed his eyes at her touch and his desire flared to a roaring flame, then he gripped her waist and pulled her closer, sealing the gap between them with a searing kiss.

Alem's agile fingers danced down her spine to her ass, gripping her cheeks as he deepened the kiss. His touch was strong, certain, but gentle all the same. But Verve didn't want gentle, at least not right now. She drove her hips against his hard length, where the thin fabric of his pants and her small-clothes sent delicious friction through every nerve. His breath came shorter.

"Verve..."

"Yes, Alem?" she whispered, as innocently as she could while they were both nearly naked and rubbing all over each other.

Alem's lids fluttered as he gazed at her. "Will you stay here?"

She stared at him, her mind blank with desire. "In Lotis?"

"Yes." He paused. "With me."

No one had ever wanted her to stick around. Before her conversation with Sohvi, she had given little thought to her life beyond the next few months. But she *could* stay long enough to make a home. She could do whatever she wanted. Her life was her own.

But of course she couldn't just *answer* him, so she slid her fingers down over his pants, caressing his hardness. He shut his eyes and sucked in a breath; she could feel his heart racing beneath his chest.

"Whatever would I do out here in the middle of nowhere?" she murmured as she stroked him.

He groaned. "You're... resourceful."

"True." She tugged down the fabric, freeing him completely, and skimmed her thumb over his tip, already wet with desire. "What would *you* do if I stayed?"

His dark eyes snapped open and fixed on her intently. "Love you until my last breath, and then into my next life, and on and on. Forever."

Love overlaid his words: a shining thread that bound their hearts. Verve, struck mute with joy and a strange surprise, could at first only stare at him. At last, she managed, "I suppose that will do."

Alem grinned at her and slid his own palm beneath her small-clothes, pushing down the fabric. His skilled, strong fingers found her soaking center and toyed with her, making her gasp, sending chills of pleasure across her completely. They faced one another as they pleasured each other, until Verve couldn't stand it anymore.

"Alem," she moaned into his ear. "Please."

His index finger circled her pearl, deviously, deliciously slowly. "Please, what?"

Utterly at his mercy, she gave a soft whimper. "I need you inside me. Now."

"Oh." His lips pressed so gently to her forehead even as he worked her into a frenzy with his hand. "Well, I suppose that will do."

"Ass," she hissed, but the word came out as more of a laugh.

"Mmmm. Maybe next time." He sat up and pulled her legs apart, and angled his body over hers. Slowly, so slowly she wanted to scream in frustrated joy, he slid inside her. An exquisite feeling of fullness shattered the very last of her control, and she cried his name, gripped his waist to pull him closer.

Their bodies moved in tandem, perfectly attuned to each other's pleasure. Verve's body wound itself tighter and tighter around him, her bliss stoked to a blaze as much by her own pleasure as his. Alem drove into her with strong, measured strokes at first, before his pace quickened and he stared at her with fire in his eyes. Verve met his gaze and together, they found their release, gazes and spirits as connected as their physical forms.

After, Alem held her close, but his touch was not confining. In his arms, she was someone precious, someone worthy of love, but she was still Verve. Even as their spirits merged, they remained themselves. And she could think of no better place to start the rest of her life.

* * *

Want more Verve & Alem goodness? Head over to laloga.com/bonus-chapters to sign up for a bonus chapter only available to my newsletter subscribers.

Thank you for reading! Your support is invaluable to independent creators like me. Please share your experience with other readers and leave a review wherever you got this book. If you like what I'm doing, visit laloga.com/newsletter for more.

Keep reading for a sneak peek of the next book in the Chaos Moon series!

29

Ellory, Alone

Ellory couldn't see for the blood. Despite the healer mage's best efforts, her wound had not yet closed and blood poured down her face, blurring her vision and making each step burn.

But she ran anyway. She had no choice, no other place to be than *away*. In her ummaroc form, she could run to the edge of the world, leap right off, and fall forever.

If only.

Pain tore at her face, her shoulder, but her legs moved anyway, carrying her far from her most recent mistakes. But no matter how far or fast she ran, she'd never shake off her past. The taste of human blood tainted her mouth, but she had no regrets for killing that sodding miserable excuse for a priest. That woman was better off dead.

Unlike the fellow mages that Ellory had tricked into Legion's hands — and surely sent to their deaths.

The thought of Legion made her steps quicken. She sped through the pine forest, heading for the border of Silverwood Province. If she didn't slack off, she'd be there in a few hours, and then....

Then she'd decide.

But running like the wind while still bearing injuries—even mostly magically healed injuries—took much of the fight from her steps, so soon she had to stop. Breathing hard, Ellory paused at the edge of the pine forest, staring at the last stretch of open marshland before the ground gave way to the prairies of Silverwood Province. One of her stockpiles of supplies was only a few days' travel away. She inhaled; no trace of hematite, which meant Legion wasn't around. A small mercy.

But another inhale brought the scent of magic: a faint tang of ginger at the back of her throat. Ellory's stomach dropped, but her shoulder throbbed and the lost blood from her head wound made her dizzy. She had to rest, and soon.

Leave now, her better sense urged. *It's best for everyone if you go on alone.*

Ellory hadn't been able to stop rogue mages from destroying her clan, so she really should have been smarter than to seek the kinship of other mages—or anyone—now. But even her brief time with Verve had reminded her of how good it felt to share a meal and a fire with someone you could trust. Sort of.

In her ummaroc form, her vision was only a little better than her human shape, so she relied more on her sense of smell. And each inhale told her a story: the other mages weren't too many or powerful, and they were close. A warm fire, maybe a hot meal and some company, beckoned.

Ellory forced herself to keep a slower pace as she followed the trail. Once she slipped out of the forest and onto the open marsh, scents of water and lilies diluted the smell of magic, but even so, she followed it, until at last she reached their encampment.

The mages had built a small fire at the center of an island in the marsh, and clustered their tents around it. Only three mages were visible, although Ellory could smell another half dozen or so in the area. Closer now, she could smell the other mages' shared blood; they were related, at least loosely, and their green eyes meant they were shape-changers like her. Hope flickered in her chest. Perhaps they'd accept a fellow shiftling, at least for a day or so while she rested. After that, she could head for her nearest bolt-hole and regroup.

She ensured these other mages spotted her before she changed form, then allowed the change to happen slowly, gradually, more so than she normally did when faced with strangers.

Changing didn't hurt, at least not anymore. By now, her bones and muscles were used to being stretched and molded, so only a mild tingle swam through Ellory's body as she shifted to her human shape. When she looked at the mages again, they had all risen, their faces hard, their hands clenched.

"I know you, traitor," one of the mages hissed. "Get the fuck out of here."

Ellory raised her hands, trying not to grimace at the searing pain in her shoulder. "I mean you no harm. I just need a place to rest for a day or two. In return, I'll hunt some game for you when I'm recovered."

The other mages' glares deepened. The first one spoke again. "Your health is no concern of ours. Leave. Now. Or else we'll make you."

The grass all around her parted as the rest of the mages surrounded her. A few had shifted already, so she found herself staring into the green eyes of a huge urslan, a lion, and a wolf. Low, dangerous growls rose from them in a feral chorus.

Ellory's heart was too tired to sink. What else had she expected, really? The other mage was right. She was a traitor.

So she bowed and backed away, her legs splashing in the cool water. Once she was safely out of clawing range, she shifted back to her ummaroc shape. The energy cost was high, but the risk of being caught as a helpless human was far higher. Her body, although still screaming with pain, moved more easily now, and she hurried away from the other mages, racing toward the province border.

By her own doing, there was nothing for her here any longer. Perhaps she deserved nothing more than to find Legion and let them take her away, with all the other mages she'd handed over to them to save her own sorry skin. Perhaps her injuries would claim her life soon.

Either way, she'd face her future alone.

That, at least, would never change.

* * *

Ellory's story continues in Traitor's Oath (Chaos Moon #2)

Acknowledgments

No book is born in a void. Assassin's Mercy would not exist without these lovely souls:

Every musician and composer in my various playlists; your music keeps the muse happy.

My indefatigable editor, Isabella, for helping me make sense of the early draft madness.

My dear friend, Imke, for your editing prowess, your constant encouragement, and your thought-provoking questions that always urge me to delve deeper into the story. I know you love this 'verse almost as much as I do.

My partner and companion, Wade, for your unflagging support, love, and supply of baked goods at the perfect moments. (Surprise cookies are the best cookies.) You are the reason I believe in happy endings.

And you, my wonderful readers. Thank you as always for coming on this journey with me.

About the author

Lauren finds Real Life overrated, and has always preferred to inhabit alternate realities, both self-created and created by others. However, after being burned by certain fandoms one too many times, Lauren decided to focus her reality escape attempts on her own creations. She's much happier now, although she still enjoys fandoms - in small doses.

A believer in love, hope, compassion, and similar squishy ideals, Lauren endeavors to create stories that both gut-punch and elevate her readers. Emotional rollercoasters are what make fiction fun, after all.

When she's not avoiding Real Life responsibilities, Lauren enjoys dancing at music festivals, spending time in nature, and tending to her cat's every whim. She lives in North Florida with her partner and assorted furred critters, but can be found online at:
https://laloga.com/
@lalogawrites on socials

Other books by the author

The Catalyst Moon series:
   Incursion (Book 1)
   Breach (Book 2)
   Storm (Book 3)
   Surrender (Book 4)
   Sacrifice (Book 5)

Learn more at https://books2read.com/laloga

www.ingramcontent.com/pod-product-compliance
Lightning Source LLC
Chambersburg PA
CBHW061615190726
48288CB00007B/2335